A VALKYRIE'S VENGEANCE

The Nine Realms Duology

Talia Clayton

Cover Design and Planet Map by Jaqueline Kropmanns

Formatting by Imagine Ink Designs

Editing by KDL editing

Content Warning

This book contains explicit content and dark elements that may be triggering to some. It includes depression, violence, mature language, explicit romance, murder, nudity, abuse, and blood. This book is intended for mature audiences 18+.

To the authors who inspire me.
Thank you for helping me understand
it's never too late to start.

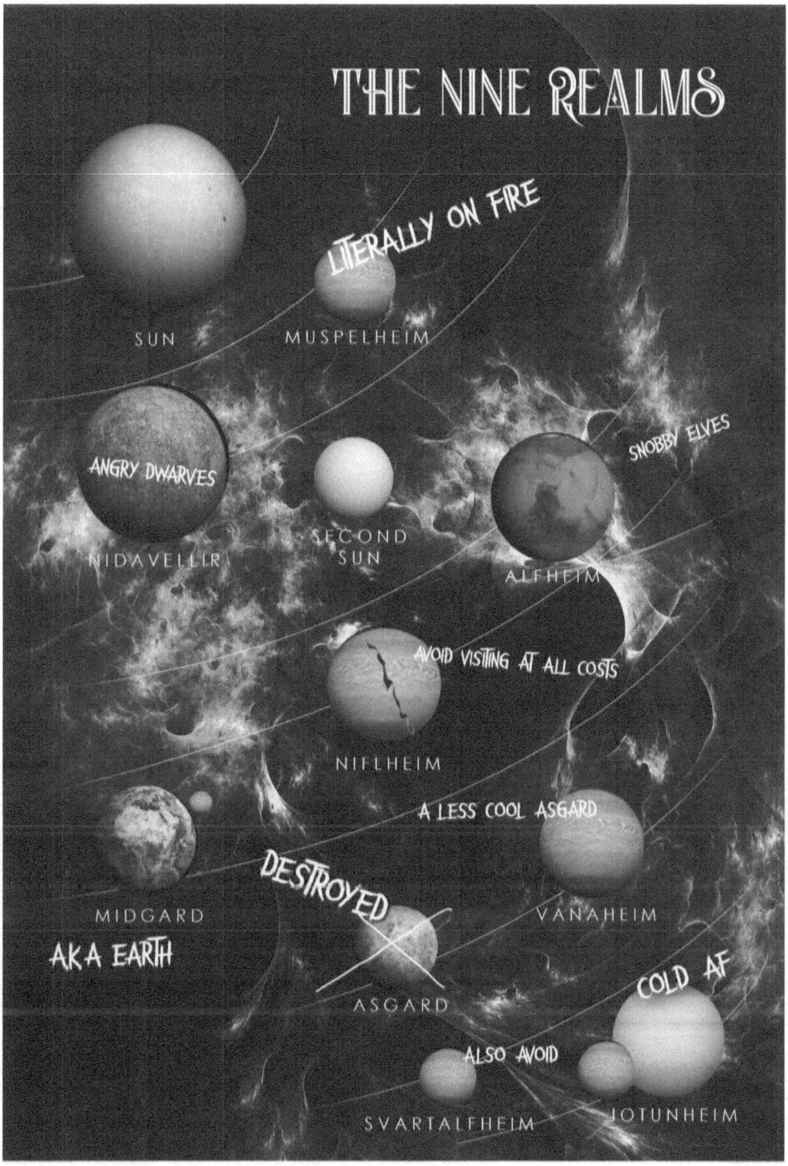

THE NINE REALMS
LITERALLY ON FIRE
SUN
MUSPELHEIM
ANGRY DWARVES
SNOBBY ELVES
SECOND SUN
NIDAVELLIR
ALFHEIM
AVOID VISITING AT ALL COSTS
NIFLHEIM
A LESS COOL ASGARD
DESTROYED
MIDGARD
VANAHEIM
AKA EARTH
COLD AF
ASGARD
ALSO AVOID
SVARTALFHEIM
JOTUNHEIM

Alfheim
Kyrzik
Tripoli
Salaza
Hallaz
Railen
Merin
Haratine
Knoul
Islas Dragones
Vanike
Port of Yulame
Basc
Montisan
Toresk
Lucia

Chapter 1

DEATH IS NOT TEMPORARY. ITS permanence is well-known to me as a Valkyrie. And yet I find myself unable to embrace it as I am flung through space and time. I pop into existence in the middle of nowhere on Alfheim, judging by the barren desert surrounding me.

Shadows cast over me as I plummet through the air into a massive ravine. There is no way to stop my death now. I wonder if it will be recorded like other Valkyrie deaths in the halls of Valhalla. 'Vera Hjelmstad - died falling into a ravine'. How embarrassing.

The wind howls in my ears and reminds me of what it once felt like to fly. *What a waste*. To have the power to travel to different realms, without a way to land somewhere safe, or in an area with actual civilization.

At least before, I had my wings or the use of the Bifrost portal on Asgard, but Asgard is gone and so are my wings.

The ground races to meet me far too quickly and I brace myself for the impact that would surely kill an average human from Midgard. Landing feet first, I grimace at the sickening sound of my shin bones crunching on impact. Mulberry-colored dust plumes up around me.

I clench my teeth so hard I am certain they will break apart. Maybe I will look more menacing if they do. As I contemplate this, I land hard on my back, my breath rushing out of me.

I catch my breath while staring at the bright sky above. Propping myself up on my elbows, I let my body quickly mend the wounds I can't convince myself to look at. I am lucky, I remind myself. Even after Odin's death, his gift of fast healing, given to all Valkyrie, remains.

If only I had the ability to regrow my wings. I blow out a breath of frustration. Maybe I am not so lucky after all.

The sun beats down as sweat slips over my shoulder blades, gliding past the fresh scars where my wings were sheared off. My shirt is already soaked, and the heat is almost unbearable, but shade is close by. Soon I will be in the shadow of the ravine and honestly, it is the small things that get me from day to day.

The fact that I didn't die on my landing—might as well call it a win. I dust off the odd purple dirt coating my pack and dig through it for some food I managed to snag from Nidavellir, the realm of short-tempered dwarves.

A soft breeze blows through the ravine, a welcome reprieve from the scorching heat, as I gnaw on some week-old bread. I hate how much I miss the food in Asgard. Hate how much I miss everything about it, honestly.

Stopping the complete destruction of Asgard, what we call Ragnarok, had been a nice dream. Until I woke up on a totally different planet with enough wounds and memories to know every effort I'd made was not enough.

I didn't save a single Asgardian, other than my sister Edda and my sorry ass. But I, a Valkyrie, am not the only one who survived. I watched space transports leave long before the planet imploded, I remind myself.

After realm-jumping from Niflheim, realm of the dishonored dead, to Nidavellir and now Alfheim, my hopes of finding survivors slowly dwindles with each passing day. It's been two months and I have yet to meet anyone other than some creepy dead people and cranky old dwarves who wanted nothing to do with a Valkyrie.

I groan and eventually convince my body to move my toes and my ankles. They pop at the movement, but everything has healed nicely. I finally stand and bite my lip to keep from letting out a bark of pain as I straighten my back. Sighing for the millionth time today, I pick up my shit and start walking.

At this point, I've been hiking for at least a few hours, based on my Valkric. The small device tells me useful information about the realm, including my geographical location. The holographic image ripples as I tap the side of the device. I pray the battery lasts long enough for me to get to my destination.

In theory, I'm close to some sort of desert outpost, whose name I can't pronounce even if I try. Which I don't. How far I am in reality is an annoying unknown.

Sunlight glints off the scraggly bushes and trees as the sky turns a deep pink just before the second sun dips behind the mountains in the distance. As both suns disappear over the horizon, I let out a sigh of relief and continue to shuffle along a semblance of a dirt path. I only remembered Alfheim had a second sun when I was still boiling in the shade of the ravine.

The second sun in our solar system is only visible on Alfheim, Nidavellir, and two other realms. The remaining five realms only see the main sun of our nine planet—now eight since Asgard is all but bits of dust floating through the cosmos—solar system.

Of course, Alfheim, land of the immortal, snobby, and stupidly beautiful elves, would have two suns. Luckily, both set around the same time. I can't imagine living where it's sunny all the time; it would clash far too often with my mood.

It's dark when I reach the town if you can even call it that. A patchwork of wooden shacks crowd together as if huddling close for warmth, each leaning against the other. Only one dirt road cuts the town in two.

I stroll into what is supposedly an inn, but it looks more like a barn. Hay is strewn over the wooden floor in an attempt to soak up spills and hide the smell of sweat and something... coppery. *Blood.* Nausea rolls through me at the intensity of the aromas.

I am greeted by silence as the din of conversation dies. I should be used to it—it was the same in Nidavellir—but apparently not. Trying not to cringe, I take a seat at the nasty bar. The barkeep, an elf who looks older than time itself, gives me a wary look.

"Don't get many of your kind around here," he grumbles in Elvish. He must be referring to the fact that I am a Valkyrie, not Asgardian.

Even without my wings, it's obvious what I am. My runes are the remaining visible sign. The light blue tattoo markings, old Norse, appear in vertical and horizontal lines traveling along my upper arms to my shoulders and upper back, ending with the smallest writing at the back of my neck. That coupled with the scent Valkyrie give off, we always stand out. The scent is hard to miss if you've smelled it before, and elves have a very keen sense of smell.

It takes me a moment to speak. I try to remember Alfheim's language, Elvish. One I care so little about.

"I suppose not," I manage to get out, but the lilt in my voice is off.

"Still at Odin's beck and call?" he asks, pouring me some amber liquid I pray has alcohol in it. I try hard not to roll my eyes before I take a tentative sip from the mug. Definitely beer.

"Not likely, unless someone learns how to resurrect him," I mutter mainly to myself, but the barkeep nearly drops the glass he started cleaning.

Swearing under my breath, I remember elves have impeccable hearing even at a distance. The barkeep stares at me as if I've grown another arm. I cock my head to the side, scrunching my eyebrows. Does he not know of Asgard's fate?

"H-how?" he stutters.

"Ragnarok, thanks to Loki." Any longer of an explanation would have me roaring my rage through this tavern. I don't allow myself to think of that god. Loki. The emotional wounds from him had healed before this all happened, but these new ones cut deeper and hurt far worse than any he delivered before.

"I… I thought it was a legend." The barkeep shakes his head in disbelief, his dreaded silver hair brushing the grimy bar top. "We don't get much news of the other realms in these parts." *Clearly*.

"Well, it's real and it really happened." Sarcasm drips from my voice. I take another sip of the tepid beer, no longer interested in this conversation.

"How did you get here?"

I shrug. "Just arrived from Nidavellir."

I don't bother explaining the powers given to all Valkyrie by Odin that allow us to teleport from one planet to the next, what we call realm-jumping. Elves can be wary of any type of supernatural powers other than their own elemental magic. Nor do I feel like explaining the annoyingly eventful journey I've been on to find survivors since I woke up in Niflheim.

Switching the subject, I ask, "Do you know if there's a place to stay around here for the night?" I try smiling to seem nicer, but it comes out more of a grimace.

"A pity, we don't have any vacancies at the moment," the barkeep spits out without hesitation. I know full well any rooms in this place are empty, but apparently, he can see I will be more trouble than it's worth. Smart elf. "This is the only inn in town," he adds.

Well, I tried.

The elf's reaction isn't unusual for me. I'm aware very few elves, or really any race from most realms, will be interested in talking to me. Offending people seems to be what I am best at and Valkyrie aren't necessarily everyone's cup of tea anyway.

We have done things for Odin, the all-father, that deem us less than suitable company to keep. When the gods called, we answered, and for a long time, we ignored the consequences and repercussions of those actions.

I frown. I hate sleeping on the ground, but it seems to be the only option. Hoping it'll help me sleep, I order one more beer. Normally, it would take much more alcohol to put me out, but these months on the road I've been focused on one thing and one thing only—finding the Asgardian survivors.

I drag myself out of the tavern and through the town, until I spot a small nook in the hillside to the south. It will shield me from sight and the blustering breeze that picked up during the hour I spent in the bar. I settle down, putting my pack behind my head as a pillow, and try to get some sleep.

———

Screams and shadows haunt my dreams, every night the same memory.

Ash and smoke clog the skies, mingling with the wisps of falling snow. The golden palace in the middle of the city is engulfed in flames, a beacon through the dark. Bells ring through out the city sounding the alarm. Hundreds of space transports take to the skies, not to fight, but to flee.

Screams of Asgardians and booms of buildings collapsing reach my ears, even here. I sprint out of the field I'm in, leaping into the skies and flying towards the city. Towards the chaos.

The Valkyrie in me seeks to protect Asgardians at all costs, but my mind is on just one. Edda. I need to get my sister out.

A glance to my left confirms that those who can make it out are running along the docks. Crews are quick to pull people into ships, shouting for them to hurry. Any remaining transport ships hover a few feet above the ground, ready to take off in a moment's notice. I spot other Valkyrie ahead, blasting into the sky only to land in other areas of the city, trying to control the chaos.

The dark sky above rains more fire. As I glide closer, I can make out Asgardian soldiers, holding back some of the fire giants with water, but just as they start to gain ground, more fire giants swarm from behind them. I want to look away, but instincts make me watch, helpless, as their bodies turn to piles of ash so quickly I doubt they felt anything.

I finally spot my mirror image, helping an older woman to docks, shouting and yelling to keep moving. I am thankful for the strength Odin gave me as I dive, scooping both her and the older lady up.

"What are you doing?" Edda exclaims.

"Saving your ass," I retort over the wind that whips around us. I fly low, amongst the roofs of the buildings before setting her and the elderly woman down near docks.

Edda turns defiantly back towards the city as if she thinks I'll let her go back in there. I block her before she gets two steps.

"We cannot leave them." Her green eyes are wild.

"And you cannot stay." My grip on her arm tightens. "I need you to stay alive. The others will need you, Edda. You are

integral to our people's survival." Her expression changes, as if in the pandemonium she'd forgotten all she'd done to help the Asgardians. After Odin's death, she became a leader, one we desperately needed, working with city officials to keep the city running day to day.

Another boom shakes the docks, lava rock landing closer to the ships.

"Safe travels," is all I can stay before I turn to leave. Edda may be my only family left, but I was never good at goodbyes, even temporary ones.

She grabs my wrist, turning me towards her. Fear and sadness shine bright in her eyes. I reach out, placing my right hand on her check. My left one grips her upper arm, where she shares the same tattoo as me. I pull her forehead to mine.

"All will be well, Edda." I swallow trying to get through words I wish I didn't have to say. "I will find you on any planet, in any galaxy. We will be together again, and we'll create a new future. One where you can be the princess you always wanted to be." I smile as she rolls her eyes.

"Find me, Vera. I will be waiting," she says before drawing me into a tight embrace.

She pulls away too soon, wiping her eyes as she goes towards the ships. I watch her go. I can spare a moment for that. To make sure the ship she boards makes it off the planet. She does not turn back, nor do I expect her to, but I still wish she would. She is stronger than me, always has been.

The ship's engines rev as it idles for a moment longer before blasting into the sky. I turn back towards the city to see more fire, death, and destruction. I don't even have armor on, but my sword is with me and that's all I need. I run towards the chaos, as I always have and always will.

Dry brush snaps nearby and I awake suddenly, fire and death ebbing from my mind. I peek through the slits of my half-open eyes before making any movement. Bright eyes sneak closer and steel glints in the moonlight. I shift casually as if moving in my sleep while reaching for the dagger in my boot.

The creature crouches on all fours, creeping closer. I recognize it is an elf, but different than the ones in town. Its skin is as dark as midnight and its hair white as snow. Only a grimy cloth covers its boney body. A dark elf.

Their home world of Svartalfheim, far from this planet, has not seen the bounty of life it once had for many centuries. Now it's no more than a planet of gray, hard-packed dirt floating in space, with nothing living on it except dark elves. Their kind seeks to conquer any realm with more plentiful resources than their own, using them up and killing the inhabitants until the planet is left as barren as their home world.

On Odin's orders, the Valkyrie were often sent to deal with them, to take them out by any means necessary before they got too far in their invasion. I wonder what will happen without our intervention. At least on Alfheim, they are of little threat to the light elves and dwell in caves deep beneath the ground.

The dark elf sniffs the air as if it smells something delicious—its next meal. At this point, I am ninety-nine percent sure dark elves do not usually eat anything other than wild animals and plants. However, without contact with others of their kind, they become almost feral. This one clearly sees me as nothing more than possible sustenance.

It lunges for me with an unearthly screech, but I move quicker, jamming my dagger into its throat. I slide to the side to avoid its wickedly sharp blade as its body slumps beside me. Sitting up, I pull the blade free from its sinewy throat and its cool blood coats my hand. The blood gives off a putrid, almost corrupt, smell.

My heart pounds in my ears, but I don't have time to worry about it blocking out sound. I quickly scan the area to see if others are close by. Silently thanking Odin for the ability to see perfectly even in the pitch black of night.

No matter how much or often I kill, my body shakes afterward with the adrenaline surging through it. The Valkyrien blood in me calls for more death, and I work to restrain it. Breathing slowly and deeply, I shove my shit back in my bag without care.

The blood will attract larger beasts. So, I quickly wipe my knife and hands clean on a rag and stuff it deep in the pack, hoping to mask the scent. I kick the dead dark elf once for good measure before slogging back down the hill.

I could go back into the bar and sleep at one of the tables, but it's a risky move. Too risky. I'll sleep in the alleyway between the shacks along the main street, only until the sun rises anyway.

A light breeze pushes loose strands of grimy hair into my face. Thoroughly caked in purple dust, hungry, bruised, and exhausted, I swat the hair away. I slept horribly in the alleyway last night. The wind tore at my clothes, seeking to push through any gaps in them. Dirt wormed its way into my eyes, making them gritty and red today.

I squint as I look over the landscape. Something waivers in the distance and, though I'm sure it's a mirage, I check my Valkric anyways. A small city blinks into life on the holographic map. That's where I'll head next.

I'm taking a risk, standing on top of the rickety water tower. It sways with the wind threatening to keel over at any moment, but this is the highest point I could find, and I trust this decision more than trying to wrangle one of the horses standing in a row far below me.

I already asked the female elf guarding the horses about purchasing one, but in her guttural Elvish she listed a price that sounded outrageously expensive. I may not know horses well, but I have been around enough to know those are some of the saddest-looking creatures I've ever seen.

So, my surest way to get to that city is to realm-jump, but without having ever seen the place I'm jumping to makes for a tricky journey. I'm more likely to land somewhere other than my intended destination. Plus, the height of the water tower may not be enough to kick-off the realm-jumping magic.

For the most part, Alfheim is still stuck in the Middle Ages, unlike some of the other realms that have advanced technology like automobiles or hovercrafts. This part of Alfheim barely has electricity, and in my opinion, they rely too heavily on their magic to do things everyday technology can handle.

I take a breath, keep hope in my heart, and leap from the water tower. At best I'll land somewhere in the vicinity of the city, at worst, I'll crush a good number of bones in my body when I land in the hard-packed purple dirt below. The air roars around me and I scrunch my eyes closed.

I pop back into existence close to the ground and land on my butt. A rush of relief floods me that I'm not dead. Then dread as I realize I'm not near the city, but an empty oasis whose foliage is unlike anything I've seen in other realms. Vibrant blue stalks shoot straight up, as tall as evergreens, revealing several layers of green fern-like branches at the top. At least it provides some semblance of shade.

I debate using the oasis to fill my canteen, but the water is an odd shade of plum. The blue water mixed with the purple dirt below. That alone is enough to turn me away. Anything that pretty is likely deadly.

My stomach growls angrily, and, after checking the Valkric, I'm only halfway to this "city" called Vanire. With no way to jump there, I begin the walk. On the plus side, I am no longer sweating. Storm clouds converge above, mercifully hiding both suns. I tilt my head up to the soft rain that begins to fall. It trickles down my face, running rivulets in the purple dirt coating my golden skin.

As it comes down more heavily, the earth soaks up the fat drops quickly as if it's been starved for a millennium. I quickly unbind my hair from its braid. It has been stuck in the same style unwashed and uncombed for longer than I care to admit.

The honey-brown color is lighter in parts after spending two months on Nidavellir, the bright suns bleaching it. I run my fingers through its medium length, combing out a week's worth of dirt and grime, and grimace as my fingers fight to undo knots.

Checking my Valkric, I find I am far to the south of the kingdom of Railen's capital city, Haliaz. I make my way through its remote desert region. Panning out on my Valkric, I view the whole of Alfheim, which is made up of about ten or so different kingdoms, spanning over five continents. Railen is one of the oldest and largest empires, yet the most underdeveloped because of its harsh landscape.

I pray the larger city will receive me more favorably than the small outpost did. I dread dealing with more unfriendly elves, but I push my worries to the side. Odin knows I need some new clothes, a good night's sleep, and a hot bath.

Chapter 2

It DOWNPOURS BY THE TIME I reach the city of Vanire. Thunder rumbles in the distance as drops of rain plop on tin roofs and smack against cobblestone paths. The guise of night and rain benefit me and better suit my mood than the heat of the day.

I pull the hood of my cloak tighter around my head as I walk through the now empty streets to find the best inn. While I've afforded myself little luxury since waking up on Niflheim, the realm of the fog and death, today I need a little bit of that.

This inn will likely be the most expensive part of my stay here and my Valkric yields information on Alfheim's currency, Gild. The gold-plated brass circles, stamped with the Elvish words 'Strength, Honor, Loyalty', are accepted across all the kingdoms in this realm. Luckily, elves will accept pure gold and silver pieces just as readily—both far more precious metals than Gild.

I reach the center of town, and once I find what I am looking for, I hide in a dark alley. After counting my dwarven gold and silver from Nidavellir, I use a rag from my pack to collect rainwater that pummels the earth and wipe my face, hands, and clothes clean, hoping to appear less grimy.

I take in the haphazard wooden buildings shoved in between more formal brick ones and colossal stone structures as I wait for my moment to strike. It's as if the city couldn't fit housing anywhere else so they just shoved it into all the alleys in between. Elves run gracefully from overhang to overhang to keep out of the rain.

Then he appears. A tall, pristinely dressed Elf walks out of the inn and into the rain purposefully.

He'll do. I wait for a moment before making my move.

I enter the same inn the male walked out of hours earlier to find its entryway walls swathed in ornately designed emerald velvet. Looking down, I wince. Murky lavender water beads off my cloak onto the plush white carpet underfoot.

There is magic cast on the inn. Elven to be sure. Even with the odd feel of it wrapping around me, I am grateful for it. The magic regulates the temperature while also keeping the humidity out. I breathe in the scent of fresh linens that wafts through the inn and already feel my tense shoulders loosen.

When I reach the reception desk, the female elf sitting behind it lifts her gaze. She has to be well into her fifth century with her graying hair, though it's hard to know age with elves. The more magic they have the longer they stay young.

"Hello, welcome to the Treeline Inn, how many I help you?" The Elvish dialect she speaks is just as choppy as what was spoken at the outpost. I watch her face transform from polite curiosity to shock and disgust as I take off my hood.

I discreetly pinch my arm causing tears to spring in my eyes and sniffle, getting into character.

"I'm returning a key, my lover... I mean my ex-lover dropped when he was leaving." Shaking slightly for good measure, I add, "We got into a big fight you see. I slapped him and I... I've been so selfish, thinking that I could keep a male like him all to myself."

I nearly barf at the tale I weave, but it is a tried-and-true method of getting what I need. Elves are known for their loyalty to their mates or lovers; it is rare they stray even if the relationship isn't serious.

Once they find their mates, they are a pair for life. My stomach rolls at the thought of being with someone for more than a few days.

The receptionist purses her lips in displeasure as she takes the silver key from me. She turns over the silver engraved marker, and her eyebrows shoot up as she reads the room number. I let tears fall down my cheek and can only hope it adds to the helpless image I try to portray, though I hardly have the look of someone defenseless.

"I-I wasn't able to find him but was sure he'd return here."

The receptionist's golden gaze scans me from head to toe warily before saying, "I didn't know Sir Holland had any lovers. He's been a long-time guest of ours, and never have I seen him bring someone home."

"Yes, well, he usually finds them in the alleys and corners." The receptionist lets out a gasp placing her hand on her chest. Her face fills with concern.

"My dear, a man who does not respect the confines of a relationship or a female's heart, does not deserve you." She reaches to pat my hand but reconsiders it, as if remembering what I am.

"Do you th-think I could wait for him? Maybe I can make him understand and take me back, right?" I give her the best doe-eyes and push out my bottom lip as I frown.

She sighs, shaking her head. "I'm afraid not. You should go back to your residence and move on. Sir Holland is not a very understanding male from what I know."

I sigh, giving up on my paltry act and switch to a much more comfortable performance.

Intimidation.

Flashing her a wicked smile, I draw myself up to my full height and watch her face pale. She finally remembers just what

I am, realizes just how easily I could put a blade through her head.

"You see," I say, dragging a dirty finger across the pristine desk in between us, letting the purple water smear across it. "That's the problem."

She swallows audibly as I continue. "I don't have anywhere to stay. I've only just arrived in town. I don't want any trouble," I say full of menace. "I have plenty of gold, but all the other inns are full."

The receptionist looks down at her books with trembling hands. My leg starts to bounce as I pray this works. "I-I have one room available, that's far away from Sir Holland's, but it's not cheap."

I purse my lips as if this is less than satisfactory news but lay one of the sacks of gold on the counter. The woman's eyes widen, and she gives me a trepid smile. "Welcome to the Treeline Inn, Miss…"

"Vera Hjelmstad." I give her a winning smile.

***

The hot water laps around me as I step into the stone tub and sigh. Tension leaves my body and for that alone, I cannot bring myself to feel sympathetic towards the poor receptionist I intimidated into securing this room. I reach for the soap that smells of lavender and eucalyptus and breathe in the calming scents. How I've gone this long without a proper bath is shocking.

My skin turns a deep pink from my harsh scrubbing and by the time I'm done the water is a nice shade of purple from all the dirt. At least it looks prettier than Midgard's shit brown. I drain the water and turn on the tap again for a second bath to scrub my hair clean. The rich smell of food wafts into the bathroom from the meal a servant brought in. I work quickly on my hair knowing a hot meal is close by.

I groan as I take a seat at the small table swathed in a soft white robe. My body stiff from riding. I devour the spread, sausage and some root vegetable. It's still better than most of the food on Nidavellir even if everything here is oddly colored.

From the moment I opened the door to this room, I understood why the receptionist said it wasn't cheap. The room is draped in deep reds and rich creams. The intricately carved mahogany four-poster bed, covered in pillows, calls my name and I am more than ready to dive into it. Across from the bed is a sitting area with a sumptuous red velvet settee, fireplace, and upholstered chairs. The door leading to the private bathing chamber with running water and electricity sits ajar next to the fireplace.

I rub my distended stomach after finishing the meal before moving to sit on the bench under a large bay window. Rain continues to plunk in fat drops against the glass, trailing down in rivulets and streams. I press my forehead to the cool glass viewing the now empty main city square below. Thoughts of Asgardians and Edda try to push to the forefront of my mind, but I bat them away. Keeping my focus on the here and now.

I dig through my pack, placing my dagger and sword on one of the two detailed bedside tables and consider my clothing options for the evening. All my clothing is with the laundress, so my only options are to sleep naked or in the robe the inn provided.

After pulling back the luxurious covers on the bed, I smile greedily and immediately chuck the robe on the floor. The cotton sheets are soft and divine. I am asleep before I can even turn off the lights.

Chapter 3

A LOUD POUNDING AT THE door wakes me up. The sleep that usually evades me hit me hard last night. My exhaustion pulled me under in minutes allowing me dreamless rest. I roll over and pull the sheets over my head as a voice calls out, "Open this door or I'm coming in!" A second voice murmurs something unintelligible.

When I realize whoever's outside the door is not going away, I drag myself out of bed and over to the door, annoyed as the pounding continues. I fling it open.

Shit. There stands the elf from the night before, his hand lifted as if he was about to bang on the door again. The receptionist is in tow.

"What?!" I bark out, switching to Asgardian without realizing it. The receptionist's jaw drops, and the male quickly averts his eyes. I look down remembering I am stark naked. *Nice going Vera.*

Keenly aware of all the scars that mark my body, I try not to think about the newest ones that tell more about my journey than I'm willing to say out loud or spend too much time inspecting. Our scars often tell stories of obstacles we've overcome, the horrors we faced, whether we wish to speak those stories out loud or not. Heat radiates on my face as I quickly pull the robe on from the floor and brush the hair out of my face and clear my throat.

"How can I help you?" I ask politely in Elvish. I look between the receptionist and the male.

"Miss Hjelmstad, don't you recognize Sir Holland?" I survey this Sir Holland in the light of day. His gaze meets mine and a muscle in his jaw tenses. He is beautiful.

His straight nose, high cheekbones, strong jaw, and general light aura would turn many heads in Asgard or any realm. His delicate pointed ears allow him impeccable hearing even at long distances. Those alone give away his Elven heritage. Otherwise, he could easily be mistaken for a god.

Elves in general are a beautiful, if not intimidating, race. Apex predators with a whole slew of abilities far more appealing to me than their magic—from night vision, incredible strength, and unmatched speed to quick healing, dexterity, and a quiet grace other races have never been afforded. That heritage alone gives me more pause than the saber dangling at his hip. Its brilliant silver is a stark contrast to his dark clothes.

"There must be some misunderstanding. This is not my Holland," I say with a confused look on my face. "My Holland is not half as handsome or strong."

I bat my eyelashes and give him a sweet smile. The muscle in his jaw tenses even more, his grey eyes turn to cold steel. I can't help my shameless flirting when this elf is exactly my type. I should have picked a less gorgeous target last night. "Is it possible that two Hollands are staying at this establishment?"

The receptionist huffs. "No, there is only one." She narrows her eyes at me, and I give her an empty smile. I've had two hundred years to perfect my acting and while my performance last night was paltry at best, today I make certain to seem like a total airhead.

"Maybe my Holland didn't drop the key, maybe he'd stolen it?" I tap my finger to my chin, pondering what my next move will be if they try to kick me out.

I casually place my hand on the door to slam it in their faces if needed. Luckily, I didn't unpack much so I could be out of here within minutes, although the lack of clothing would make it more difficult.

"Well, I'm sorry for the confusion Sir Holland," the receptionist says defeatedly. She understands there's little she can do about my presence without causing a scene and backs away down the hall. "I don't get paid enough for this shit," she mutters before turning out of earshot.

As soon as she leaves, Sir Holland brushes past me into the room.

"Sure, just come right in." I roll my eyes at him, closing the door.

"Didn't think I'd remember you when you bumped into me yesterday evening?" The rich, deep tenor of his voice fills the room. He takes a casual seat on the red velvet settee.

I replay the exchange in my head wondering where I went wrong. Normally my scent alone would have given me away, but luckily the stench of weeks' worth of dirt masked it. I was wearing a hood and it was night so even with his heighten eyesight I should have been safe.

"It was a gamble I was willing to make. What gave it away?"

"Your voice," he states.

My stupid mouth shouldn't have been so apologetic when smacking into him. I slipped on wet cobblestones when I turned the corner causing me to fall into him. Lucky for the both of us, he was like a brick wall, completely immovable. He caught me before I even started to brace myself for the fall. As he righted me, I kept apologizing while I reached into his pocket for the key. He hadn't said a word.

Pulling my robe tighter around me, his storm grey eyes rake over me from head to toe. Heat pools at my core and I internally berate myself. It's been a long time since I've been with anyone if one look from this elf is all it takes.

"Why did you do it?" he asks casually, crossing his ankle on his other knee. His Elvish is different from the receptionist's marking him as a foreigner. It's more lyrical, less choppy. I don't answer again. Watching his jaw tense further, I smirk. He knows why I did it, far cleverer than he is letting on.

"Do you normally chat this much before killing someone?"

He laughs, a rich, wonderful sound that makes my toes curl. *Odin above, Vera, really.* "Not usually, but I'm feeling rather generous this morning."

I narrow my eyes, but slowly move to sit across from him in a chair and decide to push my luck. "Have you heard about Asgard?"

He merely nods. "I'd heard there were no survivors, yet here you are." I swallow the lump in my throat, my heart falling to my stomach. "What fortune," he comments with a sneer. I dislike where this conversation is heading.

"If you aren't here to kill me, what is it that you want?" I ask. He blows out a breath as he pushes a loose strand of silver hair behind his pointed ear.

"Are you always so dramatic?"

"Maybe. You'd have to get to know me better to find out." I bat my eyelashes again and the muscle in his jaw jumps. "I was under the impression that elves kill without question when their honor is judged."

He scoffs, waving his hand in the air as if it's the silliest thing he's ever heard. "I merely wanted to see what creature had tried to drag my name through the mud in order to trick an old lady into a room for the evening. I had told Lady Lila that it could only be the vilest creature and it turns out I was right." I roll my eyes at his blatant disgust. Like I hadn't heard this before.

"You know nothing about me," I grit out, working to keep my temper in check.

"Yet you are a Valkyrie, are you not?"

My runes and scent are proof enough of it, but I feel it then. The question he doesn't have to ask. *Where are your wings?* It took me days to adjust to walking without them, gone was the reassuring weight of them on my back.

The memory of losing them pops into my head and I quickly push it far to the back of my mind. My stomach twists. Stupid elf. He studies me for a moment longer before standing to leave. I push my luck again.

"I don't imagine you know a good place to hear the latest gossip. Possibly about Asgardian transports in the area?" Better to ask than wander from tavern to tavern tipsy all day.

He stops near the door and looks at me over his shoulder. "I may."

With that, he walks out of the room.

I don't leave the room for the rest of the day and jump at the knock at my door in the evening. It is only a dwarven servant dropping off my laundry. Classic elves employing others to do their dirty work. I tip her extra and hurry her out of the room so I can change.

I pull out my pants and throw on a light shirt with leather boots, studying myself in the mirror. My brown hair is a mess and there are wonderfully permanent dark circles under my icy eyes. My skin is pallid, despite the dual sun exposure I had on Nidavellir. I quickly braid my hair with the efficiency that comes from decades spent at war fronts.

I still look too much like a warrior with my brown hair braided tightly and my fighting clothes. While I cannot change that I look and smell like a Valkyrie, I could try to appear less intimidating. Key word being *try*. I add new clothes to my mental to-do list as I grab the hilt of my sword from where it rests on the nightstand and slip it into my pocket. Forged by the gods, magic keeps the blade hidden until I release it. Then I head out into the evening in search of information.

———

"Don't want your kind here," the drunk next to me mutters. I ignore him and take another sip of the cool ale. By the second pub, I have become used to the immediate disgust from those around me.

As another elf comes to sit on the other side of me, he stiffens, recognizing me by scent alone. His eyes meet mine and I do not look away from his watery gaze that is so like mine, full of ice chips. I tilt my chin up slightly.

He huffs a breath. "Don't think we've forgotten what your kind did to our lands, our people," he sneers, "in the Dark War."

I rack my brain to remember the war he speaks of, but with so many fought during and before my time it is hard to remember the names of each. He pounds the bar with a hand and the barkeep quickly fills a glass of beer for him. Clearly, he's a regular. "Tell me, when Odin commanded you to go to war, did you ever question who exactly you were helping?"

"I did not fight in that war," I snip out instinctually, but I truly don't think I've heard of it.

"No, you did not because the Valkyrie did not come. When your god decided the elves weren't worth saving from the decimation of the dark elves." I swallow another large gulp of my beer, hoping to drown the elf out. "When the war was waged, our pleas fell on deaf ears," he says before spitting on the floor near my boot. "So many of our kind died before enough armies could be mustered from the various kingdoms."

I cannot think of anything to say. Nothing can console this elf's rage and I will not apologize for something that was out of my control. When I don't say anything, he continues asking questions. "How can you not know your own history?"

I let out a breath. "I know my own history quite well, but we've fought many wars over many millennia when commanded by Odin." It is all I can manage for a response, my anger boiling just below the surface. I struggle to push it down before I explode in this bar.

"And now he's dead, so what will you do with that future?"

Before I can answer or leave, the cool barrel of what can only be a blaster prods into my gut. A gun loaded with laser light. One shot could blow a hole straight through a body; not even Valkyrie can survive a shot to any vital organs. An elf presses half her body into my side, discreetly hiding the blaster from the view of others in the bar.

"What's your purpose here?" she murmurs, towering over my seat, though she can't be more than a few inches taller than I. Her face is turned toward me, but her auburn hair hides it from the room. I can see vibrant green eyes and a smattering of freckles across her high cheekbones.

I can feel my control over my rage starting to slip. "I don't think it is any of your busin—"

"Oh, but it is," she cuts me off.

That's when I notice the crest on her lapel. It's the image of a tree, similar to the one on the wooden sign hanging outside Treeline Inn—the crest of Railen. How ironic, that it's a tree when this barren land has so few. Is she a city guard perhaps?

"I can't in good conscience let you leave here alive when I'll hear tomorrow that you've gone and killed my brethren," she explains.

"Why would I kill elves when I'm here for information. Seems a bit backward, don't you think?" I snap.

She doesn't seem to care and merely asks, "So, you going to tell me why you're here?"

When I don't immediately answer, the barrel pokes

deeper into my side. It is incredibly rare to find blasters on Alfheim. They'd been banned long ago in most of the countries, deemed too savage a weapon, though I'll never understand why. Not when all sorts of weapons could cause nearly as much damage and weren't banned in those same Alfheimian countries.

While I'm sure the black markets still carry blasters, one could not be purchased with Gild alone. A person would need to have an obscene amount of pure gold. Since she has one, she is either a special type of guard, which allows her to carry it, or she is a mercenary for the monarchy.

I finally deign to look her in the eyes, but I read nothing in her blank expression. "I don't want any trouble."

"All the same, I'll need to know your purpose here," she says in high Elvish. She thinks I can't detect or understand the local dialects.

I glare at her, letting her feel the cold darkness in my eyes. "I am looking for survivors." She searches my gaze, unphased by my rising anger or my menacing looks.

Finally, whatever she sees in my face, she deems it enough to leave me the fuck alone. The minute her blaster isn't pushing into my abdomen, I calmly stand and stroll out of the bar. Though I take my time, making sure it looks like my choice instead of the damn elf with the blaster. I will not be returning to this bar again.

Chapter 4

I ONLY MANAGED TO GO to one more pub last night which yielded useless information. Unease settled deep affording me little sleep. Even now, worry fills me. I've heard no news of Asgardian space transports on Alfheim.

I stare at the gold filigree ceiling of my room, absently brushing the mark on the inside of my arm, identical to my sister's.

Find me, Vera. I will be waiting.

My sister's words echo in my head, and I send a prayer to the remaining gods. I hold onto hope that at least someone is keeping my sister safe somewhere.

With renewed determination, I push myself to get ready for the day and head out into the dry heat that already pulses down on the cobblestone streets.

As I walk through the main square, I feel eyes on me. I try hard to ignore them and avoid confrontation as I pay a vendor for what looks like fresh fruit. Biting into it, it's tart, juicy and sweet. It reminds me of an apple, but it's oval-shaped and the color is all wrong, orange instead of green or red. Colors here are everything you'd least expect them to be.

I still feel someone watching me, so I steal through weird side alleys and cut-throughs, switching my pace until I no longer feel the strange presence. Turning corner after corner, until I am in an unfamiliar section of the city. I stop short to study the unrecognizable buildings that surround me before I turn around and head back the way I came.

With the help of the Valkric, I manage to end up at my intended destination, though later than planned. In Vanire's version of a fashion district, the buildings are vibrantly painted with colors so brilliant they make my head hurt to look at for too long. I watch the shops to see which one most people go to; I assume it's the most logical way to find the best clothes.

After making my way into a puke green colored shop with a yellow sign that reads 'Hot Fashion' in Elvish, I hesitate. The styles, even in this shithole of a city, are bolder than I am used to. Clothes I'm not accustomed to wearing often. *Dresses.* Short ones.

Delicate undergarments, made of silk and lace, line the shelves along the walls. The selection of more decent clothing is sparse and I wonder why so many have stopped into this particular shop.

Pulling the most modest piece I can find; I use one of the fitting rooms. I purse my lips as I try it on and look at myself in the mirror just outside the room. I pull on the tight fabric trying to get it to sit right.

"That looks like garbage on you," the salesperson at the counter comments. I glance up at her in the mirror, taking in her pastel pink pixie haircut and caramel-colored skin as she sips her iced beverage. She is *human*. It's unusual to see humans outside of Midgard and yet she speaks Elvish fluently. She must have grown up here. "You should try on something from this section." She waves her hand at a section to my left, not bothering to look up from the magazine she peruses. I tilt my head as I look through the darker-toned dresses.

I pick up one that seems decent. "No, not that one, too boring," she snaps, now giving me her undivided attention. I smirk as I return it to the rack and pull out another one which she shakes her head at. I do it again until she sighs, rolling her sharp brown eyes as she stomps over. "This."

It is a floor-length burgundy dress with thin straps whose fabric is soft and stretchy. The petite human taps her foot waiting for me to take the garment from her hands. Hands stained in a riot of colors marking her as an artist of some sort.

I take it and try it on in a dressing room. It's far lower cut in the front than I care for, but to be nice I go out and show her. She taps a pen against her lip with her hip cocked to the side as she observes me. Her short skirt and cropped top seem more appropriate for an evening out than managing a clothing shop.

"Yup, that's the one."

"At least it has pockets," I mutter more to myself than her.

"You look hot and slightly less intimidating." She laughs, her chocolate eyes twinkling at my expression. At least I got what I wanted.

She walks toward me holding out her hand. I remember that handshakes are a common Midgardian greeting. "I'm Mai. You're a Valkyrie, right? Or I guess what's left of one?"

She notes my missing wings, the scars on my back visible thanks to the dress. *Ouch.* I tip my chin up though, masking my discomfort in her examination of me.

I shake Mai's hand. "I'm Vera, thanks for the help."

"No problem, I can tell this isn't your specialty." I smirk. Smart girl. "You wanna get a drink? You look like you could use one and I know I could as well."

"You mean, right now? Aren't you working?" I ask warily.

Mai laughs again, the tinkling sound fills the room. "I'm helping a friend while she runs errands, so yes right now." She grabs a jacket and shoes and hands them to me. "Put these on too, then we're ready to go."

When I try to hand her gold to pay, she shakes her head.

"You can buy me drinks instead. Besides us outsiders gotta stick together, right?" She smirks and while my instincts tell me to be wary, especially around humans, my stupid brain just can't say no to that. She seems familiar to me, but I'm not able to figure out how.

Mai leads us through a maze of small streets stating she knows the 'perfect spot'. Whatever that means. It looks like a shithole from the outside and surprise, surprise it's the same inside. A dimly lit bar, smelling of stale beer and sweat, with few patrons tucked into the dark corners.

"Hiya Saul!" Mai waves at the bartender who grimaces at her.

"Aren't you a little early today?" Saul, a dwarf, looks displeased by our presence, but it only seems to make Mai even happier. I already like this human, which is surprising, given my predisposition to hating most Midgardians. As I study her, I realize why. She reminds me of Edda whose give-no-fucks, bright personality always lights up the room.

"My friend is visiting, and I wanted to take her to the best bars in town." I grin as Saul turns his critical gaze to me. He plays with the small tuft of hair on his head, deciding if we are worth the trouble, before nodding.

"The usual then." He states, turning to grab supplies.

Mai pulls me to a table cleaner than the others around it, with a good view of the entire room. Saul hobbles over bringing beer and small glasses of alcohol. Damn this girl does not mess around.

She thanks him and waits as I hand him a silver piece, before asking, "So what should we drink to?"

"New friends?" I suggest as I hold up my shot.

Something like guilt flashes in her eyes before she smiles brightly and clinks her glass to mine. Concern momentarily fills me when I catch her reaction, the way her other hand is clenched on the table, but I brush it off. She is harmless to me. The liquid burns on the way down, a feeling I hadn't realized I missed.

"How long have you been here in Vanire?"

"Just arrived, you?" I keep my answers vague.

She tilts her head to the side as she thinks about it. "Four years? Give or take a few months." She sips her beer. "So, what happened to your wings?"

I blow out a breath. "Wow, really diving right into it here, aren't we?"

She shrugs. "Figured it's easier to get the elephant in the room out of the way first."

I scrunch my eyebrows at her reference. "Elephant in the room?"

"Ya, it's an expression. You know? Like a controversial issue that everyone notices but no one mentions or wants to bring up because it makes someone uncomfortable or is personally, socially, or politically embarrassing—"

"Right, I get it," cutting off her dictionary explanation. I run my hand through my hair, so soft and clean compared to the other day. Mai bounces her leg as she waits for my answer. "You heard about what happened to Asgard?" She nods and leans forward as if I am going to tell her the whole story, which causes me to smirk.

"That's how I lost them." I can barely think about it myself, no way I can tell my new 'friend' about it.

She huffs, crossing her arms as she leans back in her seat. "You are a horrible storyteller."

"Thank you," I say as I sip my beer.

"I heard some elves telling stories about Ragnthor, but what actually happened?"

I laugh. "You mean Ragnarok?" She waves her hand, dismissing my correction.

"It was prophesied long ago that there would be a day that Asgard would fall at the hands of one of its own. When that day would come or what would actually happen, no one knew, but it would occur, nonetheless. It started when Odin, the all-father, was killed by L—" I take a second shot that appeared out of nowhere before I can get out his name.

"Loki, who disappeared as quickly as he came. With Odin gone, we experienced the harshest winter ever." *Asgard is falling apart*. The mantra chanted impending doom in my head regularly after Odin died. "That's when some started to abandon Asgard, prepping cargo ships to take Asgardians off world and many of the gods had abandoned us for Vanaheim, the second god realm.

"The usually temperate climate, maintained by the powers of Odin, was replaced with frosty mornings and wind whipped afternoons. We had to ration our food and burn anything we could to stay warm."

I rub at the tightening in my chest, trying to settle the hollow feeling in me before continuing, "Two months later, Loki returned. This time with reinforcements."

I remember the moments before he returned. I was far from the noise of the main city, needing a break from the suffocating chaos that still griped it after Odin's death.

It was so quiet, it felt like the world was collectively holding its breath. Then the breath was released, and the ground began to shake, as if something large has crashed into it. Red light flashed through slate clouds in the distance. I watched in horror as a large lava rock hurtled towards the palace. More, so many more, flew behind it and I knew it could only mean one thing.

"The fire giants of Muspelheim came, turning our fires against us." Mai shudders and I understand why. Fire giants are terrifying creatures made of molten rock and little else, they are bred for war. "Asgard was overrun and the only choice was to abandon it. Some of us continued to fight so the transports got out of the atmosphere." I can still vividly see the large metal cargo spaceships taking off in groups from the different ports.

"But you got out?"

I nod. "I don't know how I did, but I watched the other transports leave with my own eyes. So, they must be out here somewhere."

"And now you look for them? The surviving Asgardians?" she asks, and I nod. Edda is out here somewhere. Talking about this brings up more memories I have yet to work through, so I change the subject.

"How did you end up here?"

She merely shrugs, creating circles in the wooden table with the condensation from the beer mug. "I don't remember how I got here, just remember waking up."

Something tells me that's not even remotely close to the truth, but I don't push it. It wouldn't be surprising if scavenger elves picked her up with others on Midgard and brought her here to serve them. I'd seen it done before and while human trafficking was highly illegal, there was no way to catch every ship.

"Do you ever miss M—Earth?" I catch myself from calling it Midgard.

She shrugs. "Sometimes...I miss the cool fashion and all the awesome entertainment. And not being treated like trash, but I like it here." She pauses thinking about it. "Who knows maybe I'll go back one day." We are both quiet for a moment.

"More drinks!" she exclaims and gracefully hops off her stool to bug Saul.

Mai tries dragging me towards another bar after our first, but I brush her off. I'm tipsy, and with the world tilting ever so slightly, I make it a goal to memorize the city's layout. Though last evening spent traversing through inns and bars was fruitless so maybe it's time to move on.

This certainly isn't the biggest city in the Kingdom of Railen, nor is it the most advanced country Alfheim has.

Looking at my Valkric for the tenth time, I pan out the holographic map to see the biggest cities aren't even in this kingdom, let alone the same continent. I sigh and head back to the Treeline Inn, maybe a nap will help.

Mid-afternoon light filters in through the cream-colored curtains I forgot to close. I squeeze my eyes shut and roll over, running my hand over the soft cotton sheet; the divine bed pulls me back into sleep.

———

I open my eyes to pitch black and momentarily panic that I've lost my eyesight. Sitting up, I realize I'm still in my room at the inn. Talking about Ragnarok brought on a resurgence of the suppressed memories and I spent my afternoon nap reliving the horror.

Apparently, I don't handle alcohol as well as I used to. Though it took me the rest of the day to sleep it off, I'm still groggy as I stretch my arms above me. I slog over to the bath and clean up, pulling on the dress I'd bought this morning. I realize I should have picked out more clothes, but the first friendly face I'd seen in two months and alcohol lured me away from my original plan.

Looking at the Valkric, I choose another district I have yet to explore in Vanire. In this city, there are eight in total and I've really only been through two.

I chose a lower class district where, what I assume are, stray animals roam the streets—creatures I've never seen before. I hear them fight in small alleyways over whatever scraps of food have been found. The cobblestone path has more dirt shoved between each stone, as if helping them all stay together. The smell of piss and refuse assaults my senses every few blocks.

Again, I feel a presence watching me, following me

through the narrow streets. I shake off the feeling; if someone was going to attack, they were certainly taking their time with it. Tonight, I tucked my sword hilt into my bag. I doubt I'll find any trouble, but reaching behind me, I run my finger along the cool steel of the hilt. It steadies me.

Turning the corner, I move towards the sounds of a rowdy tavern. Elves stumble into a large pub, already drunk. As they open the door, bawdy singing blasts out of the packed bar. I sigh, preparing myself for the onslaught of noise, and stroll in.

Here, I am not noticed. Enough drunk patrons cram in so I easily slip through the crowd. Once at the bar, I frown at the alcohol I receive. I haven't drunk so much since my days in Asgard. The dwarves on Nidavellir were a surprisingly sober bunch and plying them with gold was an easier way to get the answers I sought. The dwarves around me now are absolutely trashed, but maybe Alfheim is their holiday, and they get it all out of their system while vacationing.

The mood shifts as the lights in the bar dim, singing quiets, and upbeat music winds through the bar. As a single light is lit behind a white curtain on stage, a silhouette of a female appears. The audience goes wild, calling out to her as she sways her body to the music and slowly moves from one side of the stage to the other. The curtain drops and light is pointed directly at her, my jaw drops.

There stands Mai, clothed in nothing but hot pink undergarments to match her hair. They give her the illusion of curves I know she doesn't have. Glitter glints off her caramel skin in the light as her petite form dances around, enticing the males—all different species—who gravitate closer to the stage. Some have pushed others out of the way.

I forgot that elves are such a prude race, for being immortals. This is what males have for entertainment in Alfheim? It barely passes as raunchy, compared to the orgies Odin and his son, Thor, used to throw in Asgard. I tried to avoid them at all costs, but Loki had dragged me to a few. It took me weeks to get all the glitter out of my hair.

A stagehand walks out from the side of the stage carrying a deep red velvet divan and places it in the center of the stage. I tilt my head noticing how eerily similar the settee looks to the one in my room.

Males go wild holding up Gild in their hands as Mai appears to ponder her decision. She picks a beautiful dark-skinned elf whose hand was not raised, and she pouts when he doesn't move from his seat. The males around him berate him for his inaction while reaching out for Mai at the same time as if to comfort her.

She then chooses a much more willing participant who yelps his excitement while jumping onto the stage. He stands awkwardly as Mai stalks her way over, pushing herself into the front of him. The back of his knees hit the divan, and he sits down quickly.

The music changes into something slower. She dances in front of him, her back to the audience, and the elf's eyes glaze over. She turns to the spectators, sticking her butt out for the male on stage. After a moment, he gets the hint and smacks it. She slowly sits on his lap, still facing the crowd, and grinds on him.

Turning away from the patrons again she continues her ministrations, kissing and licking him. His eyes flutter, and the song quickly ends. As the male is helped up by stagehands, the evidence of his excitement is clear, and the onlookers laugh hysterically.

I decide to wait out her set until the next dancer is brought on stage. Mai saunters through the masses making a beeline to where I stand at the back of the bar. Some patrons outright ask her for the evening as she passes them.

"Surprised?" she asks while putting her hands on her hips, her brown eyes glittering. The bartender hands her a drink and she winks at him.

"A bit."

She snorts and knocks back the drink. "Please, I saw your face when you realized it was me. Priceless." I roll my eyes at her. "I'm done for the evening, and I have the best place I want to take you to." She walks off before I can even agree, to get changed I assume.

Where we go next is unlike anything I've seen in the other realms. I've heard of them before from Valkyrie returning from Midgard, explaining the new phenomena. I puzzle over the name of them for a moment before giving up.

Loud electronic music pumps through speakers. Elves wear less clothing than I've ever seen before, though it's all made of expensive glittery material. I am happy I wore the dress tonight.

Lights flash and move through the room where elves dance. Mai pulls me onto the dance floor, and I immediately need more alcohol. I am not drunk enough to dance especially when I've never been good at it. I down more alcohol at the bar and finally join Mai on the dance floor.

Falling into a rhythm we move to the beat, attracting attention from those around us. I'd forgotten what it was like, to have a friend or something close to it and to forget about my worries. To receive attention for a reason other than being a Valkyrie, hated by all.

One of the bolder elves with short black hair wraps his hands around my waist moving with me to the music. I throw my hands in the air as I move into him. I hear Mai cheering and I smile shaking my head.

Bolder still, he kisses my neck gently as I tilt my head to the side, giving him better access. Heat runs through me; it has been far too long. I look for Mai, her pink hair making her easy to spot, and I find her making out with a tall female elf.

The male behind me steals back my attention as he shifts

me so we are facing each other. I grasp his arms feeling his muscles through his thin shirt. His kiss is captivating and surprisingly forward for an elf, not that I've been with many elves.

I pull back breathless and grab drinks off a tray one of the waitresses in even less clothing walking by. I hand the male one and take mine without a second thought. He watches me before taking his.

As he brings his mouth to mine, I taste the fiery remnants of the alcohol. I immediately realize where this is going and give myself a second to think it over. Coming to terms with the idea that I'm wasting another evening with Mai and more likely, this male, I crush my lips to his again.

Light snoring wakes me as an arm tightens around my waist. Wonderful. In my drunken state, I thought it was a great idea to take the elf, whose name I can't remember for the life of me, back to my room. I wiggle slightly in his grasp, and he pulls me closer to his hard body. I let out a sigh.

If I'm honest with myself, I needed the release badly and he wasn't half bad. Moving to untangle myself from him, the elf rolls over. I stand quietly and walk towards the bathroom and pause to see Mai asleep on the red divan.

Was she there the whole time? Mortification rushes through me as I literally die inside at that thought. Shaking my head, I continue into the bathroom.

After cleaning up, I pull on clothes and stare at myself in the mirror for a moment. I look more like a ghost than a Valkyrie. Dark circles under my eyes hint at my eternal lack of sleep. My eyes themselves are duller, the cool gray of first light rather than their usual ice blue.

Guilt runs through me as I remind myself it doesn't

matter. All that matters is finding survivors. Yet any good leads I hoped to find here, don't seem to exist.

Bowing my head, I let out a sigh. I have let myself linger here for longer than I should have here. I need to move on to a bigger country.

Resolute in my decision to leave soon, I pinch my cheeks, trying to add more color to my face before heading back into the room. The male sits up in the bed, resting against the headboard. Somehow, he's gotten a cup of tea.

"Good morning, beautiful," he allures. I consider whether it's worth kicking out the still sleeping Mai to continue where I'd left off with the male. I slink over to him as he puts down the tea on the dresser.

"I'm taking you to breakfast," he says casually. I pause and realize my misstep. Elves aren't the hookup and never see each other again type. I wince remembering that particular detail.

"I'm not really a breakfast person," I lie as I step backward to nudge Mai awake.

He gets out of bed, coming towards me completely naked. Breath leaves my lungs at the sight of his sculpted body. He tilts my head up and kisses me slowly, tantalizing. *Stupid, stupid Vera*, I berate myself internally.

"Maybe lunch after we take a nap." His lips graze my neck and I squeeze my eyes shut, scolding my ridiculous body for immediately warming under his cool touch. As much as I'm ready to go again I can't handle the aftermath with this male.

"Mai and I have big plans today and we need to get moving. Maybe another time." Like never.

I don't take my gaze away from the elf as my hand catches Mai's head and flick her discretely. The elf nods, unperturbed by my excuse. He moves away to find his clothes strewn across the floor in a line leading from the doorway to the bed, the events of the evening clear.

"Don't think you're getting away so easily. I know where you're staying," he says slyly and brushes his mouth across mine once more before striding out of the room. *Shit*, I'll have to switch rooms. I look over to find Mai fully awake with a wide grin on her face.

"Please tell me you weren't here the whole evening?" I ask looking down at her. She's still wearing what she had on the night before.

"Don't worry you were fast asleep when I came in." she smirks, smoothing her short pink hair. "But if I had been here, we'd have had an amazing time."

She winks. I roll my eyes at her before telling her to hurry up. It's time for Mai to help me find any information on Asgardian survivors.

Chapter 5

I MOAN, WANTING TO SIT up, only to find that I already am. I try to open my eyes, but quickly closing them against the harsh light coming into the empty room. It's musty as if the windows have never been opened to let in fresh air.

What happened? I look around, trying to piece it together. How long had I been here? A couple hours?

Glancing down, I find I'm still wearing the same outfit, so it's a solid theory. I force myself to remember what happened, bits and pieces filter through my vision. My brain is working at quarter capacity and my liver is crying.

After six rounds at two different taverns with Mai, I was gone, and it wasn't even the afternoon. I have no recollection of us finding out anything about survivors. Mai and I left the bars and went to what I can only describe as a day club, similar to the club we went to the other evening. I finally remembered the damn name of them.

Elves writhed to the deep bass of electronic music, and the raised platform in the front of the open-air courtyard held a few gorgeous elves dancing. Mai appeared out of nowhere with more drinks, which we chugged, and I followed her to the dance floor. As we danced, vivid grey eyes came into my vision.

The attached face growled something unpleasant, but it was too loud to hear, and I cared so very little at that moment. I laughed at the grey eyes and danced away but was quickly pulled back to them. Lips crushed against mine and a hard body pushed even tighter to me. Did I moan? I wince at that particular memory. Odin above, I needed to get a grip on myself, but the world was spinning and spinning.

That's it. That's all I remember, and now in a room, tied to a chair, I want answers. A solid way to start off the morning. I roll my neck, hearing it pop far too many times to be only from sitting here.

Moving my mouth, I run my tongue over a partially healed split lip. I sigh through only one nostril; the other is clogged with blood no doubt. I try several tactics to get loose from the bindings, but I am exhausted and waiting for my captor to come tell me why I'm here seems like the best option.

As I shift in the chair, my back aches and rough splintered wood rubs against my scars, causing my heart to squeeze. How I miss my wings. I drift off thinking of them.

My pale white wings spread behind me as I take off flying down the narrow cobblestone street. The tips brush the rough-hewn stone lightly. My breath comes steady as years of training push through me. My blood sings, adrenaline pumping through my veins.

Rhodda flies next to me, and she winces as we climb higher than the buildings and into the direct afternoon sunlight. Her expression warps the light blue runes tattooed vertically under her left eye to her jawline.

As we gain altitude, my vision blurs slightly and my head throbs. At least the nausea has subsided, but the city tilts and whirls below me. I blink a few times to realign it. I am very hung over and we are very late to Odin's Birthday party. Ahead, our destination looms, a golden palace juts above the surrounding buildings at the heart of the city.

"Is Edda coming tonight?" Rhodda asks over the wind

that whips around us. I merely nod as she glances at me. Her charcoal hair flies around her face, while mine is tied back into its usual braid.

I'm sure Edda will appear late in the evening when the party has spilled into the city beyond the palace. Without Edda, there is no celebration at all. She is the life of the party, vivacious and outgoing. While I am the sharp-tongued sister, Edda is warm and kind.

We pass the guards at the gated entrance to the palace, and one calls out, "Valkyrie! You're late!"

His comrades laugh as Rhodda waves them off, annoyance alighting her lemony green eyes and we continue towards the main throne room. We glide through the large, open-air hallways. Sandstone pillars line either side with blossoming gardens beyond them. Floral scents float through the quiet halls, where only the rustling of our wings can be heard.

As we pass a square golden building containing the Bifrost portal, the hum of the engine causes the air around us to zap with a mix of electricity and magic—both items are required to power the machine. Guarded by the watchman of the gods, Heimdall, the Bifrost allows those with permission to travel to and from Asgard from any of the Nine Realms. Though more worlds exist than nine, these are the planets closest to us in our galaxy, Yggdrasil.

Rhodda and I tuck in our wings and land in front of the open doors to the throne room. The Valkyrie stand at the back of the gilded room in formation, ten rows by ten columns. We fall in line with our sisters-in-arms. Our armor shines like the molten gold in the afternoon sunlight, casting a faint glow in our corner of the room. We are Odin's immortal female warriors, who ferry the dead from battle to Valhalla, the final resting place. We decide who lives and dies on the battlefield and can turn the tide of a war in a matter of minutes.

I awake from my dreams of home as a group of elves walk into the room. I swear under my breath when Mai is dragged in. Tear stains coat her cheeks, pink hair askew, and clothes rumpled. These elves are the same type of elves as the one I killed near the outpost.

Not the normal elves from Alfheim, these are dark elves from Svartalfheim. Their skin is the color of the night sky, black with a bluish tint. Outcasts and barbarians, they fight nasty.

I am pulled from my study of them as the elf in the center whistles. He looks as if he's never seen the sun. The color of his clothes, in stark contrast with his skin, match the color of his milky white eyes. His moon-white hair drapes across his face as he tilts his head.

"What a prize you brought me, my little fairy. So, this is who you want to trade for your freedom?" he says in languished Elvish.

I glance at Mai. She mouths "I'm sorry" as fresh tears track down her face. Anger and betrayal rush through me like lava. I should have known better than to trust her. Fucking humans.

I survey the males—only six of them plus their leader. A doable job if these were regular elves, but these won't hesitate.

"Does it have a name?"

"V-Vera, Sir Jasper," Mai squeaks.

"Vera, what a pretty name, and how unusual for a Valkyrie to be so stunning, even with the split lip." I frown in disgust.

Sir Jasper looks to his henchmen. "Did you have trouble getting her?" A few shuffle their feet.

He sighs striding closer, his black boots thudding against the squeaky wooden floor. Only one of his guards trails him a few steps back. Bad move on their part, but I mold a look of fear onto my face, giving the appearance of weakness.

He comes close enough that his rank breath fans across

my cheek. I force myself to remain still, to hold his oddly colored gaze. Jasper ever so lightly brushes a coarse midnight finger over my lip, and I try not to wince.

"We'll fix that," he murmurs.

I'm too tired to find any enjoyment in what I do next. It is too early for fighting, but here we go.

Smiling my warmest smile at Jasper, he traces a finger over my other cheek, pulling his face level with mine. I seize the opportunity and rear my head back, smashing it into his face. My chair tilts back with the force and I push my feet hard on the ground forcing my fall backward. My weight smashes the chair and though pain lances through my back and stars dot my vision, I ignore it.

Jasper curses and holds a hand to his crunched nose, gushing blue blood. His guard draws his sword and rushes me. My arms, still tied to the arms of the chair, block his first blow. Picking up the remains of the shattered chair, I smash it over the back of the guard's head and dodge his next blow. As he falls forward, I kick out his legs. His arms flail before catching himself, sending his blade skittering a few feet away.

"Get her under control!" Jasper rages.

I race to snatch the blade, jumping to my feet as another guard advances. I twist out of his reach and move back towards the first guard. He tries to stand, but I swing the sword down hard on the back of his neck before he can. Cool, indigo blood sprays across my face.

I hear the steel slice through bone and cartilage, and I feel the catch of the blade as it snaps through nerves and tendons. Though I don't mind fighting, I dislike this part; their blood on me or the sound of a sword as it pushes through their body. It's all part of the job, I guess.

"Don't kill her, I need her alive," Jasper commands from where he now leans against the far wall holding his nose. One of the other dark elves keeps an tight hand on Mai's arm.

The other guard knees me in the stomach and I double over as air is pushed out my body, but I don't lose hold of the sword. I swipe out at him blindly and he leaps back, joining the remaining four guards to rush me at once. I back up quickly and assess the guards. I block the first attack with the wooden armrests, but another guard slices into my upper arm.

Fire burns through the cut and though it's shallow, something in me shifts—something I haven't felt for a long, long time and my vision goes red. I am a harbinger of death and I have pushed my body's screams for vengeance down for too long. My control snaps and I become death incarnate.

Twisting and dodging the onslaught of swords, I use the stolen dark elf's steel to cut through openings and holes the elves leave in their attacks. They are sloppy. Two more are down in minutes as I split one's chest wide open and catch another in the throat as my sword whips around.

I long for my real sword, the one built for me by the gods, but it is, hopefully, still in my pack. If I make it out of this, I am ordering room service and a very hot bath. My mind drifts as I fall into the rhythm of killing. Once I have started there is no stopping me. A curse or a blessing, I am never sure.

A whimper pulls me out of it, and as the red fades from my vision, Mai's face filters in. I have her pinned against the wall, my hand tightening around her throat on instinct. She claws at my arms trying to push me off her. Rivulets of blood drip from where she scratches deep, but I feel none of it. Anger is my armor, and it burns through me.

I watch her lips turn blue, caramel skin ashen. She still kicks, trying to fight me off. I purse my lips and decide I cannot kill her. I loosen my grip slightly and she takes a massive breath, no longer fighting me.

Still holding her pinned to the wall, I survey the room. I've even killed Jasper without realizing it. Oops. I let Mai go and she slumps down the wall putting a hand to her throat.

"Please, I'm so sorry," she wheezes out.

"I don't care," I snap. "Where is my bag?"

She shakes her head. I almost slip on the blue blood covering the floor as I walk out of the dank room. Humans. So useless.

There is no one and very little furniture as I push through the hallway opening all the doors to various rooms. I pause near the front door of the building where shafts of light filter through the boards covering the windows. My bag is shoved in the corner next to a mirror. I wince as I peer at my reflection.

She is a hellish portrait of me.

Blue blood covers the runes on her golden skin. The red, bloody scratches deep in her forearms and a slice on her upper left arm are already healing. Sallow cheeks with purplish circles under her eyes betray her exhaustion. Her honey-brown hair is an absolute rat's nest, and she has a split lip with a new black eye to really round out the picture. Her new dress is somehow still intact but spattered in blood, red and blue. Super cute.

I shake my head before turning back to the task at hand, rummaging through my bag to feel the cool hilt of my sword. Letting out a sigh, I walk back through the building to find a bathroom. Splashing water on myself, I wash off as much of the blood from my skin as possible and clean up my lip as best I can. I'm not worried about more dark elves coming, not now that I have my sword again. Mai comes to stand in the doorway watching me as I finish up.

"Where will you go now?" she croaks, throat still sore from when my hands was crushing it moments ago.

I don't respond, still too pissed to form coherent sentences. I walk out of the building into an alleyway without looking back to find I am close to the Treeline Inn.

I swear loudly as I wretch open the back entrance to the Treeline Inn through the stables. After seeing myself in the mirror, I couldn't use the front door, there would be no way to get past the receptionist without a million questions. I pass by a small library where Sir Holland reads a book. He doesn't look up and I don't stop my march to my room up the backstairs.

My earlier wish is granted as I order food and take a hot bath, scrubbing myself clean and taking a closer look at the damage. Not bad. The scratches on my arms are healed, the skin knitted back together without even a pink line of proof it ever happened. My lip is getting better by the minute, though the black eye is still the star attraction.

By later today I'll be back to my usual sour self. When the servant brings up enough hot food for three people, I hand him my newly bloodied clothes; while he doesn't say anything as he takes them, I know what he is thinking. Nothing but trouble. I crawl into bed and let the hum of the city lull me to sleep.

Chapter 6

A BLADE SCREECHES, MOVING ACROSS a whetstone as I walk through the smiths in the middle of the city. Not just any city, but my home. I take a deep breath in, remembering the metallic scent that wafts from this district, so much like the smell of mine and Edda's home.

Brushing my fingers along the grey and white stone wall as I turn the corner, I halt suddenly at what I see, or rather who I see. My beautiful baby sister Edda, sweat dripping from her brow as she concentrates on her consistent grinding of the metal. Her tan arms and face are covered with black ash as she moves metal across stone. In the distance, I hear other smiths work. The rhythmic pounding of red-hot metal against the anvil matches the beat of my heart.

I wonder why she's at the city forges rather than our home. She made me put a forge in it after all. She prefers to be alone while she works and doing it at home gives her fewer distractions. Though now our home smells just like this part of the city, metallic and ashy.

It feels like ages since I've seen her, but I saw her only this morning. She looks up and smiles at me.

I've forgotten how much we look alike, the same golden skin and honey-colored hair. It is in the eyes where we are different. Hers are warm grass fields while mine are calculating pools of ice.

She says something to me, but I am not able to hear her. Moving closer to her, she seems somehow farther out of reach. I pick up my pace, but she is gone. Dread pools in my stomach, where is Edda? I hear the blade move across the whetstone again, but it is much closer.

I sit up from the bed, shaking off the sleep and bruises from earlier this morning, to find Sir Holland sitting on the red settee, same as he had the other morning. Pulling the covers tighter around me, I internally berate myself for sleeping naked again. His beautiful saber is balanced on his knee while he runs the whetstone across it in loving strokes.

I frown, realizing that's why I dreamed about the smiths on Asgard. Why I dreamed of Edda. My chest the tightens at the thought of her. *Where* is Edda?

"Good afternoon," his melodic Elvish breaks the silence. He doesn't bother to look up from his task.

"Hi, ya, sure. Can I help you with something?" I shift uncomfortably in the bed, feeling only slightly less exposed than when I opened the door naked the other morning.

How long has he been in my room watching me sleep? Unwelcomed heat runs through me. I should be more concerned by how he got into my room without me waking up. But to be honest, he's so pretty I wouldn't have been too upset if he finally decided to kill me.

He shrugs. "I thought I was supposed to help you with something?"

Tilting my head, I scrunch my eyebrows not deigning to answer until he looks at me.

"I've decided to take you to the best place to hear gossip." His lips tug at the corners as he sees the shock on my face. As if that's the most emotion he can show.

"Why would you do that?" After yesterday's events with

Mai, I don't trust anyone—no matter how handsome.

His face is a mask of calm as he says, "I have my reasons."

Not a good sign.

"I'll have to pass; I don't accept help freely."

"I thought you might say that." He stands suddenly, wiping his blade across his arm before sheathing it. "I want to make a deal then." My fingers tap against the sheets as I wait for him to continue.

"I saw how well you handled those dark elves. I could have told you not to trust the little human, any that survive around here are always indebted to someone." So, he was the one tailing me. Figures.

"Gee thanks, you were that close and couldn't help?" I ask, rolling my eyes.

He shrugs. "I knew you could handle it." I suppress a shudder. Wariness creeps across my skin like a gust of cold wind. I don't like how he talks as if he knows me. "I need help tracking someone down. I've been close, but I'm always just missing them."

I run my hands through my hair. "So, you want me to track someone for you and you'll show me the best bar in town? I don't really feel like that's a fair trade. It could take me weeks to track someone down, especially in an area I don't know."

"You wouldn't be tracking them on your own. I'll go with you."

I snort. "I don't work well with others." A far cry from the truth, but he doesn't need to know that.

"I only need a second pair of eyes." He scans my arms. "And someone good with a sword. Maybe there's even some money to be made from it. Besides, you'll look less suspicious if I am with you to get whatever information you need. I'll help you, not just show you the best bar." I narrow my eyes at him, thinking it through.

"I don't think you'll be helping me look any less suspicious." I'm well aware that while my appearance in a dress may be less menacing, most know what I'm capable of. His appearance is far more intimidating than mine, though he is an elf.

"How much money?" I ask when he doesn't respond. Running low on funds, I already planned to receive unwilling donations soon.

"Depends."

"On what?"

"How much help you are."

I smirk seductively. "You'll find I can be very helpful with the right motivation."

He ignores my flirting, merely rolling his eyes. "We'll see."

"Do you promise no harm will come to me?"

He huffs a breath. "No."

I smirk. Smart elf. It could take weeks, but maybe we could do both concurrently? He watches me closely as I mull it over. "As long as we do both simultaneously. I can't waste any more time."

"Like you did at the day club?" His grey eyes pierce mine and my stomach drops. Had I kissed him? My eyes widen. I was too far gone that day to be sure, but those were the eyes I had seen through my drunken haze at the club.

I school my face into neutrality when I respond, but his lips curl as if he knows the thoughts racing through my mind. "Exactly... well Sir Holland, I accept."

He strides closer to the bed and holds out his hand. I sigh but shake it, keeping the blankets tucked tight around me. He is close enough that his scent wafts towards me—cedar and warmed bay leaves.

"It's Braun, and please don't forget to put some clothes on and not the ones you got from the lingerie shop," he comments wickedly as I scrunch my eyebrows. He barks out a hoarse laugh. "You mean to tell me you didn't know the shop where you met the human was a lingerie shop?" I suck in a breath as realization dawns on me. Heat rises to my cheeks at my ignorance.

"We start now Miss Vera," he adds with a smirk.

<hr>

I follow Braun to a district of the city I haven't visited yet. Its smaller alleys are more cramped, as if everyone truly lives on top of each other. The buildings seem impossibly tall, especially in the darkness of night. Streetlamps glint off the windows on ramshackle houses. I hop over the occasional puddle to avoid stepping in what clearly is not water.

Exteriors constructed of different materials, from wood, to metal, to brick, to canvas. As if the owners used whatever was available at the time to patch a hole, fix a leak, or simply place a barrier between them and the alley we walk through.

Braun stops suddenly and I run into his back.

"A little warning next time," I mutter as he turns down an even tighter alley ignoring my comment.

At the end of it are steep steps leading down to a small door. He begins the descent, ducking to avoid banging his head on the narrow opening. My stomach becomes queasy. The tight opening and small space below make my palms sweat.

I let out a breath, running a finger over the hilt of my sword in the pocket of my pants. I couldn't leave it in my pack, not after the events of this morning.

Braun mutters something and the door opens with a pop, as if he's used magic to force it. He disappears into the dimly lit room beyond. I take another deep breath, calming myself, having no choice but to follow.

Magic on the door presses against my skin as I walk

down the stairs. Elven magic to be specific. I am again grateful for Odin's gifts bestowed to Valkyrie. We can to not only detect magic, but the type as well.

Elves have the ability to wield the elements: air, earth, fire, or water. Or as they refer to them: Veoor, Terra, Ignis and Laukaz. This magic on the door screams at me to not enter, to avoid the danger ahead, to go elsewhere, but the feelings dissipate the moment I step inside. The tavern spelled with Veoor magic keeps unwanted visitors out.

My eyes adjust quickly, revealing all types of species congregating like at the burlesque house Mai works at. My temper surges at the thought of her and I push it to the back of my mind.

Dwarves play a card game with tiles while bawdy music spills out of some archaic speaker system. Grime that certainly looks toxic spreads halfway down the walls from the ceiling. I shiver at the greenish yellow fuzz.

The stench of stale beer, sweat, and blood hits me and I try not to gag. In the center of the room a human balances on a rickety wooden crate, telling a story. Elves seated at tables seem enraptured by whatever he explains.

I listen as Braun leads us to a table in the back. The story is about some Midgardian war the human survived—is this what passes for entertainment here? He takes notice of us and winks at me. I give him a look of pure disgust before sitting next to Braun. Fucking humans.

"So, who are we looking for?" I keep my mind off the fact that we are in a crowded tiny basement, where the ceiling could collapse at any moment burying us alive. Not how I want to die.

"No one, we are here for your information," he says before ordering us both beers.

When it arrives, I give mine a look of trepidation. I'm unsure if I want to even sip this with my current hangover. I push it away for a moment to work up my courage. I run my fingers over nicks and gouges left on the surface of the wooden table, surely from the many pointy objects stabbed into it over the years.

Braun notices my hesitation. "Still hungover?"

I roll my eyes at him and survey the room instead of answering his question. "You're not from here," I state. I noted his accent the other day but forgot to ask. After speaking so much Elvish, it is more distinct to me now. He shakes his head. "So where are you from?"

He looks at me skeptically. "I'm only here to help you with gathering information."

I smirk. "If we don't look like we are having a casual conversation, we won't seem approachable."

"I don't think having a casual conversation will help us look approachable," he says as he sips his beer. He's right; with my runes visible thanks to the tank top I have on and my hair braided, I look more like a casual warrior than a patron.

My appearance continues to mark me as a Valkyrie. His appearance doesn't help either as beautiful as he is. His white hair, pulled back into a messy bun, makes his facial features more severe. In his leathers with his saber at his hip, he is an idyllic picture of a sellsword.

Nevertheless, I persist. "It couldn't hurt to try."

To this Braun says nothing as we listen to the story the human weaves.

"I am from Haratine and I've only been here for a few months," Braun says, finally breaking the silence. My eyebrows raise. Haratine is far to the east of Railen, on a completely different continent.

"What brought you here?"

"Work," he bites out.

I try not to wince, talking to him is like pulling teeth. "Will you go back to Haratine once you are done here?"

"Not unless I want to be hung from the capital gates." Ahhhh, that explains it.

There had to be a good reason he is a sellsword. He seems far too decent, sparing my life when most elves would have killed me for less than sullying their name—though maybe he'd already sullied his own in Haratine. Everything I've heard about elves describes them as honorable, loyal above all else, and I know from experience that sellswords are not.

"Want to tell me the story?"

"No."

"Why not? What do you have to lose?"

"I don't know you and I don't trust you." Ouch. It shouldn't sting, but it does.

He is right though. I am not to be trusted; under different circumstances, I would have no qualms double-crossing him to make some money by selling him back to Haratine. Odin knew I needed it. He gazes at me as if he knows every thought that crosses my mind. He narrows his eyes, but I ask another question before he can worry about my motives.

"Do you still have family in Haratine?" I hope to push the conversation forward, not thinking about what I'll say if he asks me about my family. Edda's unknown whereabouts.

"A brother, a sister, and my mother still reside there."

"Younger or older?"

He gives me a quizzical look, not understanding the question. "I meant your siblings," I clarify while rolling my eyes.

"Both are younger," he clarifies. "You?"

"A younger sister, Edda."

"I'm sorry for your loss," he grits out as if showing sentiment causes him physical pain.

My eyes snap to his. "She's alive, somewhere out there."

He opens his mouth to say more but closes it as the human appears in front of our table.

A string instrument in his hand, the human strums a jovial tune. I immediately hate him.

"Can it be? What do my eyes see? A beautiful Valkyrie sits before me?" the human sings. I roll my eyes and I can see Braun smirking at my annoyance out of the corner of my eye.

"How can it be true? Are all dead but you?" My annoyance quickly shifts to anger, but he continues, my icy rage not a deterrent for the idiot.

"Asgard has fallen, and the gods are dead, so it is said. Perhaps another tale shall be told, how the Valkyrie reign supreme, no dead left to ferry, their ultimate dream." Memories rise from the back of my mind like bile in my throat, coated in acid. I swallow and push them down.

He toys with me as I fight to control my breathing. "Perhaps the Valkyrie started it all, wanting to see their realm fall."

My anger snaps through me and I kick the empty chair between the human and myself on instinct, needing to inflict harm. It grates against the floor before smacking into him. He doubles over the back of the chair, hitting his head on the seat before flipping over it.

Around us, elves laugh riotously and place Gild on their tables. I realize my mistake; he was baiting me for entertainment. Even if he gets hurt, he is still making money.

He shakes his head as he stands, stumbling back towards his wooden crate stage, making the crowd laugh again. He winks at me once more before starting another tale and I turn away.

"He's right you know. Odd that you survived when all rumors say no one did," Braun comments offhandedly.

"Others did survive."

"Oh? And where are they?" He looks around the bar as if he'll spot one.

I shouldn't be bothered by this. I know how Valkyrie appear to the outside world. I am used to the hate we would get while off-world, but before I had my comrades with me, my sisters-in-arms, to laugh it off.

Now there is only me here and I hate how lonely that makes me feel. It hollows me out. Unable to deal with this desolate feeling I have so rarely felt, I place a silver piece on the table and walk out. Braun does not follow.

———

The next afternoon, I trudge through the heat of midday on a mission to find real clothes. Not that I really mind the dress but looking at it reminds me of that two-faced human. Besides I need more clothes anyway.

After a discussion with the receptionist, she points me to the correct district of the city. Just off the main square where Treeline Inn sits there's a large alley jammed full of elves. They dart this way and that, moving gracefully through the crowds.

Each side of the alley holds different clothing shops. Some show off vibrant colored dresses, much more decent than the options at the lingerie shop. Others display armor and leathers for fighting, but those are crowded by city guards. After my run-in the other day with the female guard in the bar, I don't plan on testing my patience with the guards so soon.

I work quickly to scan the area, checking for any alert, on duty guards. Then I take what I need, slipping my fingers into pouches and money purses of shoppers. In their mad dash from store to store they barely notice my presence. I am a phantom taking what I need, and what I need is more money to pay for these clothes.

After making my way from one side of the alley to the other, I make it appear as though I'm done perusing the street and now plan to venture back in to shop. A calloused hand lands over my wrist, pivoting me to face a city guard. His light stare makes me feel uneasy.

"Something wrong?" I ask in Elvish, keeping my voice light and even toned.

He narrows his eyes at me. "You look familiar."

Panic rises in me, but I tamp it down. Tilting my head to the side, I give him the sweetest smile I can muster. "I've only been here a week; I don't think I've met any guards."

I keep my breath even, steady, knowing elves have incredible hearing. With his hand is around my wrist, I don't doubt my pulse would give me away.

He comes close enough that his scent of fresh linens and clean sweat washes over me. "Yes, it was you. The other night at the club, you were with my friend."

I have no idea who he's talking about, but it couldn't be Braun; there's no way he has friends. There are precious seconds to decide how to handle this, but then I remember the elf I brought back to the inn. "Oh yes! I didn't know you were friends."

He nods. "Are you still with him?"

I almost snort, possessive arrogant elves. Though it's no joking matter to them. "No."

Loosening his grip on my wrist, he steps even closer and at this my heartbeat picks up. He smirks and I know he's noticed the shift. Though he seems to misunderstand the meaning behind it.

I'm about ready to grab a dagger and jam it in his throat when he says, "Good. I was hoping I'd run into you again and get my chance."

Groaning internally, I smile politely before pulling out of range. "I'm sorry, I'm already with someone else." Gods damn elves.

He swears under his breath defeatedly, and I have to pinch myself to make sure I don't bark out a laugh. "Well, come find me if the situation changes."

I smile demurely and nod before heading back through

the shops. Once I'm far enough into the alley, dragged by the crowd, I let out a breath before picking out a shop.

I slip into a quieter one with only a few patrons inside, and while the clothes are plain, they are much more my style—neutral colors. The bustle of noise from outside filters through the cheap grimy glass windows. For a store with such good supplies, it is dusty.

I skim through the items. Buttery leathers and supple suedes slip through my fingers as I run through a stack of pants. I grab two that will probably fit and a few different shirts. I head toward the back and take my time trying on everything in a dressing room.

Once I've decided on what to buy, I head back to the storekeeper. A withered old dwarf sits atop of a precarious stack of books on a chair. He paints item numbers with prices next to them on vanilla paper at the small desk, signs for the different clothing in the shop.

I watch the dwarf work, fascinated with his perfectly straight letters and numbers. His hands are knotted with old age and wrinkles cover his body. The scraggly patch of white hair on his head is waywardly parted in the middle and combed down each side. Big dark eyes scan the work as he stops and scratches his chin, smearing blue ink across the area.

Dwarves are known for their excellence in any medium, whether it be art or jewelry or dangerously sharp swords. Whatever trade a dwarf picks up, they own. Their skill honed into refinement. All of it handled with a gruff finesse that is the dwarven way.

He finally looks up at me, wearily, and I take in the ink-riddled sleeves of his shirt and dirt-smeared pants. He has to be well into his first millennia. Dwarves have a potential lifespan three times that of an elf.

While any race with a lifespan of a thousand years or longer is considered immortal, elves only live until their second millennia at most before passing on, like Asgardians, but dwarves are practically ageless like the gods. Not even appearing to be an adult until their second century, they age at a slower rate.

The dwarf looks at the items in my hand, holding out a finger to do quick math. He croaks out a price. It's cheap enough I don't haggle, especially after my sudden—and completely innocently obtained—influx of Gild. It takes me a moment to realize the Dwarf had spoken in Dvergr, the dwarven language, rather than Elvish.

I'd become so used to hearing it during the two months I spent on Nidavellir, I didn't think twice when he spoke in it. I thank the dwarf in Dvergr, the language so harsh compared to Elvish it sounds like rocks being smashed together. Slipping back out into the chaos of the street, I sling the bag of newly obtained garments over my shoulder.

Chapter 7

IT HAS BEEN TWO DAYS since I've seen Braun. I finally work up the courage to face him and we head to where he is sure his target is staying. I wasn't sure I could handle being around him without wanting to punch him in his stupid face, but I've wasted more time than planned and I am no closer to hearing any news about survivors on my own. This ridiculous bargain seems to be the only hope of finding any information here before moving on.

The moment Braun sees me, he has me change into something nicer. Luckily, I haven't burned the dress I got from Mai's shop yet. I meet him in the lobby of the inn, and he gives me a look I can't read before turning on his heel.

We approach an inn located in the same district as ours. Its exterior is a little worn but still a beautifully structured building with white trimming running along the sides, windows, and doors. When Braun starts to head inside, I grab his arm.

"Why, exactly, are we going inside?"

"It's where he's staying."

"Why not wait outside the inn to see the target, then tail him, instead of trudging in and asking everyone about him? You raise more suspicion doing that than observing."

He ignores my advice and strides into the inn. His jaw practically wired shut, I'm sure he'll crack his teeth with the force he's pressing on them. It's the only show of annoyance he'll allow. With a sigh, I follow him inside.

"Which room is he staying in?" Braun asks the shaking receptionist in a deadly calm voice.

I lean against the back wall and let him handle this. The musty lobby is empty except for us and the receptionist thanks to Braun's loud announcement, telling everyone to get out in the next five seconds or he'd burn the place to the ground. I shake my head at Braun's handle on the situation.

After a thorough interrogation of the poor receptionist, who looks like he may piss his pants at any second, he hands over a copy of the room key. Braun storms up the stairs with no subtlety and doesn't even bother to use the key.

He kicks in the door with his sword drawn. Upon inspection, there is no sign of anyone here. The bedsheets are rumpled, but everything looks in order. I place my hand on the bed, finding it stone cold. I check the fireplace, but there are no ashes in it, though it is the middle of summer so it's not surprising.

"No one has been here for a while," I comment.

Regardless of my statement, the room is thoroughly searched by Braun. He angrily flips over the mattress, chairs, and table. I lean against the door frame enjoying the view of him displaying emotion for once. The room looks like a major weather event hit it once he finishes throwing his fit. I trail him as he stomps out of the inn with absolutely no concern for the damage he's caused.

When we head back to the Treeline inn, I pause as we pass a small square feeling eyes on me. As I look around, Mai steps out of the buildings' shadow. I ignore her as she calls out my name. She does not follow when I continue after Braun.

"How long have you been tracking this person anyway?" I ask as I catch up to Braun. He grumbles a response. Clearly, it has been longer than he cares to admit.

"I have an idea. Maybe this person knows your face, he

knows who to look for. Let's figure out the next place he'll stay, and I'll tell you the plan as we go." Braun looks at me skeptically before nodding. He appears to be a decent enough mercenary, but spying is clearly not his calling. He is a bull in a china shop anytime he becomes the least bit frustrated, and with this job, he seems constantly annoyed.

I sit in the little library of the Treeline, pouring over the information Braun gave me on the target, which, in fact, is incredibly useless. It doesn't mention the appearance of the target, only his name and the last ten places the man has stayed. No wonder Braun is so annoyed with this job. He gruffly smacked the information he had onto the library table before briskly walking out. He'd apparently had enough for today.

Pins stick in a city map for each of the places Braun's target has stayed. There is no distinguishable pattern in the target's selection of inns, and in a city this size there are an infinite amount. I pinch the space between my eyes, wishing my sisters-in-arms were here, especially Kellin. Her face flashes through my memory.

Dark mocha skin, charcoal lined inky black eyes, and hair braided tight against her scalp on one side above her right ear. The rest left to hang loose, covering her left eye, and making her one of the more terrifying Valkyrie. She and Rhodda would be helpful right about now, both excellent at deciphering the indiscernible.

Kellin could pick up more information from a twig than I could in the last three months I've spent looking for them. I long for their insight, their ability to see everything from all angles.

Pushing the map to the side, I plop into a chair at the wooden table more dramatically than needed. I rub my chest at the thought of the Valkyrie. Where are you?

I shove my thoughts aside before I spiral too deep into myself and look at the map again. I tilt my head. *Shift perspective.* It's what Kellin said whenever I couldn't wrap my head around something.

I stand abruptly, almost knocking the chair back as I quickly turn the map clockwise, moving North to East. My heart rate picks up and I feel closer but not quite there. I turn the map clockwise once more. Ha!

I sprint out of the room and up the stairs before halting, realizing I have no idea where Braun's room was. I swear under my breath and walk the halls, racking my brain to remember the number on the key I had stolen from him my first night in Vanire.

I stop on the second floor at a room sitting just above the little library I sat in moments ago and don't even bother to knock before entering.

The sound of a blade being unsheathed is the only thing I have time to register before I'm slammed into the wall next to the door. Stars dance in my vision from the force of being thrown back. When they clear, I stare into eyes white with rage. I'm so shocked it takes me a minute before I can talk.

"Speak."

I swallow, causing the blade to dig a bit into my skin, but it doesn't draw blood. "Is this any way to treat your business partner?"

He growls, baring his teeth and leans closer.

I huff a breath. "Fine, I figured out where he'll stay next."

His face morphs into, what I assume is, surprise, though the only change is his raised eyebrows. He drops me and moves with swift grace out of the room and down the stairs, no doubt headed back towards the library.

I rub my neck where the knife was, where a bruise will surely bloom, but my quick healing will have it gone in no time. I casually follow Braun down stairs and Lady Lila pops her head out from the reception area as I step onto the first floor. She's likely heard the commotion of Braun on the second floor. I give her a tight smile and a wave from down the hallway before entering the library. Braun stares at the map.

"That fucker," he grits out as he stares down at the carefully placed pins in the map. The path of all the hotels and inns the target has stayed at forms an erect phallic shape over the city map.

"I don't know, I think it's pretty inventive." I smirk as I watch Braun's anger boil. I cross my arms and sit down, prepared to enjoy another spectacle of him throwing furniture around. I can only imagine Lady Lila's face when she sees his masterpiece.

He surprises me by plopping down in the chair across from me, rubbing the space between his eyes.

"So, you ready to hear my plan?" I ask.

It is another two days before we enact what is, in my opinion, a foolproof and brilliant plan. One that requires little to no bloodshed, which is great because I'm tired of giving the laundress bloody clothes. We sit on the rooftop across from the inn we believe the target is currently at, waiting.

"So how old are you anyway?" It is always so hard to tell with elves. The more magically gifted they are, the more likely they are to stay looking younger longer. I have yet to see any of Braun's powers other than opening a door. Though I doubt that's his only ability with the magic I can feel within him.

"How old are you?" he counters.

"Two hundred and three. My birthday is coming up, you better get me a nice present," I say, poking him in the side. Pissing him off has practically become a sport over the past few days. By the end of the first day, he looked ready to murder me for my antics. I was sure he'd slip into my room and end me.

He snorts. "Not likely." He doesn't answer my question, but I leave it for now.

"What will you do once we finish this job?" I ask, trying to keep boredom at bay.

"If I'm done helping you get your information, I'll take another job."

"You know they say all work and no play makes a grumpy old elf incredibly boring company." I watch his jaw tick, knowing I've managed to annoy him.

"They don't say that and I'm not old."

I roll my eyes, muttering, "Well they should. It might help you with the ladies."

He shifts, finally looking at me. "I don't have any trouble with the ladies." His cool gaze dips to my mouth before meeting mine again. "You would know."

My eyes widen as mortification runs through me. Gods it had been him at the day club. Not that I minded kissing him, but that idiotic moan that came out of my stupid mouth. Unable to get out a quick retort, his lips curl in his victory before turning back his gaze back to the plaza below.

"Are you going to tell me how you survived?" he asks.

"Only if you promise to give me a bigger cut of the reward for this."

His lips curl again, causing butterflies in my stomach. I pinch the inside of my arm trying to bring myself back to the conversation.

I run my hand through my sweat-slicked hair. "Honestly, I don't know how I survived. I woke up on Niflheim—"

"The realm of the dishonored dead?"

I hum in confirmation, suppressing my shudder at the thought of that planet. While one side of the realm is covered in lava, rock, and ash, the other is cloaked in eerie fog and mist. If the oddity of the planet's perfect split in landscape isn't enough to immediately dislike it, then the minor fact that the entire planet is inhabited by the dead and ruled by Loki's daughter, the goddess Hel, is.

"I could barely move. I must have been thrown from the transport on re-entry. It was completely burned up and all I had with me was this pack... and no memory of how I even got on the transport."

He narrows his storm-colored eyes. "What was the last thing you remember on Asgard?"

I swallow hard and only shake my head, unable to share that memory. I glance at him and notice a shift in his expression. Is that concern? His brows are knitted together as if he's solving a particularly difficult word puzzle.

When I don't answer he asks another question. "So, you went to Nidavellir?" He must have marked the silver pieces I used at the tavern the other evening.

"Yes, I couldn't stay on Niflheim for longer than it took to heal." It is not a place for the living and while Valkyrie can ferry souls there, we cannot stay long. Without the ability to realm jump I never could have left. "So, I realm-jumped to Nidavellir as soon as I could."

"Nothing useful there?" He does not seem remotely interested in my ability to jump.

"Only the rumor that most of the Asgardian transports that got out in time went to Alfheim, Midgard, or Vanaheim. Though no one seemed certain of anything when pressed for more information."

It is his turn to nod. He probably understands better than most how shitty word of mouth information can be. "Not a fan of humans, huh?" He gives me whiplash with the quick change of topics.

I raise my eyebrows. "You noticed?"

He nods. "Not that I disagree with you, but care to explain?"

I shrug. "Humans are weak-minded and evil-spirited more often than not. Getting nearly killed by one will certainly leave a bad taste in your mouth." I don't bother explaining that it's not even myself I'm referring to, though I've dealt with my fair share of crazy humans. It's not my story to tell.

Rhodda always had poor taste in men, but what that Midgardian soldier put her through turns my stomach just thinking about it. How could anyone become so obsessive? Breaking to the point where they convince themselves locking someone in a metal cage in their basement for a month is a good way to keep them safe.

I shudder thinking of how we found her, emaciated, hollow cheeks, dark bruises with a dull sheen in her normally bright lime green eyes. He went mad, locked Rhodda up after drugging her, then killed himself. Fucking crazy bastard.

As Valkyrie, we understand the terrors of war. The demons that come from nowhere but are everywhere, haunting us long after the fighting is silenced. Men are not built to endure such horrors and live peacefully afterwards, but Rhodda— Rhodda was in too deep. She thought she could help but instead got caught in the man's tornado.

I am pulled from my thoughts when Braun murmurs, "There." He points to the short, sturdy white-haired elf who hobbles into the inn.

I bite my lip so hard to keep from laughing, I draw blood. *This* is who we've been looking for? An elf who looks older than dirt and certainly not capable of keeping up a two-month chase with Braun. My shoulders shake as a tear of laughter slides down my cheek. I glance at Braun to find no amusement in his too beautiful deadpan face.

I try to keep it together as the old man comes and goes during our surveillance, but I burst out in laughter every time he appears. "What exactly are we doing with him once we've got him anyway?"

"Giving him to the elf who hired me."

"And who exactly is that?"

"The less you know the better." I look at him

suspiciously. Braun seems to be too wholesome and high elven to be a soldier for hire. I say as much to him, but I immediately regret it.

He doesn't deign to answer, but the smirk he gives me is menacing. I have yet to see him in action. *Don't underestimate him*, I chide myself. He is probably older than I can guess and more experienced. I turn back to watch the street before it becomes noticeably awkward that I am staring at him.

Wearing all-black outfits midday on a roof was definitely one of the worst ideas I've had in a long while. The twin suns blaze brightly overhead, mocking me. If I stand up there will surely be a perfect imprint of me in sweat on the roof. Proof of our stakeout if we get caught.

Keeping my mind off the heat, I watch the ornately carved clock in the city square mechanically move its hands as the hours pass and the suns sink behind the roofline. We spent the better part of yesterday tracking the old man's movements. Now we sit on a different roof which provides a different angle of the square and inn below. Tonight, we will make our move.

"You ready?" Braun asks as the clock chimes early evening. I nod, but it doesn't seem satisfactory for him.

I sigh before reassuring him, "Everything will be fine."

It seems to be enough for Braun and he heads down to enter the inn once we watch the target go in. Even as he keeps an even pace across the open courtyard, elves must feel his power. They career away, swerving to avoid him.

I roll my eyes before leaping off the roof and onto the next. Slipping through darkness until I am on the roof of the inn the target is staying at. I climb down the drainpipe attached to the stone building and peer into the room we are certain he'll be in.

The room is pitch black, but the window is conveniently cracked open. Rustling and sounds of quick packing fill the dark space. I wait until the target opens his door before shimmying back to the roof, just in time to glimpse him barreling out the backdoor without even a glance backwards.

After mapping the possible inns that would complete the old man's inventive shape, we have a solid idea of where he's going next. I follow him from above, making sure he can't catch my scent and switch his plans.

He weaves through crowds of nightlife that spill out of taverns and restaurants into the streets. Narrowly avoiding getting beer splashed on him, he moves with refined grace. Tracking him from the ground would have been near impossible.

I land hard on my right ankle after leaping onto the next roof, the jump farther than the previous. I muffle my grunt of surprise and ignore the shooting pain that runs up my leg with each step. When I look down again, he's gone.

Swearing under my breath, I stare at the scene below me, looking for his stupid white hair. When nothing stands out, I keep going, hoping to either catch up with him or catch him at the inn we believe he'll try to stay at next. After jumping between more roofs than I'd care to, I finally reach the roof of said inn and hop to the next one. I have a perfect view of the back of the building.

I see far more into some elves' bedrooms than I wish to, but I keep my eyes peeled for changes. What feels like hours later a light in one of the upper floor rooms flickers to life, and a bellhop walks in with a bag and the old man in tow. Just after the elf tips the bellhop, he turns off the lights.

Odd he would want it to be dark, but maybe he's about to sleep. Hopping back to the roof of the inn, I pull the black ribbon from my hair and loop it on the front of the building. It flaps in a lazy breeze that runs through the city, but it's enough for Braun to know where I am.

I wait for another hour or so before using back stairs that run along the outside of the building from the roof to the ground floor. It's almost too easy. I creep on silent feet and am thankful Braun isn't with me. His thunderous footfalls would have given us away in seconds.

I test the window seal and find it's closed, but I slip my knife under it and it gives way without resistance. Pulling the window open is another challenge. As I lift it, it lets out a muffled squeal.

"Who's there?" a gravelly voice asks from within the darkness.

I pause, hidden underneath the window ledge. When the elf doesn't get up to close it, I drop into the darkness without sound and wait for my eyes to adjust. The old man sniffs the air as I find him sitting on the edge of the bed. He continues to look straight at the window. How has he not noticed me? Elves have exceptionally good vision even at night.

I creep closer to see the man's eyes are milky white. I pull back, before realizing they are not like the dark elves I've seen. He is *blind*. So not only has it taken Braun two months to track this old ass elf, but the elf is also blind! I literally can't wait to give him so much—

"I know you're still here." The old elf interrupts my thoughts. "I can smell you. I know what you are." I suppress a shudder at his quiet voice.

"Valkyrie… I could never forget the scent of your kind— glory and ash. You are not who I was expecting this evening. Are you here to determine whether I live or die?"

I stand in shock for a moment before responding, "I am not here to decide your fate."

"No matter, it would seem another has already decided it for me." He sighs, running his hand over the velvet bed cover.

"Tell me Valkyrie, before you hand me over to that gods-awful sellsword, how is it you are alive when Ragnarok has already come?"

"I've been wondering the same thing," is all I say back.

"I heard an Asgardian transport landed in the Port of Yulamic a few months ago, but something tells me you were not on that transport." My heart pounds in my chest. I know he is stalling, and he could very well be lying, but it still gives me stupid hope. It lifts my spirits even when I know it shouldn't. I have no idea where the Port of Yulamic is, but I tuck that knowledge away for later.

I shake my head then remember he can't see me, so I whisper, "No."

"What is your name, Valkyrie?"

"Vera."

"Truth, Faith." The meaning of my name sends a shiver down my spine. "Tell me a truth, Vera, then we shall go." I swallow audibly.

I don't understand why I am even entertaining this elf. Maybe it is because he is one of a few to speak to me without hate or malice in their voice. Maybe I am feeling vulnerable and making confessions to soon-to-be-dead strangers is easier than telling anyone I care about. Though it's not like I have any of those here either. So I speak a truth, a truth so truthful it shocks even my own ears.

"I was born and bred to kill, to decide whose lives mattered and whose lives didn't. But everything I know is gone and I don't know who I am anymore. I only know I must find the survivors, but I am terrified of what I will find."

The elf finally looks at me, and his eyes seem to pierce my soul. Deeming my truth acceptable, the old elf groans while standing. Slowly hobbling towards me, he holds out his hand.

"Lead the way." I take his gnarled hand in my own and he pats the back of it. I can't help but feel like a true Valkyrie again. Leading him to where fate will decide whether he lives or dies. Whether I will lead him to Valhalla, or to where he would wash away to Niflheim.

Braun meets us right outside the room, posted up against the dark hallway. He gives me a curious look but says nothing as he trails behind us out into the warm evening. He probably heard my confession in the room, but for some reason, it doesn't bother me.

Now that I've said it out loud, it makes it real. I will need to come to terms with it, but for now, I have a purpose. No matter how much the truth scares me, I must find the others.

Chapter 8

First light breaks over the buildings as we walk to the Treeline Inn, heat already starts to encase the day. I can't stop thinking about the old elf, whether he will live or die. I hadn't gone in with Braun when he walked the old elf into once of the fancy brick buildings and I don't know why he was sought after. Maybe I should have pushed Braun on it more, but I couldn't bring myself to ask.

My ways are so ingrained in me, normally I could barely bring myself to care, yet this time feels different and unease courses through me. On Asgard, everything was black and white: decide the fate of men, protect the gods, and bring glory to Odin. It was simple and easy until everything wasn't—until now.

Braun nudges me as we stroll, pulling me out of my head. "Four hundred and eight," he says quietly. I scrunch my eyebrows thinking that's the price he got for the job, but that seems incredibly low.

"Four hundred and eight for the elf?"

He smirks. "No, that's my age. You asked how old I was, remember?" I had forgotten that he never answered and for a moment we are silent.

"Wow, you are old as hell," I criticize, though he doesn't look a day over thirty with his perfectly flawless marble white skin stretching across high cheekbones and glorious muscles. I smirk at him as he pushes me to the side.

"I want to change our agreement," he states.

I whirl to him, my anger immediately rising. "Listen buddy, I helped you fair and square. Now it's your turn to help me!"

"That's not—"

"I thought elves were supposed to be all honorable or some bullshit like that," I snip out, cutting him off. I'm in his face, but now that we are standing so close, he's got at least half a head on me. Tall stupid elf.

"Look—"

"I've already been betrayed once here, I'm not about to put up with it a second time!" I spit. He crosses his arms over his chest. "Well?" I ask.

"Are you done with that little outburst?" He sneers. I narrow my eyes at him, but I falter. Maybe I misunderstood him?

"What I meant is I want to help you find the survivors, not just information." He watches for my reaction, but I hide my wariness. "What you did for me is more than what I would be doing for you. This way it's more even."

I roll my eyes. "We agreed I'd get a cut of the reward and now you want to help me find survivors instead?"

"No, I still plan on paying you, but I want to help you find survivors."

"Why?" I narrow my eyes at him again.

"Let's call it Elven honor or some bullshit like that," he mocks me with my own words.

"If you want it to be even, just give me a larger cut of the reward money. I don't need help finding them, just getting information about their whereabouts."

"What will happen when you move onto the next city on Alfheim looking for clues? You think people there will treat you any better than they do here?" I huff a breath at that. "Exactly, you need an elf, someone that can pass easily through bars and taverns to collect information."

"We'll see," is all I manage to say before I turn around.

We walk in silence for a bit. I don't want to take anyone with me and I prefer to only work with Valkyrie. And if I can't work with them, I don't want to work with anyone. The worry chafes against my heart. I hope I can find them soon.

He pushes a small bag of Gild into my hand before murmuring, "Thanks."

I wave my hand. "All in a day's work."

We approach the inn and I look up as a scream cuts through the air. Mai. Her face is as pink as her hair. She twists her wrists and kicks her legs to wrench out of the guards' grip. The receptionist stands there with her arms crossed over her chest watching the scene unfold.

"Lady Lila, everything alright?" Braun inquires as we approach.

"Oh yes." She brushes down her skirts and tucks a stray hair behind her pointed ear. "Quite alright, just taking out some trash," she explains while eyeing Mai who is being dragged away.

Mai notices us and begins shouting, "Vera! Please, I have to talk to you!" I watch as she's pulled farther away. Braun ignores Mai completely, only pausing his walk towards the inn when he realizes I have not moved. I am still watching Mai be dragged around the corner by elven guards, thinking of that stupid old man. I sigh, roll my eyes, and walk after Mai.

"Is this a wise idea after what she did to you?" Braun murmurs as he grabs my arm spinning me towards him.

"You gave me a second chance, didn't you?" I throw back at him, referring to our earlier conversation.

He chuckles, and the sound is foreign and grating. "This is a business arrangement. I don't trust you any more than I did when you first ran into me." It feels like a slap in the face the way he says it.

"Then you have no reason to follow me," I snap. He growls, realizing his mistake, and lets go of my arm before turning away.

I catch up to Mai a few blocks away where the city guards have dumped her on the ground and are taunting her. They are finely dressed in leather armor with beautiful broadswords at their hips, hilts glinting in the early morning sunlight. I don't really know how to start this conversation; I am never the savior.

"Enough," I say in a deathly quiet voice. One of the guards turns to me, a younger elf with tawny hair and vibrant green eyes.

"What's it to you?" he asks, crossing his arms.

"Leave the Midgardian alone, she's not worth it."

He moves to show his cutlass as he says, "Make us." They are clearly itching for a fight. No doubt Mai's antics have riled them up.

Why is it always fighting in the morning here?

I casually place my hand in my pocket and walk closer. My fingers touch the cool metal in my pocket, the one I cherish and am now glad I've brought with me. The male unsheathes his blade and gets into a fighting stance. His friends move to circle us.

I roll my eyes; here I am thinking they all want to fight, but these are elves. It'll be only the young male and me. So honorable. I just have to get him to yield. So, I pull out the hilt of my sword from my pocket and laughter erupts around me.

They assume this will be a quick fight. They would be correct in that, just not in the way they think. The young guard circles me as I stand still. I close my eyes, just for dramatic effect, but I can feel him perfectly. I know his movements before he makes them, even with my eyes closed.

He yells as he charges from my right, but I dodge his

swing and punch him hard in the ribs. Nothing cracks, but he yelps in pain. I straighten as I wait for his next attack, this time keeping my eyes open. He snarls as he rushes me again swinging his broadsword high over his head as if to deliver the final blow.

I twist just out a reach but watch as the slice cuts through the ends of my braid, causing it to unravel and fall around my shoulders. Wonderful. A haircut I didn't need. He doesn't wait this time or make noise as he moves towards me with grace only elves can achieve.

Moving too slowly, he nicks my upper thigh with the tip of his blade. I grimace as pain lances through my leg. Warm blood spills out, ruining my pants, and I frown. That's enough.

One glance at the hilt in my hand and my gladius shimmers into being from its hilt. Forged by the gods themselves, it can only be wielded by a Valkyrie. Never requiring sharpening or polishing, it is made of the strongest metals on Asgard. I flip it in my hand once, testing the weight that is so familiar to me it is merely an extension of my arm. The elves around us back up a pace.

Now it is my turn.

I bring my sword overhead, catching his. The weight of his body jarring against mine. His body is close to mine so I kick him in the stomach. Air whooshes out of him as he doubles over, a costly mistake on his part. I make quick work of him, using the hilt of my sword to hit him hard in the temple. I knock him unconscious, and he clatters to the ground.

The elves roar at me, but none are brave enough to jump in and take the unconscious elf's place. The audacity! Some even boo, but I merely roll my eyes. I've always fought unfairly, using anything and everything to my advantage. I have no honor, no dignity, and I don't care about these weak pathetic elves.

Pushing past them to where Mai sits on the dirty cobblestones, I offer her my hand. She takes it without hesitation, jerking her head for me to follow.

We wind our way back to the Treeline Inn, but when I stop there Mai keeps walking, albeit with a slight limp. I follow her as she leads us through the city, coming to a halt in front of a breakfast spot.

We sit in silence for a while, as if both contemplating all that has happened. One glance at my thigh confirms that it's completely healed over, though my pants have seen better days. Once the food comes, my stomach rumbles loudly, announcing its hunger to those around us. Nothing works up my appetite more than fighting in the morning, though I don't know if I'd call that much of a fight.

I look down at my plate of eggs on top of a stack of waffles and smile. While the bizarrely colored landscape is nothing like Asgard's, the food is similar enough albeit the wrong color. I was ecstatic to learn that waffles, though the color of cement, are a common breakfast item in cities. I sigh happily as I shove my favorite food into my mouth. Honestly, it doesn't matter how it looks if it tastes the same. Buttery, fluffy heaven.

Mai coughs, a choking sound following it as she shovels her eggs and purple potatoes into her mouth faster than she can chew. It's as if this is her first meal in a while. Seemingly recovered from her self-induced choking, she continues to eat happily. I watch her for a moment, wondering just how she managed here on her own for as long as she did. Even when she was in servitude, it couldn't have been easy coming from a realm like Midgard.

"Tell me a story Mai," I say, this time in a Midgardian language. I can't remember its name but when she looks up, surprised by my switch in language, it's clear she understood me. She swallows her massive bite of eggs and potatoes.

Her chocolate eyes drift to the ceiling, and she twirls a piece of short pink hair on her dainty finger as if trying to decide where to start. I grimace at the fading finger-like bruises across her tan throat. *I* did that.

"I was 18 when I was taken. I lived with my family in a small apartment in a big city on Earth." She takes another bite, luckily a smaller one, as she stares out the window. She watches the busy street beyond as if she's trying to parse out what to say. "My dad was a doctor, and my mom was a lawyer." I don't know what a lawyer is, but I don't to interrupt her for an explanation.

"My grandmother would sit in our small living room, reading passages of her favorite books to my grandfather. Some nights I swear I can still hear her voice in the wind, reading those stories. I shared a bedroom with my younger brother.

"He was such a nerd, he only ever worked on computer programs with his friends and thought up crazy theories about how aliens were real, and they could contact them. My parents thought it was adorable, I thought it was annoying." I can hear the pain in her voice as she continues.

"I was finally about to leave and start college, getting away from our overcrowded apartment. Then one night, we awoke to our apartment building shaking. We all thought it was an earthquake, all of us yelling and hiding under tables and beds if we could fit. Then a blinding blue light flooded the rooms and the door burst into a million pieces. Zapping went off in the main room where my family was screaming. I was hiding in the bedroom with my brother when the shouting stopped.

"I hid my brother deep in the recess of our closet. The bedroom door was flung open too quickly for me to hide again. A hulking dark elf came in and he pointed a blaster at me." I shudder at the thought of the destruction those laser guns could cause. "He inspected the room and I prayed he didn't find my brother, but, when the other elf grabbed me, my brother jumped out of the closet to help. They shot him square in the chest. The laser cutting a hole straight through him, where his heart would have been. I was knocked unconscious shortly after that." Unshed tears brim her brown eyes, but she blinks them back

"I was promptly sold to Jasper, the dark elf you killed, when I arrived here and have been working for him ever since. It took me months to learn Elvish and even now I can hardly read it. Jasper always promised me that if I could find a better replacement, he would give me my freedom. When I first saw you, I knew you'd be a perfect fit, but the more I talked with you... I just—I couldn't do it." She pauses as if unsure where to go next. "The problem was that I'd already tipped off one of his cronies about you so they found me and you anyways."

I nod and stare out the window unable to look at her for a moment. She lost everything, so similar to me, and yet she stands here strong. A survivor. She gives me hope. I feel her scan my face for a reaction.

"If you'd just told me your situation, I could have helped you," I say. The words shock me as they leave my mouth.

She laughs. "Sure, you would have."

She's right.

Only a week ago, I would have laughed in Mai's face if she'd asked me for help, but something has changed. She reminds me too much of my sister and I know if my sister was in my position, she would have helped her. I brush the Rune on the inside of my arm again, missing Edda.

I realize, today I acted like my sister by going after Mai. Sometimes I'm floored by how much humanity I've lost in all the time I've been a Valkyrie.

"You know Hayden found me the other day at the clothing shop and was asking about you," she comments offhandedly, and I crinkle my eyebrows. She rolls her eyes before saying, "You know the elf you slept with from the club?"

I let out a snort, realization dawning on me. Elves are so incorrigible. "And?"

She waves her hand in dismissal. "And nothing. I told him you left town."

I nod, moving what's left of my waffles through the egg

yolk on my plate, before taking a bite.

"I also heard an interesting story the other evening." She quickly tells me about several city guards discussing an Asgardian transport that landed in the city of Merin, which is in a completely different kingdom.

I mull this over as we finish our breakfast, which was quite delicious. I have not looked into the location of the Port of Yulamic either. Something I plan on correcting today.

"So when will we leave?" Mai asks, pulling me out of my thoughts. I raise my eyebrows at her.

"You're not coming with me." No matter where I go next, I don't want to bring along someone else I would have to look after.

She crosses her arms. "Why not? You saved my life; I'm indebted to you. Besides I clearly know more about navigating Alfheim than you. I can help you until you find the survivors."

"I'll be too busy making sure you don't get carted off by the next gang that turns the corner," I say while staring out the window.

"I'm coming with you, whether you want me to or not," she states. Stubborn girl.

"I'll think about it." She grins as if she's won, like I won't sneak out of the city whenever it's convenient for me.

Chapter 9

I POUR OVER THE MAPS Mai brought to the Treeline inn. After discussing it with the receptionist, Lady Lila, Mai is once again allowed to come and go from the inn. We sit in the small library on the first floor of the inn and like everything else in Treeline, it's lavishly appointed. Oak bookshelves wrap around the room matching the wood table in the middle with plush blue velvet seats around it. In the corner a small table currently holds the food and drinks I ordered.

I sip the drink, letting it cool me from the infernal heat here. Afternoon light casts shadows on the map where I stuck pins, marking the port and city locations. The two points could not be farther from each other even as the pins shadows stretch to draw them closer. I pinch the space between my eyes, not sure whether to trust the old elf or Mai.

This information is all hearsay. Maybe I should do more investigating before moving on? Though the thought of having to step into another nasty bar in this town has my stomach roiling. Besides most of the places Braun and I visited revealed very little in the way of information. Maybe a change of pace to one of the larger cities on Alfheim would afford better information.

I twirl a piece of hair around my finger, before running my hands through it. Mai helped fix it up after the hack job it got from the city guard earlier. It now sits on my shoulders, and I already miss its length.

Footsteps approach and I look up as Braun passes by, looking gorgeous in a simple crimson tunic and leather pants. His skin shines like the whitest marble in contrast with the dark tones he has on, and his shoulder-length, silky white hair is pulled up in his usual messy bun. He stops short when he spots us and slowly walks into the room.

"Hair cut?" he asks.

I smile broadly and shake it out. "You like it?"

When he ignores my question, I scrunch my nose sticking out my tongue at him.

"She'll be more trouble than she's worth," Braun comments offhandedly while leaning over to review the maps spread in front of us. Mai gives him a vulgar gesture in return causing me to smirk. I watch the muscle in his jaw jump. "How old are you anyway, fifteen?" I snort a laugh.

"I'm twenty-three, asshole," she states and runs a hand over her pink locks, smoothing them.

"It's not your call to make," I say to Braun.

"If I'm going with you then it is."

I bark out a laugh at this. "Who said anything about you coming with me."

"We had a deal, you help me and I help you." He crosses his arms turning his stormy gaze towards me.

"Then I'm ending our deal, I told you I don't work well with others and I'm not taking either of you," I state with finality and stomp out of the room before anyone can argue with me.

I can't be worried about others, and this isn't about them, or me for that matter. Braun catches my arm in the hall before I make it to the stairs. I turn towards him as his eyes pierce mine and I try to remember to breathe. When I do, all I can smell is his lush scent, causing me to forget what we were even arguing about. Behind him, Mai leans against the wall.

"We *are* going with you, whether you like it or not," Mai quips and Braun nods. Seems he has decided not to argue Mai's presence anymore.

"We'll see," is all I can whisper, before gently pulling my arm out of Braun's grip and heading to my room.

Rhodda and I thought we were late, but it's been ten minutes since we arrived and not a single Valkyrie has moved. Gods mill about, talking amongst themselves while Asgardians flock to them, drawn by either their power or beauty. Probably both.

The room quiets when Odin appears from behind the altar where his golden throne sits. Odin, the all-father, is the ruler of our realm and, just as the old texts say, he is creation. He created the realm of Asgard, and many of those who live in it. His grey beard, braided neatly, is nearly as long as the ruby red robes that swish around him while he makes his way to the throne. His dark eyes appraise the room of subjects standing at attention before him, all his to command.

"Thank you all for being here to celebrate my birthday. Is it my twenty-first?"

A chuckle runs through the room at the use of a Midgardian joke, though it's a known fact that he is over twenty thousand years old. His powerful gods, noble Asgardians, and loyal Valkyrie listen intently as he continues. "Let us celebrate our hard work and dedication to Asgard and its health. We will continue to ensure peace in this realm and others. Those who opposed us have fallen, and we now stand supreme."

A servant hands Odin a goblet; he takes it gently and holds it up. "A toast to Asgard and our dominance over all realms." Cheers erupt around us, followed by a loud bang that echoes through the room. Smoke billows in front of the altar.

I roll my eyes as the smoke clears, revealing Loki, the

trickster god. His theatrics are ridiculous. Clad in his usual Asgardian attire, he looks like a bird of paradise. He wears a purple fitted jacket with long coattails falling to his lower thighs, swathed in black suede breeches that highlight his fit form. His jet-black hair, pulled back by a leather strap, is not quite long enough. Strands fall out of their hold to curl at the base of his neck. Dark hazel eyes search the crowd and I try to shrink into Rhodda's side, hoping to avoid his gaze.

He always pops up when I least expect him to, always trying to win me back. It's a game he's lost every time, so far. He was once my whole world, and now I can barely stand to be around him. It took me years to get over the relationship, which I knew was doomed to fail from the beginning. Hard to be with the embodiment of trickery.

As his gaze finally locks with mine, he smirks and throws me a wink. I frown and subtly give him a vulgar gesture. Rhodda squeezes my arm in warning, but Loki's smirk morphs into a grin. I should have listened to Edda about avoiding him. Loki breaks eye contact as he pivots in place towards Odin.

"Apologies for being so late to the party, Odin. I was in Vanaheim getting some affairs in order." He strides towards Odin but stops mid-step as several guards draw closer. A warning. Odin now lounges on his throne and merely waves Loki away.

The din of conversation picks up again as servants pour into the room carrying trays filled with all types of liquor, as if they were given some silent signal. I grab two glasses from a tray passing by, handing one to Rhodda. We clink the glasses and throw back the alcohol in unison, while the other Valkyrie break formation to mingle.

I'm reaching towards the next servant to grab more, when an arm ropes around my waist and pulls me backward against a hard body. His scent washes over me; I stiffen in disgust as jasmine and lies stuff up my nose.

"Vi, my treasure," he purrs, his nose grazing the line of my neck.

Set on ignoring him and the use of my old nickname, I push out of his embrace and walk away without a glance in his direction or Rhodda's. I don't want to drag her into this. Nor do I speak a word to Loki. Either of those actions will likely get me into more trouble.

He lets me walk just far enough away before miraculously appearing at my side, keeping pace with me as I move through the crowd. Spotting who I need, I make a beeline towards them; Loki stops walking then with a scowl forming on his face, unwilling to move closer to those who wish to kill him.

"Vali." I nod my head as I approach the golden god. He nods back, continuing to scan the room with his pine green eyes. His looks mirror those of his brother, Thor, and there is no safer place to hide from Loki than near a son of Odin. Since Loki killed Vali and Thor's other brother, Baldr, Vali has made it no secret he seeks revenge.

While I have no love for his brother Thor, Vali and I have come to see one another on the same side when it comes to Loki. For a crime that severe, we expected Odin to punish him, but, for whatever reason, Odin will not strike Loki down for his son's death.

Outside of Vali and, unfortunately, Loki, I'm not close with any other gods in particular. Even with Odin, our closeness more like a king to a loyal subject. Blessings and powers are given by him to all Valkyrie once we pass our ten years of training. That alone connects us to him, giving him our loyalty.

As a servant passes by, I grab another two drinks. I down the first, hoping to combat my nerves with Loki here, before handing the second to Vali, who nods his head again. I appreciate his comfortable silence; I'm not even sure what we would talk about given the chance.

We both survey the room, and I catch movement near

Odin as Loki attempts to speak with him once more. The guards halt him again. I smirk. Of course, Odin figured out something I learned the hard way. Ignoring Loki will annoy the trickster god far more than swift justice by Odin's hand.

"It's like he forgot that Odin is furious with him for killing Baldr," Vali murmurs. "I swear he has been slowly losing his mind ever since you two split." It's the most I've ever heard Vali speak, but my stomach drops at what he insinuates.

The hairs on the back of my neck prickle as I notice clear rage on Loki's face for being rebuffed a second time. Loki rarely becomes angry. Usually, he delights in small defeats. "It allows me to take the game further, making my victories even sweeter," he once explained to me. Something in him has shifted and not in a good way. Maybe Vali is right, and Loki is losing his grip on himself. On his magic.

Dread curls in my stomach. I have a bad feeling Loki is about to do something reckless that will probably have a terrible ending.

In a matter of seconds, he disappears only to reappear close to Odin's side, too far from the guards around Odin to be stopped. "I am sorry to say I am not here to celebrate your birthday, dear Odin." He seethes as he reaches into his coat, revealing a blade I hadn't noticed he was even carrying. His trickery blinds us all. "I am here to celebrate your death!"

Vali makes a strangled sound and starts to move towards the pair just as Loki plunges his sword straight through the all-father's heart.

"And so Ragnarok begins!" Loki hisses the last statement in Odin's face, which drains of its usual golden color.

Shouts ring out through the room as we witness the end of our ruler's life. Only a god can kill another god, and it must be with a weapon forged by the gods. The sword Loki produced happens to be just such a blade. Blood pours down Odin's chest, turning his red robes a darker crimson. My heart stops. He will not make it.

Chaos erupts around us. My sisters-in-arms and the soldiers bellow in anger and loss as they charge Loki. I run towards Odin, unable to keep my rage quiet either.

Loki has taken so much from me, yet he always seems willing to take more. I am pushed to the side by the torrent of gods and soldiers flowing past me, moving in the same direction. Loki vanishes before any of us can stop him, not even bothering to make a dramatic exit. Ahead, Vali trembles with rage as slips his hands under his father, catching his fall. The other gods, woefully unable to heal Odin, surround their creator to say a final goodbye.

A feeling runs through me I have so rarely felt. Fear. What will this planet become without its creator?

If Ragnarok is truly here, I am afraid this is only the beginning.

With a gasp, I awake, my heartbeat thudding in my ears. A fine sheen of sweat coats me, my fear in the memory leaking into my body's reaction as I slept. Though sleep always feels like a nightmare these days. Those last months on Asgard plague me, haunt me and I cannot escape them.

I should not have been shocked that Loki started Ragnarok, it was only a matter of time I suppose. But I had hoped he would be better after we separated, I know I certainly was. No longer drowning in his ever-changing moods and personality.

I sigh and push those thoughts, those memories, from my mind. Instead, I return to the debate of where to go first. Both places are far enough away that the quickest way to get there would be to realm-jump, but doing so without my wings and trying to take two people with me seems like a recipe for disaster. The other option would be going by ship.

Here ships are the massive hovercrafts, but aren't nearly

as fast as those on Asgard, so it would take us a few days to reach the Port of Yulamic. The port is located in the Kingdom of Haratine where Braun is apparently no longer allowed.

Maybe going there would get him to not come. I smile at the thought, though he is more useful to bring along than Mai, whom there is no getting rid of. She has nothing holding her here at this point.

I'd already made up my mind to take her with me. Partly because she reminds me so much of my sister, Edda, with her no-bullshit personality, quick temper, and sassy exterior. And partly because if Edda were in my position, she would not leave Mai here.

Besides, it will be nice to have someone else around since Braun's emotional range is that of a carrot, and he's made it very clear this is just a business transaction.

Before I notice what I'm doing, I've changed and am heading down to the stables. I need time to think, but something to do with my hands. I walk down the row of horses to find a stallion asleep with his head in a feed bag. Classic.

Honestly, I would do it too if it wasn't considered impolite. I grab a brush from a bucket in the corner, but as I approach, he awakes and stomps his hoof. I roll my eyes at the stupid horse and hum an old lullaby my mother sang to my sister and me as children as I approach more slowly.

Finally, he settles, and I brush him. Falling into the rhythm, I let myself think about my sister. The only family I had left in Asgard even before Ragnarok. Our parents died when we were young; I was barely twenty, and Edda was only thirteen. We have taken care of each other ever since.

When I followed in my mother's footsteps and became a Valkyrie, Edda had raged. She hated the Valkyrie for what they did. For what they had taken from her, from us. She never understood what it was really like; she never wanted to. She was always so sure I'd die just like mother had.

Though after our first century, she no longer held onto that fear and anger so tightly, her sharp edges fading over time. She was an amazing blacksmith and I hope she still is one wherever she ended up in the nine realms. She's meticulous in her craft, and it shows in each piece she makes, crafted with the intended user in mind. All my armor had been forged by her. I frown remembering it is gone.

"That's a beautiful horse," a voice murmurs from behind me. I whip around to find the young human that Braun and I saw at the bar with the enchanted door. I hadn't noticed someone watching me. I cross my arms as he approaches saying nothing.

"And that is a lovely tune." I roll my eyes at him as he grabs a bucket of brushes. "Thanks for making my job easier," he states while walking to the stall next to me just as I turn back to continue brushing the stallion.

I struggle to hide my shock. "I wouldn't have had to do it if it wasn't done so poorly by you."

He looks up from the dapple-gray horse he brushes and smiles at me. He knows full well I'm lying. I pat the horse one last time before turning to lease.

"I'm sorry," he blurts out and I turn back to him slowly. "For the other night. I was only trying to make more Gild. Plan to go back to earth soon."

I nod, unsure what to say.

"Sucks about what happened," he says more quietly and I'm not sure if he's referring to Asgard or my wings. He looks for my reaction, but I have none. I am too raw after my dreams and the thoughts of my sister. I merely shrug and walk away.

I stand in front of Braun's door for a minute before knocking, as if preparing myself for battle. A muffled "come in" has me pushing open the door. Braun's room is more sparsely appointed than mine, yet he sits on a similar window bench overlooking the city square below.

"You're going to the Port of Yulamic," he states, not taking his eyes away from the scene outside. I move to sit next to him, my knee lightly brushes his as I curl one leg under me. I follow his gaze, curious about what he sees out there. "I won't be making your trip any easier by accompanying you there."

"You don't have any friends there that can cover for you?" He only shrugs like he's unsure if they would help. "Well, you know more about Haratine than either Mai or me, so I think you'll be useful enough." He nods at that, so I continue, "Besides if you get into trouble, I'll come rescue you, princess."

He barks a laugh at that, an emotion I am sure is displayed so rarely he barely knows how to do it. The sound is scratchy and missing the telltale sign of practice.

Chapter 10

BRAUN BOUGHT US TICKETS ON the next transport out, and Mai packed enough clothing to get her through to next year and an apocalypse, as well as some for me. I gave some money to the human, much to the annoyance of Braun, who knew we would need it later.

He even said as much. I'm still not sure why I did it. Maybe because I felt bad for the human; I understood not being able to go home.

From Vanire, it is only a half day's walk to the transport on the coast, so we set out early the next morning. Darkness cloaks the landscape as we walk along the purple dirt road that cuts through an oasis. A small river babbles close by, and birds chitter in the wiry trees.

I walk in silence; it's too early for me to have conversations with anyone without snipping at them. Meanwhile, Braun and Mai currently argue the merits of eating vegetables, which Mai is vehemently against. I rub my head at the headache already forming from listening to these two idiots.

Suddenly, Braun grabs my arm, an order to stop walking. I nudge Mai, but she continues walking, still bringing up any valid vegetable substitutes. The trees have fallen silent and besides the crunch of Mai's boots on the dirt and her words there is silence. She looks back when she realizes we've stopped walking.

Braun puts a finger to his mouth, and I watch fear enter her brown eyes. Braun notches his bow with an arrow and scans the area with it. I pull out the hilt of my sword from my pocket, checking the trees for anything, but I see nothing.

A screech and something brown and leathery bursts through the tree line from above and it dives straight for Mai. There is a twang as Braun fires off an arrow. It finds its mark in the side of the beast, who pulls up and out of range.

"What the hell is that?" Mai asks hoarsely, coming closer to us.

"Harpy," Braun murmurs. "And where there's one there are more. We need to move now." I shudder.

Harpy. I didn't know they occupied Alfheim or any planet besides their home world of Crowinal. The surface there is too hot for even immortals to withstand, with its caves of steam and pits of tar. I haven't seen a harpy in years, but their appearance is unforgettable.

Creatures with leathery skin and wings, brown as mud, and the body of a woman tapering into bird legs with talons. Eyes, dark and ominous. Razor-sharp teeth, ready to cut into anything in its sight. Gaunt faces like they've been starving for years. Their favorite meal is human hearts, of course.

We run off the main path, Mai pants trying to keep up with Braun's long strides. After a few kilometers we stop in a small clearing and reassess. Setting down our packs, we take a quick break. It doesn't seem to be following us as we look up through the trees. I hear no rustle or flap of wings, but suddenly Braun's hand is around my waist pulling me backward. When I follow his gaze, I see why.

"Odin above, are you serious Mai? This again?" I give Mai an exasperated look.

"I didn't do this!" she hisses back.

In front of us are at least ten dark elves, and in the trees,

I spot two harpies. The one from earlier has removed the arrow. Black blood oozes from the open wound, but it doesn't seem to mind.

I groan and mutter, "It's too early to fight." Why is it always in the *morning*?

"All right, what is it you want?" I resign myself to do this again. The dark elves look surprised at having a chance to talk. "We don't have all day," I add. I tap the tip of my sword on the dirt.

"We want you," croaks one, who wears rags for clothes. His moon-white hair is almost piss-yellow. He's clearly not bathed in weeks. His Elvish more guttural without the usual lilt, as if he's halfway to becoming completely feral.

"Wow, super original," Mai says with sarcasm, but I catch her hands shaking as she pretends to study her nails.

"Loki sends his regards." I flinch as my head snaps up to the harpy sitting in the tree. She speaks to me in Asgardian rather than Elvish. Her eyes, wholly black, seem to stare through me as a wide wicked smile pulls at her lips, revealing two sets of needle-like teeth. Barely contained anger pulses through me. I grip the hilt of my sword tighter. That asshole.

Braun pulls Mai behind me and gives me a look that says, *protect Mai and I'll deal with this*. I roll my eyes at him but hold up my sword. Then the dark elves rush Braun, while the harpies hop off the branches they're on.

Their bird-like legs hit the ground lightly, but their sharp talons gouge deep gashes in the dirt, slowly stalking towards us sizing up their prey. The clash of Braun's sword against the dark elves' steel rings in the clearing.

I spin my sword. "You sure you want to do this?" I ask the harpies.

They look at each other for a moment, and I realize they are sisters, possibly even twins. Their tar-black hair is tied back in braids and their onyx eyes look at us as if we are the tastiest treat they've seen in a while. I hand Mai my dagger from my boot as the harpies advance. One clutches a rusted and chipped sword in its serrated, taloned fingers.

The one with the sword attacks first, swiping to cut me in two, but I dodge the attack and slice my sword at her exposed left side. She lets out an earth-shattering screech as black blood gushes out of the gash in its torso. The smell of her blood stuffs up my nose, reeking of rotten fish.

The second, who Braun shot earlier, doesn't waste any time as she whirls with talons out, hoping to sink them deep into my skull. I grab her wrist before she comes too close and knee her hard in the gut. As she stumbles back, the first brings down her sword overhead. The vibration of steel meeting steel runs through my body.

Our bodies collide and I kick her where the gash is. Black blood from her wound soaks into my pants as she crumbles to the ground. This time she doesn't scream, as if the pain has already soaked through her and she no longer feels any of it. She crawls away and I'm one move away from killing her, but the second one engages me before I can.

She picks up the rusted sword the first one dropped. I meet each blow of the second harpy's sword. Out of the corner of my eye, the first pulls herself to stand, clenching and unclenching her taloned fist. Before she draws nearer, a dagger is flying past the right side of my face too close for comfort.

The dagger embeds itself deep into the first harpy's head with a sickening thud, who slumps forward. I raise my eyebrows and look over at a pale-faced Mai whose hands shake. At least she's got good aim.

The second lets out a scream full of anguish and rage. She attacks me with such force, I'm put on the defense. I parry a strike aimed for my heart, but the harpy doesn't pull her attack and the rusty blade thrusts into my left shoulder as it slips over my sword. I stagger back and the rusted blade comes with me.

Tripping over a rock, the harpy takes advantage of the situation, and her taloned feet dig into my shins pinning me in the dirt. I grunt out a breath as fire sweeps through me. Her clawed hand curls over the hilt of the sword in my shoulder and the other hand's nails gouge deep into my right shoulder. Blood spills out where she's dug into the soft flesh and tendons. I gasp short breaths, reigning in the throbbing pain pulsing in my body.

"Poor little Valkyrie, can't fly away." The harpy looms over me, sneering, and twists her sword in my shoulder.

I grit my teeth together as I pant, not letting out the scream my body aches to release.

"Why don't I just take yours?" I hiss as I pull my leg free.

Her talons rake lines down it, drawing more blood. I wince, getting my knee between us and kick her off me with all the strength I have left. She is shot backward, tearing the sword free of my shoulder. It skitters over the dirt landing a few feet away. My vision dances and pain lances through my body. I stumble to stand as the harpy gets to her feet.

She snarls and decides I've not got long to live as she turns her attention to Mai. My heart in my throat, I watch the harpy hurtles towards her. The scene before me unfolds in slow motion.

The harpy flaps her wide brown wings and Mai lurches backward, but not quick enough. The harpy's clawed foot cuts into Mai's shoulder and drags Mai with her. I grab the rusted blade and heave it like a spear as hard as possible, ripping more tendons in my shoulder in the process.

Mai is only a few feet off the ground when the harpy's own sword goes through her chest. She doesn't even have time to scream before the blade pierces her cold dark heart. As Mai and the harpy drop to the ground, her talons rip out of the tender flesh in Mai's shoulder. Mai moans in pain as they hit the ground. I look over to see Braun finishing off the last dark elf, not even a bead of sweat on his forehead. Of course, he's fine.

I stumble over, my legs aching from the puncture wounds the Harpy dealt me. I strain to push off the dead harpy, who landed halfway on top of Mai. Mai rolls onto her back. She pants with her eyes squeezed shut, the pain in her face obvious.

Braun takes a knee next to her within seconds and white light rings his right hand. As he places it lightly on Mai's bloody shoulder, she winces and inhales a sharp breath. I watch mesmerized as Mai's arteries, tendons, and skin knit together as if the wound was never there at all. I had no idea elves could heal.

Once she's healed, he turns to me, but I push his hand away. He frowns. "Your wounds will heal, but can your body handle the infection from the rust on that sword?"

I roll my eyes. "If that's what takes me out of this world, then so be it." I stand, the pain in both my shoulders no more than a needle prick. Though the same cannot be said for my legs.

Braun sighs. "Are you always so stubborn?"

"Are you just figuring this out?" Mai asks from her position on the ground. She pokes her tan shoulder in awe at the completely healed wound.

Braun uses my momentary distraction to drop his hand on my shoulder, and I wince as his magic pushes through the wound, cleaning it out before my body can heal the hole. His magic increases my already quick healing, and I barely mumble out thanks as the pain finally subsides.

I mull over what the harpy said about Loki while I change into clothes not stained with my own blood behind a nearby tree.

"So, are we going to talk about what just happened? Because that seems like something we should maybe worry about." Leave it to Mai to bring up the hard topics. I only grunt in response as I walk over to pick up my pack from the tree where we left them, feeling better with new clothes on.

"I wonder if he's going after survivors in other realms as well." Braun muses and my heart lurches to my throat.

"If that's the case then no one is safe," I murmur. "Though this could have been personal," I mutter more to myself than anyone else. I certainly hope it's the latter.

Mai's head whips around to look at me and narrows her brown eyes. "Why?"

"Because she was his lover," Braun says casually, causing both Mai and I to turn towards him.

"How would you know anything about that?" I hiss, annoyed that anyone knows about it. It was years ago now. I start walking towards the main path.

He shrugs. "A solid guess considering your reaction to hearing his name, and I heard that he had taken a Valkyrien lover." Gods dammit Loki would have told people about it, that ass.

Mai's mouth hangs open. "Wow, I literally have no words."

Braun snorts. "Well, clearly, you have words, you just spoke them."

Mai gives him a withering look without explaining that it's a Midgardian expression. I smirk remembering how Rhodda taught me it after her last stint in Midgard. We spent days saying "literally" in front of every word, driving the others crazy.

"You must be out of your mind if you got involved with Loki," Mai says and while I'm certain she knows very little about him, she speaks true.

I huff a laugh, running my hands through my now dirt crusted hair. "Something like that," is all I manage to get out. It was crazy to think about how I acted around him; how alive I felt.

Being with him was like being a drug addict. One minute you're having the best time, then the next you're crashing so hard, spinning out of control. Every time is the last time, until the next time. I couldn't get enough, yet I was constantly overwhelmed and out of my league.

I imagine it's like that with any god of that magnitude. His very essence is to confuse and manipulate, to trick and create grand illusions. How he painted ours so vividly, us together forever. His treasure he couldn't be without. You would think his previous choice in wives would have deterred me, but instead, it only drew me to him. Remembering my time with him was like being drowned in technicolor rainbows. So beautiful, yet so destructive.

I am pulled from my thoughts as Mai and Braun argue over the weather today. Is it considered fair or good? I pinch the space between my eyes and decide killing them both will put me out of my misery.

Chapter 11

OF COURSE, THE TRANSPORT IS an actual wooden ship, its hull covered in sun-bleached crustaceans, as if it was sailing on the open ocean only yesterday. Now, magically, it hovers about twelve meters above the water's surface. Elven magic lives in the manipulation of the elements, but it is spread so thin amongst the race, it must take more than a few Veoor elves manipulating air to lift this boat. So impractical.

Braun glances back at me as we move to the lower levels, walking along the cramped hallway. I narrow my eyes at him when he does it again. "Something to say, Braun?" I hiss.

He gives me a blank look. "Just wanted to make sure you didn't have a panic attack." I clench my jaw. He must have noticed my hesitation when heading down the stairs to the underground tavern. Those gray eyes of his miss nothing. I frown causing the corner of his mouth to tug upward.

My frown deepens as we arrive at our room on the ship. There are only two beds. One could barely fit Braun and the other would only be comfortable if he could magically shrink himself to Mai's petite height. Mai winks at me as if this was planned, though I can't imagine why. The quarters are tight and musty, and a small wash basin stands in the corner with a mirror next to a large cabinet for our belongings.

"Nice going Braun," I mutter and throw my pack into

one of the cupboards.

"It was the best I could do in the time you gave me; besides, you and Mai can share the bigger bed."

I sit tentatively on the edge of the slightly larger one, and Mai flops down next to me causing dust to fly everywhere. It filters through the light coming in from the porthole above the bed. As Braun sits primly on the smaller bed, Mai covers her laugh. He will barely fit in that bed even if he sleeps tucked in a ball. His discomfort makes me feel better; at least we'll all be suffering.

"Let's go, I want to check out the rest of the ship," Mai says, dusting herself off. I follow her out but stop when Braun doesn't. He merely waves his hand at us to go on without him.

"I thought he'd suggest you two share a bed," Mai comments causally. My eyebrows must have disappeared behind my hairline because she busts out laughing.

"I'm joking," she adds as she nudges me.

"I'm fairly certain he dislikes me," I comment as if it doesn't bother me.

She snorts. "Hardly." I stop, studying her for a moment as she continues walking. "Trust me, I've been around elves long enough to know when they hate someone, and Braun does not hate you."

We stroll back through the narrow corridor lined with doors on one side, other passenger cabins. Walking up a level on creaking stairs, we enter the main dining and sitting area.

This part of the ship has been updated since being on the water, and warm, buttery afternoon light spills in through the floor-to-ceiling windows casting the room in gold. Worn couches and chairs next to coffee tables are placed around where we stand and a more formal dining area with wooden tables and chairs is on the other side. The doors across the room must lead to the kitchens.

We head up to the top deck where the crew moves to

hoist the sails. It is odd to me that they even have to do that when the boat is magically hovering. I sigh, shaking my head at the decisions these elves make. If I had any magic other than what was gifted to me, I would not waste it on such frivolous things when hovercrafts powered by technology are readily available and used in other kingdoms of Alfheim.

Mai and I lean against the rail letting the breeze tease our hair. The salty brine of the ocean sits heavy in the air. "What's it like?" Mai asks as she stares at the horizon. "To be immortal, I mean."

"Long," I state, and she smacks my arm laughing. I shrug, not sure if I even know the answer. "Most of the time, it's just life. You live day to day. I think it only catches up to you when you return to a place and find it is completely changed. I see it on Midgard—I mean Earth. Their technological advances in the last century skyrocketed them past Alfheim and similar realms, but they use their tech differently than anywhere else. It's fascinating but sad. Sad to see traditions, people, and places die. Sad to watch time move on, but to find yourself stuck forever in your existence just as you are."

Her brown eyes study me for a long moment before she turns to face the horizon again. "I used to wish I was immortal."

"And now?" I ask.

"Now..." She runs a hand through her pink locks. "Now I am grateful to be mortal, to only have to live this one life. The impermanence of life makes us do everything with more gumption, more passion. I love that. Besides, immortality sounds... lonely." I nod, far more intimate with that feeling than ever before.

"It wasn't lonely on Asgard," I counter, "not when everyone around you is immortal. It was nice."

"Do you miss being a Valkyrie?" She turns propping her elbows behind her on the rail, now facing the deck.

I tilt my head from side to side before saying, "I am still

a Valkyrie."

"Are you?" Mai asks and I meet her gaze, finding only curiosity in it.

I sigh. "Yes. I still have my abilities, no matter that Odin died. The Valkyrien blood from him and Asgardian blood from my parents still run through my veins. I am what I am, no matter who I receive orders from."

"With Asgard and Odin gone, who do you receive orders from?" Mai presses.

"I suppose I answer to no one now."

"Sounds dangerous," she says with a smirk. "Letting you have free will."

I snort, brushing a finger over the Rune on my inner arm and remembering the promise I made. "That was always the plan. At least, eventually."

When she gives me a confused look, I merely shake my head and push Edda from my thoughts. "I don't miss killing people or just blindly obeying Odin's orders, but I miss my sisters-in-arms. I miss that bond, and I miss fighting with them. We were a lethal force to be reckoned with, and I would go to battle for them any day."

I don't say what I truly miss, more than all of those things, my wings. Without them I am no longer a true Valkyrie, without them, I am no longer me. Just a shell of the person I was before. "I can't change the fact that my home is gone, that Odin is gone, but I am still a Valkyrie."

"But you can change your actions and decisions. You could decide to not be a Valkyrie anymore." I flinch. It's exactly something Edda would say.

"I can't decide that any more than you can decide to be human. I would be nothing if I were not a Valkyrie." My heart aches for my wings. "I am nothing without that."

Mai smiles at me placing her delicate caramel hand on my tan forearm. "You would be Vera and you would be my friend." I place my hand over hers and squeeze it.

Never in my wildest dreams would I have thought I'd be friends with a human. *Never say never*, the stupid Midgardian phrase runs through my thoughts. We stay on the deck watching the suns fade into the west.

———

I sit in the corner of the main level on the transport watching the crowd with Braun seated in front of me. He wears close-cut pants and a loose white shirt while reading a book he's picked up from somewhere, the picture of simple elegance. A scuffed mahogany coffee table lies between my squeaky chair and his threadbare couch. The rug underneath is just as ragged as the couch.

At least the elves on this ship don't seem bothered by my presence or Mai's for that matter. She sits across the room, practically on one elf's lap, telling some story to a group of males. She has them riveted in their seats and they lean close when she lowers her voice, then booms of laughter ricochet off the walls of windows. One elf cries from laughing so hard. I turn away, pretending not to have noticed.

"I wish I had that kind of charisma or the ability to capture males' attention the way she does," a female elf remarks as she takes in the scene. Mai's bright personality and easy laughter light up any room she walks into, while Braun and I hide in the dark corner. "Is she with you?" the female turns to ask us.

I nod as Braun remarks, "Unfortunately." He doesn't even bother looking up from his book.

The female smirks and sits down, uninvited, in the chair to my left. She moves her wavy black hair over her shoulder in a graceful movement. Calling her beautiful would be a discredit; she is beyond that, as most elves are. Her willowy form and brown eyes set her apart, especially from other elves, whose eyes generally come in a spectrum of pastels or lighter tones.

Braun seems to notice the female for the first time and sets down the book on the coffee table in between us. His attention is what the female was waiting for as she now beams at him. While I have watched others in the room, both female and male, stare longingly at Braun from a distance, none have been so bold as to approach. I expect Braun to ask her why she is here, but he doesn't; he merely waits to see how she will act.

"You're a talkative pair," she comments jokingly.

I already don't like her, but I shrug at her response and turn to look out into the darkness of the ocean around us.

"Would you like to have a drink, my *prince*?" she asks. My shock isn't masked quickly enough as I snap by gaze back to Braun, and she laughs leaning closer to Braun whispering, "Don't worry, it'll be our little secret."

Prince? I can feel my hands begin to shake with rage as I cross my arms. He omitted that information when he told me he wasn't allowed back in Haratine. Is he out of his mind? Did he not think someone would recognize him?

He could jeopardize this whole trip if he gets caught by local authorities. I don't have the time to go galivanting through Haratine to find him either, no matter if I told him I'd save him should something happen. Braun holds my gaze, trying to convey something, but I am too pissed to care. I'm sure it shows on my face. He gracefully unfolds from his seat and offers his hand to the female.

"Shall we?" he says without looking at her, his eyes still boring into me. She hops up from her seat like a giddy schoolgirl and places her arm in the crook of his elbow instead of taking his hand, practically hanging on him. I roll my eyes again and turn to look back out into the night.

It is late and I toss and turn in bed. Mai is sound asleep next to me snoring like an angry bull and Braun still hasn't returned. The last time I saw him the female was all over him while he stood there stoically. At that moment, I felt bad for him, but he lied to me.

Though I understand why he hadn't told me, I am still angry about it. He said he doesn't trust me, and this is a business transaction. He knows I now could sell him to the highest bidder the moment we land in the Port of Yulamic.

I huff out a breath and get up to get some fresh air above deck, needing a moment of quiet from the devil sleeping next to me.

There is no one on the main deck save for one person, and I frown recognizing the silhouette cast in moonlight. I consider going back inside, but I end up taking up a spot next to him along the rail. We stand in silence for a long while, and he seems to be waiting for me to speak. We play the silent game for a little longer until I sigh, giving up.

"How was your evening?" I am unable to hide the venom in my voice.

He doesn't respond for a moment, and when he does, he doesn't answer my question. "If you're planning to double-cross me—"

"I'm not." I cut him off. He turns to study my face then, his eyes ash gray and alight with rage, searching for something, though I'm not quite sure what.

He lets out a breath I didn't notice he was holding and turns back to the ocean before murmuring, "Thank you."

We lapse into silence for a moment. "I get why you didn't mention it, but this changes things, Braun. We'll need to be careful who we talk to, who we see."

A nod is all he manages to give me as he continues to gaze at the calm waters around us. I can tell he still doesn't trust me, and I don't blame him.

Yet somehow these past few weeks I've come to trust him a little more. His stoic expression and steady cynicism now comfort me. It has become a small familiarity, a new normal in my life.

"You'd think it would be just as fast for us to sail to Yulamic," I comment, still annoyed about the whole magic-powered boat.

Braun huffs a breath but doesn't say anything.

"How does it work? Your magic, I mean." I switch topics.

He takes a moment as if deciding how best to describe it. "I am a Veoor elf as well as Laukaz," he explains casually, like the ability to manipulate both air and water is just so normal.

Which I guess is true, though I doubt many are as powerful as Braun. Ignis, or fire elves, are just as common as Veoor and Laukaz elves, but Terra elves—who can manipulate flora, fauna, and all that accompany it—are very rare.

"When I'm near the element, it calls to me," he continues. I nod, understanding the feeling of being called to. "It's familiar, like I am a part of it, and it is a part of me. I can manipulate it with merely a thought." At that, water springs up the side of the ship before misting into the night. "It took a long time to master the concentration needed to use elemental magic, but it is useful. Veoor magic is what I use the most, as air is all around us."

When he doesn't add anything else, I prod further, "I didn't know elves could heal."

He sighs. "It is an inherited trait in my family, very unusual among elves. It's believed to be passed down from the Sacred Ones." I remember learning about the original elves that first settled Alfheim, called the Sacred Ones.

On Asgard, we were taught that the elves received some of their powers from Vanaheim gods who procreated with them in this realm, in turn, creating their Sacred Ones. Though I don't say that to Braun, who'd likely consider it blasphemy or sacrilegious.

"What a group we make, an exiled prince turned sellsword, a pink-haired, burlesque dancing human, and a wingless Valkyrie." I smirk and nudge him. He chuckles and I hate how it takes my breath away. What happened to him to make him this way? I cherish the show of emotion, tucking it into the corner of my dark heart.

"Do you think she knows how to fight at all?" he ponders aloud, his expression turning impassive once again. "Beyond using her words."

I shrug, doubting it. We will test Mai in the morning.

I shove Mai out of bed the following morning, earning another chuckle from Braun. Two chuckles in less than twenty-four hours are a feat. She groans as she lands soundly on the floor, covering her eyes from the bright sun leaking through the porthole in our room.

"Time to get up!" I exclaim loudly, causing her to cover her ears and earning me a whispered "shhhhh".

Braun rips the covers out of her hand, and she snarls at him, "Fuck off, asshole!"

He merely tosses the blankets back onto the bed.

"Meet us down a level in twenty minutes. If you're late we're leaving you on the ship when we land," I state before turning on my heel and walking out. I won't actually leave her, but she doesn't need to know that.

"Not the main deck?" Braun asks as he follows loudly behind me.

"We don't need to attract any more attention to you." I raise my eyebrows at him in accusation.

He puts his hands up in defense and I smirk. The level below is storage for passengers' larger bags and boxes. I already took the liberty of clearing a space between everyone's trash for us to see if Mai has any skill and if not, to teach her.

Exactly eighteen minutes later, Mai stomps down the wooden steps, eyes barely open. She pauses at the bottom and calls, "Hello?"

Braun waves his hand above the stacks of crates and she tromps over.

"What's going on?" she asks, eyeing us suspiciously.

"Do you know how to use this?" Braun holds up a short sword, barely longer than his forearm.

She cocks her hip to the side, crossing her arms. "Ya, stick the pointy end into the bad guy." I roll my eyes at her and she grins.

Braun tosses her the sword, and she yelps, moving away in time for it to clank to the ground. "What the hell? You could have just handed it to me!" Braun gives me a look, *I told you so.*

"Pick it up." I lean against the crates, crossing my arms over my chest.

"Fuck you, no," she spits out and turns on her heels. Braun blocks her path, his sword in hand.

"Get past him and you can leave," I explain, picking up on what he is trying to do.

"I hate weapons and fighting, plus I'm hungover from last night," she pouts while looking at me with big brown eyes and a frown.

"Then you shouldn't have come," Braun states, not moving a muscle.

She sighs as she sees there is no getting out of this. She finally walks over to the sword and picks it up, turns and yells, charging straight at Braun. The sword is awkwardly raised over her head in both hands. Braun's sword connects with it before she even has time to start her downward movement. He merely shifts his sword and Mai's clatters to the ground behind her.

Braun hasn't moved at all. I imagine watching him fight is like watching a dancer, albeit a heavy-footed one. Each of his movements practiced and concise, never using more effort than needed.

Mai picks up the sword and rushes again, this time swinging the blade from left to right before cutting up sharply. Again, it's blocked by Braun. This continues for a few more minutes until I become tired of watching and Braun explains, "Your eyes are moving to where you intend the blade to go. It gives up your move every time."

She throws up her hands in exasperation as she stands next to the blade that's been knocked out of her hands for the fifth time. "Where the hell am I supposed to look then?"

"For openings in his stance where you can slide the blade in," I comment offhandedly before turning back to picking my nails. I catch her giving me a vulgar gesture out of the corner of my eye before she turns to Braun.

"Fine, just teach me already," she says defeatedly. Braun brightens up and moves her through basic stances.

An hour later, she is sweat soaked, panting, and laying on the floor. I smirk and push off the crates to head back up when a sword is lightly pressed against my throat. Braun's grey eyes are bright and alert as they watch me from the end of his sword. *Really?* My expression says.

He smirks, *unless you're too afraid.* I roll my eyes at that and pull my hilt out of my pocket, willing the blade into being. It shimmers as it appears, and I slash the air to get a feel for it. It's a shorter sword than most, similar to a gladius, but it's perfect for me.

I size up Braun and his longer broadsword. He attacks first, moving with speed I can barely keep up with. I block closer to my body than I'd like. His strikes come from every angle imaginable, changing so often there is no predictive behavior that I can see.

I change the pace with his next blow, and when he comes close enough, I kick him in the stomach. He doubles over for a moment, giving me an opening to move into the offensive.

My blade slices through the air toward him from the right, but he leans back, and it misses his chest by inches. I use my momentum to follow the path of my slash with a kick that just barely knicks him in his left shoulder and hits his sword hand. I twist in the air, landing in a squat before popping back up.

He is already striking again, winding his sword around him to confuse me before aiming to spear my left shoulder. I perry his blow, and this back and forth continues for several long minutes. A bead of sweat winds a path down the side of my face.

I finally spot an opening and rush towards him. Our blades sing as they collide above my head, but I don't stop moving as I crash into him, taking him down to the floor. My sword is at his throat as I straddle him.

"Yie—" I freeze realizing his sword is at mine as well. I narrow my eyes at him and his lips tug upwards slightly. He puts the slightest pressure on the blade and a rivulet of blood runs down my neck. Leaping off of him to stand, I glare at him as he twirls his sword. I sigh in annoyance but offer him my hand. As he takes it, warmth spreads through my arm at the contact.

I turn to leave, trying to get that stupid feeling out of my body, but his hand still holds mine and turns me back to him. He runs his left finger, ringed in white light, across the cut on my neck. The blood smears, causing me to wince, but the pain ebbs from his healing touch.

His gaze is intense when he meets my eyes, more emotions flitting through them than I've ever seen before. I freeze, unsure what to do. I look around to avoid his gaze and see that Mai is no longer here. Before either of us can say anything, he lets go of my hand. I don't move as I watch him head up the stairs.

Chapter 12

WE LAND AT THE PORT of Yulamic early in the morning and it's unlike any city I've seen before. The port is built on the mouth of the great Ijan river, and the waterway stretches farther east than the eye can see. Houses stacked on top of one another and supported by wooden stilts, keep the buildings just above high tide. Planks and gangways lead from one structure to the next, and the air is filled with the smell of seafood and heavy seasoning.

I am careful where I step on the waterlogged planks as we descend the ramp from the flying ship onto the dock. Around us, elves wait to pick up their belongings the crew throws out of the ship's cargo hold. We have so little with us, we don't have to wait before continuing into the city. Mai and I follow Braun, who wears a hood to conceal his face. He looks menacing in all leather—*and hot*, my ridiculous brain feels inclined to add.

Narrow waterways between buildings are filled with small boats overflowing with vibrant spices, potions, and food, as merchants shout their wares. Pedestrians in fine, vivid silks and linen, stroll along the walkways inspecting purveyors' goods.

The color and chaos of it all is in stark contrast with the gray sky above and murky water below. We weave through people heading towards an inn where Braun was sure no one would recognize him. Sweat slides down my brow; the humidity here is practically suffocating. Mai says as much, complaining quietly while we walk.

Braun stops suddenly and I almost crash into him. Mai collides into my back with an 'oomph'.

"Wait here," he explains.

We are far from the crowds and the fish smell has dissipated slightly. I study the property before us, noting there is little chance that this is an inn. He enters the small, shingled, two-story home that leans slightly to one side, almost as if it's reaching to touch the next building. I get a bad feeling about it almost immediately.

I reach into the pocket of my pants and run a finger over the warm metal of my sword-hilt for comfort. Mai leans against the side of the building tapping her foot impatiently. She seems to be taking note of our surroundings, just like we taught her. I smirk.

Over the third day of our journey, Braun and I had explained to her more useful tips for surviving. Such as blending in and being more aware, marking how many exits are in a room, and noticing unusual or distinguishing features about an area to help you remember it, the number of people that pass by and what they wear. I wasn't sure if she actually listened when we told her, let alone if she'd actually use any of it, but it seems she got the message.

We will not always be there to protect her.

A few more minutes pass before Braun opens the door and jerks his head at us to follow him inside. My stomach drops farther, and I fully grip the hilt of my sword in my pocket before going in. Mai appears more wary than I, forcing me to lead the way.

Incense, used to ward off the outside smell, and magic assault me as we enter. My eyes adjust to the dim light inside where it, magically, isn't nearly as humid as outside, and I hear

Mai gasp. The room looks fit for a king. Rich tapestries hang from the walls, making the room cozy if not a bit stuffy.

I walk over to one, brushing a finger along it. Intricately woven, it depicts an elf on horseback riding into battle.

"That one is from four thousand years ago, the battle of Mt. Pyran." I turn to see a handsome male elf. His skin is the color of brushed bronze, and his rich black hair is braided into a thick plait falling to his mid-back. His eerie turquoise eyes study the painting with intensity.

"It's beautiful," I comment quietly.

"No, my dear, you are beautiful, that is a masterpiece." He turns to me with a smirk which I don't return. I feel a rush of unease as he studies me. My instincts scream at me to get the hell out, but I don't move a muscle.

His aqua eyes roam down my body. "It's been a long time since I've seen one of your kind." He breathes deeply. "Since I've smelled one." It's the magic, the Valkyrien powers, that gives off a particular smell, mixing with our own scents. I remember when Edda first saw me after I became one. She said I smelled like myself, bitter apples, but now with subtle notes of smoke, cloves, and cinnamon.

"Where'd you find this one, Braun?" he comments. I frown as he turns to where Braun leans against an ornately carved dining room chair.

Braun studies me for a moment. "In Vanire."

His friend snorts. "What were you doing in that shithole?"

"Work," Braun comments.

Mai finally stops gawking at all the furniture and puts her delicate hands on her hips. "Aren't you going to introduce us?" she sneers at Braun.

Braun's friend chuckles. "What interesting company you keep these days, Braun. I am Count Pierre Van Louis, but you can call me Pierre. What is your name, little fire sprite?"

Mai narrows her chocolate eyes in scrutiny and glances at me as if deciding whether to give her real name or not. "Mai Zhao."

"And you are?" Pierre inquires, turning to me.

"Vera," is all I say as I cross my arms. He doesn't press me for my last name, it's not important anyway.

"Well, Miss Mai and Miss Vera, welcome to my humble abode. You are free to stay as long as you need." I look incredulously at Braun.

"I thought we were staying at an inn?" I ask Braun through gritted teeth. Pierre seems far too friendly towards a Valkyrie and a human for my taste.

I don't know him, and I don't plan on making the same mistake of trusting someone right away. I can see Mai sizing him up in my periphery.

Braun only shrugs but gives me a rather pleading look. *Please, just trust me.* I narrow my gaze at him, and he huffs a breath, knowing full well I plan on yelling at him the first chance we're alone. I don't like this, but I sigh heavily and nod.

Pierre seems to take the hint and leads Mai and me to a room we will share on the second floor, which is equally as ostentatious as downstairs. I am grateful it has two beds as I cannot stand another night of Mai snoring directly in my ear. I wash up first in the en-suite bathroom leaving Mai to explore the treasures in the bedroom.

Looking at myself in the mirror for the first time since Vanire, I no longer have such dark circles under my eyes, and I've put a bit of weight back on my lithe form—all signs of health returning to my body. My blue eyes look less sad than before.

I can't help the guilt that surges through me, that I should thrive while all of Asgard suffered and died. I push the guilt to the back of my mind, as well as the longing to find Edda, and head out the room feeling more refreshed than I have in weeks.

I catch Braun at the top of the stairs and grab his arm, dragging him back into the room he just came out of.

"Are you out of your mind?" I hiss. "We can't stay here. I don't trust him."

"That's not my problem," he scoffs while crossing his arms.

"Actually, it is your problem." I cross my arm as well.

"And how is it my problem?"

"You threaten this mission with your inability to properly judge character—"

"Oh, and you're an expert on character, huh?" he snaps back defensively, grey eyes sparking with anger. "You trusted Mai when you barely knew her and look where that landed you." I bare my teeth at him, but he continues before I can say anything else. "Pierre is an old friend, he won't betray my trust." I narrow my eyes and he runs his hand through his silver hair. "Pierre helped me escape."

I frown, realizing I still don't know anything about that. "Yes, you have yet to tell me that story."

"And you have yet to tell me your story," he counters.

"I told you I don't remember how I survived," I grit out.

"I'm not talking about that story, I'm talking about your last moments on Asgard," he says exasperated.

I flinch, jerking back as if he physically hit me. A torrent of memories try breaking through the dam I've created to keep them deep in my subconscious and my dreams.

"Exactly," he says. His scent wraps around me as he brushes past.

I smile widely over my shoulder at him. "I'm sure the city guards would love to know that a certain Prince of theirs has returned." It's a wildly absurd thing for me to say, and highly unlikely I'd do it.

"Is that a threat?" He whirls towards me, growling in my face, his anger breaking through. He's so close, our noses practically touch, and the heat from his body seeps into mine.

"You bet it is." I poke his chest with my finger. "The moment I feel even the slightest bit of deceit from Pierre, I won't hesitate to leave."

"Fine," he snaps.

"Fine," I snap back, and I watch him pound out of the room and down the stairs.

A few hours later, Mai and I stroll through the waterlogged city. It seems the weather here, while humid, also coats the coast in constant cloud cover. It casts the city in dull light, making the dark wood of the buildings appear gray and washed out.

We try to quickly orient ourselves with each part, knowing our current accommodations are precarious at best. At least I'm not alone in this feeling. Mai immediately disliked Pierre as well. It reminds me why I brought her along, back up in case my sanity actually fails.

The humidity presses in on us. I immediately wish we were back inside Pierre's, but that would mean interacting with him. Something I'm not in any rush to do. How can Braun trust him? I think of our earlier altercation. I feel lighter now having gotten some frustration out about something, even if it was only over lodging.

We walk through the waterway where merchants on flat bottomed boats show off their goods. As we peruse, Mai and I both take advantage of the distracted elves, slipping any coin we can get from them. We are almost out of the gold, silver, and Gild we pulled together. While Braun financed the ridiculous floating ship transportation, I don't think he has enough for much more.

When an elf with a big barrel belly bumps into Mai, she pouts dramatically. While he apologizes profusely, I slip my hand into his bag, rooting around lithely until I feel a leather pouch. I gently pull it out and start to slip it into my pocket as Mai and I continue on our way, when suddenly my wrist is caught.

My eyes snap up to a golden-haired guard. His sea-blue eyes narrow when he feels my pulse flutter in surprise and his grip tightens as he halts in front of us. I don't drop my gaze from his and tilt my head up slightly. "Planning to rob me of my coin, guard?"

He seems surprised by my reaction, as if he now doubts me stealing the coin. He opens his mouth to say something but is cut off. "Leave them be, Jacque," a familiar voice commands from behind us. "They are with me." *Pierre*.

The guard narrows his eyes further, as if warning me he'll be watching, before letting go. Pierre must be a high ranking officer here if he's able to dismiss the guard so easily.

"So rude," Mai huffs.

Pierre snorts. "I'm going to pretend like I didn't just watch you both rob these poor people blind," he adds once the guard is a safe distance away.

I roll my eyes, pushing past him. "They are hardly poor."

"They have plenty more where it came from," Mai mutters at the same time.

She follows me back down the path we walked, this time staying in the shade of the building as the suns breaks through the clouds. I hate how much I'm sweating.

"Where are you going?" Pierre asks, his tall form easily keeps up with the pace we set. With Braun nowhere in sight, his suspicion is clear. He's just as wary of us, as we are of him.

"Wherever we please." Mai sniffs, not deigning to look at Pierre. He follows us, a silent shadow, as we walk through the city.

We stop in front of an inn. It's not the nicest one, but it looks decent enough.

"Should we ask for a room here?" Mai switches to Midgardian as she asks the question.

I shrug. "Let's pretend to debate staying here."

She nods before rambling off in Midgardian, so quickly I'm not able to follow what she's saying. As if she's laying out points of an argument, she lists reasons while holding up a finger for each. I nod and rub my chin as if I'm contemplating it.

"You can't seriously be considering staying in this dump." Pierre, exasperated with our performance, steps out of the shadows. Mai, overly committed to this act, gapes at him as if she had no idea he'd been following us.

He rolls his turquoise eyes. "You can drop the act."

I turn to face him, crossing my arms. He sighs and runs a dark hand over his braids. "Look, I don't trust you and you don't trust me—"

"We never said that," Mai comments airily.

"You think I couldn't hear your little lover's quarrel earlier?" He waits for me to deny it like I cared if he had. It was certainly not a lover's quarrel, but I don't deny we argued either. When I don't respond he continues. "I may not trust you, but I trust Braun. If he trusts you, then so do I."

I snort. "That's the thing. Braun doesn't trust us."

"He most certainly does if he came with you here."

I'm already tired of arguing and apparently so is Mai when she mutters, "Whatever." He shakes his head and walks away, giving up on convincing us.

"What do you think?" Mai asks.

I shrug. "I think we're safe at Pierre's for now."

"So, you're looking for survivors?" Pierre asks, breaking the awkward silence of dinner. I nod swallowing my food. "Then we'll check the transport depot soon, if a transport came through here, it'd be there."

"Why not at the main city docks?" Mai asks.

"That would mean Asgardians are still in town.

Everyone would have been talking about it and we haven't seen any come through here in the past few months." My heart sinks and I gulp down the rest of my wine. I don't let his words set in too much.

Pierre pours me more wine and Mai clinks her glass with mine. She winks playfully at me to which I roll my eyes.

"What will you do once you find survivors?" Pierre asks.

"Settle." I snip.

"Have you ever thought that far in advance?" Braun asks curiously, though it sounds more like an insult. He's clearly still pissed about our argument earlier.

"When I need to. Clearly you cannot properly judge character." I retort. He only growls in response.

"Why are elves so pretty?" Mai whines, cutting off our impending argument. Her chin is propped on her fist as she stares at Pierre.

Pierre somehow smirks while wincing, and I can't help but laugh.

"You don't need to yell," Braun mutters, rubbing his ears. The downside of superior hearing is people yelling next to you hurts more.

"Sorry!" she exclaims loudly. "Is there music we can put on? It's so quiet in here."

Pierre runs his hands over his braids before getting up to fiddle with a box in the corner. It looks familiar, Midgardian tech.

Mai gasps, "I haven't seen one of those in years!" Braun gets up and moves onto the couch across the room. "Why are you leaving?"

"I can hear you perfectly from here," he grumbles, plopping down, and acts like he's dealt with more than he wanted to today.

Jazzy soulful music comes on which Mai crinkles her nose at. "Not this type of music." She hops up and brushes past

Pierre to push different buttons on the machine. It switches to a pop-ier song, and she giggles and starts twirling around the room.

I chug the contents of my drink, certainly not drunk enough to handle Mai right now. Pierre has moved to sit across from Braun in an armchair. He swirls his wine but before he can take a sip, Mai plucks it from his hands and drains the contents. I quietly grab the remaining unopened wine bottles to hide them before Mai tries to get her hands on more.

"No more wine for you, fire sprite," Pierre murmurs. Crossing his legs, he watches her petite form spin around the room. The music changes and she jumps into his lap. She dips herself back, her magenta hair nearly brushing the luxurious carpet as she contorts her body into an arch like an acrobat.

Braun pinches the space between his eyes, leaning his head back. "Gods Mai, calm down," he comments. Pierre's face is priceless, torn between shock and not hating having her on him. I laugh as she hops off him and he lets out a long breath. She starts to slink over to me.

"Absolutely not Mai," I warn her. She pouts but sits next to Braun. She wraps one tan leg over him and pets his arm. He looks ready to dump her on the floor, so I decide to spare these elves from Mai's antics. "Come on Mai, let's go out."

She hops up clapping her hands. "I'll go change!"

As she runs up the stairs Braun looks at me skeptically. "She'll be asleep before she finishes getting dressed."

"I'm counting on it," I say with a smirk as I move over to the music player and change it to something calmer.

Twenty minutes later, Mai still hasn't come downstairs. When I go up and check, she's passed out on the floor next to her pack, clothes strewn through the room. I pull her into the bed, tucking her in.

When I go back downstairs, Pierre hands Braun Gild. Apparently, they'd taken bets on it.

Chapter 13

"Ｔｈｅｙ ｗａｉｔ ｆｏｒ ｙｏｕ, ｙｏｕ know?" I halt on the stairs listening to Pierre in the dining room the next morning.

"Who?" Braun asks with reluctant curiosity.

"Those still loyal to you."

There is silence for a moment before Braun snorts. "I am not going to take the crown. They wait in vain. For nothing."

"So, you will continue to follow around that human and Valkyrie as if you are not above them?"

"I am not above them," he grinds out. "I abdicated my title the minute I acted against my father, and I am glad of it." Pierre huffs but doesn't seem to push it.

They lapse into silence, and I resume my descent.

"No braid today?" Braun comments from his seat at the unnecessarily fancy dining room table. I run my hand through my hair, surprised he's noticed. I merely shrug, taking a scat next to him. The cool gray light of morning seeps through gaps in the heavy curtains on the windows.

"Anything interesting?" I tilt my head to the book in his hands.

"Reading some folklore. Pierre has hundreds of these ancient texts lying around." He waves his hand through the room. I scrunch my eyebrows as I read the cover and sit down. Braun explains, "I think it may give us some context on Ragnarok, maybe help us locate the others." I doubt it, but I lean back in the chair and pick up a book on the table next to him, skimming it. I feel his stare. Looking up, I catch his eyebrows rising. "You can read Elvish?"

I nod. "I can read all languages. A gift from Odin, though I can't honestly say I've found it very useful in situations other than this."

"And how often are you in situations like this?" he teases, and I almost fall out of my chair in shock. It seems he's gotten over our fight yesterday.

Recovering quickly, I smirk. "More often than I care for." He smirks back and is about to say something more when Pierre walks into the room from, what I assume is, the kitchen, carrying freshly baked rolls with jam on the side.

The moment he sets them down, I greedily rip into one, not caring if it burns my mouth. "So how do you two know each other?"

Braun and Pierre exchange a glance before Pierre explains, "I was the Captain of Prince Braunryn's guard." I never realized Braun is a shortened version of his full name.

"So they make you an officer here?" I inquire and something like sadness flits through Pierre's aquamarine eyes before he responds.

"Something like that." He picks up a book Braun has pulled from the desk, brushing off the dust. I give Braun a look conveying my suspicions about Pierre aren't unfounded. He merely rolls his eyes in return.

"Looking for something in particular?" Pierre inquires and Braun only grunts in response.

I take that as my cue to finish skimming the book in front of me for information. This one tells me very little I don't already know. That Ragnarok would be started by a god killing Odin, the all-father and god of gods in Asgard. Blah, blah, blah, old news.

I feel as though I can barely remember Asgard's beauty

before the frost and the fire. The rich, intoxicating smells that wafted from the spice district always made my mouth water. The constant beating of steel against steel or a whoosh of arrows followed by the thud of them hitting targets in the practice are—

"Anything useful in that one?" Braun pulls me out of my daydream.

I meet his stormy eyes and find them studying me. I merely shake my head, placing the book on the table to pick up another from the pile.

We continue this for another hour or two. Mai comes down to see what we are doing, looking like death. She immediately goes back up the stairs claiming she's going to take a nap, though she's only just woken up. I don't blame her. She's probably got a massive hangover, and she can barely read Elvish. Most of these books are in the ancient language, which is far more difficult to read.

"Hmmm," Braun hums for a moment as he flips back a page in his current book. I give up on the one I'm currently sifting through. He looks up at me and shoves the book my way. "Read this." He points to the part of the text.

"'Ragnarok will sweep through Asgard, caused by one of its own. The battle ensues, the remains of Asgard will sink into the sea. There will be nothing left but the void,'" I read from the book aloud. "'Creation and all that has occurred since will be completely undone, as if it had never happened. Arising from the void will be the new world. Mightier than the one before, ruled by a new god.' A new god?" I scrunch my eyebrows in disbelief. "Odin is gone, no new gods can be created."

"What about the offspring of gods?" Pierre asks, munching on a roll.

I wave my hand dismissing the possibility. "None would be powerful enough with creation to create a whole realm even if there are others with that power. Besides, a new god hasn't been created by Odin in a long while. He was creation itself; no other gods are that powerful. None that are still in existence at least."

Braun leans towards me. "That word," he says, pointing to the page for emphasis, "has a double meaning, new or creation."

I shake my head. "Any other possible god with the power of creation is long dead."

"But you don't know for sure?" I shrug at Braun's question. Knowing all the gods and goddesses is harder than it sounds. With both Asgard and Vanaheim being god-realms, there are too many to track. "So it's possible Asgard will arise from the ashes by a new god."

I shrug again.

"It's not impossible, but the odds of it being true are slim."

"If it is true, it's all the more reason to find survivors. So, you can restore them to their home."

"Will it even be their home anymore?" I ask, thinking that if there was a new world built by a new god, it may look nothing like Asgard once had. I lock eyes with Braun for a moment and know he can see the devastation in mine, but he says nothing.

I have shoved back my trauma for so long, suppressing the memories that now threaten to shoot to the surface, like bile in my throat. I am dragged into them without warning.

Smoke and ash clog my nose and the ringing in my ears will not stop. I shake my head and my vision blurs, causing the buildings in front of me to sway from side to side, like drunken dancers. Once my vision clears, I can see the devastation.

Stone buildings are smashed to pieces, and the golden palace in the distance is engulfed in red hot flames. All around me are piles of ash in the shape of bodies. I throw up the contents of my stomach as I recognize they are, were,

Asgardians, burnt to a crisp upon contact with a fire giant.

Stumbling, I walk through the street to see if I can find any others still alive. Tears I barely feel trail down my face as I pass more and more dead. Stopping, I see my appearance in a broken window and vomit again. My wings.

My wings have been completely charred and pieces of them flake off in the breeze that blows. I know there is no saving them. I close my eyes for a moment, trying to collect myself.

When I look up, Loki stands in front of me—once my lover, my heart, and now my enemy.

I somehow still have my sword and I raise it as much as I can. Pain shoots through my arm, which I must have broken and only partially healed. As he strides closer, I can see my distorted reflection in his silver helm. I am a wreck, but he looks untouched by all the destruction, as if he hadn't been a part of the fight at all.

His armor glints in the fires that burn around us. His expression is one I've only seen a few times, completely empty and void of feeling. My anger boils to the surface. How could he? I shriek as I charge at him, barely able to lift my left leg, but I no longer care. All I want is to end this, end him.

I am shaken out of my memory by strong hands on my shoulders and I gasp for air. Braun swears under his breath and runs a hand through his silver-white hair as he flops back down into the chair next to me. Pierre's bronze face is a few shades lighter. "Gods above, what happened?" he asks shakily.

I open my mouth to speak, but it feels as though ash is stuck in my throat and I cough. I feel it coming and bolt to the bathroom upstairs before I puke all over Pierre's fancy table and ancient books. I barely make it to the toilet. Mai rushes in and I wave my hand at her before she can say anything. She seems to understand and closes the door giving me privacy.

I crouch there for a while longer, gagging and spitting,

before heaving myself to the sink to wash my mouth out. I splash water on my face. My hands shake as I place them on the lip of the cool sink and take deep breaths, steadying myself.

I glance at my reflection in the mirror and grimace. I look haunted. Maybe I am, by memories and dreams I can't seem to shake. Tightness fills my chest as I think about Edda. She could be anywhere. I huff out a breath and force myself to push the worry back and face the others.

Mai sits on the edge of her bed, bouncing her foot, and Braun paces in front of the bathroom door. They stop as I step into the room.

"I'm fine," I say with a small smile as I lean against the doorway, trying to play it cool.

Mai snorts. "Sure you are."

Braun walks towards me, placing two fingers under my chin and tilts my face to his. His eyes are stormy as they search mine.

"Flashbacks?" he murmurs as if he's had personal experience with them.

I can only blink, confirming. His scent hits me, calming my roiling stomach. It seems to be enough for him as his fingers trail up the side of my cheek, heating the skin beneath, before he strides out of the room.

Mai walks over and squeezes my hand. "I'm here if you need me." I smile at her and squeeze her hand back, not ready to discuss what I just witnessed again.

The rest of the evening passes without incident, and I am grateful when they all act as though nothing happened. I lay in bed, memorizing the ceiling, afraid to fall asleep. The nightmares I am unprepared to relive lay waiting in my subconscious. So, I stare at the ceiling and pretend I am not tired at all.

———————

There is no fooling anyone, not even myself, when I am exhausted the next day as we tromp through the intensely humid port to where Pierre says the Asgardian transport was last seen. I grumble my annoyance as both suns burst through the cloud cover and turn the temperature up far too high.

We make it to the western edge of the city closest to the ocean. The salty brine smell washes over us as we continue south along the sloping blue hills for a few minutes until we come to an area filled with unclaimed transports.

All docked on rickety wooden planks, it's more of a junkyard than an active transport hub. I am mesmerized as we walk through row after row of transports. All contain spray-painted symbols on the side that note the ships' origins. All wait to be claimed, wasting away, collecting rust.

I stop at one that is completely covered in ruby dust and tilt my head as I study it. My heartbeat doubles as I run a hand over the side, removing the silt, and recognize the runes marked on it. This isn't just any transport. It is a *Valkyrien* transport. In its prime, this space transport would have been the color of cedarwood, with accents of burnt amber running along its edges.

It is small, only large enough to carry five people at most with a two-man cockpit. My stomach is in my throat as I brush off the keypad on the door. I smile sadly as I remember we only ever had one passcode, a running joke amongst the Valkyrie.

My hands shake as I punch in the numbers, 1 2 3 4 5. I hear the clicking of the electronics coming to life inside and a pop as the door unlocks. It screeches as I push it into the pocket fold.

I can't decide if I'm excited or disappointed to find that there is little inside, but everything seems to be working. I turn on the display console and Braun spots me from the gangway through the glass.

He whistles as he comes aboard. "Is this it?"

"No." I shake my head, but don't look up from the

display. "This is a Valkyrien transport, but it's in good shape." I type in code trying to pull up the ship's log. My heart drops as I see the last entry was recorded five years before Ragnarok. I play it anyway.

A holographic video of a woman appears on the screen. Her long blonde hair is braided back, and she wears Valkyrien armor. The runes along her neck peek out just above the collar of the armor. "Captain's Log, day 184 of ALF1829 Mission in Alfheim." She runs her hands over her face. "This place is honestly a shithole. I've found nothing that leads me to believe the rumors that the..." She trails on describing the mission and latest reports in detail.

It is not a mission I knew of, but I know this woman. Yssil, a former Valkyrien captain that had died under mysterious circumstances off-planet. I wonder if she died here. She and I hadn't been close, but I remember her; we were still sisters-in-arms.

She had several children with an Asgardian soldier. We were all sad when we learned of her death. I pause the video and type in more code to find the route they were taking and any other information. It seemed like she was alone in this mission, which was odd. Valkyrie were normally in a group of at least five for smaller mission.

I ponder the oddity of it until I see Mai wave a hand to us from across the way, her pink hair like a beacon making her easy to spot. Behind her, Pierre walks the gangway to a large transport that I immediately recognize. Quickly shutting down the systems, I drag Braun out of the transport with me and slam the door shut. I enter the number code again.

Braun snorts. "Nice passcode."

I give him a vulgar gesture before sprinting to where Mai and Pierre are. The ship, triple the size of the Valkyrien transport, is in bad shape. There are dark blast marks along the side and one of the wings is bent at an awkward angle. Somehow it landed without issues, possibly from autopilot kicking on after sustaining too much damage to continue space travel.

I stride up the gangway but am stopped by Pierre. His eyes are sad as he turns to keep me from looking into the cockpit window, the door still locked tight behind him. His bronzed hand grabs my wrist as I move to press my fingers on the scanner.

He only shakes his head. "You will not like what you find inside."

I wrench my hand out of his and place it on the scanner. I need to know, even if the truth terrifies me. The door slides open and stale air pushes from the main room. I put a hand over my nose and mouth as I move inside the cabin.

It smells of death.

My heart aches as I see bodies lying on the floor, dried blood in pools around them. I count ten in total on this level, and I move quickly down the hatch to the lower level to find more of the same.

My body shakes as anger courses through me. Somehow the locked door had deterred any elves from searching this ship. There could have been survivors when it landed, if only they pried open the doors.

"Vera," Mai calls from the main deck, "you should come to see this." I reluctantly head up and find Braun placing tarps normally found in the back of the ship over the bodies.

"Wasn't this ship here for months?" Braun asks, not understanding how these bodies are so well preserved.

"It's as if the air system kept them in a suspended state, not allowing them to decay," Pierre comments through a handkerchief covering his nose and mouth.

Mai pops her hot pink head out of the cockpit. "In here."

I walk towards her and stop as I see white feathers on the ground just beyond the door.

I scarcely breathe as I enter to find a Valkyrie face down

on the floor, her wings partially coated in blood. Gently kneeling by her torso, I turn her over in my arms. I close my eyes, looking away for a moment, trying to compose myself. Rhodda.

My dearest friend. My hands tremble as I stroke a hand down her beautifully serene face and close her now dull green eyes for the last time. I brush her charcoal hair to the side and adjust her so her wings and body are not at odds with each other. After rubbing away the blood spattered on her left cheek, the line of light blue runes running from just below her eye to her jawline appear.

Gently, I place her back down on the cockpit floor, needing to clear my head. I move to the console display and find recordings from the same week as Ragnarok, only the audio recording though. Seems like the video was knocked out. I take a deep breath in, preparing myself for what I'm about to hear, and hit play.

Rhodda's voice comes through clearly on the display as she calls on the transponder for help over and over again. Tears slip free that I don't try to hold back. The ship's blaster cannons go off in the background and the jolt of the transport's shields as something fires upon it.

I hear the hushed whispers of survivors huddling together at the back of the ship. Rhodda swears, and I smirk remembering how often she did that. The crashing of steel meeting steel rings through the recording as if whatever was attacking them outside had gotten in.

As unearthly screeches erupt, I know what they are from. The sound is so familiar it makes me shudder. Braun was right.

Loki *is* sending out dark elves to hunt down survivors.

The screams continue until it is silent and there is only a shuffling sound before the tape cuts off. I place my forehead against the console, unable to move. How could I have let this happen? I should have been there to save them, or at least been with them to die amongst my own. How did *I* survive?

A small, warm hand gently lands on my shoulder and I look up through tear-stained eyes to see Mai, looking just as devastated. What does she know about this? These aren't her people. I hate her at that moment. I hate all of them. For being here, to see me fall apart like this. I hate the support I feel from them.

I brush her off and kneel next to Rhodda, gently lifting her off the ground and carry her out of the ship. She is heavy in my arms, but I ignore it as I take her out of the shipyard. Even as they begin to ache, I continue to carry her up the slope her wings almost drag on the ground to the crest of the knoll. Gently, I place her on the scraggly, blue grass and cross her arms over her chest, laying her sword on top.

I go back to the ship and begin to pick up another, placing him to the left of Rhodda. This time Pierre and Braun each carry one and place them in the same manner on the other side of Rhodda. Once we finish moving the rest of the bodies to the crest of the hill, we are coated in sweat. I stare at the dead for a long moment.

When I had my wings, I would have ferried them to Valhalla. Now, I'm not even sure what to do, but I know I can't bury them here. Asgardians are not meant to be put in the ground, our bodies, and souls only rest when we reach Valhalla. I pull out my sword from my pocket, and the blade shimmers as sunlight again breaks through the clouds, bathing us in its golden light. I drive my blade into the purple dirt at Rhodda's feet and kneel with my head bowed, both my hands on the hilt.

"Make no truce or treaty with foe," my voice shakes as I say the words. "Kinsmen to kinsmen should be true. Reach your destination though you have traveled slow."

More tears fall as I finish, "Valhalla calls."

Mai gasps from behind me, and I look up to see light shimmering around Rhodda and the others.

As the shimmer fades, the clouds block the sun and the dead are gone.

Chapter 14

It takes Mai and the others a long time to convince me to move. I sit there on the crest for so long, my legs are numb when I try to stand. It is pitch black with a chill in the air. I don't want to talk to anyone and don't want to be around anyone, so I immediately sprint up the stairs when we arrive at Pierre's and take a long bath.

After sitting there for so long, my fingers wither and the water tepid, I carry my waterlogged body to the sink and dry off. Staring in the mirror, I turn around to see the ridge of scars along my shoulder blades from where my wings used to be. Whether they were removed by someone or whether they withered off, I don't know. I just remember waking up without them in Niflheim.

I manage to throw on a cream shirt and underwear, too exhausted to even fix my hair. Hushed whispers in the hallway reach my ears, so I sneak to the closed bedroom door and lean my ear against it.

"Seriously Mai, let her be. She doesn't want to be around anyone right now, especially a human who has no experience with this sort of stuff."

"That's rich coming from you, statue man." I almost laugh at her response, but I'm so hollow I barely feel anything.

"That doesn't even make any sense," Braun hisses.

"You wouldn't even know what emotion was if it hit you

in the face." I sigh and decide that none of it matters.

Crawling under the covers, I fall asleep immediately.

Edda appears before me, her eyes wild with fear. She runs towards me, something dark as a void in space creeps towards her. I scream but no sound is emitted and I stretch my arm towards her and my heartbeat pounds in my ears. Anxiety ratcheting to the highest level until my fingertips brush her extended ones.

I grip her fingers hard, pulling her to me. I encase my wings around us, hiding us from whatever is chasing her. The darkness envelops us but does not feel like it will do us harm. Regardless, she shakes within my embrace, and I murmur assurances, unsure if she can hear me.

It reminds me of when we were kids, and she would get scared during thunderstorms. Of course, natural thunderstorms were rare in Asgard, and I knew Thor had caused most of them. I've punched him in the face on more than one occasion for his antics. Such an asshole.

She would hide in my bed with me, tucking her small body close to mine. "All will be well, Edda." I would tell her, half asleep from being woken in the dead of night.

"Tell me a story." She would whisper. She would always ask for a story, but she only ever wanted to hear one specific story.

A story I concocted when she was sick as a toddler, and I was barely nine yet somehow she remembered it. The story of two sisters who were not separated by differences, or distance. Ones who grew together, laughed together. Who did not fight about hard choices or snap at each other when they were hurting.

I tell her the story now of two sisters, princesses who live in a golden palace, even as darkness encases us, even as the wind of it howls around us. I can no longer see her face or body, but she is still tucked tight against me. We will weather this storm, this darkness, as we always have. Together.

When I awake, I am too raw to do anything. Mai tries to get me to eat, but I am not hungry. I cannot stand another night of seeing those closest to me in such peril or finding my friends dead. I do not want to go on, but as I stare at the ceiling sleep pulls me under. Dragging me through memories I now wish never occurred, all of them hurt, regardless of the memory being terrible or happy.

————

By the third morning, Braun pulls open the door with a bang and storms in. He throws back my covers and I yelp in surprise.

"Get up."

I narrow my eyes at him. "No."

"Get up right now, or so help me I'll drag you out of this bed." His grey eyes are filled with rage.

I give him an Alfheimian vulgar gesture, hooking my pointer finger at him, before rolling over, taking the sheets with me. He huffs a breath and rips the covers back. I'm thrown over his shoulder and carried into the bathroom before I can begin to protest.

He sets me down in the tub and turns on the water. It is ice cold, but he seems not to notice as he gets in, sitting in the tub with me. Our knees touch. He is fully clothed but doesn't move to do anything about it.

"What are you doing?" I croak, my voice hoarse from disuse.

When he doesn't answer I try to stand only to be held in place, his palms flat on my thighs. My teeth chatter from the cold as the tub fills, but his fingers send warmth along my thighs. Braun takes my chin between his thumb and forefinger, and his cloudy gaze holds mine.

"You cannot give up."

I want to wrench out of his grip. I want to be left alone and I hate him for pulling from bed.

"Just because you found one transport of those who did not make it, does not mean there are not others filled with those still living. You must keep going. You cannot give up on finding Edda." I hiss a breath at his mention of Edda.

A sob pushes its way out of me, but my eyes stay locked on his. "I can't," I whisper. I don't care if it makes me a coward. How can I continue when I feel so sure that all I will find is death?

"If you give up now, I promise you'll regret it every day," Braun says quietly.

"How would you know anything about regret?" Anger snapping through me faster than my grief.

"Because I feel it, every day." My eyebrows shoot up at that. "I was a coward and now I have to live with the consequences of that." He runs his hands through his silver hair and stands. He glances down at me as the icy water runs down his clothing. "Don't make the same mistake I did. I won't let you give up."

"I thought you didn't care, this is just an arrangement," I spit out, needing to direct my anger and my sorrow at something, someone, even if they are undeserving of it.

"Well, I do and it's not," he throws back.

As he storms back out of the bathroom, I catch Mai struggling to hide her surprise in the other room. He's shown more emotion in the past five minutes than in the last month I've known him. However he did it, my thoughts no longer spiral to death as they had earlier.

I sigh, letting go of my anger, pushing down the grief that threatens to engulf me, and shed my soaked clothes to clean up in the cold water.

Once I pad back into the room, Mai is flipping through a book on the bed, pretending to ignore me. I put on a flowy white blouse and black leather pants. I know she's upset with me for blocking her out, so I attempt to make amends.

"Can you help me with my hair?" I ask. She looks me up and down, judging whether it's worth it.

She rolls her brown eyes. "Fine."

She moves to the edge of the bed, and I sit on the floor below her. We are silent for a while as she combs my hair, untangling parts. I close my eyes and it's almost as if Edda is here instead of Mai. My chest tightens at the thought of Edda.

I wince as Mai pulls on a sensitive area. Even with its shortened length, it gets tangled daily.

"Sorry," she murmurs.

"No, you're not," I say, and she chuckles.

"What was her name?" she asks softly. I close my eyes, remembering her. Her apple green eyes and thick raven black hair. Runes marking her arms and down her left cheek.

"Rhodda," I whisper as a tear falls unbidden down my cheek.

"What was she like?" Mai asks, and I take a big breath. Then I tell Mai about Rhodda and our adventures together many years ago. How her filthy mouth was always getting us in trouble and how she would take on anyone who talked down to us.

I have not wanted to talk about Asgard or any of it for so long but pushing back the memories did more damage than good. It hurts to even think of Rhodda or home. I feel raw after talking about it, but as the stories flow, I also feel a small piece of my heart light up.

Mai pulls my hair into a pretty plait on my head, and we head downstairs. Pierre sits alone at the dining room table, and Braun is nowhere to be seen. *Good*, I'm not ready to face him after that. Mai chats politely with Pierre as I eat for the first time in three days. I am starving, but I know better than to overeat,

I'd be puking my guts up in an hour.

Mai and I leave to walk the city, and my thoughts wander to the Valkyrien transport. I want it. I mean technically it belongs to me, as one of the last Valkyrie, but I doubt that will have much sway here.

Mai nudges me once we reach the main market waterway, dragging me from my thoughts. She jerks her head to the side, and I follow her eyes until I spot Braun. He's got his hood on, but at this point, I could recognize him in a bear costume.

I wonder if others notice him as well. I look around to see most people minding their business and vendors mill about near their goods. Braun talks with a male who wears finer clothes, like Pierre. Maybe another palace guard?

My stomach drops and I get a bad feeling. Glancing at Mai, she keeps her calm brown eyes on passersby, but I notice her leg bouncing. The male sneers at Braun and brandishes a knife from behind his cloak that Braun doesn't notice.

Before I even realize what I am doing, I hurtle towards them as I watch in slow motion. Braun turns his head and when his gaze finds mine, his eyes narrow perceptively. He glances back at the male, and then blinding white light explodes from where they stand.

I am blown back by the magic, landing hard on the wooden walkway. Screams and shouts fill the air. I pop up, racing to where Braun and the elf were standing. The male seems unscathed and struggles with Braun over the knife. I run straight into the male, tackling him to the ground as Braun stands there shocked. I struggle to keep the male's arms pinned and having not eaten much in a few days I am weaker than normal.

Mai is already grabbing Braun's arm, but he doesn't budge.

"Run you fucking idiot!" I yell as I land a blow on the

male's head with the hilt of my sword, knocking him unconscious.

Braun snaps out of it. He is leaping away with his hand gripped tight around Mai's, dragging her, and I am hot on their heels. Guards are alerted to the explosion by bells that ring through the city and the pounding of their armored steps jolts through the walkways. I follow Braun as he turns down an alley only to find it's a dead end.

I turn around, running right into a city guard. The guard quickly recovers, and three more guards appear behind him. I back away slowly, my sword appearing from its hilt, but they aren't looking at me as they brandish their blades. They only stare at Braun, whose hood has fallen off. *Shit, shit, shit.*

They say nothing as they charge toward us, but wind rushes at them before I can move, tearing at their clothes and armor. I gape at Braun. White light rings his hands as he moves them, shifting the torrent of wind, pushing the guards out of the alley entirely. Suddenly water beneath the walkway shoots up through the planks where the guards stand, sending them sky high before crashing down onto the wood that snap under their weight.

We are moving out of the alleyway before the guards even hit the water below. Mai gasps for breath, trying to keep up with us. We turn the corner close to Pierre's now and stop dead in our tracks.

There stands Pierre, clad in full armor with at least thirty guards behind him. I swear under my breath.

"It's over Prince Braunryn, time to face the consequences," says a male elf that comes to stand next to Pierre. Clearly, he's in charge.

Pierre's eyes are filled with sorrow, but Braun only looks at him with disgust. Braun doesn't have his sword with him, but I am already pulling the dagger from my boot and pressing it into his hand.

He seems to remember Mai and me then. Emotions flit over his face, too quickly for me to read before he says to the guards, "I'll go with you, as long as you leave these two alone." The male in charge looks us over before nodding.

I scrunch my eyebrows. "What the hell are you doing?" I hiss at him.

He smirks at me. "Saving your asses."

"We are in this together, Braun, even if I dislike you most of the time," Mai mutters.

"Don't do this, we can easily take these guys," I plead.

He smiles at me, a genuine one that makes my heart hurt.

"It looks like I won't be holding up my end of the bargain, but this," he says, jerking his head to the group in front of us, "is something I need to deal with."

I shake my head, not understanding, not wanting to understand. His hand brushes down my cheek as he presses my dagger back into my free hand.

"Do not give up." He stares at me for a moment longer before he turns towards the males and holds his hands out in front of him.

Glancing at Pierre, who jerks his head at the guards, I realize these men won't spare us based on our association.

I gaze at Braun one last time, memorizing his features, before grabbing Mai's hand and pulling her around the corner. Guards yell in shock, but I don't bother stopping to see if they follow. I sprint along the wooden walkways with Mai just behind me until we reach the backside of Pierre's place.

We need to grab our things and leave now. I smash in Pierre's back window and crawl inside, hoisting Mai through it after me. We bound up the stairs, and I throw my shit into my pack while Mai does the same with her stuff. I run into Braun's room and grab all his items, shoving them into his bag as Mai comes to stand at the door, both our packs slung over her shoulders.

"We aren't going back for him, are we?" I ignore her question at first while I keep packing.

"Not yet, we need to get somewhere safe first."

She shakes her head. "They'll kill him before we can save him." I pause what I'm doing and sigh, running my hands through my hair.

"What do you mean?"

"Braun killed his own father, the King of Haratine. They will execute him for it." I never knew why he wasn't allowed back here or what he'd done to be exiled. I was too focused on my mission to even think about it, but now I realize my mistake in bringing him here. *Stupid Vera.* Somehow even Mai knew Braun's past.

"She's right," Pierre comments from behind Mai. My sword is out in an instant and I've pulled Mai farther into Braun's room behind me.

Pierre merely holds both his hands up. "I'm here to turn you in, but I'm partial to you. So why don't you knock me out before the guards show up here."

"How long?"

"Minutes," he says, moving closer to me, his hands still up.

"No, how long until they execute him?"

He shrugs. "Could be a week, could be a month. Depends on what his brother, the king, decides. I'm sure he'll make a spectacle of it."

I nod and sling Braun's pack over my shoulder. I let my blade disappear and Pierre misunderstands the movement as surrender. He surges towards me and I dodge, hitting him hard on the side of the head with my hilt. He collapses to the ground, and I breathe out a breath and look at the ceiling, which gives me an idea.

Smirking, I ask Mai, "Do you still have those maps?"

Minutes later we are jumping from roof to roof traversing across the city the only way I know we won't run into trouble. Mai looks ready to barf, but her fear of getting caught keeps her moving. She yelps as she slips and barely catches the roof I've already jumped to. I haul her up, almost losing my grip on her sweat-soaked hands, and we sit there panting for a moment.

"Are you sure about this plan?" she asks skeptically, and I nod.

"We can't stay here, but we will come back for him. I promise." I watch Mai's brown eyes turn determined as she nods, even as she shakes slightly.

Heights are clearly not her thing. We continue our journey, luckily without incident, as we make our way to the transport depot. We sneak past the guards at the main gate and wait until night falls before creeping to the Valkyrien transport I'd looked at the other day. It should have plenty of fuel in it, and just in case it doesn't, Mai nicked some from the guard station hours ago.

In the cover of darkness, we move on quiet feet to the ship. I already miss Braun's loud footfalls. His quiet intense presence. I wait until the guards are far enough away on their patrol, they won't hear the clicking of the keypad as I enter the door code. It opens and I test pushing it into the pocket when it lets out a loud groan. *Stupid fucking door.*

Luckily, neither of the guards have looked this way. I get it open enough for Mai to slip in and hand her the packs. Quickly, I add the stolen fuel into the chamber while keeping an eye on the guards. My heart beats in my ears as I finish and slip through the door.

When I try to close it, it lets out a sharp whine, and I grimace. The guards turn towards the sound. I push Mai into the second pilot seat while I quickly hit the buttons, starting the engine. It sputters to life as the guards run towards us. Mai clicks on her seatbelt.

"Faster, faster," Mai urges.

"Grab the joystick in front of you." She complies while I try to get the ship off the ground.

"See the button on the top." She nods her finger brushing the red button that blinks. "If the guards get too close press that button."

In moments I've got us hovering on the platform and am waiting for the damn light on the control panel to turn green, which will allow us to bust out of here. It blinks yellow and Mai glances nervously at the control panel as the guards get closer. She lines up the shot right as the light blinks green.

"Hold on." I push the engines to full power, and we are flung into the back of our seats as we surge forward, almost clipping the ship in front of us. Pulling up hard on the lever, I launch us straight into cloud cover.

Once I see no one is following us, I switch it to cruise control and get up to search for the maps of Alfheim. Mai looks like she's going to be sick.

"Not a fan of heights?" I ask as I spread out the map over the table in the back and I pinpoint the city of Merin's location.

"Something like that," is all she says, not averting her gaze from the darkness around us.

I snort. "You'll get used to it."

"Doubt it," she comments. I type in the city coordinates into the navigational systems and the ship automatically redirects itself.

"Don't worry, looks like we'll make it to Merin in a few hours."

"Then we look for survivors?" Mai asks, finally opening her eyes.

I nod. "And we figure out a way to get Braun back."

My mind drifts to Edda. I hope Merin has more answers than Yulamic did.

Chapter 15

Mai and I both doze in the cockpit, but I awake when the control panel alerts us, we are close to our destination. I nudge Mai as we approach the Democratic Republic of Salaza's capital city of Merin. My Valkric tells me it's one of the few countries in Alfheim that doesn't have a monarchy but rather a body of representatives for each city, district, outpost, and port who make all the decisions a monarch would.

Its people also differ from other countries. Here, there are a wide array of races—from dwarves, to humans, to elves—all living together equally rather than as servants for elves. It is also the most technologically advanced country in Alfheim, similar to Asgard in that sense.

Mai gapes as I take the ship off cruise control. We merge into the traffic of brightly painted transports moving throughout the city, like automobiles on a road in Midgard, but here everything is hovercrafts and space transports. The buildings, made of shiny metal, practically touch the sky and reflect the early morning sunslight. Each structure has docking platforms on different levels for ships to enter. Lanes of traffic hover at varying heights above the ground as they move around the buildings.

"It's like New York on crack twenty years in the future," Mai comments.

I have no idea what she's talking about.

To me, it looks like a more modern Asgard, one that I know Edda would love to see. I have no idea where we should go, but Mai finally unbuckles her seatbelt and studies the navigational map on the console more closely.

"Looks like we are close to the city center," she murmurs, examining the screen. The buildings here sit tightly together and the lanes of traffic give them wider berths.

"We need to find the main shipyard, search there first. See if any Asgardian transports landed here." Mai nods at my instructions and using her fingers, she scrolls through the map for a moment.

"There!" she exclaims. Though the map is in Asgardian, the icon underneath the words shows a transport landing. I steer us towards the port that is as tall as the buildings around us and land in one of the open docks.

"Don't look down," I warn Mai before we disembark the ship.

We are high above the ground with only a skinny walkway keeping us suspended. I can already see the concern filling Mai's eyes. Carrying my pack and Braun's, while she shoulders her own, we approach the dockmaster.

Near the main entrance to the building, the dockmaster is a young-looking elf with bright red curls framing an iridescently white face. The elf looks nervous as we approach, but Mai smiles and bats her eyelashes. When we stand in front of him, she looks up at the elf with her warm brown eyes. I let her handle this, she's better with people anyway.

"Hi handsome, we plan to dock our transport here for a few nights, how much do we owe?"

"1,000 gi-gild," he stutters.

"Done!" She plops one of the bags of Gild we stole and parsed out in Yulamic. The elf's eyes widen, and Mai gives him a winning smile.

"Th-this is more than what is owed," he says inspecting

the bag.

"Well, we figured you could keep the rest." Mai leans against his stand with a digital console that allows him to log comings and goings of transports on this part of the dock.

"Re-really?" I try hard not to roll my eyes at the elf.

"Mhmmm," she says looking at the elf while twirling a piece of his fire-red hair around her finger. "Say, my friend here is interested in finding out if an Asgardian transport landed in the city in the past few months, would you be able to look up that information for us?"

He looks at me for the first time, rather skeptically. I pretend he's a friend and smile at him. His face blanches of color, and I immediately regret it.

Mai puts a finger under his chin turning his attention back to her. She leans in closer to ask, "What do you say, can you check that for us?"

He gulps and nods, his fingers flying over the keyboard. "It looks like one came through here about three months ago, but only stopped for refueling on the way to Midgard."

My heart stops, then picks up double time. If it has an ID number, I should be able to locate it on my Valkric.

"Does the transport have a serial number or some sort of ID?" I demand, and he winces at my tone but looks at his screen.

"AS14278," he reads aloud.

I pull out my Valkric and type in the number to see if it can locate the ship, anxious energy filling me. I pinch the bridge of my nose as I get an error message. If the Asgardians knew Loki was searching for them, they could have turned the tracker off. Otherwise, the tracker itself could be broken. Either possibility doesn't instill much hope in me.

Don't give up, Braun's words echo in my mind. Stupid elf.

"Is this the only transport center for the whole city?" I ask. As the male nods, I sigh through my nose.

The old blind man hadn't lied when he'd said an Asgardian transport was spotted in Merin, but it makes sense for Asgardians to go to Midgard. They could blend in and assimilate much better there than here, where they would always be outsiders.

I nod to Mai who gives the elf a kiss on the cheek and murmurs, "Thank you for your help."

We are halfway to the main building when he shouts, "Wait I didn't write down a name?"

"Miss Smith," Mai calls back and I give her a confused look.

"I thought your last name was Zhao?"

She rolls her eyes. "Ya, I'm using a fake last name. Duh!" I scrunch my eyebrows not understanding what 'Duh' means. I shake my head at her. "So, since Merin is more or less a dead-end, what now?"

"We figure out how to get Braun back."

Mai tilts her head to the side. "Does Alfheim have public resource centers? Like where you can look up any information? Maybe we can find some more information on Braun that might help us?"

"Possibly." I pull out my Valkric again and start searching keywords to see if anything close by references that. Eventually, I get a ping and it's located near the city center we passed earlier.

Hovertrains run through the whole city, so Mai and I hop on one heading downtown. It's dark when we arrive, and it feels like a whole different city. Elves stroll by, technology altering their appearances. Their clothes or hair transform, shifting color and style as they move. Eyes flick from blue to brown to purple in a matter of seconds. I roll my eyes in annoyance at their frivolous use of technology, but Mai merely stares at them enviously. Some even wear clothes with lights in them that change color.

I study the Valkric and follow it until we reach our destination: an impressively tall white stone building that stands out from the others around it. It's completely dark inside.

"Ugh, it's closed!" Mai exclaims.

I bound up the steps, reading the plaque next to the entrance. "Opens early tomorrow morning though!"

Mai's stomach growls loudly and I smirk. We find a place close by to eat and locate a place to stay as well, continuing to use the name, Miss Smith.

I'm honestly not sure why it matters, but it's fun to pretend to be someone you're not. Someone who isn't searching the realms for Asgardian survivors or finding their sister or trying to save a stupid elf from execution.

We awake early the next morning, both eager to find information to help Braun. As we head back to the white building, the loud hum of the transports overhead echo through the city. The ground lacks roads or paths for transports and elves move quickly as if all late for something important. We stride along open pathways for pedestrians, hoverbikes, and scooters and when we pass through the boundaries of one district to the next, the divide is marked by the color change in the stone we walk on.

The ever-present calming smell of fresh linen lingers in the air, thanks to whatever Veoor magic is cast here. Its presence brushes against my skin, settling me. Large open parks with flowers and trees bursting with color stand proud at the center of each district. Flora definitely kept alive by Terra magic as the weather here is far cooler than Yulamic or Vanire. We had to find an apparel store this morning and purchase heavier jackets as Mai and I brought none.

Just like the outside of the white building, I am blinded

by the stark white of everything inside as we enter. Walls, floors, desks, tables, chairs, and lamps are so white it gives me a headache to look at for too long. Mai doesn't bother asking for directions at the main desk, just wanders until she finds a kiosk. I type in 'history' in Elvish on the screen and it pulls up a myriad of topics.

"Here," she murmurs, seeing one option for Haratinian history.

She taps the icon, and it exclaims, "Back right corner of level one-eighty-one."

Mai swallows her annoyance and mutters, "Of course it's on the one hundred and eighty first floor."

We walk towards a bank of moving platforms that will shoot us to the correct floor. "Close your eyes once we get on," I tell Mai as I watch one of the platforms shoot at unsafe speeds to the levels above.

An elf gestures to a platform on the left and we move to stand on it, only a clear piece of glass separates us from the impending doom of falling off the edge. I tap 1-8-1 on the glass number panel in front of us.

It gives a countdown, which I find odd, and I glance at Mai whose face is ghost white. I smother my smile, the poor thing.

My stomach drops and Mai lets out a squeal as we are blasted up to the one hundred and eighty first floor. The city, metallic and shiny, comes into view as the platform propels us upward.

Mai is green and heaving great breaths when we arrive at our destination. I grab her hand for support as she wobbles off the platform.

This level is much like all the ones below, but instead of being all white, it's all blue. Maybe in honor of Haratine's colors?

Void of life, its silence and filtered air give this floor an unwelcoming feel to it. There are no books—nothing like I imagined a library or information center to look like—just a few large black tables with chairs around them.

Mai and I approach one, realizing the entire tabletop is a screen. When Mai taps the glass, it comes to life, and an image of the Haratinian flag, grey with a blue star in the middle, appears. I am grateful everything here is digitized.

Another touch to the screen and it pulls up suggested topics to search. Mai plops into one of the chairs and I follow suit, typing in 'Prince Braunryn'. Several books appear on the screen as well as a video file. Under each item, the date of publication is listed.

My heart drops as I see the video file is only a few days old. Odd.

"So, they do have movies here after all," Mai murmurs mostly to herself, selecting the video file. It zooms out to cover half the table, and as Mai presses 'play' I stand for a better view.

The video angle is looking down into a room filled with courtiers. The stark grey stone walls are swathed in royal paintings and tapestries depicting battles, much like Pierre's apartment in Yulamic. At one end stands double doors, probably leading to the hallway or antechamber, and on the other end sits a raised platform.

Lazing in the silver throne encased in crushed blue velvet is a slightly shorter version of Braun. Outside of the height, the two could be identical. The King of Haratine, Marcus Theron Holland.

The doors at the other end of the room burst open and Braun appears. He is not cuffed nor dragged; he merely strolls in, hands in his pockets as if he's taking a leisurely walk, with guards on either side of him.

He stops ten feet away from the king and makes no move to bow. Mai and I share a look before turning back to the screen.

"Brother, finally you have returned to us," the king

announces, his face shifting to annoyance as Braun says nothing nor bows.

"Kneel before your king!" a guard demands, but Braun continues to stand there until two guards kick the back of his knees forcing him to kneel.

"Do you have nothing to say for yourself?" There is a strain in the king's voice and the look on his face shifts to sadness.

Braun looks at his brother for the first time since entering and says, "He deserved to die." Gasps echo in the room and some courtiers pull out fans. I roll my eyes at them.

"You are a better king than he ever was," Braun adds quietly.

King Marcus rises from his throne and descends the steps stopping right in front of Braun. "You were supposed to take the throne, not I," he murmurs. "Why did you do it?"

Braun looks up at his brother and something in his expression shifts. "Father cared for little other than wealth and glory, you know this." King Marcus nods in agreement. "He told me that in order to become king, I would have to kill my own family to prevent any doubts of succession."

The king's face looks pained, though not shocked by Braun's candor. "I knew the moment I turned the blade on you all, I would never be the same person." His father must have meant his sister and mother too, to kill anyone possibly in line for the throne. It's a cut-throat way to rule. "I would never be fit to rule, but I did as I was commanded. I killed our father, so that you could rule better than him or I ever could." The king looks away as if collecting himself before nodding.

"Your candor has brought to light our father's traits that many did not see and even I chose to ignore," he remarks as he slowly climbs the steps back to the throne. "However, it still stands that you have murdered our late King, and for that the punishment is death. No matter that you are the Prince or the heir to the throne of Haratine. You shall be executed in seven days, at the altar of Hylaxion." The king looks right at the camera. "Until then you will be held at the lowest level of the dungeons."

The video goes black, and I check the date; it was recorded two days ago.

Mai sighs propping her chin on her hand. "If the King believes Braun did the right thing, then why execute him?"

"Elves are honorable to a fault, if killing one's brother rights the wrong of losing the former king, they will do it no matter blood relation," I comment. I move the screen back to the homepage with the search bar.

"It was what, seven years ago? Why bother with it now?"

I shrug. "Seven years for an immortal is like a week for a human, time moves differently for us."

"It's stupid," she states, and I nod in agreement.

We are silent for a moment before she asks, "Is it just me or was it odd that the king looked right at the camera when he said where Braun would be held?"

I smirk at her. "You're catching on. Clearly, he's hoping someone will rescue him, though it'll be a big surprise when it's us and not his supposed supporters."

I finally take a seat across from Mai and begin to pull up maps of Knoll, the capital of Haratine, where the King's palace lies. Mai pulls up digital history books and begins paging through them. I'm not sure how far she'll get before she gives up trying to translate it, but we sit there for hours combing through information.

Later in the evening, we lounge in a pub across, staring at nothing. Both our brains hurt from the amount of information we sorted through today. While finding blueprints to the palace and city were out of the question, we looked through digitized books of when the city was originally built which showed tunnels underneath it.

We decided it was the best way to get in and out of the palace undetected, but we would need to test them out before running in blind. Who knows what's down there?

Pierre. My brain says but I push away the thought. He already double-crossed Braun; I doubt he would have any qualms doing that to people he barely met a week ago.

I sigh, making dark circles on our table from the condensation of my beer. We leave in the morning for Knoll, and I cannot seem to think of anything other than Braun.

I look over to see two dwarves sitting together, looking as miserable as Mai and me.

"I just can't believe it's gone, we'll never see it again," the female dwarf with a mass of chestnut-colored curls murmurs in Dvergr. I roll my eyes, they probably lost something valuable.

The second dwarf, a male with a thick tuft of black hair at the top of his head, hums in agreement and raises his glass to toast his partner. "To Nidavellir, may we always remember it as it was."

I perk up at that, scrunching my eyebrows together. I glance at Mai who's enraptured by the conversation happening next to us, though she has no idea what they are saying.

"Excuse me, but what are you referring to?" Mai boldly asks them in Elvish.

They both eye us, quickly turning disgusted as they see me.

"Like you don't know all about it?" The male bites out in broken Elvish before spitting on the floor near us.

"I've been here for a month, and I was on Nidavellir before that," I clarify. My stomach hollows out as my nerves build. Something has happened.

"Oh, were you there helping them prepare for Ragnarok?" My heart stops in my chest. No, it can't be. He pauses as he sees the absolute dread on my face. "You really don't know?" I shake my head.

"Ragnarok has swept through Nidavellir and found its kind unworthy," he sneers, spitting on the ground again. I close my eyes slowly, trying to swallow the lump in my throat.

"The entire planet exploded not a day ago. It happened within hours of Loki appearing," the female dwarf added in softly.

"I am so sorry for your loss," Mai said sympathetically.

"I don't understand, I thought Ragnarok was only supposed to happen to Asgard." I shake my head, muttering more to myself than anyone else.

"You and me both. Don't get me wrong, I was glad to be rid of you haughty Asgardians, but not at the cost of losing Nidavellir and our entire way of life."

I glance at Mai who's chugging the contents of her glass as if it's her last. I know she'll be bringing this up as soon as we leave.

"What's the plan?" Mai asks as we walk through Merin back to our inn.

"Save Braun. Find Survivors."

"That's it?" Exasperation fills her voice. All I can do is nod.

"So what? You're going to do nothing about Loki?" Mai asks heatedly and I only shrug in response. "You have the power to fix this, you have the power to stop him. What if Midgard is next?"

I stomp down the street ignoring her as she jogs to keep up with me. "Hell, you're the one who dated Loki, can't you just talk to him and tell him to back the fuck off?"

My temper rises. "It's not that simple Mai." I am a coward for this, but I don't care. I made up my mind back at the pub.

"Oh? And why is that?" I don't give her an answer, only shake my head.

She stops walking. "I thought you were better than that. I thought you cared. You're just a coward. You don't care about anything or anyone, but yourself." There is such anger in her brown eyes, they almost look black in the evening light.

"I'm looking for survivors, Mai! I am looking for my sister, my people! That is it. I can't deal with Loki. He's not *my* problem and he has not been for a while."

Mai shakes her head. "He is *your* problem. He's already attacked us once. Now he's everyone's proble—"

I cut her off. "Yes, well I don't see anyone else volunteering to do anything about it so why should I?"

"Because you know him better than anyone!" she shouts at me. "Why are you being like this? You know you could help."

"Why should I care if he destroys planets whose inhabitants won't give me the time of day. Hell, they won't even look me in the eyes. I have dealt with their criticisms and their impressions of me. Even when I've tried to be better, they don't see it as an effort, and I'm tired of dealing with all of these people!" I shout back gesturing to the elves walking around us.

The ones who keep their eyes straight ahead or on the ground to avoid being pulled into my fight with Mai. *Pussies*. Such a passive race, most would settle for compromising over an argument or fight.

"Then prove them wrong! Because right now, you're proving them right. That you only serve one person and right now, that's yourself." I huff a breath and turn away from her heading towards the inn.

I roll over in bed and sigh, watching Mai's petite sleeping form as she sounds like an earthquake with each breath. I cannot believe how incredibly used to her loud snoring I've become. She and I ignored each other for the rest of the evening, but it is not my fault I'm not stopping Loki. I have other things to worry about and besides, I am not the hero in this story.

Chapter 16

I HATE TO LEAVE THE Valkyrien ship behind, but it will be far more suspicious than taking a passenger transport to Knoll. Plus, we'll have an easier time blending in with a large crowd. We sit through the rather bumpy ride to Knoll in Haratine. Mai has a death grip on my hand as we start our descent over the city a few hours later.

Luckily, she and I are both too preoccupied to dwell on the previous night's fight. I blow out a breath, taking in Knoll. It's expansive—larger than I expected—which could be a good or bad thing. Bad if we must traverse the entire city to get to Braun and then get him out, more pitfalls to our plan. Good because it means it'll be harder to catch us with more possibilities for reroutes.

In the afternoon, we take our first walk through the city, starting from the inn we are staying at, in the scummiest part of town, all the way to the main palace gates. It's a forty-minute stroll between locations. Mai and I note alleys along the way as we walk the main route through the city, but we hopefully won't have to take any above-ground routes to and from the palace dungeons.

The weather is temperate for an inland city in summer. A light breeze curls through its cobblestone streets, the last chills of spring clinging on. A far cry from Haratine's swampy port city of Yulamic where its southwestern location means summer is the only season for most the year.

Here there are no wooden walkways hovering above open water, but gray cobblestones to match the muted gray stone buildings. The street we walk along teems with elves from all levels of society. Like the buildings around them, the elves here wear neutral tones of greys, blacks, and browns, so unlike the riot of color and style we saw in Merin.

Children laugh and yell as they play in alleyways. Mai and I keep to the side of the main thoroughfare where it's so cramped elves push past each other. Only pedestrians pass us on our walk, meaning there must be another street filled with hover-carriages taking the elite and high society folks from one place to another.

Mai must notice this as well because moments later she casually branches off, venturing down a brightly lit alley. When we reach the other side, I pull her back as a hover-chariot nearly runs her over. The elf inside gives us a look of annoyance and Mai gives them a crude gesture in return. I smother a laugh as the elf's eyes widen, looking terrified.

We watch for openings in the traffic, but it is an endless stream of caravans. We eventually give up and head back to the pedestrian pathway.

The palace gate sits open for pedestrians, but individuals are checked by guards before entry. The only indicator that it's even the palace is the black wall marking its boundaries with a large gate. Beyond the first gate is a smaller inner gate, and both are made of thick welded metal—not an exit option. Not that we were planning to waltz back out the front gates, but it never hurts to check.

We take our time on the walk back to mark the locations of manholes along the streets on the Valkric; most are probably sewage, but they are a start to finding the original tunnels built under the palace over ten thousand years ago.

In the evening, we sit in a dingy pub near the inn, the

rowdiest one we could find, biding our time. This bar smells far worse than any I visited in Vanire, and that's saying something. The only barmaid in the pub heads downstairs to what I hope is a cellar, bringing up bottles of wine to restock the grimy bar.

I glance around the room as a very inebriated elf sways towards our table. He probably thinks he's walking towards us like a prince instead of a drunk. Once he wobbles in front of us, he smiles wickedly revealing some of his missing teeth. Gross. I see Mai turn away to grimace out of the corner of my eye. "What are two ladies like yourselves doing here?"

"No thank you, please leave," Mai says, but not in Elvish. She's switched to a Midgardian language, England? I speak Midgardian languages better than some of the others in my retinue, but I hardly remember the titles given from one to the next. The elf's face scrunches in confusion. I sigh before translating.

"We're not interested," I say, watching his face morph into annoyance.

"Fucking cunts," he mutters.

My anger slips its leash and I casually trip him. He crashes right into a table of card players, who look serious about their game. Piles of Gild fly off the table as the drunk crashes to the floor. Mai smirks and slides off her seat as we watch the card players fight with other patrons for the money off the floor.

Before we know it, we've started a full-on brawl. Shouts and sounds of punches being exchanged followed by grunts resound off the walls.

With the barmaid distracted, we creep into the cellar. It is lit by a lone candelabra attached to the entrance, but my eyes adjust quickly. We picked this part of town for a reason. It is the oldest and the least updated, therefore the buildings may have pathways to the old tunnels. We hope.

I scan the walls for anything that stands out while Mai plays guard near the stairs. I sigh as I find nothing and motion to

Mai to start heading back up. I wait for her to give the all-clear before moving up the steps casually, walking through the bar moments later.

We try this tactic at three more bars in the area before I suggest trying the sewers.

"One more, then I'll swim through the sewers all evening with you," Mai begs, and I happily oblige. I'm not eager to swim through shit either. Though I'm sure my claustrophobia will reach new heights in the tunnels we hope to find.

The last bar we try is situated closest to where the city ends and the palace begins. In a vastly nicer building than the others we've visited, the upper floors have been redone. The crudely cut stone is darker, not yet faded by the suns enough to match the bottom floor.

The patrons are better dressed and, thankfully, better smelling than the other bars, whose clientele were rowdy and drunk at best. Sultry music winds through the room from a little machine in the corner.

Here, we are noticed more. We sit for longer, chatting about nothing at all before ordering fancy cocktails. They arrive in vibrant blue and pink hues with purple salt rims and oddly colored citrus fruit twists. We clink our glasses together in celebration of nothing.

I certainly sniff mine first, one can never be too sure. Once we finish the rather delicious drinks we head to where the bathrooms are located one at a time. Finding the staircase, we slip to the cellar below.

This time I find an archway that's been bricked up, though the bricks are loose and cleaner than the brick around it. My fingers grip one tightly and remove it. I can barely see in the pitch-black beyond, but when I put my ear to it, I hear wind and water. A good sign. I pull more bricks out, silently setting them on the floor. Once the hole is big enough for me to squeeze through, I walk back to Mai who's keeping an eye on the stairs.

She jumps as I touch her arm and keeps her hand on my back while following me quietly. I suck in a breath as her hand brushes my scars. She realizes her mistake and quickly moves her hand to the top of my shoulder.

I chide myself for the knee-jerk reaction as I step over the remaining bricks, careful not to knock any of them, then hold out a hand to Mai for support as she follows suit. Quietly we restack the bricks, covering the hole we've gone through as best we can.

Once inside the tunnel we walk silently without a torch or light. Mai keeps a hand on my shoulder for guidance, this time careful not to touch too close to my shoulder blades. It's still better than having her hold my hand, which has become clammy with sweat.

We avoid the small puddles of water that dot the dirt floor. The ground bears no footprints, and the stone walls are covered with black blooms of mold and white spots of mildew, as if they wage war against each other. Dust clings on top of them all.

No one has been down here for a long while, a good sign that we won't run into trouble for this part of the rescue.

Though the air is musty here, it isn't dead. There must be an opening somewhere that lets in fresh air. I pull out my Valkric, marking this location on the map, and scan to where the palace is in relation. It's north of us, and we are heading straight east.

We walk in silence for a quarter of an hour until we come to a fork in the tunnels. The passage opens up slightly and the muffled buzz of hovercrafts can be heard on the street above.

I try to look farther down each path. Neither have any footprints or markings of someone else using these tunnels. We take the left passage heading northeast, closer to the palace.

Mai huffs an annoyed breath as we come to a dead-end, but what she can't see is the grooves cut into the stone. I trace a finger along them and pull Mai towards the wall to feel it as well.

"A way up?" she ponders.

"Possibly. I'm going to check; I'll be right back." She nods in response. Mai seems more comfortable with confined spaces than heights.

I notch my fingers into the rough stone and pull myself up. I am only a few feet off the ground when my right hand hits the rock ceiling. I stamp down the immediate panic that runs through me as I think about the amount of stone and brick stacked above us.

Running my fingers along the stone, I find it is a whole slab. I lightly prod my fingers against it, testing for weaknesses.

Putting my hand flat against it, I push a little harder. I can feel the binding around it give slightly, and debris dusts my hair.

I stop, pressing my ear to it, but only silence greets me. Shoving again on the ceiling while holding my breath, I try not to breathe in the falling dust. The stone grates against the cement gripping it in place and finally gives way. I wait a minute before thrusting up the stone to see.

It's pitch black in here as well. I push the stone fully off and quickly realize it's like the tunnels below, but instead it's dead space, like a part of the castle that has been long forgotten. Dust coats the stone flooring here and I wince knowing every step we take will show a perfect trail. Though I can only see a few yards ahead, it looks like the chamber heads west.

I hoist Mai's small body up and replace the stone over the opening. I mark the spot on my Valkric and the holographic image ripples. When it zooms out, our location blinks on the far east side of the palace.

This time I take Mai's hand and we walk slowly through the tunnel. As we turn a corner, I see warm orange light ahead, reflecting onto the wall. I squeeze Mai's hand in a silent order to wait as I pull out my sword and move towards the light. It streams through small slits in the wall near the floor, almost like an old ventilation system. Peering through the slits, an open hallway sits barren except for lights lit along it.

The tunnel we are in continues parallel to it. I get Mai and we keep moving along the tunnel until it reaches another dead end. There are slits in the wall here as well and I crouch to see through them. In front of us is a set of double doors reinforced with steel and a pair of guards monitoring from either side of the door.

I pull Mai down to see.

We sit quietly near the vent slits, dust clinging to our clothing, and wait. After what feels like hours later, approaching steps echo off the stone. A hooded man stops in front of the guards and lowers his hood.

Mai gasps at who we see, and I quickly cover her mouth. *Pierre*. Luckily, he is already speaking to the guards, and Mai's gasp is muffled in the background. If we aren't careful, elves' superior hearing could even detect our breathing or heartbeat from where we sit.

"I am here to see the prince," Pierre says confidently, but the guard doesn't open the door.

One of them merely holds out his hand and Pierre sighs before fishing out a piece of paper and handing it to him. He takes a moment to look it over and Pierre taps his foot in impatience. The guard hands it back and they push open the double doors.

I quickly try to take in every detail of what's behind that door, but unfortunately, it's a dim corridor that reveals little. The doors are heavy though, and I can see the strain on the guards' faces as they push it open. Pierre walks stiffly through the entrance turning left.

My butt goes numb as we wait for Pierre to appear again. When he does, he tells the guards to clean Braun up, whether from a beating by Pierre or someone else I don't know.

Though looking at Pierre's knuckles I think the former. I berate myself internally for not having thought of the fact that

Braun may not be able to be moved quickly.

I mull this over as we quietly walk back the way we came. We remove the stone slab and I jump through, landing softly on the dirt floor of the tunnel below before helping Mai down after. As we reach the fork in the tunnels, Mai stops me when I walk towards the tunnel we came through.

"Shouldn't we check out where this other path goes?" Mai points to the tunnel we hadn't explored.

I sigh. I'm exhausted and my claustrophobia is at an all-time high, but she's right. We only have three more days until the execution so checking every possible route is a necessity.

The trickle of water grows louder as we move farther into the tunnel. We end at an underground water system. The water looks to be only a meter deep, and high above the large cylindrical stone ceiling traffic can be heard.

Small bits of light seep in through the slits in the road above. The tunnel runs north and south. I check out our position on the Valkric; we are close to the city's eastern border.

There is an odd sound, one I didn't notice above the rushing water—the scrape of something sharp against stone. The hairs on the back of my neck rise and my stomach drops.

I turn to Mai and notice movement near the ceiling. *Holy gods.* I stand still staring at it and as Mai starts to turn, I grab her wrist.

"Don't turn around, stay very still," I murmur.

She beings to shake in my grasp as if she now senses the danger too. I reach for my sword hilt and pull it out of my pocket.

"When I say run, go back the way we came through the tunnels as fast as you can." I wait a moment as the darkness shifts and my blood runs cold.

"RUN!" I yell and Mai takes off in the direction we just came from.

The light created by the appearance of my blade shows me my foe and it unleashes an unearthly sound as the light stings its twelve onyx eyes. It's black as night and as big as a Valkyrien transport.

An arachne.

The eight-legged creature with two hollow fangs longer than my forearms lies in wait at the top corner of the tunnel we came through. Its sticky white web covers most of the wall and bits of venom drip from its fangs, corroding the stone floor below. Venom even an immortal cannot heal from.

Shit.

Panic grips me as it leaps from its web toward me. Instincts have me moving even though my brain has dissolved into mush. I slide under it as it hits the ground with its long needle-sharp legs.

I roll to the side as it shifts, trying to reach me, and I swing my sword into one of its legs. It lets out an ear-shattering screech as it lands hard on the stub I just cut, black blood oozing onto the stones before it adjusts.

It shoots one of its legs towards me and I dart away, but not fast enough. It cuts me deep along my rib cage and I curse, swinging my sword at it blindly.

I glance back at the tunnel we came through. It's not large enough for the arachne to fit through. Before I can think through my decision, I make a full out sprint for it, but the arachne expects this and stabs through my leg with one of its own.

The spear like end rips through skin and muscle, barely missing the bone, as I smack face first into the ground. I let out a yelp of pain, stars dance in my vision, and my teeth sing.

As I reach for my sword that clattered only inches away, the arachne drags me over the stones closer to its long fangs.

I feel my fear take over fully as I scream at it, clawing at the ground to get away. My nails break and tear over the stone floor as I'm dragged through its putrid blood. I am no longer concerned if its leg rips deeper down mine all the way to my foot.

I haven't felt fear like this in a long while, and I grapple to control it as I sort through my options.

Just then, light floods the cavern. The arachne screeches, rearing back, and releases my leg.

My eyes adjust quickly, and Mai stands at the lip of the tunnel with some sort of equipment that lights up the whole waterway. I crawl towards her and grab my sword, not daring to look behind me. I force myself to stand, limping.

She drops the light on the ground, and we tumble through the hallway far enough in that the arachne can't follow.

We stop and I sag against the wall panting. I am livid. I haven't had my fear blind me this badly in so long. Completely useless, I forgot how to react.

My leg is on fire as blood trickles down it. *Good*, I deserve it for my idiocy. Mai slings her arm around me, helping me walk back through the tunnel into the bar we are in before.

As I sit there using rags found in the cellar to clean up my leg as best I can, Mai places the bricks back into place. I can see her hands shake as she works.

"Thank you," I whisper and she only nods, not stopping.

We wait in the cellar, hiding behind crates and casks until the wound on my leg is healed enough, I can walk properly.

"What was that thing?" Mai finally asks as we walk back to the inn.

"An arachne." Mai shudders as I continue. "A giant spider with hollow fangs filled with venom. One bite is enough to stun anyone instantly, immortal or not, and keep them in a state of paralysis for days. The arachne will leave a victim wrapped in their silk web for as long as it pleases before devouring them whole."

Mai shudders. "If I had known that before, there's no way I would have even considered saving you."

I bark out a laugh.

Chapter 17

Light breaks across the city casting it in hues of yellow and orange. We have one day left until Braun's execution. I spent the day before hobbling from rooftop to rooftop over the city, checking any other viable routes.

While my footfalls weren't their usual night-cloaked silence, I still wasn't as loud as Braun. I asked if Mai wanted to join, and she mumbled something about preferring to face the arachne again rather than running on rooftops.

In the evening, we continued searching for more tunnels but found no others that led so close to the dungeons of the castle. My ribs are still sore from where the stupid arachne sliced me and my leg is still tender, but both are looking better.

Mai and I sit in a cafe pretending to eat our breakfast, but nerves have gotten the better of us as we push the food around our plates.

"I don't like this plan," Mai states, and I nod in agreement.

"I don't think we have another option," I say defeatedly.

"What about Pierre?"

I grimace. "He barely decided on a whim to give us a chance to run at the Port of Yulamic and I still had to knock him unconscious."

"We could always grab him and hold him at knifepoint for information?" Mai mutters to her plate.

"Why would you need to do that?" We both jump as Pierre stands at our table. My sword hilt is in my hand within seconds.

He holds up his hands and chuckles. "You have no need of that, I have no quarrel with you."

Mai narrows her brown eyes at him. "Then why are you here?"

He shrugs and slides his tall, dark form into a seat next to Mai. I look around to see if he's brought any friends with him.

"I'm alone," he states, noting that I scan the room.

"I doubt that," I snip while continuing my perusal of those around us.

He chuckles. "So distrusting, Vera. Just like Braun was when I saw him the other day."

My eyes flick to Pierre, but I don't rise to his provocation. I tilt my head to the side and study him carefully. He is a handsome elf to be sure, but he's greasy and does what he wants only to his benefit.

"Why are you here?" I reiterate Mai's original question.

"To help you of course!" he exclaims. I huff a breath, shaking my head.

"And why exactly would you want to do that?"

"I have made many mistakes in my life and wish to make right the few I can," he says while staring at his bronze hands.

"Bullshit."

He sighs, tapping his dark finger on the table before answering. "I want to go with you when you leave."

"Why would you want to go with us?" Mai asks skeptically.

He merely shrugs. "I've wasted too much time in this cold and callous place." Pierre waves his hand around dramatically. "I saw first-hand in Port of Yulamic what it was like for Braun. To be on a grand adventure."

I snort at the ridiculousness of what Pierre claims.

There's no way he wants that, but he continues. "I want what Braun has. Adventure and glory. Two things that you both seem to be chock full of."

"It's not as glamorous as you're making it sound. Besides I'm looking for survivors, not playing hero." I don't comment on the fact that his explanation is also an utter lie.

His smile turns into a thin line. "Was saving Braun a part of your plan to find survivors all along?"

"We wouldn't have had to if you hadn't been such a deceitful bastard," I sneer at him.

"A momentary lapse in judgment," he comments as if it hadn't thrown off my plans completely.

"Do you have those often?" Mai asks casually.

Pierre frowns while his aqua eyes hold Mai's gaze for a moment. When he adds nothing more, Mai and I discuss the best course of action. We silently hash out whether to add this idiot into our plans. At some point, Mai nods and I sigh, knowing I've lost the battle on this.

"Alright." I look at Pierre, whose face turns into pure delight. "If you want to help, give us a detailed description of what's on the other side of the main dungeon doors and where Braun is located. Then you can give us the best options for escaping." I cross my arms and sit back.

"Wonderful!" he exclaims. "The dungeons are primitive at best. Besides the two guards at the main door of the dungeon, there are two more inside patrolling each hall. They have Braun to the left once you go in the main door." The same way we watched Pierre walk the other night. I glance at Mai who seems to be thinking the same thing. "There are tunnels built all throughout the palace that will take you close to the dungeon. That will be the best way in and out."

I raise my eyebrows in fake surprise. "They are still accessible?"

Pierre nods before continuing, "The specific tunnel will

be to the right of the dungeon doors, there are slits along the floor where it starts. It will dead end and there's a slab of stone on the floor you can move it and it'll drop into a lower tunnel. That tunnel forks and we'll take the tunnel to the left."

I glance at Mai again whose frowning, but I turn back to Pierre and nod. He must know about the arachne there. "From there a waterway leads you to the edge of the city, where I have no doubt we'll be able to find a transport."

"Any other escape routes?" I ask and Pierre shakes his head. I tell him where to meet us tonight and go over the plan, only giving him just enough detail to keep him thinking we are playing his game. We depart, and Mai and I take the longest possible route back to the inn. We don't want any more surprises.

I sit on the bed repacking Braun's stuff between Mai's and my bags. He has very little in his pack other than a few daggers, throwing stars, and a metal spiked ball that looks like the end of a morning star as well as some clothing and a single book. The same one he was reading on the passage to Yulamic, and... and a blaster? How have we not known about this?

This weapon is high-tech for Alfheim. I read the symbols on the side, and it looks to be Asgardian.

How did he get this?

No matter. This will certainly come in handy while breaking him out of the dungeons. We planned to make bombs to blow up the wall between us and the dungeon doors, but a single shot from this gun will do the trick. Its high-powered laser beam will incinerate anything in its path.

The only issue is this model takes a full minute to recharge between shots. If only he had the newer one that takes mere seconds to recharge. I tuck it in the waist band of my pants and finish packing his stuff into ours.

Just before night falls, we head to the bar where we

found the tunnel. It doesn't open its doors for a few hours, but Mai picks the lock with ease. I practically burst with pride when she unlocks it in under a minute. She's getting good.

We move quickly and quietly to uncover the bricks. A clock tower nearby strikes fifteen minutes until six in the evening—a full hour before we planned to meet Pierre at the dungeon doors. We told him to arrive before us to casually chat with the guards, but neither Mai nor I trust him so we moved up our timeline just in case.

We walk quickly through the tunnels, careful not to tread too loudly. When we come to the stone ceiling, I leave it open. We will need it to get out. As we approach the dungeon door from inside the tunnel, it is eerily quiet. I glance at Mai who looks worried. As I crouch down, I see blue blood coats the floor on the other side. The palace guards are already down, and the dungeon doors are wide open.

"That traitorous asshole," Mai mutters under her breath.

I pull out the blaster. It's now or never. Dragging Mai back down the hall, I flick off the safety lock on the laser gun. I aim it towards the wall next to the dungeons, and it lets off a trilling sound once it's charged. I pull the trigger without hesitation. Red light streams from the blaster and the wall before us bursts open, throwing debris everywhere. The sound alone is loud enough to alert someone, so we have to be quick.

I grab Mai, stumbling over rock and dead guards. The smoke clears as we move into the dungeons. Other prisoners call out, but their pleas fall on deaf ears. I follow Pierre's instructions and turn left and signal Mai to check the right side just in case.

All the cells on this side remain empty, but I stop at one where the key still sits in one of the locks with two guards dumped inside. Shit, Pierre's already grabbed him. Mai whistles from the other side and I run to her.

"Not here, what now?" she demands, the panic in her voice clear.

"We find Braun and Pierre."

We hurtle down the only passage leading out of the dungeons and listen before climbing a set of spiral stone steps. At the top, there's a door I press my ear to. I can hear Pierre's voice on the other side.

"What I want is for you to give me the treasures you promised me all those years ago." Pierre sounds exasperated. I hear Braun's chuckle. My heart picks up, relief rushing through me. He's not dead yet.

"Just kill me already. I will never give you the crown jewels, you greedy bastard," Braun states and I roll my eyes.

He's forever a martyr.

I rev up the blaster and just as it rings, I blast open the door, sending shards of wood flying at Pierre and Braun. As the smoke clears, Pierre lies on the floor unconscious.

Braun has his arms pulled behind him, bound by chains at his wrists. The chair he sits in has tipped over and he shifts, coughing, on his side. He looks more or less unscathed but sports a black eye and a cut along his cheek, and his clothes barely pass as rags.

The blaster smokes from the barrel as I wave it in the air, stepping into the room.

"Thanks for this." His eyes meet mine, and I can see the wickedness in that smokey gaze.

My heart leaps in my throat. Mai kicks Pierre in the stomach as I haul Braun out of the chair. He's worse than I thought as he sways on his feet, his weight pushing into me.

I use the heat on the blaster barrel to melt through the chains linking Braun's hands. I consider killing Pierre right here, the pain in the ass that he is, but I can hear shouts from levels above and below.

"Time to go." I start pulling Braun back the way we came, but he doesn't budge.

"I know a better way," he says and starts moving towards

the door to our left before we can protest.

Mai kicks the unconscious Pierre in the stomach once more, just for good measure, and we follow Braun out of the room. From here it is a long flight of stairs; up and up and up we go. They must be the servants' stairs. Every so often there is a landing and a door, and eventually, Braun stops at one of the landings. He pants heavily as he opens the door slowly and, upon seeing the room is empty, strides in.

I cross my arms. "This is not a way-out Braun, what the hell are you doing?" Mai stays near the door checking the stairway for activity.

"This is my old room," he murmurs as he digs through the wardrobe.

"Now is not the time to be nostalgic." A bit of panic enters my voice. He mutters something inaudible as he finds whatever he is looking for. He walks towards me and slips it into my pack.

"Guys, we've got company," Mai whispers.

"Close the door and lock it," Braun commands.

There are no other exits in the room. Do the royals use the same stairs? How un-Elven.

I look across the room towards the bank of windows overlooking the palace; we are high above the city as well. So many floors lay between us and the ground.

"What now?" Mai demands. I hate my next thought, but we already hear pounding footsteps race up the stairs. *Shit, shit, shit.*

"Do you trust me?" I ask Mai and Braun.

Mai looks at me skeptically then nods and Braun just smirks like he knows what I'm going to suggest. I take one of the dust covered chairs and chuck it at the floor-to-ceiling windows. The glass shatters, surely alerting the guards to exactly which room we are in.

Mai frowns and steps towards the door, realizing my

intentions.

"I lied I don't trust you." Braun merely laughs and moves towards her. She spouts off a flurry of Midgardian swear words.

"On the count of three, we jump, and do not. Let go. Of my hand. For any reason," I state and take one of their hands in each of mine. Braun's fingers slip through mine interlinking them tightly, and Mai holds onto my other hand with a death grip.

"One." I hear the guards bang on the door behind us, trying to force it open. Muffled shouts rise from the stairway.

"Two." Something pounds into the door, the wood whines in protest. Guards wedge an ax into it, creating a hole to see into the room.

"Three." A buzzing sound whips by my ear, and I start losing the feeling in my hand Mai holds.

We take off sprinting towards the opening, wind whips inside inviting us to jump. I drag Mai, as she protests wildly, to where the windows stood moments ago and plummet into the darkness of night. I close my eyes as Mai screams and I block her out, thinking of the grassy field and wide blue ocean I saw on our travels here from Salaza.

Chapter 18

WE ARRIVE ONLY A FEW feet off the ground, so the drop is not far, but Mai, mouth wide open, still screams as we land, though she emits no sound. Her face, usually a rich caramel color, is ash gray and she trembles from where she sits in the grass. I try to pry my hand out of hers, but she's in shock. Braun kneels in front of her and gently peels her fingers gripping mine as he murmurs, "You're all right."

Her fingers shake, but she lifts her free hand and puts up her middle finger to us. Braun and I scrunch our eyebrows, unsure what it means.

"F-f-f-fuck you," she bites out, though far too weakly to be an actual threat. I realize she's used a Midgardian gesture.

Braun still doesn't understand as he wrinkles his nose before saying, "No, thank you."

He looks over at me and he chuckles. "What?" I snip out.

He smirks. "How did you know that was going to work?"

I give him a wicked grin and shrug. "I didn't."

"Gods, I hate you both," Mai whispers and falls back into the azure grass.

I pull out my Valkric to confirm our location and sure enough, we are on the coast of Salaza. Behind us a sheer cliff drops into the water below. While Mai recovers, muttering how much she hates us, Braun and I collect firewood.

We walk through the sparse tree line as the suns dip toward the horizon in the west. Cypress trees lean towards one another as if reaching to tell each other secrets. Gulls circle above in the warm air current and cry out every so often. I hate the jealousy that claws through me as I watch them soar. How easily they glide overhead, without a care in the world.

Braun and I work in silence for a bit before I tell him the news we heard in Salaza about Nidavellir and the transport. I watch his face become drawn, but he doesn't say anything, doesn't try to convince me to do anything about it as Mai did. The relief I expect to feel doesn't come.

He bends to pick up a stick and he winces.

"Are you hurt?" I ask. He waves his hand and mutters to himself.

I watch him wince again that evening as we sit around the campfire and Mai comments on it. His response consists of silence and rolling his eyes. He must have drained his healing powers during an earlier beating, so I rummage through my bag and throw him a tin of healing salve I picked up in Railen.

"If you won't tell us then at least fix it yourself." He lifts his shirt, and his ribs and chest are covered in angry watercolor bruises.

Mai grimaces as she turns away, unable to watch. I, on the other hand, am unable to look away. His sculpted body looks as if he was chiseled out of marble. He sucks in a breath as he tries to lift his arms high enough to pull off the rags he's been wearing since we found him.

I sigh, taking pity on him, and walk over. He gives me a defiant look as I crouch in front of him but says nothing. I cut through his shirt with the dagger from my boot before he can even protest. Running my hands along his shoulders, I push the ragged cloth off, and it drifts to the ground behind him.

Only slightly aware that I am barely breathing, I gently take the tin from his hand and pull the lid off. Notes of eucalyptus, lemon, and pineapple waft out. I dip two fingers in and dot it on his chest.

His stormy eyes bore holes into me as I try hard to focus on the task and not the proximity of him or how gorgeous he is with his shirt off even with the bruises. I meet his gaze before touching his chest to spread the salve. He winces when I place my hand as lightly as possible on his left pec.

"Sorry," I murmur and continue the movement across his chest and very carefully along his ribs.

When I'm done, I quickly stand, needing to put more space between us. I dig through Mai's pack for one of his shirts and chuck it towards him. He catches it with ease. After a while, he's able to pull it over his head, proof the salve helped.

He stands, stretching out his arms above him, and gives me a satisfied smirk. Narrowing my eyes, I'm tempted to throw a piece of firewood at him. He rummages through my bag for a moment, and I catch Mai looking curiously at him, wondering what he could be looking for.

"Here," he murmurs, before handing me a heavy metal object.

I'm unable to hold in my gasp as my fingers brush the intricate design inlaid on the handle. Runes run in a vertical line down the blade describing the intended user.

"A gods' weapon," I whisper. Its magic hums under my touch, begging me to use it. "Where did you get this?"

When Braun doesn't speak, I glance up at him, to find him watching me closely as I fawn over the blade no larger than a dagger.

He shrugs. "I found it a long time ago."

"Do you know whose blade this is?" I wave it around casually before twirling it between my fingers. It moves with practiced efficiency like the blade knows its user even before it is wielded by them. "This is Baldr's dagger."

"Bladder..." Mai murmurs, watching the dagger with as

much intensity as I do.

I snort. "Baldr. Son of Odin, brother to Thor. He was the god of light, joy, and purity. He was the summer sun." I smile fondly thinking of Baldr.

I hated him the least out of Odin's offspring. It was hard to hate someone who made you feel like nothing was impossible when they were around. Vali briefly pops into my mind, and I wonder if he made it out of Asgard alive as well.

"Was?"

I'm pulled from my thoughts and give Braun a sad smile. "I'll give you one guess at who killed him."

"Oh! Loki!" Mai exclaims, happy to finally figure out something first. "I knew it!"

Braun only grinds his teeth together so loudly I can hear it from where I sit. I stare at the weapon for a moment longer, running my fingers over the designs. My fingers love the familiar strokes of runes etched into the metal. Braun comes to sit beside me, and his thigh brushes mine as he sits on the dusty ground next to me.

I hand the dagger back to him as I ask, "Is this what you were looking for in your rooms?"

He turns his smokey gaze on me and nods but doesn't take the dagger. Mai bursts out laughing. "Here I was thinking you were looking for a ring."

Braun ignores her, keeping his eyes on me. I am unable to tear my eyes away from his gaze to question what the hell Mai is talking about.

"It's yours," he murmurs.

I snort. "Hardly. If anything, I should give it to one of Odin's other children if I find any of them."

"You deserve it more than they do," Mai mutters, poking the fire with a small twig.

I smile and realize Braun will keep putting it in my pack if I try giving it back to him. So, I quickly switch it out with the dagger in my boot, and Braun moves back to his spot across the fire from me.

As he passes, Mai wrinkles her nose at him. "By the way, you smell like shit."

I'm pulled from sleep by the light whisper of Mai's voice.

"We saw the video of your reunion with your brother."

There's no response for a moment and upon opening my eyes I see it's too early to be morning. My back towards the fire, I blink to scan the trees. I almost close my eyes again when the deep timber of Braun's hushed voice fills the air. "I don't understand."

Mai explains so quickly I only catch every other word. At one point Braun hums in understanding, about what I'm not entirely sure.

"We elves are… very set in our ways. Traditions are not easily changed. When I killed my father and fled the kingdom, some felt that no matter my transgressions, I should be the next King of Haratine. Then others felt I should die for my treason.

"The former opinion would be that of my mother's, the latter my brother's. My mother was… cruel. A trait she picked up from her upbringing and passed to my sister, Rowana, but my brother… he has always been fair and just. What my mother would consider to be 'weak' characteristics. 'Better to rule by fear than love' was the mantra she lived by. She wanted me to rule, or even my sister, but never my brother."

I shudder thinking of growing up in such a cold household. Pulling my rough spun wool blanket tighter around me, I snuggle in waiting for Braun to continue his story. "I know my brother still loves me, but he feels the weight of that crown. No matter if he still cares about me, he cannot, in his just mind, let me go unpunished. Sounds like he found a loophole with the cameras. I didn't know he added those."

"And Pierre?" Mai asks.

"He wanted to live like a king. While he was a friend, a comrade, and helped me escape the first time, he assumed I'd eventually come back to rule. He had hoped I would give him crown jewels for his loyalty to me. I may have led him to believe it when he aided me, but I never planned to go back. I'm not…"

He trails off and I can imagine him swallowing while running a hand through his grimy silver hair. "I'm not meant to be a ruler."

My heart hurts for him. Trying to do the right thing, only to leave without an explanation. He clearly cares about his brother's opinion if he was willing to die for his crimes.

"You're still a better elf than most," Mai tries to comfort him. I almost huff out a laugh at her poor attempt. "There's nothing you can do to change your past and now that you cleared the air with your brother, there's no sense dwelling on—" She stops when I shift slightly, though I doubt either of them realize I'm awake. They are quiet for a moment while they wait to see if I'll 'wake up'.

"Are you going to do something about that?" I scrunch my eyebrows; I get the feeling Mai's not talking about Braun's past anymore.

"I don't know what you're talking about," Braun snips out.

"Sure, sure." Mai sighs. "Good night." I hear her shift in her blankets as Braun grunts in response.

I close my eyes, drifting back into sleep, when I hear crunching footsteps and something warm brushes my cheek. I try to open my eyes, but they feel glued shut and I'm unable to fight the pull of the dreams I'm sure will have me screaming awake in a few hours.

Early morning light casts long shadows as I sit along the cliff's edge. I tilt my head towards the sun as they break over the horizon and soak in its warmth, its energy, and let the spray of the surf wash over me, almost hoping it will take me with it. My left hand runs absently over Baldr's dagger in my lap, and my fingers track the etched runes.

I scrub my other hand over my face, contemplating my next step. Three worlds down and no luck finding survivors or my sister. I am a coward for not wanting to help end Ragnarok.

I sort through everything I know about Ragnarok. Only Loki's greed and tricks would go this far. Who would be next? Midgard, if Loki felt like punishing Odin's son, Thor, even more. Maybe Vanaheim, the second god realm, if Loki remembered how the gods there slighted him.

I briefly wonder if any of the gods sided with him, thinking of Loki's terrifying children. Namely, the one who rules Niflheim, aptly named Hel, a massive wolf named Fenrir, and the giant, cruel serpent, Jormungandr.

Preventing Ragnarok the first time had gone so poorly, I'm not sure what makes me think I can stop Loki this time. I don't even know if the version of Loki I knew and loved is real.

I lift my head from my hands as Mai approaches. She gives me a small smirk before sitting on my right, though slightly farther away from the cliff's edge. She twirls a piece of her pink hair, now a few shades lighter and longer in length without her upkeep on it.

"Change of plans?" she asks, as if she already knows I've changed my mind about stopping Loki.

I nod. "Only slightly."

She shrugs and says, "We'll figure it out."

I can feel another piece of my heart light up at that, thankful for this new friendship, this new sisterhood, and to have someone to help me through this journey.

The newest goal on the list intimidates me. With the fall of Nidavellir and the attack from the harpies and dark elves, I cannot guarantee that whatever realm I find Asgardian survivors in will be safe from Loki.

It's a calling in my blood, that even after Asgard's fall I would always be loyal to it and its people. Now it feels like more than that, like I am somehow accountable for stopping Ragnarok as well. I can feel the Valkyrien blood in my veins calling for vengeance. To spill the blood of my foes and protect the Asgardians until my death.

"You mentioned your sister in Merin. I didn't know you had a sister," she states quietly, pulling me from my thoughts.

I run my fingers through my hair. "You remind me of her, you know?" A small smile spreads on Mai's face. "Edda is sassy and out-going. The life of the party."

I can't say more without my throat closing. I miss Edda and I know that while Mai reminds me of her, she is not a replacement for my Edda.

"Is she like you?" Mai asks.

I hum in confirmation. "Except she's… brighter and warmer. Friendlier than me."

"That's not difficult to accomplish," Mai teases.

I nudge her thin shoulder before continuing, "Her eyes are green, and she doesn't have any runes other than one that we share."

"I hope I get to meet her," Mai says after we are quiet for a moment.

"Me too," I whisper hoarsely.

I stare out at the ocean, pushing Edda from my thoughts for a moment. While I cross off 'save Braun' from my mental list of things to do, I add 'stop Loki/Ragnarok' to it. I hate that Loki still surprises me with the shit he pulls even after all this time.

The breeze shifts as Braun slowly sits on the other side of me and I glance at him, knowing he heard our conversation about Ragnarok and my sister. His stony countenance has been my constant companion these days. I didn't realize how much I missed it until he was captured. I will miss him once Mai and I leave for another realm.

"Where to next, Vera?" he asks quietly.

His pale, clean skin shimmers in the early morning suns. He thankfully bathed earlier. As he turns to face me, tilting his head to the side, his silver-white hair falls from its loose hold to cover the right side of his face.

I look away before I become entranced by those cloudburst eyes. It has happened far too often during our time together, though he never seems to notice and never comments if he has.

I shrug, finally answering Braun. "I searched Niflheim, Nidavellir, and now Alfheim. So that leaves Midgard and Vanaheim. Or possibly Svartalfheim, Jotunheim, Muspelheim, though I doubt anyone would last long there."

"Or Asgard," Braun comments absently.

I huff. "Just because we found one text saying that Asgard will rise again doesn't mean it's real. Besides does that mean Nidavellir will too? That wasn't prophesied at all."

"Just admit that if you find some of the Asgardian survivors in a recreated Asgard, you're going to feel like a total ass for arguing with us," Mai says with a smirk. I roll my eyes at her and ignore her comment.

"Vanaheim or Midgard would be the closest to visit next. I've been to both a few times. Vanaheim is another realm for the gods and could be where they took Asgardians as they fled. Plus, there is a Vanaheim god who can supposedly see the future, which may help us locate the Asgardians and figure out where Ragnarok is moving next.

"Though Midgard might be quicker since you and I know it better," I say referring to Mai, "and there's a chance we can find the transport that landed there as well as Thor."

Midgard has always been his favorite haunt. However, he and I have a fraught history, so getting help from him is a toss-up at best.

"I think we should try Earth—er—Midgard first," Mai

comments. She and I already discussed this late the other night before we left Knoll. She wants to come and continue to help, and I appreciate her friendship and company.

I stand to stretch as I feel my butt cheek go numb. Braun's face quickly flits through a series of emotions. Clearly, he has something he wants to say. "Spit it out, Braun."

He stands to face me, and I see vulnerability there that I've never seen before. "I've heard Midgard is something to behold. They have a very basic and primitive understanding of the universe and yet their technology is far more advanced than our own."

"Braun, are you saying you want to come with us?" I smirk at him, and hope grows in my chest. I wasn't ready to say goodbye yet anyway.

He holds my stare, finding nothing funny about this. I sigh and run my hands through my mess of brown hair. It would be good to have another companion on this quest but dragging him and Mai into my problems feels wrong.

"You understand this won't be a vacation? I am working towards a larger goal." Find the Asgardian survivors, find my sister, and stop Ragnarok.

Braun watches me for a moment, and I try not to dwell too much on how close we've all become. I hadn't thought of how lonely the next part of my journey would be, but now I smile as I feel as if a small weight is lifted. With Mai and Braun joining me for a bit it is as if they are sharing the burden, though failure would mean little for them and everything for me.

"Where you go, so will I," Braun answers. It feels like there is more behind that statement, but I push the thought aside. I can only nod in response.

"Are we sure we want to bring him along?" Mai asks as she brushes off purple dirt from her pants. Braun frowns at her. "Can you even speak any languages of Midgard?" she adds. He looks like he's deciding whether or not to punch her.

"I'm sure I'll pick it up better than you did Elvish," he snips, earning a glare from her.

"What language can you speak, Mai?" I ask curiously. We haven't talked much about her home realm.

"English, Mandarin, and maybe five words in French," she states.

"It'll be fine, Braun will pick it up or we'll have a fabulous time laughing at him when he tries," I say in English to her. She smirks, deciding that alone is an acceptable reason. I glance at Braun who looks at me through narrowed eyes.

"When do we leave?" Mai inquires in Elvish.

"Shortly, I have all I need with me." I pat the pack that I throw over my shoulder which now contains my stuff as well as some of Braun's.

"How do you plan to get there?" he puzzles and Mai's smile fades. I open my mouth to speak but Mai cuts me off, knowing what I'm going to say.

"No. Absolutely not. There is no way I am doing that again," she states while crossing her arms. "We can catch a transport."

Braun shakes his head. "Very few transports come and go from Midgard. The last I heard it was five years ago when one arrived." Mai grumbles some response about how stupid elves are with technology.

"Hold on tight, this will be more disorienting than last time," I instruct.

After twenty minutes of arguing with Mai, somehow Braun convinces her to jump with us. It might have been his promise to give her one compliment every day or the jewelry he claimed he'd buy her. Now, we stand hand in hand at the edge of a cliff in Salaza.

"Great," Mai mutters.

Braun looks far too excited about this part of our trip,

while Mai bounces her leg in anticipation of hating every second of it. Before I would just leap off and tuck in my wings to realm-jump. Now, to travel between realms, I have to freefall into the timeless dimension and rely only on my Valkyrien instincts to reach my destination. I can only pretend the wind on my face is from flying, not falling. It never feels the same, and it hurts my heart far more than it should that my wings are gone.

"Are you ok?" Braun looks uncomfortable sensing my heartache. I take a breath and count quietly to three.

As we jump, I pretend to not feel his hand squeeze tighter around mine. The last thing I need is his pity; I am one of the few left alive. I must stay strong and find the others.

Chapter 19

I AM BLINDED BY LIGHT as we pop into existence on Midgard. It is far, far too bright for my eyes and it takes several minutes for them to adjust.

This part of Midgard is expansive from our vantage point. We stand on a balcony of a very tall building. I am thankful that we didn't land between buildings and plummet towards the ground. Trying to jump from one planet to the next while it orbits a sun and rotates makes any realm-jump tricky at best, deadly at worst.

The bustling city teems with humans below us while the surrounding buildings stand just as grandly as the one we are on. Made of metal, stone, or brick, the mismatched structures make it feel as if this city is in transition between the old and the new.

Braun lets out a low whistle. It is a lot to take in compared to most of the places on Alfheim, whose castles and land are far behind what is here. I pull out my Valkric, checking out our location.

At one time I could locate other Valkyrie or gods on the device as well, though I have not seen another dot pop up on it in all the realms I've been to, and I doubt it will happen here. The gods and Valkyrie are difficult to find in the best of circumstances.

I move my finger across the holographic image that hovers above the screen. "Looks like we are in—"

"San Francisco," Mai whispers in wonder. Seemingly less affected by this jump than last time, she adds, "Why do we always land up so high? Can we try landing in an area that is not an 80-story building or cliff edge?"

"I'll keep that in mind for next time, princess," I say sarcastically.

"That was certainly the last time for me. Zero out of five stars; would not recommend," she snaps back before listing all the things she'd rather be doing than realm-jumping.

"Huh, an odd name for a place," Braun states, tuning out Mai as she rants. I grin at that. "Now what?"

"Humans aren't used to seeing people from the other realms, so we'd better find new clothes to help us blend in here," Mai explains while walking towards the doors leading into the building. I start to follow, but Braun's hand catches my arm.

"What?" I give him a confused look. He looks concerned as he takes in the building but then shakes his head before walking in.

"Excuse me! This bar is not open yet; you need to leave immediately! How did you even get up here?" A woman in black pants and top exclaims with a hand on her chest as if we've frightened her. We pay her no mind and continue to the elevators.

As the elevator descends, it jostles briefly. The first few times, Braun unsheathes both his weapons thinking it's an attack. Mai and I try hard to smother our laughter at a very cross Braun.

"You could have warned me," he mutters under his breath as we fight to control ourselves. I love pushing Braun's buttons.

"Oh, this is going to be fun." I smile at Mai's comment and grab Braun's hand leading him out of the building.

From the street, the resonating chatter and commotion of people is even more disorienting. Humans rush out of an underground staircase labeled 'BART'. Whatever BART is, it seems to be a popular, if not grimy, place.

I keep hold of Braun and Mai as we weave through people, trying to bring as little attention to ourselves as possible. I stop short in front of a big building with the word 'Macy's' written on it. Braun practically runs into me.

In the windows, creepy plastic statues without heads wear clothing. I can't remember the name of them now, something like manicures? It must be a clothing store. Mai walks in with us in tow and heads towards the section labeled 'Men's'. Braun stands out more than she and I with his height and looks. We ignore the humans who gawk when we pass.

"Hello, anything I can help you find today?" A man in a black button-down with a tag on his shirt labeled 'Dave' approaches us when we walk into the men's area.

"Yes actually, we need to get him into more everyday clothes. Something casual," Mai explains. "He doesn't speak any English," she adds.

The man nods and appraises Braun who shifts from one foot to the other uncomfortable with the attention, though I can't understand why. Elves on Alfheim were always staring at him, whether in jealousy or lust.

"I see, you must have just come from the Comic-con Convention, right? I can understand wanting to change out of that." The salesperson doesn't bother hiding his disdain for our clothes. Braun looks ready to punch the man. "Not a problem at all, follow me this way."

Mai and I leave Braun and walk to the women's section, but I look back and catch his gaze. *Play nice.*

He smirks and shrugs. *We'll see.*

We go up the moving stairs—the mechanism's name evades me. After picking out pants called 'jeans' and a simple black top, I grab a sweater and a jacket to layer. Since I have no idea where we are going after this, I figure it's best to have layers.

Mai has somehow thrown together a much cuter outfit than I, but far less practical. I pull a jacket from the shelf for her as well. I adjust the layer under my top again. Mai calls it a 'bra', but it feels like a jail cell for my boobs. I prefer the stretchy band of fabric used on Alfheim and Asgard to this, but Mai promised I'd get used to it. More like used to burning it.

I spot Braun as we walk back through the men's section. When the rest of his tall form comes into view, it's hard not to stare. Rippling muscle can be seen under the white shirt and deep blue jeans he wears.

I pull a black hat from a nearby shelf and hand it to him.

"Here, you'll need this." Braun takes it from me warily, but I tap my ear in explanation.

He jams it on his head, and while he seems to be hating every minute of it, the hat sadly does nothing to diminish his beauty. Stupid pretty elves.

Mai has already managed to pay for our clothes with a shiny plastic card she snagged from an unsuspecting lady's bag. We walk outside only to be plunged back into the ebb and flow of humans.

Braun grips my hand tighter as Mai presses towards what looks like a place to eat. "Where are we going?" he murmurs to me. I shrug, continuing to follow Mai.

"To eat, then for a place to stay. We call them hotels," Mai explains as she walks into a shop with a bright neon sign out front.

———

I watch Braun tear through his third massive slice of pizza, each slice making up a quarter of a whole pizza. He licks his fingers afterward like he's having the best meal of his life. This is also my first time eating this round dough piled high with tomato sauce, cheese, and whatever toppings. There's even one with pineapple and ham, which I wrinkle my nose at.

We sit in a small, grimy pizza joint, but Mai swears these dirty little places have the best food. Braun picks up the menu again, analyzing it, apparently wanting to try every possible combo they offer. I chuckle and shake my head.

"Wait until he tries cheeseburgers," she says to me in English, nudging me. "He'll never go back to Elven food again."

I have no idea what a cheeseburger is, but I shake my head. "I can't imagine anything better than this pizza right now." Braun narrows his eyes at us, annoyed that we switched to English.

"P-I-Z-Z-A." Mai gestures to the pizza as she sounds it out for him.

He frowns and his mouth twitches as if he's sounding it out in his head. "Peezzaaa," he tries with an odd accent. Mai smothers a laugh, but nods. I pat his leg, annoyed that he looks so sexy even when he's got no idea what we are talking about.

"Are you going to get another slice, or can we move on?" I tease in Elvish.

"Only if we can come back here tomorrow." Mai snorts at his response.

"We need to stop at a place to pick up a phone." She laughs at our confusion. "A communicator, to help us navigate and get around here."

We walk through a less crowded area where red and gold silk lanterns hang on wires between the buildings. The narrow street holds small stores with knick-knacks like waving cats, potted plants, and children's toys. When we come to a corner, women hand out paper flyers. Braun takes one as they push the colorful pamphlets in front of us. Mai ignores them and I follow her lead.

A few blocks later, I look over to see Braun has his hands

full of flyers. Mai sighs, ripping them out of his grasp and tossing them in the next trash bin we pass.

"Just stop taking them," I say.

"Seems rather rude," he mutters.

"Since when have you ever cared about being rude?" Mai snips.

He shrugs, before his face morphs into concentration. "You have very white teeth."

Mai and I turn to look at him, unsure we heard him right. "Your one compliment a day," he explains. I bark out a laugh.

"That's hardly a compliment!" I retort, but Mai beams.

"It's the best we're gonna hear, so better soak it up!" She winks at Braun whose impassive face reveals nothing before she turns on her heel to continue walking.

"You certainly seem to know where you're going, have you been here before?" I ask, noting how comfortable she looks walking down each and every street. She stops in her tracks. For a split second, she looks sad, but it's gone so quickly I wonder if it's just my imagination.

"I've visited here a lot." It is the only explanation she gives before turning down another street.

"Here!" she exclaims as we stop in front of a store with photos of humans holding some electronic device to their ear in the window.

"Wait out here," she states and walks in. Braun huffs and mutters something about being bossy. He leans against the light post and starts to take out a knife to clean it. I grab his hand halting him.

"You can't just walk around brandishing knives here," I warn. He looks even more annoyed. "We need to keep a low profile, remember?"

He closes his pack and readjusts it before crossing his arms. Automobiles, large and small, kick up dust and trash as they go by. I adjust Braun's hat so it's straight, and he grabs my arm when I start to step back. My heartbeat picks up as he brings his other hand up and runs it through the ends of my hair along my neck.

"Well, that was painful," Mai exclaims as she strolls out of the storefront. I am too stunned to move, but Braun casually steps away before Mai seems to notice.

"Where to next?" he asks.

"We passed a hotel on the way here, we'll stay there. But we'll need to pick up some more cash first," Mai states.

I nod and we walk back the way we came through crowded streets. On busier sidewalks, we casually slip into purses, pocketing cash, valuables, and plastic cards. The close press of bodies makes it easy to slide in and out unnoticed.

Mai says the plastic cards are directly linked to bank accounts. It sounds sketchy to me, but I trust she knows what she's doing. We turn down a smaller alley and count our loot while Braun keeps his eyes on the street, making sure we don't run into any trouble.

"Hotel Triton," Braun reads aloud as we sit in the hotel bar later that evening. He glances at me for confirmation. *Correct?* I nod.

We are all a bit exhausted from the day's activities and Mai plays with the 'phone' she got from the store. The technology has advanced a good deal since she was last here. She's engrossed while trying to get up to speed.

"So, what's the plan?" Braun asks, breaking the silence.

I shrug as Mai explains, "Midgard isn't like the other realms. Humans know nothing about the existence of other lifeforms so we can't just walk around asking people about Ragnarok, Thor, or Asgardians. No one will know what we are talking about."

I get an idea. "Mai, you said you were from this country, right?" She nods. "Where exactly?"

She takes longer to answer than I expect. Her leg

bounces as she taps on the phone.

"Washington, D.C. It's on the other side of the country." She quickly shows us a pin on a map indicating our current location and then a dotted line across it to where she is from.

Braun whistles through his teeth. "Looks like we could be there in an hour."

Mai and I both laugh at this, and she scales out the map to the world view and he frowns grumbling. From Mai's reaction, it's probably best to steer clear of places she remembers. Instead, I move on to my second idea.

"I think our best bet is to find Thor first. He should be easier to locate than any Asgardians."

"Any ideas on where he is?" Mai inquires.

"He used to always brag about this city…" I can picture him surrounded by endearing Asgardians as he tells stories of travels to the other realms like he's the hero in every single one. I roll my eyes and try to think of the name, but it slips my mind. "He always called it the City of Love?"

"Paris!" Mai exclaims but chews her lip.

"Paris is the City of Love?" I cannot fathom it. The Paris I knew was pockmarked with debris from German bombings. The city felt like a shell of itself.

"Yes, why?" Mai studies me curiously.

I shrug. "I've been there before is all."

"It's even farther away than Washington. I'd say we could fly there, but neither of you has passports or IDs."

"Could we take a boat?" Braun asks.

Mai shakes her head. "It'd take even longer to get there by boat than flying."

"It sounds like jumping will be the only way for us to get there quickly then," I add.

Mai pouts and offers, "I can fly there, and you can jump there."

"How long will it take for you to get there if you fly and

we jump?" Braun asks.

"I could be there in two days?" she offers and hands her phone to Braun who scrolls through the images of Paris she pulled up. It looks very different from the way I remember it.

"Won't it be suspicious if you just show up out of the blue—" I stop mid-sentence as two women approach our table at the bar. They wear neon-colored tops that stop just above their belly buttons and their black skirts barely cover their asses. My eyebrows raise as I look at the height of their heels.

"Excuse me," says the taller blonde one who looks only at Braun. I study her for a moment, noticing the dye in her hair and the layers of makeup she has on. "But if these ladies are boring you, you're welcome to hang out with us. We're going to DNA Lounge tonight and we'd love for you to join us." She smiles at him, and I think she's trying to be seductive, but I honestly can't tell.

Mai's mouth drops open in shock, and I smirk at their boldness, leaning back in my chair. Braun turns his head to study them for a second before he turns back to us and asks in Elvish, "What do they want?"

"You," I respond. An easier answer than explaining they want to take him dancing, which I cannot picture him being even slightly interested in.

He turns back to them, looking as if he's struggling a bit with what to say before responding, "No."

I bite my lip to keep from outright laughing, and I can see Mai's petite shoulders shake as she hides her laughter.

The tall blonde looks annoyed and flips her hair over her shoulder and walks away. Her friend follows suit, but not before saying, "Your loss."

"That right there proves my point about you being rude," Mai says in between fits of laughter. Braun only rolls his eyes and goes back to looking through images of Paris on Mai's phone.

Braun and I hold each other's hand with our packs strapped onto our backs. "Ready?" I ask and he's never looked more excited. Well, other than when he knows we are going to get pizza. I shake my head and chuckle. I wouldn't have pegged Braun as being such a thrill seeker or such a fan of food.

Mai booked her flight this morning and while I don't love the idea of us splitting up, I've already put her through two different jumps.

We stand along the cliff's edge near a rusty orange bridge shrouded in fog. Below us, the ocean strikes against the rocks in angry bursts as fog horns bleat out in random intervals. High above, the moon is barely visible through the cloud cover. A cool ocean breeze pushes against us, as if to make sure we don't jump. He squeezes my hand, grinning broadly.

I count down and we leap into the unknown.
I picture a city I've visited a few times before, one that I barely remember and am sure has changed quite a bit in almost a hundred years. I picture a structure that I am sure will still be there today

Chapter 20

I HAVE MADE A MISTAKE in my calculations and the ground is far below us as we plummet towards the hard cobblestone. Braun grabs me around the waist with his free hand, and as we near the ground, he uses his Veoor magic to slow us, and we float calmly down the rest of the way. I let out a breath of relief.

"Thanks," I murmur before pulling out of Braun's grasp to gape at the view in front of us. It's still the same as I remember it.

'Notre Dame' it reads on a plaque nearby. Built from tan stone over eight centuries prior, it towers over the square in front of it. Braun stands entranced as he gazes up at it, taking in the intricate stained-glass windows and magnificent structure. We walk the perimeter, viewing the structure from all angles, before moving on to meander through the quiet streets of Paris.

Streetlamps begin to turn off as the sun peeks over the tops of buildings. I glance at Braun who is enthralled with the sights and smells of this city. Fresh baked bread and rolls move into window displays in cafes and pastry shops as the bakers turn on their shop lights, starting their day. The early morning silence breaks as passers-by discuss everything from the weather to politics, strolling to their destinations, so unlike the people in San Francisco who constantly ran from one place to the next.

Mesmerized by it all, I forget that I am supposed to be

finding a place to stay. I refocus myself and look for signs or guides that mention hotels. A 'FOR RENT' sign hangs in the window of a quaint pink pastel building with white lace trim. I smile as it reminds me of Mai's hair and I cannot think of a more perfect place to stay.

After some negotiating, I'm able to rent the flat on the top floor of the pink building. It has only one bedroom, but it's fully furnished, centrally located, and the living room has a 'pull-out bed'. I'm not sure what that is, but it makes me laugh picturing Braun stuck in a tiny bed again. The kitchen is small, but the other rooms are spacious with white walls and light-colored furniture.

Birds chirp in the small trees behind the building and there is a small balcony off the bedroom. I open the balcony doors after changing, letting in the fresh air and morning sunlight.

How different this city is from when I was last here.

From the humid heat of summer to the bite of winter, my sisters-in-arms and I would sit on the roofs of buildings or fly high above the battles. Rifle shots, bombs, and screams could be heard throughout the day and sometimes into the evenings for months on end in the brutal and often bloody battles. The Great War took so many lives, it certainly kept us busy, deciding who lived and died, who would be ferried to Valhalla or Niflheim.

Those days were often bleak, but I relished in it. Chooser of the Slain. My blood and being calls for battle and bloodshed, even now, when there is so little left to fight for. On occasion, we would take some to Asgard to be made immortal and serve in Odin's army for whatever good that did as they were all lost in the fight against Ragnarok.

"Ready?" I am pulled from my thoughts as Braun walks in. He wears his usual outfit of a baseball cap and jeans but with a black shirt instead of white. Very original. He gives me an odd look. "Is that what you plan to wear out?"

I scrunch my eyebrows and nod. He and I have a day before we meet Mai at the airport. So, I changed into a simple red dress with white flowers on it, which Mai packed for me, and slip-on sandals. She promised warmer weather in Paris and so far, she hasn't been wrong.

The sundress has cap sleeves showing off my rune tattoos that are so at odds with the cute dress, but it's comfortable and perfect for a day like today. He decides not to say what he's thinking.

Good, I can't imagine it was nice.

"Better than wearing the same outfit every day," I mutter more to myself than him, though he hears it and gives me a very pronounced frown.

As we walk our hands almost brush each other, and a tension I never noticed before seems to be ever-present between us. We pass crowds in small cafes who spill out the doors and onto sidewalks where they chat with a coffee in one hand, a cigarette in the other.

I vaguely remember places like this from the last time I was here. Though the buildings are taller now and appear to loom over every street as if watching the activity below. The passionate yet calm energy of the city is invigorating and before we know it, we've walked from one end to the other.

I pull out my Valkric to find our location, but the screen doesn't even light up to project the map. It finally died. I sigh and put it back in my bag. "We should buy a map."

Braun merely nods. He's lost in thought, and I decide not to disrupt him, so we continue walking until we find a shop with tourist items and maps in the window.

"Bonjour, please let me know if you need help finding anything," a short man greets us in French as he hobbles towards us.

"Vous avez des cartes de la ville?" I ask for a map while taking in the number of items in the store.

He eyes us for a moment, and Braun again shifts uncomfortably at the attention.

"Of course, over here." He shows us to a small corner off the store, where maps are folded neatly into squares with different advertisements and pictures of the city on the front.

"C'est ta première fois à Paris?" He asks if it's my first time in Paris.

"Third actually, but it's been so long and so much has changed," I explain.

He nods as if he understands, but I can't imagine what the shopkeeper would say if I mentioned my last trip was a hundred years ago.

He pulls out a map from the rack. "C'est le meilleur." I take the one he recommends from him and open it up. Braun peers over my shoulder to look at it.

"These are different points of interest in the city," the shopkeeper points out. I look them over, noting the ones we already passed this morning.

"C'est parfait, merci." We walk over to the register to pay, and I notice a small TV in the corner showing the news. An ad comes on and I yelp in surprise.

There on the screen is Thor, Odin's son, and the god of thunder, modeling the latest boxer briefs for men.

At this moment, he is the epitome of a pompous god. His stupidly long golden hair flows in a non-existent breeze, and he gives the camera a smoldering look. It's a look I've seen him give many Asgardian women. It's a look I hate.

"Like what you see?" Braun notes rather sourly in Elvish, but I ignore him.

"Qui est-ce?" I ask the shopkeeper. He raises his eyebrows and turns to the screen.

"You don't know who that is?" He seems puzzled by the notion of someone not knowing Thor. "Oliver Stone? Britain's biggest fashion icon?"

"Does he live here?"

"He has a house here in Paris he frequents, yes," says the shopkeeper. Of course, Thor is just lounging around in Midgard with not a care in the world. That *asshole*.

I turn to Braun. "That's Thor," I say in Elvish, pointing to the screen. "Do you know where his place in Paris is?" I ask, switching back to French with the shopkeeper

The shopkeeper looks confused. "No, they normally don't tell people where they live, otherwise fans would wait outside day and night for him."

"Right, of course," I say, as if I've asked the dumbest question in the world. "Thanks again," I add and begin to head out with Braun in tow.

I pull out the map but realize it's useless if we don't remember where the flat is. Though looking at the streets, we are on the same side of the river as it is. I remember the place we are staying is in the 3rd arrondissement, so we head that general direction following the Seine and within an hour Braun's stomach grumbles.

"Wait here," I tell him as I spot a bakery.

I jerk my head to Braun as I come out of the shop. He follows me as I walk to the Seine and sit on the white stone wall where I pull out the pastries from the paper bag. I hand one to Braun who turns it over in his hand like he's never seen a croissant before.

"Really? You've never had a croissant before?" I ask as he finishes the third one. I leave to go back to the shop to get him more.

"This is like the pizza incident all over again," I mutter as I sit back down with extras.

"Is there pizza in Paris?" He perks up.

I nod. "Some would argue pizza in France is better than in America." Braun looks at me skeptically, making me laugh.

We sit in comfortable silence for a while. I tilt my head

towards the sun, closing my eyes to feel its warmth, and try to soak up its energy. I look back at the river, one of the other things that has remained the same since I was last here.

When I feel the weight of Braun's gaze, I find his storm cloud eyes watching me.

"When were you last here?" he asks.

"In 1916, over a hundred years ago, in the middle of the Great War."

"What was it like?" he asks, so I tell him.

The memories of a century ago come rushing back to me as I describe the city, its people, and for the first time in a long time, I talk about my sisters-in-arms. It hurts more than it should, knowing most are likely dead. I am raw when I finish, and Braun doesn't speak for a while.

"When's your birthday?" Braun asks. I scrunch my eyebrows in confusion at the sudden change of topic. "A month ago, you said your birthday was coming up, when is it?" he supplies.

Today is the 20th day in the Lyra cycle, the end of summer on Midgard. It hits me how long it's been since Ragnarok, almost six months.

"It's in three days, why?"

Braun merely shrugs in response.

"What happened to that old elf we turned over in Vanire?" I blurt out. This conversations becoming more disjointed by the minute, but it's a question that's been in the back of my mind for so long.

Braun sighs, running a hand through his silver hair before putting his cap back on. I'm tempted to reach out and fix it, but I clasp my hands together instead.

"I turned him over to the city guard."

"What did he do?"

"He killed a lot of elves, specifically females." It must have been bad if that's all the details Braun is willing to give me.

My throat dries up and I feel weird for having assumed he was innocent.

"Why do you ask?"

I wave my hand. "Just curious."

I pause for a moment, deciding if I should say anything more about it. "When we turned him in, I… I felt guilty and for the first time… I cared whether he lived or died." I stare at the river, unable to look at Braun. These feelings towards him are odd and jumbled.

He puts a finger under my chin, turning my face towards his. "Do you care if I live or die?" he whispers his question.

"I saved your sorry ass, didn't I?"

"It could have been because we had an arrangement," he counters.

I shake my head, unable to say anything. I look up at him and am entranced as he leans towards me. For a moment, I think he's going to kiss me, but instead, he murmurs, "I care whether you live or die too."

That statement does more to my heart than a kiss could ever do, and I crack a small smile. I hate that I've let him in, one more person to worry about. Stupid elf.

We eventually make it back to the flat and slog up the four flights of stairs. I'm asleep on the couch within minutes.

When I awake, I groan and roll over into a hard body. I tense before realizing it is Braun's sleeping form. Soft afternoon light trickles through the opaque cream curtains in the room he moved me to.

Braun's face is so soft when he sleeps, nothing like his hard, no-nonsense expression he wears the remaining sixteen hours of the day. I trace the lines of his face, without touching him. He'd assuredly wake then.

I can see a long white scar just under the vee of his black shirt and when I glance at his face again, his eyes are open. I jump in shock, and he chuckles.

Flustered, I blurt out, "What's this one from?" pointing to the scar on his chest.

"Mmmm," he says looking down at it. "It was in the Dark War, two hundred years ago against dark elves who declared war on Alfheim." I remember the elf who spoke of it at the bar in Vanire.

"My men were tired after nearly a week on the battlefield. It was a sloppy mistake on my part to take on the dark elf commander so late in the battle. I was cocky and he got past my guard and sliced me across my chest."

I trace my finger along it thoughtlessly, but quickly pull my hand away when I realize what I've done. When I glance up at Braun and there is an intensity in his gaze I've never seen before. My heartbeat picks up speed, but before I can say anything, Braun is already off the bed, heading to the kitchen down the hall.

I release the breath I'm holding and roll onto my back. I think of how he said he cares. He *cares*. I squeeze my eyes shut, *what the fuck are you doing, Vera? There are bigger things to worry about.* I hear my sister warning me to not let this go further.

"You hungry?" Braun asks from the kitchen. Hearing him pull out equipment, I get up and follow the noise. On our way back from being completely lost in this city, we stopped at a store and picked up ingredients for dinner. Braun pulls out tomatoes, onions, and the other items needed to make pasta.

"Do you want help?" I ask and he shakes his head. Not that I'm a very good cook, but I could at least cut vegetables.

"I didn't know you could cook," I comment, taking a seat at the tiny island.

Happy to watch him, I fiddle with the radio on the counter. I remember older, bulkier versions of this device. The need to fill the silence with something is strong, and I finally tune to a station with music. Crackling static cuts into the music every so often and, suddenly, I'm transported to the frontlines of the Great War.

Someone plays the harmonica in a trench nearby. Our group of Valkyrie is spread out, slogging through the mud of no man's land between the two armies. It is still dark out, but Odin's powers protect us from being seen by anyone other than the dead—an ability bestowed before passing through the Bifrost to Midgard and removed when we return to Asgard.

The armies worked through the day yesterday pulling the dead off the field, making our job easier or harder, I can't tell.

I slide in mud plopping on my ass, and I hear a few Valkyrie snicker. I push myself up but notice something marble colored in my periphery. A young soldier who couldn't be older than twenty. His eyes are closed, and he is encased in the mud; only his head sticks out from the ground. I kneel by him and begin digging.

Two sisters, Rhodda and Axis, come help me, noticing I've found someone. He is halfway dugout when he takes a gasping breath and bolts upright into a sitting position. Both Rhodda and I fall back. He's alive. How long has he been buried here? I don't see any wounds on his upper body, though we haven't dug out the rest of him.

Axis is quiet, looking the soldier over as if deciding his fate on the spot. I swear under my breath and the soldier looks at me, his eyes wide as saucers.

"Engel," he croaks in German, his voice scraggly from disuse.

He mistakes our wings for angels' wings when we are far deadlier than angels. Rhodda snorts, shaking her head. The young man looks at her and says the word again. I glance at Rhodda. He shouldn't be able to see us.

"Bin ich tot?" he asks, looking between us.

She merely shrugs. But he can, so fix it. I roll my eyes at her.

"You are alive," I answer in German. I give him my hand and help pull him to his feet.

Now I see why he's been stuck here. Even with the mud coating his body, it is easy to spot the nasty gash running up the soldier's right leg, though it looks like it could be fine if treated soon. I pull his arm around my neck and help him limp back to his side of the trenches unseen. We are close enough that I see, in the campfire's glow, those on night patrol.

When we are only a few yards away, I stop. "This is as far as I go. Tell nobody what you saw this evening."

He limps to stand in front of me. Seeing him up close, he's even younger than I thought—maybe only sixteen, with watery blue eyes.

"Wer sind sie?"

I smirk. "Angels... of death."

His face goes sheet white as he realizes we aren't looking for survivors. He limps back to his side, holding up his hands so they don't accidentally shoot him.

A few nights later we are out on the battlefield, doing the same thing as all the nights before, collecting and ferrying the dead. There are bodies in a pile and Axis and I sort through them. We are both covered in mud, but I could spot Axis anywhere. Her bright red hair is a beacon even in the dark.

We pull another body off the pile, revealing the young face of the soldier I helped. She swears, dropping her half of the body we hold.

"He didn't last long," she murmurs.

That is all we say on the matter, but the young man's eyes now a dull blue stare at me. I am rooted in my spot, still half holding the other dead body. Suddenly his eyes shift to the color of smoke, and he opens his mouth.

"Vera," he whispers. I scrunch my eyebrows tilting my

head to the side. I don't remember telling him my name. He says my name again with more commanding in his tone, and I swear his voice is so familiar.

"Vera!" he shouts, and I am pulled back to the present, Braun's face hovering over mine. Behind him is the ceiling. Braun lets out a breath and puts his forehead against mine, his touch cool against my feverish skin.

"What happened?" I ask, my voice is hoarse like I've been yelling for hours.

"One minute you were messing with the radio and the next you were on the ground." I try to push him off and sit up, but he holds me down. "Don't move yet, you're as pale as paper. I'll get you water."

He rushes to grab a glass from the cupboard and fills it with water from the sink. I sit up on my elbows, sipping the water he hands me. He sits beside me on the floor, worry distorting his handsome face.

"Another flashback?"

I meet his eyes that are full of concern and nod. I haven't had one since we were in Yulamic, but luckily there is no puking this time. I finally sit up and Braun keeps a hand on my back, worried I'll pass out again at any moment. He runs a hand down my cheek.

"Your color is returning," he comments as if feeling the need to say something. I lean forward resting my forehead on his shoulder. He runs his hands through my hair, heat and comfort rush through me.

We sit on the floor like this for a while before he whispers, "Tell me about it."

I lift my forehead from his shoulder and as our gaze's lock, I decide to let him in. I already had to some degree, and now it feels silly to keep him at arm's length.

He pulls me into his lap and strokes my back as I explain

seeing Rhodda and Axis again and the battlefield somewhere in France. This time, I don't feel sad about seeing Rhodda. Even if the memories seem bleak, it is nice to remember her as she was.

When I finish talking, Braun tilts my face to his, and I become acutely aware of every place our bodies touch. He leans in and my gaze drops to his mouth. He has a small white scar near his bottom lip that I never noticed before. I look back up and he closes the distance. My heart pounds and his lips softly brush across mine, electrifying me. Once, twice.

A loud pop on the stove has Braun swearing and gently putting me back on the floor before running to the stove. Pasta is bubbling over the edge of the pot. He pulls it off the heat and swears again, as some of the sauce he's made is burnt. All the while, I'm still sitting on the floor too stunned to move.

I roll my neck, feeling better, and stand to place the cup on the counter. I casually walk out of the kitchen while Braun attempts to fix the burning dinner. I act as if nothing happened before turning the corner and practically sprinting to the bathroom. I splash water on my face and place my forehead on the cool lip of the sink. Well, this is an absolute disaster, but that kiss…I blow out a breath still too hot from his touch, his lips.

Footsteps sound in the hall and there's a pause before a quiet knock on the bathroom door.

"Dinner's ready," Braun states.

"Ok, be right out," I respond through the door, and I hear him pause and clear his throat to say something. Instead, only retreating footsteps sound.

I look at myself in the mirror and tell myself to just act like it never happened.

Chapter 21

The next morning, we take the underground railway to the airport, where we will meet Mai. Last night had been awkward, to say the least. We ate dinner in total silence and, of course, there was nothing to distract us. Braun would not let me turn on the radio for fear I'd have another episode.

Exhaustion weighs on me this morning as I couldn't sleep at all last night. I could hear Braun in the living room rolling over on the squeaky pull-out bed, which was in fact hidden inside the couch.

What a mess.

I have bigger things I'm working towards, and this was not part of the plan. I don't deserve this, this respite, this possibility of happiness. Yet I cannot help worrying about Braun. He plagues my thoughts more often than I care to admit.

Braun sits adjacent to me in the railcar. He stares out the window into the blackness around us as people on either side of him read a newspaper. I roll my eyes. Clearly, acting as though nothing happened wasn't helping the situation.

I force myself to fix this and take the seat the woman to his right just vacated. Braun merely glances at me before returning to his surveillance. We sit shoulder to shoulder as the train jerks occasionally on the track. I rack my brain thinking of what to say to fix this, but no words come to me.

I look at his hand, placed on his thigh and the idea that

comes to me is stupid, but maybe the risk will be worth it.

My heart races as I slip my hand under his, interlacing my fingers with his. I look at him trying to make eye contact, but he doesn't move from his vigil. Just as I'm about to pull my hand away, his fingers curl around mine and I look away, hiding the relief that breaks across my face. I rest my head on his shoulder.

This time the silence between us is comfortable, as if the silence replaces unnecessary words. Words that would explain why we should ignore this and let it fizzle out, why I am terrified of this, and why I can't promise anything more than right now. *He knows*, a voice in my head whispers.

We walk through the airport terminal casually, keeping distance between us as we stop to wait near the exit people stream out of. Mai told us exactly where to meet her before we left San Francisco as she was sure we'd get lost with any sort of vague instructions.

The rounded shape of the airport walls and ceiling provide entertainment as I listen to Braun mention the impracticality of them for the tenth time. He seems to be in a better mood than this morning thankfully. Possibly from the train ride, but I can't be sure.

I give him a smirk and his gaze turns molten as it meets mine. Definitely from the train ride then.

"I am seriously shocked both of you are still alive," Mai says as she walks up to us with her bags. "I was sure one of you would have killed the other in my absence."

"It's nice to see you too, Mai," Braun mutters and picks up the bag Mai conveniently dropped in front of him.

"Did you get a haircut?" I ask, taking a piece of it between my fingers. Her pink hair is a shade darker and back to its pixie length.

She nodded and twirled for us, showing it off. "You like?"

"Super cool," Braun comments sarcastically and I snort.

He's clearly picked up sarcasm more than I thought he would. Mai frowns and sticks her tongue out at him.

"Are you ready to go?" I ask as she adjusts her second bag on her shoulder.

"So, what did I miss?" Mai asks as we board the train back to Paris.

Braun shrugs and glances at me, probably wondering if I plan on telling Mai what happened between us. Instead, I launch into explaining how I saw Thor on TV doing underwear ads.

She quickly searches on her phone for him using his new name, Oliver Stone. "Looks like he's supposed to attend a gala at the Louvre for an opening of a newly restored painting."

"A what?" Braun and I passed the Louvre the other day when we were lost, but I have no idea what a gala is.

"Basically, it's a big event, normally like dinner, dancing, and sometimes a raffle, where you win stuff for purchasing tickets to the event," Mai explains as her fingers fly over the touch screen of her phone.

"There," she states proudly. Braun and I look at her in confusion before she sighs. "I just bought us three tickets to the gala. It's in two days."

"How did you buy us tickets?" I ask, and she pulls a shiny rectangular plastic card out of her pocket.

"Using this." She waves it around.

"Where did you get that?" Braun asks and I read the name 'Elizabeth Plunkett' on the card before smirking.

Braun still doesn't seem to understand. "She stole it," I explain.

Realization dawns on him. "You are very sneaky, Mai."

Mai gives him a wicked smile. "I'll count that as my compliment for the day."

We make our way through the city back to the flat, which

Mai instantly loves solely based on the building color. Braun lounges in the living room while reading the same book he had on our way to the Port of Yulamic, and I wonder how many times he's read it.

As I pull out sandwiches we picked up at the store, I ask, "Braun, are you hungry?"

When I don't get an answer, I walk into the living room to find him sound asleep on the pull-out bed, apparently exhausted from the lack of sleep the night before. I bring Mai a sandwich and we eat quietly on the balcony that overlooks the gardens below.

Mai shifts to shut the balcony door before asking, "Seriously, what happened while I was gone?"

She looks at me seriously and I merely shrug, picking at the French bread. "I can tell something happened, you two have been acting all cool and calm since I got here. Spit it out."

"Aren't we always cool and calm?" I counter and she gives me a look. I sigh, looking up at the trees before explaining the flashback. Her face becomes worried as I continue. I pause as I contemplate telling her what happened afterward.

"So, what did Braun do?"

"His voice pulled me out of it. I just sat there until I felt better and that was it." Mai narrows her brown eyes at me.

"You're a liar." My jaw drops open and I pretend to be offended. Mai doesn't buy it for a second and rolls her eyes.

"Fine. He kissed me."

Mai jumps to stand. "What!" she exclaims loudly. I shush her, worrying Braun will wake up in the living room even with the door closed. She sits down.

"I knew it! It was only a matter of time." She crosses her arms smugly.

"You did not."

"Did too," she counters and pauses. "I'm happy for you," she says a little more quietly.

"Not much to be happy for," I mutter back. She stares at me with raised eyebrows, waiting for me to explain. "It's not that simple. He's one more person I must worry about, I can only handle so much of that. Plus, what happens once I find the survivors? He goes back to Alfheim? Not much of a future there."

"The fact that you're thinking about a future with him is a big deal. We have no way of knowing what the future holds," she counters, "and there's still the issue of Ragnarok. You deserve a little happiness Vera, just run with it and see what happens."

She pauses before saying, "If nothing else, do it for me." Her eyes reveal what she isn't saying. It's been too long for her as well.

I think about what she's said as we sit in comfortable silence.

"We should go to the Louvre and take a look around before, plus we need fancy clothes for the gala," she adds, and I nod in agreement.

The Louvre is massive—something I anticipated when Braun and I passed it before—but, in person, walking through the halls of artwork is overwhelming. Mai walks up to the large sculpture carved in grey marble. I watch her look back and forth between it and me.

"She looks like a Valkyrie," she murmurs to no one in particular. Braun merely glances at it before returning to survey the room with his general stoic expression. He watches the humans who stroll through the gallery and acts more like a security guard than a bored tourist.

I snort as I read the placard on it 'Winged Victory of Samothrace'.

"A victory that most certainly was not." Mai raises her eyebrows. "Why do you think she has no arms?" I watch Braun's lips twitch.

I have decided to make it my personal goal to get him to crack a smile. If I get a real laugh, I'll never ask for anything else again.

He turns towards me then. "I'm going to look in the next room." I bite my lip to keep from laughing as he practically sprints to the next room. I doubt he will ever get used to the casual pace humans keep to in museums.

Mai and I move on at a more leisurely pace through Greek and Roman Antiquities that overlooks the Cour Carree. Mai says the gala will be held in this square. The fountain in the middle sits dried out with roped walkways, barring people from cutting through the middle.

"I wonder what it will look like for the gala," Mai murmurs. I hum my agreement. It's not much to look at right now, so I turn back to the artwork around us.

Mai lets out a chuckle, and I follow her gaze to where Braun sits half asleep on one of the benches. Next to him is a pile of chatting tourists. I kick his foot as we pass, and he opens one eye frowning at me. How he knows it's me I'll never know.

"I thought you liked art?" I tease in Elvish.

"This stuff isn't even a few thousand years old," he mumbles before closing his eyes and leaning his head against the wall again, clearly, it's unworthy of his appreciation or attention.

"Such a snob," Mai snips. Braun lets out a small growl, causing the group next to him to stop talking and move away from him.

"We'll leave soon," I promise as I turn back to walk through the sculptures in the room.

A few hours later, we make our way back to the flat and Braun is asleep again within minutes.

"Apparently his museum nap wasn't long enough," Mai comments, rolling her eyes.

———

The next afternoon, after Mai dragged me to a salon where they did our hair and make-up, we help each other get the dresses on we bought the day before. The slinky material slides over my body as Mai helps me into it.

The dress's long sleeves cover up the runes on my arms and shoulders. It dips in a deep vee between my breasts and down my back but hides my scars along my shoulder blades.

The fabric wraps over itself to gather on my left hip. The glittery, sky-blue material pools at my feet with a slit running up to where the dress comes together at my hip. The color matches my eyes and complements my golden skin tone perfectly.

I strap Baldr's dagger and sheath on my right thigh—the side of my dress that doesn't have the slit—just in case. I slip on a pair of sparkly white heels that match the sparkle on my dress and move to view my profile in the full-length mirror in the hallway.

The stylist pulled my chestnut hair into a low bun and smeared glittery makeup on me to match my dress and eyes. Though it isn't my outfit, hair, or makeup that surprises me.

It's my smile, genuine for the first time in a long time.

Braun's footsteps echo from the living room and abruptly stop as they round the corner. I glance to my right and do a double take. Braun stands there in a tailored grey suit and his white hair is pulled into his usual messy bun, but it hides the tips of his ears.

He looks magnificent and I can't even speak. *Get ahold of yourself, you're gawking,* I scold myself. He swallows as his eyes roam the length of my body, and he seems at a loss for words as well. I open my mouth to speak, but Mai comes barreling out of the room.

Mai chose a strapless floor-length number with a deep vee as well. The color reminds me of my wings, pristinely white, and it hugs her body in all the right places. Lace detailing curls along her waist and small breasts like wings crossing her body, holding her close. She grabs her bag before striding towards the door, only stopping when she notices neither of us has moved.

"Yes, we all look hot as fuck. Now that that's cleared up, can we go?"

Braun breaks into a smile, the genuine one I've been dying to see. It takes my breath away. He walks towards me and takes both my hands in his. I still can't speak.

He raises one eyebrow. *Ready?* he silently asks. I bite my lip, holding back a beaming smile, and nod.

"Seriously, our ride is here, and they will be pissed if we are late." Mai now has her arms crossed standing by the door. Braun interlaces his fingers with mine and we stroll out the front door.

I am floating on a cloud as we pull up in the rented automobile Mai had me order this morning. She sits next to me telling us exactly what to say and do tonight.

"There will be a lot of photographers when we get there, so lots of flashing lights," Mai warns. I'm sure she's worried about Braun brandishing the sword he's hidden somewhere on his person.

"I mean we aren't famous, but people will definitely be taking pictures of Braun." She eyes him and he frowns. "Just pretend you're at a fancy ball in Haratine," she adds.

She is right; as we exit the car, Braun steps out first and a million flashes go off. He extends his hand to Mai to help her out and then to me. My heart races when he holds his hand out for me.

He looks at me as if I'm the only person around, the only one that matters. He tucks my hand in the fold of his arm and we stride tall, following Mai into the Louvre. She stops and poses at a designated area and cameras flash.

She turns to us and mouths, "Smile". I glance at Braun who takes the hint and blinds the crowd of photographers with his too-white smile. I laugh and smile with him as we stop in the same spot Mai had, facing the cameras.

We slowly walk inside the Cour Carree, following the line of people. It looks like a totally different place than when we saw it the other day. The usually empty square is now dotted with tables and a dance floor placed near the back.

The fountain in the middle, now filled, has water shooting into the air in intricate designs; the lights underneath change colors every few minutes. Lights placed at the base of the building illuminate it, so it glows against the darkness of night.

The tables are numbered, and we head towards ours. Each one is draped with fine white clothes and more silverware than I know what to do with. Servers bring out dinner while a host jabbers on about the painting restoration we are supporting tonight.

I nudge Braun, who immediately starts eating while everyone else waits politely for the speaker to finish. He sighs and puts his spoon back down. *For a prince you sure don't act like one*, my look conveys to him. He merely grumbles in response.

Without much thought, I place my hand on his thigh to distract him. At first, he stiffens, seemingly unused to being touched so casually, and I worry that maybe I should have ignored Mai's advice about seeing where this goes.

He relaxes after a moment, flipping my hand so my palm is face-up. He traces on it with his finger, sending heat and a shudder through me. He smirks, seeing my reaction out of the corner of his eye.

Soon the speeches are over, and we dig in. The food is

delicious, with three decadent courses placed in front of us at perfectly timed intervals. Luckily, Mai steals the attention of those at our table, leaving Braun and me to eat peacefully without much small talk. She explains that she is a wealthy heiress from America and met Braun and me here in Paris. I whisper her story to Braun in Elvish and he huffs a laugh, rolling his eyes.

Throughout dinner, Braun's chair scoots closer and closer to mine and by the end, he has his arm casually draped around the back of my chair. He toys with a piece of my hair that came loose from the updo at the nape of my neck.

As the dinner ends, dancing begins. People mill around to other tables, talking with friends and acquaintances.

For us, the real work of finding Thor begins. Normally it wouldn't be too hard—he's always surrounded by women—but looking around the tables at dinner, I didn't spot him.

"Do you want to dance?" Braun murmurs in my ear and I glance at him surprised.

He smirks. "I was once a prince."

"Clearly not with dinner," I mutter, but he ignores my jab as he takes my hand.

He weaves us gracefully through the rows of tables to the dance floor where a few other couples sway to the music. He bows and I smother my laughter at his formalness.

Taking my right hand in his and looping his left arm around my waist, he pulls me close. It's closer than what I'm sure would be considered proper decorum in Alfheim, but I have never been one to follow the rules anyway.

The music starts and it's a waltz. Gods, I forgot how to do this, but before I can overanalyze it, we are off. Gliding across the floor, we steal the attention of those around us. He doesn't miss a beat and leads me lithely even as I don't remember the steps.

"See anyone that looks like an underwear model?" I ask,

trying to keep the conversation light.

He doesn't even bother looking around before saying, "Not particularly."

We lapse into silence until he leans in so that our faces are mere inches apart. "You look stunning tonight. I couldn't even get the words out earlier."

I blush, startled by the confession. He runs the tip of his nose along my cheek. "A blush? I never thought I'd see one of those on you again." He chuckles, reminding me of when we first met, and I opened the door naked.

My blush deepens as I say, "Someone's feeling bold."

We are silent for a moment, before he whispers, "Happy Birthday Vera." I look up at him in surprise. I was so wrapped up in preparing for tonight I completely forgot, and I can't help the smile I give him.

Boisterous laughter rings out from the other side of the courtyard, and my smile falters. I stop dancing when I recognize who it belongs to, and Braun gives me a concerned look. Without explaining, I pull him off the dance floor with me as I stride towards the source of the voice. I pause at the edge of the circle of humans that surrounds the being, taking in the one and only Thor.

I've forgotten his pull, his allure of magnificence, that can only come with being a god. He is radiant in a white suit with silver trim. His sunshine blonde hair is cropped short with only the top left long, the wavy locks pulled to one side. Seeing him without a beard is…surprising.

A woman on his lap whispers something seductively in his ear and he smirks against her neck. I take a deep breath, letting go of Braun's hand, and move through the crowd. It parts for me and as I get closer to him, he notices me. I remind myself to play nice but am thrown off when his smile widens upon recognizing me.

"Vera Hjelmstad!" he announces and stands, practically

dumping the woman from his lap onto the ground. His forest green eyes never leave mine.

"I never thought I'd be happy to see you, but there's a first time for everything, isn't there?" he says in French, stopping a few feet away from me. I try to collect my thoughts enough to speak without yelling at him. "What is this? Not happy to see me?"

His smile is sad. "Are we still at odds, Vera, after all this time?"

I smile and shake my head. "I don't think so, though it depends on where your allegiance lies." He could very well be on Loki's side, I remind myself.

"You wound me, Vera," he says, switching to Asgardian, and puts his hand over his heart as if I've actually stabbed him. "I am always loyal to my father and Asgard, even after his death."

People around us have started to move on as if Thor mentally suggested they find somewhere else to be. I feel Braun's arm come around my waist causing Thor to raise his eyebrows.

"Finally moved on from the bastard god, have we?" Braun's arm tightens imperceptibly. How Braun even knows what Thor is saying, I can't fathom.

I ignore Thor's question. "Where are the survivors, Thor?" I ask quietly in Asgardian.

"Vera, Vera, Vera, has no one told you?" He tilts his head to the side. "Asgard is gone, and we are all that is left." He gestures between us. "There are no survivors, other than a few gods," he says with confidence, as if he watched them all die himself.

"How can you be so sure?" I say, crossing my arms defiantly. He opens his mouth to speak only to shake his head. Not a good sign.

"Vali?"

"He's in Vanaheim, with some of the other gods," Thor supplies, remembering my alliance with his brother.

"What about Loki?" I ask and watch as Thor's face distorts in rage and anguish.

"I have not seen him since the day Asgard fell. He has taken much from me. If he decides to show his face, I will be the last thing he sees before he dies," he spits out.

I'm counting on that. He turns to sit down at his table, and I follow.

"You heard about Nidavellir?" I ask cautiously. Thor's perfectly groomed eyebrows scrunch together. "It's fallen." Thor doesn't seem to understand, and I briefly explain. "Loki took Ragnarok there. Nothing remains."

He barks out a laugh as if I just said the most hilarious thing. "You jest! I was there not more than a month ago!"

"See for yourself Thor, then come find me." I hand him a slip of paper with the address to the flat. "We're staying here in Paris for a while."

He takes the slip of paper and reads it before shoving it in his pocket.

"Who's we?" he asks, and I merely point to Braun who stands nearby with his arms crossed, highlighting his muscular arms and torso, and watches Thor's every move. Then I point to Mai who I spot heading our way. She has a cool glint in her chocolate eyes.

Thor raises his eyebrows upon seeing Mai. "A human? Vera, I thought you despised humans?"

I purse my lips before saying, "People change."

"Indeed, it would appear so," Thor comments as he glances between Mai and Braun.

I know this is the end of our conversation, and I can honestly say we were more cordial than we've ever been with each other. I stand and nod before taking Braun's hand and walking away.

"Vera," Thor calls out, and I look at him over my shoulder. "I'm sorry about your wings."

I suppress the shudder that runs through me, at the sorrow in his voice as he says it. He knows how much they mean to a Valkyrie. I nod once more to him before turning away.

Mai is almost to us now, but I see Braun shake his head at her in my periphery and he pulls me back onto the dance floor. It's a slow song, and we just sway to the music. He leans his forehead against mine, our breath mingling.

"I know what you're trying to do," I tell him.

He smirks. "And what is that exactly?"

"Distract me," I barely get out as he moves to nuzzle the crook of my neck.

"Is it working?" His storm eyes lock with mine and I am entranced. It's a full minute before I remember to nod, and he chuckles.

We relax in hard metal chairs on the apartment balcony drinking champagne straight from the bottle. We nicked a few before leaving the gala, and the first one lies empty next to me. I take a swig before passing the bottle to Mai.

Mai perches cross-legged in her pajamas, though she's given up on trying to do more than change before coming out here. Braun sits on the ground in front of me, his back resting against my legs.

His hair is out of its usual bun, loose around his shoulders, and I play with it giving him a dozen or so small braids that stick up every which way. His eyes are closed, content to let me mess with his hair. Mai snickers at my masterpiece before taking a sip.

"Well, if nothing else, at least we got to have a nice evening," Mai says while passing the bottle to Braun.

"At least Thor is on the same page as us, which is more than I hoped for," I counter. Braun grunts in agreement.

"I liked your dress tonight, Mai," Braun comments. True to his word, he continues his one compliment a day, though no sign of the jewelry he promised. I think Mai forgot about it anyways.

"And I like yours too. Do you want to see your new hairstyle Braun?" Mai giggles as I finish the last braid. She hands him the phone, and he looks shocked when he sees himself in the camera.

"You don't like it?" I pout and his face drops as he turns to me.

I laugh loudly and he realizes I am joking. He grumbles and stomps to the bathroom to fix what I've done. Mai hums poorly to herself as we relax there.

I gaze towards the stars, and it feels like they are holding their breath, waiting for something.

Chapter 22

"Geez you two, get a room," is the first thing I hear as I lie in bed, not ready to open my eyes. I'm slightly hungover, and the body tangled with mine growls something unintelligible back. The vibration has me shifting closer to its origin, and someone softly laughs before padding away.

They bang around in the kitchen as a hand gently moves my hair out of my face. The touch is so soft, I move into it. A quiet chuckle, one far too familiar to be related to whoever runs their hands through my hair, has my eyes opening quickly. I blink a few times, wincing as I am blinded by the light streaming into the living room behind... *Braun.*

I don't remember falling asleep on the pull-out bed next to him. He watches me for a moment as I take in the lines of his bare chiseled chest and jagged silver scars where wounds hadn't healed perfectly. I trace one with my finger and when I lift my eyes to his, I see the heat in them. A blush rises on my neck.

He brushes a calloused hand down my cheek, making my heart rate skyrocket. He leans in slowly, his stormy eyes never leaving mine as he brushes his lips across mine.

For a heartbeat, I am nowhere and everywhere.

He pulls back studying my face for a moment, and whatever he sees in it makes him hesitate. He starts to get out of bed.

"What was that for?" I manage to get out as he crosses

the room, practically naked.

He shrugs. "Thought it might make you feel better."

My mouth hangs open as I watch him pad into the bathroom. Rage courses through me. That *asshole*. I stomp to the bathroom to give him a piece of my mind, not caring what he's doing in there, and as I fling it open, he pulls me in.

He presses me against the door to close it, his body lining up perfectly with mine, and his lips crash onto mine. The anger I felt moments ago melts into something hotter. I moan loudly, because, gods, I want him. I *want* this.

Braun chuckles, taking the opening to sweep his tongue across mine. Fire runs through my veins, and my breath becomes rushed. His hard body pushes me up the door, and I wrap my legs around his waist instinctively.

"She told us to get a room," he mutters into my neck, by way of explanation, in between soft kisses and I let out a breathy laugh. I hear Mai walk through the flat loudly and close the front door with a bang.

His length presses against me and need charges through me. I grind against him, and he lets out a growl of approval that rumbles through me. I feel it in all the right places. He makes just enough space between our bodies to pull off my shirt, and I move my arms to let him. He takes one of the already firm tips of my breasts in his mouth before the shirt can even hit the floor, his tongue circling the hardened pebble.

I tip my head back, eyes half-closing in pleasure. His hand caressing my other breast is gentle and exquisite, so at odds with his outward appearance of hard edges and sharp lines. He removes his mouth and I almost let out a whimper. Carefully he places my feet back on the ground as he takes off his shorts, and I am greeted by his impressive length. *Gods*.

He is gloriously naked without an ounce of self-consciousness. I follow suit, taking off my sleep shorts and underwear. He keeps his cloudy gaze locked on mine the whole time, and I feel myself melt in the heat of it.

We stand there gazing at each other for a moment, tracing our eyes over one another as if committing our bodies to memory. Silver scars litter his torso, more than I've noticed before, causing his white skin to sparkle in the bathroom light.

He moves towards me slowly and caresses my breast with one hand, then continues his sinful touch up my chest to brush my neck and cheek. My heart pounds in anticipation.

"You are so alluring," he murmurs before kissing my neck.

I snort, closing my eyes, and tilt my head to give him better access. My hands run up the rigid planes of his stomach and chest, tangling into his soft silver hair. "Is that the best you can come up with?"

He stops his ministrations, and I open one eye to find him regarding me seriously for a moment. "There aren't any words in any language that can best describe your beauty."

I know he's serious, and it warms my heart more than it should.

"That's better," is all I manage to get out. He smirks as he lowers his mouth to mine and when our lips meet, the world slips away. His tongue and lips move in time with mine, in perfect synchrony. He kisses me with such passion, with more feeling than I've ever seen in him since we met. He winds his arm around my waist, lifting me to his height, and I wrap my legs around him again. I lose myself in him, in this moment.

I think he's heading to the shower, but I get turned around as he opens the door and strides to the bedroom that Mai and I share. He lays me down with near reverence onto the bed before getting up to close the door. Not even Thor in underwear is more captivating than watching Braun now as he strides towards me, completely naked.

I realize there's significant meaning in this act— something so primal, so instinctual, I almost miss it. He bares his scars to me, for me, shows me his past while seeing mine, and he does not balk at it.

As he moves on top of me, he pauses, and I see the question in his eyes. *Are you sure?* To which I nod. There is no turning back. No going back, even if we don't go any farther. I no longer see him as part of a business arrangement. My friend, my shadow. *Mine.*

He holds my gaze as if he knows exactly what I'm saying, though I've not made a sound. He kisses me softly, sweetly, as if in promise, and shifts down the bed, kissing and licking his way. A trail of fire and ice is left in his wake as he moves lower and lower until his head is between my thighs. He lightly bites the inside of my thigh, then brushes his lips across it.

The switch between the sharp pain and teasing pleasure has me shifting restlessly, needing more from him. He teases me for a few more agonizing seconds before moving his tongue over my bundle of nerves in one great swoop. My back instinctively arches off the bed as I let out a gasp, bliss soaring through me.

He follows it with his thumb, continuing to switch between the two every few strokes. The coiling need in me tightens further. I run my hands through his silken strands, keeping him close as my body experiences the ecstasy of his touch and tongue.

He stops his ministrations and moves back up my body until his face is hovering over mine. He slowly kisses me, and my hands are instantly in his hair again. My eyes close and he positions himself at my opening, but he pauses.

I open my eyes to see why he's stopped, and his white fire gaze bores into me, into my soul. I give him a wicked smile as if expressing how I want it and his returning smirk is practically feral as he slams into me.

I cry out in surprise, and he stays grounded in me for a

moment, letting my body adjust to him. Gods above, he is perfect.

He begins to move and instantly I feel like I'm on the edge. I need the release so bad; it tries to barrel through me within minutes as though my body will burst apart into a thousand pieces, but I hold on.

He doesn't stop as he pushes harder and moves deeper into me. I moan his name as he pants hard, as affected by me as I am by him. My nails dig into his shoulders as my release bursts forward before I can even try to ride the edge any longer.

He growls in rapture as he feels me tighten around him, riding the waves of ecstasy that flow through me. Braun flips me over with impressive speed and pulls my hips up to him, driving deep inside. I swear into the pillow, causing him to chuckle. He moves slower now, more luxuriantly.

The need to be closer to him has me sitting up so we are both kneeling. He kisses and sucks my neck, right along my runes. While one of his hands kneads my breast and the other gently skims down my body, stopping at the apex of my thighs. He growls in satisfaction, sending vibrations through my body, and thrusts deeper. My body tightens in pleasure again, trembling with want, in a matter of minutes.

Just as I'm close, Braun pulls out and sits back, pulling me into his lap. I straddle him, slowly lowering onto him. His eyes are closed, head tipped back in ecstasy. I grin, loving the open display of emotion from him. I pull up to the point where he's almost all the way out and slam back down onto him.

He swears and his eyes fly open. Now he knows how it feels. Our heated gaze locks as I move up slowly and thrust down again.

Together, we are a white fire and golden light.

Stormy skies over glacial peaks.

I feel him pulse inside me and I know he is close. I pick up speed and I am on the brink once more. He grits his teeth, trying to make this last longer, as he continues to watch me. Our bodies move in a symphony of sounds, and soon I shake with restraint as I race towards the crescendo. As if he can see it on my face, he pulls my hips down hard on him, and I cry out as my orgasm rushes through me, and he growls through his own.

He lays me down but remains inside me, kissing my cheeks, chin, forehead, anything he can get his lips on, and I smile.

We lay there for a long while, switching between tracing each other's bodies with our eyes, mouths, and fingers and moving with him deep inside me like today will be our last day together. Elves' sexual appetites run high, making Braun an excellent match for me. Luckily, Mai hasn't come back from wherever she went earlier this morning.

"Tell me about your sister." I realize I've only overheard him talk about his brother and mother.

"Rowana... She's a bit..." I open my eyes to see him contemplating how to describe her. "A bit of an asshole." I bark out a laugh as he continues, "She's pleasant enough with family, but she cold and aloof with any outsiders—"

"Must run in the family," I mutter and for that, he pinches my side but pulls me into his chest. I close my eyes, breathing in his woodsy scent, as he continues.

"Rowana's excellent with political strategy, and she sits on my brother's high council. Her ruthlessness is well known, but my brother keeps her in check for the most part." He clearly kept more tabs on them while in exile than I thought. I wonder if she looks much like his brother and him, but before I can ask the question, he asks me one.

"What's this one for?" He traces a rune, two upside-down vees one atop the other, on my inner arm. Unlike the others that crawl up my arms and shoulders, it is alone with no others near it to tell a story.

I smile before explaining, "It means 'create your own reality'."

"Isn't that kind of contrary to the whole 'follow Odin's orders' Valkyrie thing?" he asks.

I nod, propping my head on my hand. "Edda always hated that I became a Valkyrie, but she understood my decision on some level. She made me get this one with her to remind me—remind us—that I can always change my path. My bonds to the Valkyrie are not permanent. She has always wanted more for me. I promised her that I would leave the Valkyrien life someday and choose a different path." I smile thinking of her strong will and stubbornness. He hums his response.

"I think I would like your sister," he comments.

I snort. "Everyone loves my sister; her charisma and energy are magnetic. People are drawn to her." Braun continues tracing his fingers down my body and I shudder as he reaches between my legs, as if to say he's ready again. I look into his eyes and see the fire there.

It's a long time before we eventually are pulled out of bed by hunger and the need to clean up. We get ready slowly though, as if not fully ready to be near each other without a bed close by.

I'd honestly be fine with a quiet alleyway, and I shudder in pleasure at the thought. I look at myself in the mirror and I can't stop smiling. Idiot. My skin has a glow to it that didn't exist before.

Braun takes my hand as we walk through the streets. Turning the corner, we practically run into Mai who gives me a knowing smile. I roll my eyes at her and we continue until I find a spot for us to eat.

"How was sightseeing?" I ask.

"It was lovely, though probably not as lovely as your sightseeing this morning," Mai says wiggling her eyebrows. I roll my eyes again but can't help the smile that spreads across my face. I glance at Braun who seems intent to stare into the distance and tune us out.

"So where did you go?"

She lists a few places and talks about some people she passed, but she becomes unusually quiet after only a few sentences.

My thoughts drift to the cool fingers that have found their way onto my thigh and trace intricate patterns across the surface. I shift in my seat, angling slightly more towards Braun, lost in the movements he makes.

I almost hiss out a breath when he stops, but he seems to notice I'm not listening. As I look up, I find Mai with her arms crossed.

"Did you hear what I just asked?" she snaps.

I wince. "Sorry."

She huffs a breath, shaking her head. "I said, what do we do now?"

I shrug. "I'm not exactly sure. Thor seems to believe no one is left, so maybe we just wait until he finds us."

"You don't think we should check out another planet?" Braun asks.

"There's a chance there are survivors on Vanaheim, it's the last place to check. However, I don't want to miss the chance to enlist Thor's help in killing Loki. I cannot kill him on my own."

Mai scrunched her eyebrows. "What do you mean?"

"Only a god can kill another god. With Baldr's dagger I can do some serious damage, but nothing that will actually kill Loki."

"Well, that's rather annoying," Mai says, crossing her arms.

She seems quieter today than usual, as if her mind is far away. When I ask her, she merely waves her hand and says she's fine. Braun watches her with concern too as we eat lunch in the restaurant.

I push the worry from my mind. She'll tell us when she's ready. A glance at Braun tells me he's thinking the same thing as his expression relaxes. He munches happily on a personal pizza that would normally feed six.

And so, we wait.

Chapter 23

IT IS A WEEK LATER when I run into Braun in the hallway as he comes out of the bathroom wearing his clothes from Alfheim.

"Feeling nostalgic?" I joke in Elvish.

Then I catch his eyes, shifting colors between grey and hazel. I grit my teeth and put my dagger to his throat. He doesn't even look phased. *Loki.* Panic runs through me as I scan the apartment for Braun.

"Where's my friend, Loki?" I grit out in Asgardian, pushing him against the wall.

Before my eyes, Braun shifts into a man of similar height with distinct green-brown eyes and slate black hair. But one cannot truly describe Loki as a man. Even in his Midgardian attire, a sharp black suit, I feel the power rolling off him.

"Surprise!" he says with an easy smile.

My anger slips as I punch him square in the nose, never moving the dagger away from his throat. The satisfying crunch I expect to hear never comes, even as drops of blood spill down, popping onto the front of his shirt. He merely gives me a wicked grin as if he expected nothing less from me. I try hard not to roll my eyes at him.

He pushes off the wall coming closer unconcerned about my knife still at his throat. The trickster god is not to be trusted, especially after the damage he has caused my people and my heart.

"Miss me, Vi?" A pet name he'd given me that now causes me to grind my teeth, but I reign in my anger.

"Certainly not after what you've done."

He chuckles and pushes a stray hair behind my ear. It takes everything in me not to shudder in disgust before I put my dagger away. I'm lucky he doesn't notice the dagger isn't mine. Braun, Mai, and I cannot win against Loki alone, though shoving Baldr's knife through his heart sounds like a great idea in my head.

"Are you referring to your broken heart? I see you've mended it," he comments airily as he looks around.

At this, I let out a breath of air and step away from him.

"I meant starting Ragnarok. Now, what did you do to my friend?"

He shrugs and flits his hand through the air. "I did nothing to him. I'm sure he's around here somewhere."

Not giving him time to think of what to say next, I turn on my heel and go in search of Braun, Loki follows close behind me. I spot Braun in the kitchen, Mai tucked behind him, while he casually holds a butcher's knife in one hand. I can already tell he's heard the whole conversation. Wonderful. He keeps his eyes on me, scanning my face for something, though I'm not sure what.

"Who the fuck are you?" Mai spits out.

"Well, it has been terrible seeing you as always, Loki," I say at the same time as Mai. "Please leave."

I turn to face the god of mischief. He gives a small, knowing smile. The one I hate. Well, I hate everything about him. I sense Braun moving closer to me with the butcher's knife at the ready.

"You know I could help you, Vi," Loki says, ignoring Braun and Mai completely.

"I don't even know you anymore, Loki. How can you even show your face to me after what you've done?"

He flicks a piece of lint off his pristinely tailored suit, seemingly unbothered by the blood that now stains it, and comments coolly. "I did what needed to be done. Asgard needed to fall. It was prophesied and I knew long ago I'd be the catalyst for it." I am stock-still, trying to calm the rage building in me.

"And what about Nidavellir? Why there?"

He sneered. "Those dwarves were useless. They stood in my way, so I wiped them out."

"What did they stand in the way of?"

"My rule."

I keep my face neutral, but I am appalled. The Loki I knew was sometimes cruel and harsh, but this is a side of him I don't know. His demeanor changes back to calm, and I'm getting whiplash from his ever-changing moods as he asks, "Are you going to accept my help?"

His shifts in temperament are far more obvious and fraught than before, as if something in him broke.

I huff out a laugh. "You are the last person I want or need help from. Leave or I won't hesitate to plunge my blade through the area where your heart would be if you had one."

Not that a knife to the heart can kill Loki, but it could certainly do some damage. I move to push him out the front door, only steps away.

"I know where they are, Vi." I stop dead in my tracks as he comes closer. "I know where the Asgardians are."

My heart stops in my chest and I'm torn.

I think of Edda's warnings to not make any deals with Loki. But if it means getting her back, I'll do it. I cock my head to the side while watching Loki, who stands calmly with his hands clasped in front of him.

If I ask him to take me to them, he will be in a position of power. It's a dangerous move to make. Braun, as if sensing my indecision, presses his solid body slightly into me as he closes the distance. He places a hand on my lower back for the support I didn't realize I needed.

We would have to play Loki's game better than him. Something I used to revel in, which is why we were so good together. Yet I'd grown out of it, and he never could. He is the god of games after all. A god who even tricked himself into thinking he didn't need anything but his games. No room for love, only power.

"No consequences or repercussions. I will take you to them. They are here on Midgard."

"How did you find us?" I ask.

He merely shrugs, looking bored. "I happened to see you on the television. Fascinating thing, television. It was easy enough to track you down after that." He smirks as if rather proud of himself.

"I don't like this," Braun murmurs warily as he crosses his arms.

"I wish I could trust you," I whisper to Loki hoarsely, unable to look at him.

Loki shakes his head as if struggling to shake out his multiple personalities warring under his calm surface. His mood shifts again as he reasonably says, "Think about it, I'll come back in a few days."

As he turns to leave, I ask, "Why?" He merely shrugs not giving me an answer.

Not a good sign.

Once he leaves, Braun lets out a breath resting his forehead on my shoulder. We stand frozen in the doorway of the kitchen for a while.

"Well, that guy was an asshole," Mai mutters. We are all silent after that, mulling over what just occurred.

———

We argue for what feels like hours. Braun paces in front of the pull-out bed while I sit on the edge, watching his every move.

"What if it's a trap?" Braun counters.

I sigh and tilt my head to the ceiling in exasperation.

"It will most definitely be a trap, but the one thing we can use against him is that any promise he makes, whether verbal or written, he can't break. If we get him to promise our safety, then we lose nothing by going with him."

Mai just sits there with her arms crossed over her chest. For once she doesn't add kindling to the fire of this fight. At some point, she leaves the flat more in a daze than I've ever seen her in before, as if her thoughts consume her. I begin to worry, but Braun pulls me back to the present.

"What if he takes us off-world and abandons us there?" Braun throws his eighteenth 'what if' scenario at me.

"Then I will realm-jump us back here. Easy."

I stop him from his march placing my hands on either side of his face. It doesn't matter how many times we sleep together, any time I'm near him my pulse quickens and my need for him feels almost unbearable.

I close my eyes and try to stay focused on the conversation, pulling his forehead to mine. Our breath mingles as his hands move down my torso, stopping at my waist. I open my eyes to find him watching at me.

"I've come too far, and searched for too long, to not accept any opportunity to find survivors, even if that puts us at the mercy of the god who got me into this mess in the first place." I pause, brushing my thumb across his lips. "Loki won't hurt me."

Braun shook his head. "You don't know that for sure." He swallows as if deciding whether or not to say something else. "And I've come too far, and searched for too long, to lose you."

I ignore my stupid heart that flutters at his words. "It's a risk I'm willing to make."

"I'm not," he whispers back.

"Then don't come with me," my voice cracks as I say it.

Braun growls. "I'm not leaving you alone with him. Just… just take until he comes back to make a decision." His eyes plead with me.

I nod once more, unable to deny him that. He sighs and pulls me into a hug. He buries his face in the crook of my neck and I close my eyes.

He holds me for a moment before I ask, "What will we do until then?"

He pulls back. A wicked grin spreads across his face and I feel flush. He nips my jawline as he murmurs, "I can think of a few things."

He throws me over his shoulder faster than I can react and carries me into the bedroom.

———

"Found you!" a disembodied voice says.

Out of thin air pops Loki. His hands reach for me as I squeal running down the hall. My laughter bubbles up and my adrenaline spikes as I turn the corner quickly, only to come face to face with the god.

He gives me a knowing smirk as I turn to run away, but he wraps his arms around my waist, tossing me onto his bed.

I am embraced by silken sheets and his heady scent. One that I've dearly missed while he was away.

He is on top of me in a second, pulling my hands above my head as he nuzzles my neck.

"Finally found my treasure," He murmurs, tracing a hand down my body which goes taught under his touch. My dress slips to the side, showing just a peek of my breasts, but that's all it takes to snap Loki's restraint.

His lips crush mine and I writhe beneath him, needing him to fix the hollow ache that's been building in me all week.

He groans when his hands slip between my thighs to find I'm not wearing underwear.

"So naughty, Vi," he chuckles.

"I was hoping you'd come." It's been a week since I've seen him and the thought of what he does when I'm not around makes my stomach turn. He is mischievous and unpredictable, but without a person of reason nearby, he is chaos at best.

"I always come when I'm with you." He insinuates, but I don't have time to retort before he plunges his fingers into me. I cry out as pleasure courses through me.

My fingers slip through his inky hair, pulling hard. He groans again, loving when I'm rough. My other hand reaches toward his pants, making quick work of the bindings, pushing them down.

With disorienting speed, Loki buries himself deep inside me. My body lights up in rapture, and I no longer have thoughts or worries. In this moment, he is not a god, and I am not a Valkyrie. He is just Loki, and I am just Vera.

He shucks off his shirt and tears the fabric of my dress, bearing me to him wholly.

"Vera," he says, plunging in and out of me in a dizzying rhythm. I can barely keep up, but there's no need to. He always takes care of me, leaving his pleasure to be secondary. It's probably the only place in which that occurs.

In any other situation, he would come first, he would be higher ranked. He is a god after all.

I whimper as my need peaks, and I know I'm close. Loki sits up realizing the same thing. He loves to watch me fall apart for him. Always, only for him.

"Come for me, treasure," he commands, it's a light one but I feel its impact on me. The Valkyrie in me begs to give in, to submit to a god, but he is not the one who controls me. So, I hold on for as long as I can before I'm screaming his name and rainbows burst in my vision. He grunts, following me into

ectasy.

We pant, catching our breath as he traces the line of my cheek. He lays next to me, sweat glistening on the small patch of onyx chest hair. His sculpted body on display. All mine… right?

"I heard Angrboda gave you a hard time yesterday," Loki prods and catches my gaze. I see the wrath in those hazel eyes. That someone would try to cause me pain to get to him guts him as much as it infuriates him. He may be mischief, but he can be vengeful when something happens to those he protects.

I can never lie to Loki, so I shrug and say, "Nothing I couldn't handle."

I can tell he doesn't buy it, but this wasn't my first run-in with the mother of monsters, Loki's ex. I have the skills to get out of the situation quickly.

"You know you can always tell me. I can deal with her," he murmurs, continuing to trace his fingers along my body. "It's me and you always, Vi."

"Is it, Loki?" the question tumbles out of my mouth before I can stop it. Now that we aren't in the throes of passion, our reality crashes into me.

I wince, I don't want to fight with him today. He pauses his tracing, a silent order to look at him. When I glance up, I find no anger in his gaze, but sadness.

"I know it doesn't always feel like it, but all I am is yours." The conviction in his voice is so real. I told myself before that he was not to be trusted. Not with my heart, not with my body, but both betray me every time he is near.

How many times have we fallen apart and gotten back together? Too many, my mind whispers to me, but my heart still firmly believes in him.

I wonder if one day there will be a final straw and if letting go of him will break me in an irreparable way.

He pulls me on top of him, pushing inside me, ready to go again. I ride him as he whispers, "you and me". Over and over, until our bodies are slick from exertion. Until his voice becomes garbled, words muffled and distant.

I know this cycle will have to end, but right now I don't care. This is the Loki I love. Full of mirth and giddy from winning the chase. This is my Loki.

As our pleasure climbs, I decide.

Tomorrow.

I'll figure out what to do about this tomorrow. Or maybe the day after that. Or maybe the day after that. But either way someday, I will have to choose. My heart or my sanity.

I awake sick to my stomach from the dream. I roll into Braun, snuggling into his warmth and thanking the gods over and over I got away from Loki. I finally had the sense enough to end it with him and move on with my life.

He will be here sometime today and though it's still early, there's no way I'll be able to sleep. So, I pull a blanket from the bed, draping it around myself as I go sit on the balcony. I run through what I need Loki to promise, to keep both of us alive.

"I need a promise Loki, otherwise we're done here," I say to the terribly magnificent god in front of me with my arms crossed.

It's been two days since he appeared in the apartment as Braun. Now, the real Braun sits close by strapped with more blades than I realized he owned. Mai left the apartment early this morning, I woke her up not long after I got up. We all agreed we didn't want to risk her safety where Loki was concerned.

Loki smiles, excited that I remember his games. "No fun Vi." His use of my old pet name makes me want to punch him again. He pouts playfully.

There was a time when I would do anything to play games with him and now, I can barely tolerate him. "Alas I promise no harm or misfortune will fall upon you as I take you to the Asgardians"

"And?" I cross my arms.

He sighs and pinches the space between his tumultuous eyes. "Fine, I promise to take you there as quickly as possible and without delay. Now if you'll follow me." He begins to walk out the door towards the elevators of the apartment building.

Braun catches my hand as I start to move. I turn to find his eyes searching mine, looking for certainty I know he doesn't reciprocate. Braun does not know Loki as I do, and he has every right to be wary of him, but the promise should protect both of us from his chaos.

After a moment, Braun nods as if finding what he was looking for and walks towards the apartment elevator and Loki. I am still terrified that this is a trap somehow, but I can't pass up an opportunity for help from Loki even if it comes with terrible consequences. I have come too far and searched fruitlessly for too long.

I once thought he did things for me because he loved me. Only after did I understand it all came at a price, one way or another. Braun walks into the elevator in front of me, putting space between Loki and me, for which I am grateful.

"Hold on tight," Loki mutters to no one in particular, looking extremely bored with this adventure already.

Moments later, the elevator doors open, not to the first floor of the apartment building, but to open space. Stepping out, we stand in a field of the greenest grass I've ever seen outside of Asgard, it billows around my waist in the light breeze that flows over the valley. The air is crisp and light, unlike the city we've come from.

I take a few steps before my foot runs into stone. I curse under my breath and look down to see the stone has a name carved in it. My heart sinks as I look at the engraving. *Heimdall.*

My pulse quickens, and I look around spotting more and more stones, similar to this one, all with names engraved.

I have been tricked again.

Loki promised to take me to the Asgardians, but I never thought to ask if they were dead or alive.

I hurdle past the rows and rows of stones looking at the names. Flashes of their faces fly through my mind. It is too much. Then I see a name I hoped to never see on a stone, one that I had hoped was still alive.

Edda Hjelmstad.

My baby sister didn't survive but somehow, I had. How is this possible? Is this even real? I turn to see Loki behind me; his face is drawn.

"Tell me this isn't real; promise me this isn't real." I choke out, barely feeling the salty water that trails down my cheeks. Loki shakes his head.

"Vera, I wish with all my heart that this wasn't real." I cannot fathom he didn't want it when he created it.

"What happened? I saw so many make it on transport ships, yet there are no survivors?" He doesn't speak, instead he just stares at the name on the grave behind me. "How come I survived?" I whisper. "How come I survived, Loki!" I yell at him.

He runs a hand through his hair before saying, "The transport ships made it out of Asgard, but the fire-giants of Muspelheim and dark elves of Svartalfheim made sure the transports didn't make it to any other realms. There are no other Asgardian survivors other than a few gods who were already off-world." My mouth falls open. Innocents, so many of them dead at the hands of this god who started it all. "This was fate Vi, there was nothing I could do to stop it," he whispers.

"And that's supposed to help me? Knowing you had no choice but to participate? You killed thousands of innocents, for what? And what about the other realm you destroyed?" Loki says nothing, only continues to stare at the ground.

This doesn't make any sense. How has everyone died and I'm still alive?

"Why am I alive Loki? How am I alive?" I walk towards him and lift his face to mine meeting his mercurial eyes that have turned a deep green like the grasses around us. "You took away everything I loved, the least you can do is tell me how I survived."

A single tear slides down his perfectly sculpted cheek. I have never seen Loki show any emotion other than mirth, anger, and ridicule before. His face flits through emotions so quickly I cannot follow.

"When I found you, you were so sad and angry. So, I took that away from you and made you sleep. Your wings were—" He swallows, not able to say it.

So, he was the one who took them off. My heart aches, but my wings were beyond saving anyway. "You were still alive, barely, and I-I couldn't bear losing you after all I'd lost." Never have I heard Loki stutter. "I pulled you from the city and into an unmarked transport just before the planet erupted. I knew you'd never forgive me, but I couldn't let you die too. You are mine and I am yours, but I tricked myse—" he breaks off and is quiet for a moment.

As I watch him shake his head, his eyes flickering through emotions again, and it finally dawns on me. Vali was right, whatever snapped in Loki means he no longer understands his illusions from reality. Whether from our breakup or something else, it was a slow unraveling.

Five years—if our split was truly the start of it—is a long time to spiral inward and break the very fabric of one's mind. It seems Loki has done just that. He's lost so deep in his head he can't control what he does from one moment to the next. It explains his ever-changing temperament. It explains why he saved me only to rip everything away. A small part of me feels sorrow for this god, but rage pours through me, blocking out all else.

"I am not yours, Loki," I spit out in my fury and agony.

"I just couldn't let you die," he whispers.

"You should have," I mutter, and his face turns to rage, but I no longer care. I don't care if he decides to kill me now that I have well and truly lost everything.

I start to walk away but whirl around when Braun yelps from behind me. Before I can move or yell light flashes from across the field.

Loki is gone but so is Braun. He has *taken* Braun.

Panic rushes through me as if someone has kicked me in the gut. I have no way to follow Loki. I could jump to a million places and still not find Braun, but I cannot lose him too.

So, I realm-jump without thinking about where I'm going. I jump right into the middle of the throne room in Knoll on Alfheim. It's dark and empty, and I have no idea why I thought Loki would go there. I jump again, to another planet, an old haunt of his.

Then another.

And another.

And another.

I will tear this universe apart to find Braun.

Chapter 24

I SIT UP IN THE bedroom of the Paris apartment, but I have no recollection of how I got here, no idea how long I have been gone. I've lost all concept of time. Still fully clothed, I've managed to smudge grass and dirt across the sheets. I want to believe that what happened was a dream, that Loki hadn't taken us to the graves.

I reach across the bed to find it stone cold. Loki stole Braun from me. As if to ensure I felt alone. Isolated. In my desperation to find survivors, I had only agreed to my safety and return, not Braun's.

Selfish.

Numbness settles over me as a light inside me—the one that held onto hope so tightly these past months—dies. My mantra, 'find the survivors' that I repeated over and over again for so many months, quiets and the silence of my mind envelopes me. Edda is dead, everyone I know is dead, and everything I know is truly gone.

Since I woke up on Niflheim I hoped there were others out there. I saw the transports take off with my own eyes; they are supposed to be somewhere waiting for me. And they were, just not as I had hoped. The asshole hadn't even given them the proper burial. Rotting in graves is not the Asgardian way.

I press a hand to my chest as the intense pressure continues to build, and I wipe my hand across my cheek to find

I am crying.

What am I to do now?

It isn't fair that I survived while everyone else died, all because a selfish god couldn't bear to lose me. If I thought I hated Loki before, it is nothing compared to how I feel now.

Defeated.

Exhausted.

I can barely breathe, let alone think of a plan.

Mai pads into the room, and the bed shifts as she sits down next to me. "Loki killed them all, Mai, then he took him. He took Braun," I say with a tremble in my voice I can't hold back.

Either I've told her this or she figured as much because she only mumbles a response. Something about me being gone for several days, but the ringing in my ears is too loud for me to truly hear her. I lie back down, and she runs a hand over my hair murmuring soft words.

I fall asleep pretending none of it ever happened.

Someone screams as a splash echoes across the lake. I turn and see a few girls giggling as they watch someone fall into the water. The person sputters, struggling to swim in the deep part of the lake.

"Vera!" the person calls out, and my heart races.

I could pick out that voice anywhere.

Edda. I hurdle towards her and jump in seconds later, treading through the murky water as she goes under and doesn't come up. Even at fifteen years old Edda is not a strong swimmer. I pop up to take a big breath before I dive under to grab her.

The water is frigid, causing my body to lock up the deeper I go. She sinks faster than I thought possible as I claw through the depths towards her. My lungs scream at me for air, and I let out a few bubbles of precious oxygen just as I brush my sister's fingers. I swim deeper until I snatch her wrist and drag her with me back to the surface.

Gasping and sputtering as my head pops above the water, I pull Edda up next to me. While I make sure her head is out of the water, I kick hard to the shallow area. The ache in my arms builds as I carry her the last bit to the shoreline, but I ignore it. I lay her down and immediately push on her chest.

"Come on Edda!" I command.

"Wake up." I blow a breath into her mouth as I pinch her nose before going back to chest compressions.

"Wake up!" I yell at her. Just as I'm about to hold her nose, I feel her convulse. She gags and I force her head to the side as she coughs up half the lake.

I rest my head on the coarse sand, and relief sinks in as she heaves giant breaths.

"You're okay, you're fine," I soothe, pushing the wet hair out of her face. Tears prick the sides of her eyes as she begins to shake. The girls who pushed her in are long gone, but I know their faces and will deal with them later. I help Edda sit up, and we are quiet for a while.

"Thanks," she croaks, and I can only nod. My rage at those girls simmers just below the surface of my calm facade. They pushed her in, in the middle of winter. Assholes.

We sit at home that night with a big fire in the hearth. Edda shivers as I hand her a mug of tea. Her nose is bright red, and I have little doubt she's sick, though the doctor won't stop by until the morning.

I watch her as she stares dejectedly at the fire. "I saw them you know," she whispers. I cock my head to the side confused.

"Mom and dad." My eyebrows raise as she looks at me and I move to sit next to her. "They told me it wasn't my time... they said they miss us very much." Now I understand the tears

when she awoke.

Whether it was real or just her imagination, I don't voice my questions. Edda is strong-willed and stubborn like me, and I don't feel like fighting with her. I'm just happy she's alive.

"When I die, I want you to be the one who ferries me to Valhalla. Just like the two sisters in the story you used to tell me."

I snort. "That's assuming you die before me, Edda, which I highly doubt will happen." She merely shrugs. "Besides I doubt you'll get into Valhalla." She barks a laugh at that. I pull her into my arms, and we sit like that for a long while.

"I'm glad you're my sister," she murmurs, and I hum in agreement, thinking I'll always be there to protect her.

I awake from a voice commanding me, "Vera, get up!" It's Braun's voice. He nuzzles my neck, his cedar scent wrapping around me as he murmurs, "Do not give up." My eyes pop open and I am hit with grief. Braun's voice pulled me from my dream, but he is still gone. Like a second punch to the stomach, my sister is dead.

I climb out of bed and get dressed in a zombie-like state, cooking breakfast only to push it around my plate. Mai stands in the doorway watching me quietly, her brown eyes full of concern.

The silence is so loud.

Lost in my thoughts, my sick twisted mind allowed me to see Edda again in my dreams when I know she is gone. It allowed me to hear, smell and feel Braun without him actually being here. Though the dream made me realize what I need to do today. I try to force down some of the food, keenly aware of Mai watching every move I make. She sits down next to me.

I turn to her and her worried gaze searches mine. "I want to go back," I tell her. She rests her delicate hand on top of mine. "I..." I pause, unable to say the words without my voice breaking. "I need to say goodbye."

Mai and I jump there and land without issues. I perfected it while searching for Braun and no longer need the fall to move from place to place. She gasps as she moves away from me to take in the scenery.

Quietly she walks through the tall grasses as strong winds gust through them. I stride past gravestones while trying not to look at them too closely, not ready to bear the sight of the names of each who have passed. I find Edda's and sit down in front of hers.

"Why did it have to be you?" I whisper and move some grass off her stone, tracing my fingers along the outline of her name. I don't know what else to say or where to begin. "Remember the day Mom and Dad died and we stayed at their transcendence site until they were taken to Valhalla? We cried in each other's arms for days, but you picked yourself up first. You decided to get up and move forward.

"You've always been the stronger one of us. You can't be gone, how…" I gulp. "How will I go on without you? You were the one good thing in my life. I was in awe of you, your strength, and your courage. I am still in awe of you."

I have so much I wish to tell her, but I don't know how. How do you convey the love and heartache you feel over someone's passing? I am quiet for a moment before remembering what she'd love to hear most.

A breath shudders out of me and tears flow as I begin. "Once upon a time there were two sisters who lived in a golden palace by the sea. They were always happy and the best of friends…" I tell her the story one last time. Our sisterhood was the story, but it had all the messy bits too. All the best sisterhoods have a little bit of both. Ours most certainly did.

"I will see you again my dear Edda. I will see you again." I take a breath and pull out my sword. The blade appears, but its shine seems dull today with the clouds looming above. I dig it into the ground in front of the stone. "I wish I could take you to Valhalla like you wanted, but this is the only way I can do that now."

I turn to find Mai with tears in her dark eyes as she walks towards me. She sees the names and understands my loss. I give her a sad smile when she is close enough. She kneels next to me near Edda's stone and says something I don't catch. Something, I realize, not meant for me to hear.

I close my eyes and move to kneel before beginning the same Valkyrien prayer I did for the dead we found in Yulamic. My sister is not a Valkyrie, and neither are the Asgardians nor gods that lie around her, but they deserve the prayer just the same.

"Make no truce or treaty with foe. Kinsmen to kinsmen should be true. Reach your destination though you have traveled slow. Valhalla calls." It is quiet for a minute until the grasses around us burst with light. It is so bright I have to shield my eyes. I gasp as I see all the graves are lit. As the warm white light fades, I slowly stand. I pocket my sword and Mai takes my hand as she stands before we jump back to the Paris apartment.

I am exhausted when we arrive, and I don't even bother taking off my clothes as I crawl into bed. I drift in and out of sleep on the dirt-smeared sheets.

When I awake next, the numbing silence hits me before I've even opened my eyes. The pit in my heart yawns wide, and darkness flows out, filtering through my veins and spreading quicker than poison. I push myself into a sitting position in the dark room. Unable to be alone here any longer, I walk to the living room.

Moonlight gleams through the curtains as Mai sleeps on the pullout couch. I sit on the floor next to the bed, resting my head against it. I watch her for a moment, taking in the calm stillness in her usually fiery features. I smile and brush my hand along her outstretched arm lying across the mattress.

Her eyes blink open at the touch and she smiles sleepily. She scoots closer and runs a hand through my hair.

"We'll find him," she murmurs, her voice heavy with sleep. "I promise, we will find him."

Guilt rushes through me that I worry more for Braun at this moment than the death of my sister. I hate what that says about me.

"I'd invite you to sleep with me, but you're covered in grass and dirt," she grumbles. "And you smell." Her eyes are closed within moments and her breathing evens out.

I lace my fingers through hers that lie close to my head and shut my eyes.

"Come on Vera, time to get up." I blink to find I'm curled up on the hard floor of the living room with a thin blanket draped over me. Mai squats in front of me and rubs her hand over my shoulder. "Let's get you cleaned up."

I nod and follow her to the bathroom. She runs hot water in the tub, and I pull off my clothes, uncaring if she sees me naked. I step into the tub after Mai pours in some soap. Sapphire bubbles float along the surface, and she helps me scrub my hair while I wash my body. Needing something to distract me, anything, I ask her about her family.

Her hands still in my hair at first and I glance at her, but her expression is unreadable. "What do you want to know?"

"What were they like?" I ask.

She huffs a breath. "Annoying... loud. Judgmental. Kind. Protective. Loving... they were all the things a family should be. My brother constantly annoyed me with his science experiments that threatened to blow up our apartment more than once. I never thought I'd miss him yammering on and on about the molecular structure of an atom. Or the scientific theory behind the cosmos and gravity."

She smiles sadly, before continuing, "I miss my mom's cooking. Homemade Chinese food for dinner every night was heavenly. I'm surprised I didn't gain a thousand pounds from how much I ate. On special occasions, we would get a roast duck from the market. It was always my favorite. I'd go for seconds or thirds every time. Mom would always tell me to slow down when I ate. She would say, 'We are not pigs eating from a trough, so we shouldn't act like one.'"

I laugh. "I think I would like your mom."

"She was stern, and she would have chewed your ass out for your Rune markings while stuffing you full of food. She'd say you were a foolish girl who will never get a good job or husband." I smile, thinking of how proud my mom had been when I got my first one. "My dad would have liked you though. He's the only one who went against conventional thinking. My Wai Po, my er—grandmother, hated him at first, but he was a good match for my mom, and he came from an upstanding family. Something even my Wai Po couldn't deny."

Mai continues talking about her family as I get out of the bath and dry off. She adds more about her family still alive in America and continues telling me stories over the next few hours until my stomach hurts from laughing and my eyes are heavy with sleep, even though it's only mid-afternoon.

My mind is full of her memories, reminding me to replace my horrors with my triumphs and favorite moments. Clinging to those good memories, I hold her hand as I fall asleep, feeling like maybe I didn't lose everyone. After all, I did gain a new sister.

Chapter 25

A WEEK LATER, MAI AND I get absolutely trashed, taking drinking to a whole new level. She forces me to put on the shortest dress she brought and does my makeup before we go out to a bar, but not before taking far more shots of alcohol than necessary.

The music in the bar winds through us, over us, around us as we sit there. I can think of nothing other than Braun and Edda. The thoughts block out even the murmuring voices of conversation around us.

Mai sighs. "Ok, this clearly isn't working. Let's go to a club." Maybe the press of bodies and beat of the music will help. So, we walk into a club close by.

As we move to the music, I force my mind away from all that has happened, living solely in this state of drunken stupor. No more tears from me, I made a promise to Edda.

"At least you haven't started crying yet!" Mai yells to me over the music, before turning to make out with a random woman.

I keep moving to the rhythm as if it will somehow take away the hollowness in my chest. A man pushes up against me, but in my drunkenness, I jab him in the throat.

"Sorry," I mumble and move away from him. I cannot stand to be touched by strangers and, suddenly, the room becomes too full. Too many people, too little space, and I cannot move without someone brushing against a part of me.

Before I realize what I'm doing, I am pushing past people. I make my way out of the front doors of the club, gulping in deep breaths of fresh air. The chill of the night clears my head even if the world still tilts and whirls.

I'm sure I look ridiculous, weaving back and forth on the sidewalk as I stumble home. Home. What a ridiculous thought that this could be my home. In my state, I can accept that I may never find home again, even though it leaves me feeling raw.

The stairs tip from one side to the other as I make the slow trek up them to the flat, apparently the elevator was too difficult to try and use. I fumble with the keys, swearing as I drop them twice, and have to use two hands to put it into the slot of the door while closing one eye. Exhausted from the long dizzying journey home, I fall asleep on the couch, too lazy to pull out the bed from within it.

The sound of wood splintering into a million pieces has me bolting awake and in a fighting stance within seconds. My head pounds like I banged it against the wall for hours, and I'm still in my revealing dress from the prior night. Mai stumbles into the room still in her clothes from the prior night as well, her pink hair matted with sleep.

Thor groans as he rolls off Vali, who landed directly on the coffee table which is now smashed to smithereens. Next to him, a lean, pale man heaves great breaths. As he rolls over his grey eyes pierce mine and I yelp.

I launch myself on Braun and he lets out a pained sound. I pull away only to assess the damage. The left side of his face is covered in purple and red bruises, and he stops my hand as I move to lift his shirt to continue my inspection.

He murmurs something unintelligible, and Mai drops to

her knees beside me. A glance at Mai tells me she is just as hung over from last night's debauchery as myself. We help him up to lay on the couch before I grab Thor's hand and help him up.

"Couldn't use the front door?" I mutter as I pull him to his feet.

He's dressed in traditional Asgardian wear now. His massive hammer, Mjölnir, in one hand. He brushes off splinters of the wood from his silver armor that gleams in the early morning light; lined with runes down it for protection, it is some of the strongest armor ever created in Asgard.

I swallow the lump in my throat knowing my sister helped create the chest plate. Thor doesn't speak as he takes in the surroundings. Nor does Vali who is already standing by the time I get to him. We smirk at each other before clasping forearms. I'm glad he's still alive.

"Nice outfit," Vali comments. I grin and bat my eyelashes.

"Who the hell are you?" Mai asks in English crossing her arms.

"This is Vali, Thor's brother," I explain.

Vali turns his gaze to Mai and assesses her quietly before nodding his head—the best kind of greeting you can get from him. Though Mai only narrows her eyes before going into the kitchen.

I turn back to Braun, running my hand down his good cheek, and place the ice pack Mai hands me on the left side of his battered face. He wheezes on the couch as he tries to breathe deep breaths. I sit on the arm of the couch closest to Braun's head, tapping my foot. Mai perches on the other arm, keeping her gaze wary.

"How did you find him?" I ask quietly in Asgardian, running a hand through Braun's disheveled, dirty hair. It is matted with blue blood and gray dirt. I pull out a piece of gravel that reminds me of the ground on Niflheim.

Thor huffs a breath but looks at Braun with concern. Not a good sign. "I went to Nidavellir and saw it for myself..." He shakes his head, unable to continue.

"I told you it was bad," I mutter. Vali hums in agreement

"There's no time to waste, we must go to Alfheim," Braun grits out switching the conversation to Elvish, the only language all of us have in common. His complexion is paler than usual in my periphery.

"What happened?" I ask hoarsely.

Vali shakes his head. "Not what has happened, what is going to happen." I suck in a breath and squeeze my eyes shut.

"Loki has picked the next victim of Ragnarok."

I let out the breath I'm holding and swear.

"How long?"

"Two weeks at most," Vali explains. Braun lifts his good eye to mine, mulling over something.

"You were right, Vali." I state as I glance at Vali, who scrunches his eyebrows together. "Loki is no longer in control of himself. He's completely lost it."

I explain how Loki was the one to pull me from Asgard and how he hadn't tried to kill me when he saw me again. Vali swears when I mention the transport I found Rhodda in on Alfheim and Asgardian graves Loki took us to. How Loki seemed barely in control of himself.

Thor nods as if he expected as much as well. "He spared you twice though, you must mean something to him still."

I shrug. "After our last conversation, I doubt that he will spare me again."

"I hate being right," Vali murmurs.

"So, what exactly are you planning to do?" Mai asks. "It's not like the four of you can take on the entirety of Loki's forces alone." Clearly, she doesn't count herself in this group.

"We need to inform the different kingdoms on Alfheim. Maybe some of those unable to fight can be transported off-world before it begins," Braun notes stoically. I smile down at him. Even while in pain, he still lacks emotion—a good sign he'll be better soon.

Thor nods. "Exactly. Vali and I will work on the rest." I raise my eyebrows unimpressed. Braun and I and the rest of Alfheim stand to lose a lot more than Thor and Vali if this ends badly. Thor looks at me annoyed. "Give me a break, I only found out an hour ago."

"You're the god of war, so…" His expression darkens further and a booming thunderclap echoes through the quiet streets of Paris. Vali merely smirks, he always enjoyed watching us bicker.

"And you're a Valkyrie. You've been in just as many wars as I." I roll my eyes at his statement. "Care to help with a plan?" he sneers.

I push all of Thor's buttons and I'm about to push more when Braun pinches me, reminding me to play nice.

We are silent for a moment before Thor finally answers my initial question, "Found him in Niflheim." My blood runs cold. "After I saw Nidavellir, I thought a visit to Niflheim would reveal some enlightening information on Loki's whereabouts."

I grit my teeth thinking of the goddess Hel, Loki's daughter and ruler of Niflheim. A nasty bitch— "You can imagine my surprise to find your latest conquest in one of her cells. She took very little convincing to give him up once I started asking questions about Ragnarok." I would have never been able to get Braun out of Niflheim alone.

"I am indebted to you for bringing him back," I say to Thor without taking my eyes off Braun.

"What will you give me in return?" Thor's eyes have a devilish gleam to them when I look up at him surprised. I feel Braun's fingers grip my leg closest to him. "Perhaps marriage? Won't that enrage Loki even more?" he muses to himself more than us, but he doesn't miss Braun's arm tightening in annoyance. I know Thor's just trying to rile me up, tit for tat.

Vali smirks. "I forgot how overprotective elves are when it comes to their partners." He eyes Braun for the first time since smashing the coffee table and a low growl slips from Braun. Not helping.

I roll my eyes, ignoring the last comment. "And where have you been Vali?"

His face falls a bit. "Vanaheim. Locating survivors there."

"Any luck?" I ask, though no longer hopeful. He merely shakes his head. "Fine." I sigh and run my hand through my tangled hair.

"You should rally the gods from Vanaheim, we'll need all the help we can get." Thor and Vali nod at the same time, as if one is real and the other a reflection. "We certainly can't expect any help from Midgard, so that leaves only those on Alfheim. How likely are they to be useful against frost and fire giants?" I direct my question at Braun.

He shrugs. "Depends on the kingdom, some will be more prepared than others. It depends on whether they heed the warning we bring them."

Thor runs a hand over his chin, where his beard usually rests. "Vera, I know you can send out some sort of call to the other Valkyrie. Can you try it? Even if there aren't any left, better to try than not."

I nod. "I did it the minute I woke up on Niflheim over six months ago, but no one came." I explain.

"Just try it one more time. Besides if you tried it only on Niflheim there's a good chance the magic there blocked it. It blocks most users' powers, otherwise, how would Hel keep the dead from hailing a transport to get off-world?" Vali points out with a smirk.

I huff a breath at his poor attempt to joke. "I'll try one last time."

"Do we know where in Alfheim Loki will strike first?" Mai asks, but neither Braun nor Thor have an answer. I freeze. What if Loki is doing this to spite me? Haratine would be the first place he'd hit. I say as much to them.

Thor shakes his head. "He likely thinks he's already hit you where it'll hurt most. I doubt Hel will mention the small prison break to her father unless she wants to incur his wrath," he says, referring to Braun. "The kingdom of Salaza seems the most logical location. He has had several run-ins with the republic leaders and would be more than enthused to wipe them off the map." I let out a breath and a glance at Braun confirms he was thinking the same thing.

"Then we'll start there," Braun murmurs hoarsely, again seeming far away in his thoughts.

Thor holds out his arm to me, and I grip his massive forearm in my hand as he does the same. "Never thought I'd be on the same side as you." He smirks. "It's a nice change."

"It's only because we are going to battle," I remind him. "Besides killing Loki has always been a dream of mine."

Thor lets out a belly laugh as he disappears into thin air, another round of thunder rolling over Paris as the skies light up with lightning. Vali merely nods and, to my surprise, winks at Mai before disappearing as well. It's only after they both leave that I think of their brother's blade stashed in Braun's bags.

Mai goes to the kitchen to make some food for Braun as I force him to sit in the tub, not trusting he won't tip over from using too much magic while trying to heal himself. Slowly I pull off his shirt, and my throat makes a noise trying to hold in my gasp. It's so much worse than when we broke him out of prison.

Lashes run across his chest, shoulders, and back. Rage burns through me. They *whipped* him. My hands shake with fury as I turn on the tap and fill the tub with warm water. I help him lean back as he dunks his head under the stream.

The tub is barely large enough to fit him alone, but I move to sit in it with him while I still wear the ridiculous dress. Unable to avoid physical contact. As if he'll be taken from me at any moment if I don't keep close.

I lather his hair, which is full of grit and dirt, with shampoo. Suds run down his chest and back, and he sucks in a breath as it stings his tender open wounds. He leans back again, and I run my fingers through the silky strands, getting out all the shampoo.

We work in silence. I know if I open my mouth all the words I cannot and should not say will rush out. I know my rage is not what he needs right now.

Eventually, I get out and let him finish the rest, allowing him a minute alone. I change clothes before walking into the kitchen. Mai made eggs and potatoes even though it's early evening.

She shrugs seeing my expression. "It's all I know how to cook. Deal with it."

I throw my hands up in surrender, and Braun comes into the kitchen after changing into a pair of pants. He wraps his arms around my waist as I lean my head back against his shoulder lightly, trying not to cause him pain.

"I thought I lost you," I murmur hoarsely. "I looked everywhere for you." I take a breath swallowing the lump in my throat. No more tears. "I went to so many planets."

He nuzzles my neck. "I know." It's all he seems capable of saying.

"Good to have you back, old man," Mai says lightly, putting Braun's plate of food on the kitchen island. I work on bandaging his open wounds while he scarfs down his food and I can feel his exhaustion rolling off him.

Braun naps while Mai and I walk through the empty city. Both of us need to clear our heads. With the rain still pouring overhead, few Parisians are out, but neither she nor I seem to mind the wet or cold. We stop at a cafe, shaking off as much water as we can, before stepping inside to order tea.

Mai pushes her teabag around in her drink as she mulls over something.

"I've been thinking…" She pauses, appearing torn. "I'm thinking of going home—back to the U.S. I mean." Mai only glances at me before turning to stare into her drink. "I-I think I need to go back and figure some things out."

I frown but can see this is a tough decision for her. "You've been distant the past week. Is this what you've been worried about?"

She swallows as she explains, "I was planning on leaving sooner, after the gala, but when Braun was taken, I couldn't leave you."

"And now he's back."

She nods. "And now he's back."

"And he and I leave for Alfheim soon," I add.

I know she'll never want to go back to Alfheim, nor would I want her to come with us. She's gotten better with a knife, but she'll be no use in battle. Besides, too many years stuck in one place will make a person restless to be anywhere but there.

"How soon until you go back?" I ask. Mai tilts her head, her brown eyes sad.

"Maybe tomorrow, maybe the next day. I was looking at some flights last night. I still have family there that I want to reconnect with. Some friends too... maybe."

She looks up at me and there are tears brimming in her eyes. I gulp and don't allow myself to think about what it will mean not to have her around. A true friend.

A sister.

"Thank you for bringing me home, Vera," she whispers.

I only nod, unable to say anything. I can't tell her that I will miss her rants, her drunk singing, and her pointless arguments with Braun. I can't tell her because I know it will only make it harder for her to leave.

I reach over and squeeze her hand. We sit in silence for a while and I can't help but feel I'm losing another sister, one that I had hoped would meet Edda someday. I'm reminded that will never happen now.

Chapter 26

BRAUN PATS MAI'S SHOULDER AWKWARDLY causing both of us to laugh at him. "You will be missed, even if you are a pain in my ass," he comments quietly.

Before Mai departs, she sets us up with our own cellphone so we can keep in touch, not that it will work in Alfheim, but when we come back. I hug her fiercely. "Call me," she murmurs and squeezes me in a tight hug before she pats Braun on the shoulder and walks away.

I will miss her, but I am relieved. If Loki ever brings Ragnarok here, we can easily find her and get her out. Since he plans to take it somewhere else, she is safe and out of harm's way.

Braun puts his arm around my shoulders and kisses my hair. I lean into him for comfort. He always seems to know what I need in that moment without having to ask, which I haven't decided if I love or hate.

After she leaves, I pull Braun into the bedroom and close the door behind him. He's healed enough that neither of us can put this off any longer. My need for him feels cataclysmic as I slowly peel off his shirt, careful not to brush the tender parts of his chest and back.

His fingers brush the runes on my upper arms, tracing them up to my neck. Goosebumps spread over me as he trails their path. He gently tilts my head up to his, and the minute his smokey gaze crashes into my icy one, I can't breathe. His eyes convey emotions not yet ready to be voiced, emotions I'm not ready to hear or process.

I push his silver hair behind the delicate tip of his ear, and he leans into the touch, softly closing his eyes. My eyes and fingers run down the planes of his chest, careful to avoid the blue and purple bruises marring it. His skin heats as his heartbeat thuds under my touch.

"Vera," he says my name like a prayer as he pulls off my top and tosses it to the ground. I shudder, his lips igniting my skin as he drops a tender kiss on my shoulder then runs those sinful lips up my neck where his hands were moments ago. He grazes his nose along my jawline as I tangle my fingers into his silver locks.

I draw his mouth to mine and brush my lips across his as I murmur, "I need you."

Whatever tether he holds on his control snaps at hearing those words and his sweet touches turn savage. His lips crash onto mine, tongues and teeth warring against each other. He pulls my bra off with little effort while I fumble with the buttons of his pants as my fingers tremble. He bites my neck, leaving teeth impressions on my tan skin, and I hum my pleasure against his neck.

I finally free him from his pants and palm him through his boxers. He hisses a breath through his teeth before bringing his mouth to my breast. He teases the sensitive skin, causing my back to arch. I drag his boxers down, and my hand finds his velvet wrapped steel before tightly pulling on it. His groans send shivers through my body.

Braun withdraws his hand from my breast to the front of my pants and makes quick work of the buttons before sliding a calloused finger over me then in me. His mouth finds mine and his touch sends fire racing through every nerve ending in my body. I yearn to drag my nails down his back, but I am careful not to do more damage.

Instead, I press myself lightly against him while his fingers still pump in and out of me, dragging me closer to the edge I dearly want to fall from. I shudder again as if in warning that I won't be able to hold on much longer. Something Braun innately understands as he pulls his fingers away and backs me up until the back of my knees hit the bed.

I crawl up it before he settles over me and I trace the silver scar near the middle of his chest. As he slides into me, his eyes blaze with white fire. I cup his cheek before running my fingers through his hair. He moves slowly, chest heaving slightly, as his body shakes with restraint.

I kiss his jaw, and right as I lift my hips to meet his I whisper, "Let go."

Braun growls, thrusting deeper, harder. Heat pours over me, into me. We move together painting a masterpiece, each stroke of his paintbrush harsh and intense yet beautiful. I ride the edge for as long as I can, loving his powerful body that moves so perfectly with mine.

As I stand on the precipice, he pinches the tip of my breast, and it sends me tumbling over the edge as a breathy moan escapes my mouth. He keeps moving, wringing the pleasure out of me with each loving stroke. He jerks, unable to hold out any longer as his own release courses through him.

He sighs and his weight settles comfortably on me as he leans his forehead against mine, our breath mingling as we catch it. I close my eyes and deeply breathe in his cedarwood scent. His hair falls in a curtain around us, blocking out the world that exists outside of this, outside of us.

I can't find words, can't form thoughts. I can only think of him, and as he fills my mind it pushes all other contemplations from it. I sigh at the moment of reprieve from the sadness and cynicism that rages inside my head. The thoughts that try desperately to pull me under the dark waters and drown me.

He presses a gentle kiss on my raw lips, and I feel him hardening again. I lay a hand on his shoulder, a soft request to change positions, and he lies on his back. I bite his lower lip before moving between his legs.

I take him in my hand and run my tongue along his shaft. He huffs out a breath, and before he can process it, I take him in my mouth. He bucks slightly, pushing in further. I can barely fit him.

I wrap my hand around his base and pump in time with my mouth. Sucking and lightly running my teeth along his length has him writhing under me. I look up at him as he watches me. Braun runs his hand lovingly over my head, swearing, which causes me to smile. I continue my ministrations until he growls something unintelligible.

He twists his fingers into my hair, holding me close as he thrusts into my mouth. He calls my name through pants until he spills into my mouth. I swallow him down before crawling up him to lie on his side and rest my head on his shoulder. He brushes his mouth against the top of my head before wrapping his arms around me. I close my eyes and listen to the steady beat of his heart.

I awake from a dreamless nap to a pale arm roped around my middle and a hard, warm body pressed against my back. As I roll into him, I nuzzle Braun's neck, hoping to wake him. I've already decided it's time to try sending out a call to the Valkyrie. Something I haven't even tried to do since Niflheim. I whisper this to Braun earning only a grunt in response.

Soon I have both of us clothed and in the living room, as rain slides down the windowpanes in slow rivulets. The constant pitter-patter of it on the roof allows a calm to wash over me. I sit on the floor in the living room where the coffee table once sat. Taking deep breaths in and out, I feel Braun's eyes on me, and I open one to see him smirk.

Let me focus, I chide him subconsciously, and he closes his eyes but still smiles. It's a smile I can't help but constantly stare at. I somehow broke through his tough, unforgiving exterior these past few weeks, and I melt when he smiles, knowing it's just for me.

I close my eyes again, focusing on my sisters. The glory, the love, and the bond between us. Fierce, stark, and beautiful, we are built for battle. Our skills honed to a sharp edge. We live for the battles we watch. Picking the winners and ferrying the dead.

I keep my thoughts on them as my blood calls for vengeance, calls my sisters to aid me. *Valkyrie, if you can hear me, if any of you are alive, Loki plans to bring Ragnarok to Alfheim next. I need your help, sisters. Help me avenge our fallen home. Help me bring that bastard to justice for his crimes. Thor and Vali will rally the Vanaheim gods, but I cannot do this without you. Fly well.* I keep my eyes shut for a moment longer, as if that will help get the message to anyone still out there. I open my eyes to find Braun looking at me as if I'm a ghost.

I cock my head to the side, but he says nothing. "Everything ok?"

"You… you just were glowing." I gape at him as he shakes his head. "Not very brightly, but as if someone turned on a light inside you." I laugh at his description of it.

"Huh, I had no idea that happened," I murmur, looking at my hands before running them through my hair and rolling my neck.

Later in the week, rain still pummels the city as if Thor's storm is a warning. Braun has said little since his return. He seems to know there are no words to console my moods.

Instead, he lays his head in my lap where I sit on one end of the couch. I give him a small smile and run my fingers through his hair. He hums and closes his eyes in pleasure. His face has healed almost completely, but his chest and back will take a few more days. I've already denied him multiple times when he protested that we should leave for Alfheim. I wasn't willing to go anywhere until he'd healed.

As I watch him, I am keenly aware of how deep this has gotten since he was taken from me. How protective I've become. Just the other day a Parisian woman smiled at Braun, and I almost tore the poor woman's throat out. I let out a sigh, tracing his face with my fingers silently. I will be in Thor's debt forever for bringing him back to me.

Braun is the only thing that helps me get up in the morning now that Mai is gone. His strong silent presence keeps me from spiraling down in the dark thoughts that occupy my mind. We don't talk about the graves, or any of it, unless I bring it up. He gives me the space to decide when I feel up to discussing it.

The rest of the time he keeps me distracted by taking walks with me around the city or pulling me into the bedroom. Some days I feel like a wholly different person, so at odds with who I was. I'm not sure which version of me I am anymore. Maybe I'll never know, but there's always tomorrow.

"You ready?" he murmurs, jerking his head to where our packs rest across the room. They've been packed since this morning, but I couldn't bring myself to realm-jump us back to Alfheim quite yet. So, we sit here in silence and breathe each other in. The silence doesn't seem to haunt me as much as before.

I decided to keep the flat. I prepaid for six months with a checkbook Mai swiped, which the landlord surprisingly accepted. I like it.

Maybe because it reminds me of Mai, or maybe because the memories here are far better than any I've made in the past decade. I look down at Braun who nods in agreement. I can't be sure about what, but, at this point, I'm convinced he hears at least half of my thoughts.

Chapter 27

The twin suns are blinding as we land in the city center of Salaza's capital, Merin. Braun grabs my hand as we weave through elves wearing outrageous clothing. Their tech shifting their hair from green to pink—whatever suits their mood—or reconfiguring their outfits.

"Do you know where you are going?" I ask him as I try to keep up with his long, purposeful strides. I imagine it's nice for him to be back on his home world where everyone walks as quickly as he does.

"I've got a contact in the Republic that will get us in front of the necessary people."

We take a hovertrain towards the government district in the city. I remember the last time I was here when Braun had been captured. Anxiety grips me as I think about the idea of going to the Haratinian kingdom again. I wonder if he cares about telling his family to prepare or not.

We get off the hovertrain fifty stories up a building. All around us elves move at top speed to their destinations. I haven't had to try so hard to keep up with Braun in a while.

We reach the front desk of the building and I veer off to the side, casually surveying the room. I note the elves that pass as if I'm preparing for an attack at any point, so used to being on guard in other realms. A moment later Braun strides over and pulls me to the waiting area across the way.

"Braunryn Holland!" exclaims a soft female voice.

I tense as a drop-dead gorgeous female elf walks towards us. She wears a business dress similar to those in Midgardian fashion that shows off her long lean legs. She flips a piece of her deep brown hair over her shoulder and flashes a beaming smile at Braun. Her cocoa skin shines in the lighting, and her big blue eyes look him up and down, not sparing me a single glance.

Braun smirks at her and stands. She kisses his cheek and holds onto their embrace for longer than I care for. I grind my teeth together but casually stand as they break their hug. A foreign emotion rakes through my body, *jealousy*. She and I are almost the same height; I'm only an inch shorter, maybe.

"And who do we have here?" She purses her lips as she looks at me curiously. I instantly dislike her.

Braun slides an arm around my waist which causes the female's eyebrows to shoot to her hairline. I hold out my hand to shake hers.

"This is my Vera." I mentally chide myself for preening at the possessive tone he takes. "Vera, this is Meli Emarin," Braun explains.

Meli looks at my hand as if it's covered in dirt and gives it a weak cold shake. *Pussy*. I almost chuckle as the thought pops into my mind, but I keep my face neutral.

"Well, please follow me this way." She gestures to the hallway she just came from.

Meli's black high heels tap on the floor as she sways her curvy figure from side to side. Braun laces his fingers through mine, and I am instantly calmer—or at least less likely to kill the female.

We walk into a well-maintained office space that overlooks the city. I press my lips together to hide a smile as I think of Mai dealing with being able to see the drop below. I miss her. She would have already trashed this female for her rudeness.

"So," Meli starts, leaning against her desk directly in front of the seat Braun takes rather than sitting behind her desk. "How can I help you?"

"We have some information that needs to be brought to the attention of the council of representatives for the Republic." Her eyebrows raise as she waits for Braun to continue.

He takes in a big breath and explains Ragnarok and Loki's plans. I watch the beauty's face transform from curiosity to disgust to worry while Braun explains. She purses her lips and looks out the window as Braun finishes.

"Well, this is interesting information indeed… but how can we trust that it's true?"

"What do you mean?" Braun asks, confused.

"You're a prince on the run, are you not?"

He grits his teeth. "I'm not running. We got the information from Loki's daughter, Hel. I can't imagine why she would lie."

She shrugs. "Possibly to throw you off Loki's real target, maybe a completely different planet."

"Gods can't lie." His tone takes an edge. "She specifically told us Alfheim."

Meli shrugs, twirling a piece of her dark brown hair around her finger. "But you can. It could just be a ruse for you to throw your happiness in my face, Braun." Braun tenses as she finally meets my eyes.

She sneers. "We used to be lovers; you know?" I pray my body stays in the seat and doesn't try to throttle her as I huff a breath.

"I don't doubt it, but I've never known Braun to be spiteful," I counter, appalled she'd question Braun's motives. "Look, believe us or don't. Ragnarok is coming whether you're ready for it or not. We have it on good authority it's coming here first, so we came to warn you."

"And which side will you be fighting on? With or against Loki? Last I heard Loki had a Valkyrien lover." Meli spits and Braun's fingers grip the arms of the chair until the wood beneath whines from the pressure.

I stand quickly, and Braun's hand immediately lands on my shoulder, creating space between Meli and me.

Meli's eyes go wide before turning cold as I calmly explain, "You think this is some kind of joke or trick? Just wait until Loki rules over you, because without our help, without my knowledge, you'll never win against him and his army. They are coming and they will overwhelm your forces. The dark elves will take over your land, rape your women, kill your men and you will be helpless to stop it. Loki will have you all in the palm of his hand, his playthings to do whatever he wishes with until he turns your planet into space dust. You'll never know what is real and what is illusion again, but I promise you whether it's real or not, it will be a nightmare."

I leave the room before I can make a bigger mess of this meeting, annoyed that she got under my skin. Rage courses through me as I stride towards the exit. I have become comfortable with people knowing me well enough that they don't judge. I forgot how horrid it feels when people question my allegiance or my choices. Even worse when they dare question Braun's.

Braun calls my name, but I shut him out as I cross the entryway and race for the main doors. I fling them open wide and am blasted by the cool winds at this height. I pace back and forth along the sidewalk to calm down.

"Vera!" Braun calls and jogs up to me.

I stop my pacing but can't look him in the eyes. I wince thinking of how ridiculous I just looked. He puts two fingers under my chin as he tilts my face to his. I continue to keep my gaze distant.

He gives me a sultry smirk and whispers, "Vera, look at me." My little self-control melts under his intense gaze, and I lock eyes with his stormy ones.

"I thought I would never have to meet one of your previous lovers," I pout.

He chuckles and runs his nose along my jawbone. "Desperate times call for desperate measures, love."

I ignore his choice of words and sigh through my nose. "I almost punched her. I'm used to people questioning my motive, but how dare she question yours. I couldn't even listen to her after that." I cross my arms as my rage resurges. He nips my jaw.

"I wouldn't have stopped you if you had." My eyebrows rise at his comment, and he chuckles. "I like your jealous side. She's quite dominant. Maybe I'll introduce you to a few more women."

I huff a breath. "You'll be dead along with them if you do." He laughs and pulls me to him, and I lean my head on his chest.

"Do you think she'll alert the council?" I whisper.

"She already has. We are to report here tomorrow morning for the initial discussion." I pull away and Braun laughs at the surprise on my face. "You were perfect in there. You scared her enough to believe it." I shake my head and roll my eyes.

———

We sit in a theatre-shaped room with wine-colored leather seats lining each of the different levels where the hundred council representatives now sit. The cream carpet beneath us is worn with use, and the walls are a buttery white color.

We are positioned just to the left of the main podium where issues are brought forth. I bounce my leg nervously being in full view of the council. I wish Thor was here to help convince these elves. He is much better at swaying people to do just about anything. His charisma as well as his general power of persuasion are things I have never possessed.

The head of the council approaches the podium, his deep blue robes billow around him. Other council members wear varying shades of different colors. To represent their territory, Braun mentioned when we entered the room earlier.

Murmurs settle as the head councilor clears his throat and begins speaking. "Today's agenda was originally to discuss the water issues between Nymir and Jeleni in the northern territory. However, the agenda has changed in light of recent news. Today we will be deciding on the best course of action regarding the news of Loki bringing Ragnarok to Alfheim." Gasps and murmurs pick up again as the council member pauses. "We have it on good authority that Loki will be striking Merin first."

More whispers erupt and I almost roll my eyes as the head councilor pauses again, which I have a feeling is more for dramatic effect than anything else. "I vote to call in all city troops and ask that the other territories in Salaza give us twenty-five percent of their forces. If Merin falls, the rest of our country may not hold out."

Shouts erupt around the room as council members argue over the validity of the claim. I want to plug my ears against the calamity of noise that reverberates through the space. Chaos in its finest form. Braun grips my thigh to keep my leg from bouncing. *You're putting me on edge*, his look conveys.

"Is there no reasoning with him?" someone from the council asks.

The head councilor looks in our direction and I shake my head. He beckons me toward him, and I freeze up. I don't like being the center of attention.

Sensing my discomfort, Braun nudges me for support. I let out a breath as I walk towards the center of the stage. More chatter breaks out among the members as I suppress the urge to run.

"There is no reasoning with Loki. He will spare no one," I state loudly and the room quiets down a bit.

"You're a Valkyrie?" an elderly female councilor asks from the first row.

"Yes." I nod. "And I've experienced Ragnarok firsthand. It's not something I'd wish anyone else to go through."

"He spared you! What makes you so sure he won't spare us?" Another yells from across the room.

I bark out a laugh. "Spared me? I lost everything that day. What is left of me is a shell of my prior self." I take a breath, to center myself, before continuing, "So yes he did spare me, but I am the only one. The only Valkyrie left; the only Asgardian left for that matter. So will you be the one in a million that he spares?" I cross my arms and snip, "Not likely, I think."

"What would you have us do?" asks the elderly female councilor.

"Fight. Fight for your homes, your lives. Loki is blinded. He is blinded by ambition and greed. He has taken the prophecy of Ragnarok and twisted it to fit his needs. He uses it as his justification for coming here and creating chaos and war.

"He calls it fate instead of what it really is. One god's quest for glory, to rule all others. I have known Loki for a long time, but he is—he has changed. There is no reckoning with the god he has become. I ask you—no, I plead with you to heed this warning and help me right his wrongs. Help me stop Ragnarok and kill Loki before it is too late."

I want to tell them about Thor and Vali and the gods they may bring, but I cannot give them hope. Not when the Valkyrie and Odin's armies did not come last time the dark elves descended upon their world. What if Thor and Vali don't come through? What if they don't show in the elves' time of need? Better to not say anything than disappoint them later.

"Why should we believe you?" someone shouts from the crowd.

I open my mouth but close it. I shrug. "People will die, either way. Don't make the same mistake we did and assume you'll win without preparing. Don't let your people die in vain. If I'm wrong, then all you've lost is a few days of work."

More shout at me, and I feel my temper rise as I hear words spoken in anger and fear. My vision starts to go red, but a hand tugs me off the stage and out the door. Braun is in my face, saying something, but I can't hear him above the ringing in my ears. His cool hands frame either side of my face, holding it tightly.

"Breathe," he mouths. I try to pull oxygen into my lungs to calm the rage that came over me.

Eventually I calm down, but we stand in the hallway for long minutes before that happens. Braun lightly runs his hands up and down my arms, attempting to distract me. I tip my head back to lean against the cool stone wall. Braun takes my hand and leads me out of the building once he's decided my temper is in check.

Once we arrive at the hotel, Braun turns to lock the door and leans back against it. He watches me with hunger in his eyes. The predatory gleam sends a shiver running through me.

"Strip," he murmurs, crossing his arms.

The command is as clear as the intent.

Distraction.

I give him a sultry look before I trail my fingers along the hem of my shirt. His growl tells me I'm going too slowly, but I'm intent to make him wait a little longer. I take it off leisurely, throwing it on the couch behind me then move to the buttons on my pants.

One by one I unbutton them, not taking my eyes off him before pulling them off. His stormy gaze roams my body, lower lip drawn between teeth, as I arch slightly to unclasp my bra. My fingers trace lightly over my body as I saunter towards him, and when I'm within arm's reach, he shifts us seamlessly, so my back is against the door.

I let out a small breath in surprise, and the returning grin he gives me is wicked. His eyes don't leave mine as his fingers ghost along the seam of my underwear before hooking his fingers into the silky material. He lowers himself to his knees, taking the last piece of clothing I wear with him.

My breath hitches at the sight of him on his knees before me. The look he gives me tells me all I need to know. He plans to worship me.

I tremble as my body turns molten for him, my heart beating loudly in my ears. He nips the soft flesh on the inside of my thighs, before licking his way up to where I'm most sensitive.

My head instinctively falls back against the door with a bang at his first touch. He chuckles, and his breath fans against me as I rub the back of my head. I thread my fingers through his silver strands, needing him closer, needing him to finish what he's started.

As he turns back to the task at hand, heat rushes through me as he sucks and swirls his tongue across me. His hands move from my hips to angle my body towards his glorious mouth. His other slips calloused fingers in and out of me in a consistent rhythm.

I moan loudly, not caring if anyone in the hall hears us. I crave more, need more. I arch my body into his face, practically riding it, as I teeter on the precipice of my orgasm.

Pleasure rushes through me before I can even try to hold out any longer. My hands curl tight in his locks as I murmur his name over and over again. Tremors rack my body as the orgasm barrels through me. Braun holds me through it; my knees buckled long ago.

I lean against the door, panting, while he pulls away and strips naked with an efficiency I appreciate. He lifts me off the ground, and I wrap my legs around his lean, muscled waist.

His lips find mine, and I taste myself on his tongue. I writhe as I feel his hard length against my thigh, so close but not where I need him.

He pulls back slightly and clicks his tongue. "Patience."

I swear at him as he chuckles and shakes his head. He reaches down positioning himself, and I brush my lips along his neck up to his delicate pointed ear.

"Now," I whimper, unable to wait any longer. At my plea, a growl of pleasure rumbles out of him as he slides into me to the hilt.

I grind against him, moving with him, my back pressed hard against the door. I pant his name. He pushes deeper inside with each thrust. Our foreheads touch, breath mingling as we become one.

Our bodies are slick with sweat as he pulls me off the wall and carries me to the bedroom. He situates himself back against the headboard, sitting on the pillows. I unravel my legs from his waist and reposition myself on his lap. I draw myself up and down on him slowly, marking his scars with my fingers.

When I catch his gaze, his eyes carry an emotion I'm unable to identify. His hands roam my body, tracing the runes on my neck and upper arms lovingly.

He sets fire to each part of me with his cool touch as he caresses my breasts, grabs my ass, bites my earlobe, pushing me closer to the edge.

I change the pace as I feel another orgasm on the verge of bursting through me. I slam down on him and move quickly. He guides my hips and lifts his up to meet my thrusts. He groans as his head hits the headboard with a thump. I increase the speed and he sucks in a breath.

When I feel myself crest the edge, I bite his shoulder. Release pulses through me. I scream and he thrusts a few more times before following me into oblivion.

We sit still for long moments afterward. He stays inside me, a sign we will be at it again soon. I smile as I bury my face into his neck. He smells the way he always does, of cedar and bay leaves. No matter what soap he uses, his natural scent lingers.

I could never tire of this, this bond that had formed between us, that goes deeper than just distractions. Even if I'm not willing to admit it out loud, I care for Braun when I know I shouldn't. He mumbles something I can't hear, and I pull my head up to meet his gaze.

His fingers trace the line of my cheek, but he only shakes his head not willing to repeat the words. Soon we are moving again, satiating our desire for each other. If the world wasn't falling apart, I'd happily stay here with Braun, just like this, forever.

In the early evening, Meli informs us that word has been spread throughout the kingdoms and countries across Alfheim. Another meeting will be held in the morning that they would like us to attend, this time with the royals and emissaries from each country.

———

We enter a large room, decorated similarly to the auditorium we were in yesterday, but with a massive table and chairs. More chairs are placed around the perimeter of the room. Braun described the royals we'd be meeting today and more information about Alfheim than I cared to know late into the evening the night before.

We take a seat but consistently stand as more and more elves flood into the room. I follow Braun's lead on this as I don't know the normal decorum when meeting royals on Alfheim.

I tilt my head as I recognize a woman in Railen's entourage. It's the woman from the bar in Vanire. Taking in her regalia, I notice a small emerald crown resting atop her auburn locks, denoting her heritage.

She certainly isn't a city guard; she is the *princess*. No wonder she could afford the blaster. She nods to me with a smirk, her vivid green eyes sparkle with mischief, before taking a seat next to her father, the King of Railen.

My heart stops and blood runs cold as Braun's brother, Marcus, The King of Haratine, walk into the room with two royal guards and a gorgeous woman trailing behind. Her hair is the same silver-white as the King's and Braun's, but her eyes are an eerie lavender color. *Princess Rowana.*

She is all angles and edges like Braun, but lither where he and his brother are hulking. She gives me a smile full of ice, and I hold it in my glacial gaze while tilting my chin up slightly, not daring to show fear. After a moment she grins, giving me a wink, before taking a seat across from me. I frown, unsure what that interaction meant.

The King appears much as he did on the video in Merin. However, in person the energy he emits is far heavier, as if I can feel his magic wrap around me, blanketing me, but not pleasantly like Braun's magic. It feels intense, electric.

His gray eyes skip over me, landing on Braun. I swear currents run through the room as they note each other's presence. I put my hand into the pocket of my skirt, feeling the hilt of my blade. It warms against my skin, helping my pulse even out.

The King says nothing but takes the seats directly across from Braun, next to his sister. He smirks darkly at Braun until he seems to notice me.

I feel his gaze rake over my body in an unpleasant way, and I suppress the shudder that runs through me as I again lift my chin slightly. I don't dare look at Braun. Marcus turns his gaze back to his brother, raising an eyebrow, and Braun lets out a low growl in response.

Their silent conversation is not lost on the royals and emissaries around us who have leaned forward in their seats, as if they can actually hear them speaking. I am doing it too as I glance between the two brothers. Marcus purses his lips in discontent while Braun merely grins wickedly and leans back in his chair.

Someone at the other end of the table coughs, and those around us snap their attention to it. It is the same head Salazan councilor that spoke in the meeting yesterday.

"Thank you for joining us today. As you are aware we are preparing for an attack on Merin from Loki, the god of mischief, and his cohorts. Salaza has a hundred thousand soldiers, half of whom are inexperienced in battle. We need more soldiers if we are to take on Loki and Ragnarok," says the Salazan representative. Only twenty brigades? Not nearly enough.

"How many would you have us give?" King Marcus asks as he sits back in his chair, the mirror image of Braun in so many ways.

"How ever many you feel comfortable sparing…" the councilman comments. Murmurs go around the room as they confer on whether they even want to help.

"How many soldiers did you have when you fought it?" the older councilwoman from the day before directs towards me.

"Fewer than twenty thousand. We were taken by surprise, plus some of our troops were off world, dealing with political discord elsewhere. As were many of the gods. Loki is smart. He likely knows we are aware he's coming, and he will have already recruited many more to his cause if he was able to take down Nidavellir," I mention as nods of agreement pass through the chamber.

"I can only give you twenty thousand soldiers for this. The rest are too far spread across our cities and regions to get here. We have no transports to offer," King Marcus comments. My eyebrows raise in surprise. I didn't think he'd be the one to offer anything.

"So you expect us to give you some of our soldiers? What if they attack us first instead of Merin?" an emissary of Kyrzik counters, sounding astounded as though no one told him what this meeting would be about.

"It will be easy enough to reposition troops to your borders should Loki strike you first," Marcus counters. The emissary shifts in his seat, uneasy with the direct attention from the powerful elf, but Marcus is right. Kyrzik, a small country who borders Salaza, is only an hour or so away by transport.

"I have a thousand starships and two thousand soldiers to pilot them," says the Royal from Montisan.

I have seen very few starships on Alfheim; I'm surprised they even have them. Different from transports, they are solely meant for battle in atmosphere on a planet and are unable to fly great distances. However, they are incredibly fast, and their laser cannons are some of the most powerful.

"We can give you sixteen thousand," states the wiry old King of Lucia. The royals from Toresk give a quarter of that amount.

"I will be able to spare eight thousand," the Queen of Islas Dragones adds. The small island chain teems with life and breeds hearty warriors. I feel a small breath of relief leave my lungs.

"We won't have enough soldiers to even protect our own borders," the Kyrzik emissary confesses, shaking his head in disappointment. "But we will drop off any weapons and supplies we can tomorrow."

The emissary from Basc tacks on to the Kyrzian emissary's statement and expresses their inability to provide troops as well but promises the same. Tripoli is all but silent in the discussion.

The Princess of Railen stands. "We will only be able to give one thousand and I will lead them." Her father pats her hand proudly as she sits down next to him.

After a moment, those who are unable to help and provide troops bid farewell and walk out. It leaves us with a handful of royals and emissaries from seven of the ten countries to go over plans.

I notice Marcus glancing at Braun every once in a while, and now I understand why Marcus has offered to help. Whether Braun realizes it or not is a mystery, but there's something in Marcus' gaze that tells me all I need to know. It's the same way I looked at my sister. No matter how bad the conflict, love and blood run deeper.

"Your troops need to be here by tomorrow morning. We do not know how soon this attack will occur, so we need to prepare," the Salazan Councilman states.

"We will house troops in tents just inside the retaining wall with medical tents as well. That will be the area we need to focus on protecting. If they get past that wall, then all is lost."

"I will keep to the skies with my men," the Montisan Royal comments. "I will also take whatever starships the other countries have and put them in with mine."

We sit there for hours discussing how to split up the troops and where to station them throughout the city. Then move onto troop formations once Loki comes. Depending on what manner of creatures he brings, it changes our plan.

Our need for those gifted with magic becomes clear. It will be one of the only ways to defeat fire or frost giants if Loki brings any. We argue over the location Loki will attack from.

Though instincts tell me he will come from the oceanside, Loki is too unpredictable to be certain.

The next day flies by as troops settle into the city. Transport ships clog the skies as soldiers come in and civilians flee for the countryside. Tents are set up just behind the retainer wall for troops. We move through the camp, helping set up where needed. It keeps my mind off the waiting.

The second day is quieter, and I become more nervous as we wait and wait and wait. Troops train on the ground, preparing for the battle to come and learning the new formations to keep everything as uniform as possible though these soldiers have never worked together before.

There is no sign of Thor or Vali, and I fear they won't arrive until far too late.

By the third day, I begin to question whether Loki really plans to come here. Thor could have been wrong. Hel could have easily misled him about the location of the next attack to throw us off their scent. Though Thor and Braun seemed sure the information was accurate, and it is nearly impossible for gods to lie.

Rain clouds have gathered overhead, but not a drop has fallen as if it's waiting for the perfect time to downpour.

I awaken as my skin prickles, hairs on the back of my neck stand up in warning. It's still dark out and the city is quiet, but I slip out of Braun's embrace and pad to the front room, pouring myself a glass of water. I turn to the window to study the early morning sky.

I choke on the water as I see the darkness before me. Not the darkness of early morning, but the darkness of hundreds of thousands of dark elves and harpies waiting at the edge of the city.

My heart pounds as I count and recount the numbers. Farther than the human eye can see, they stretch from the edge of the beach to only fifty yards away from the old retaining wall around Merin. More than three hundred thousand against... I sigh.

We have half the number of fighters, some completely inexperienced in battle. Though we have the laser blasters on the starships as well as laser cannons mounted along the retaining wall facing the ocean, I doubt that will help much.

The dark army stands at attention, waiting for the signal, which I have no doubt will come from Loki himself. That *asshole*. He'll show up when it's most convenient for him.

My hand trembles as I put the glass of water on the table and stride into the bedroom to wake Braun. I find he's already sitting on the edge of the bed. I pause, surprised he's up.

"Loki's army is already here," he comments after studying my face for a moment. He runs his hands through his silver hair as I walk towards him and straddle his lap. He buries his face in my neck, inhaling deeply, as if I'm a drug he can't get enough of.

"What if I don't want to fight?" I mumble into his shoulder, and his laugh reverberates through me.

"We must, but we will do it together," he comments. His hands slide to either side of my face gently stroking my cheeks. "No matter what today brings—"

"Don't." I give him a stern look, and my heart aches that he even brings it up. "Don't finish that sentence."

He opens his mouth, but I fix him with the evil eye until he swallows and nods.

"Fine. We'll do it together, nothing more." I smile as I get my way and kiss him passionately.

There is enough heat between us to burn a thousand suns. I aim to distract us, but he growls, gently putting space between us.

"There is not enough time," he says hoarsely. I pout, but he ignores the look and lifts me to my feet. "Get ready, we must go."

Chapter 28

Braun and I stand hand in hand on the retainer wall that surrounds the city of Merin. The massive skyscrapers tower over the original stone wall, built centuries ago.

This is it.

Braun gives my hand a squeeze as if reading my thoughts. The darkness in front of us is expansive, but Loki's army is silent and waiting. Behind them, the ocean seems to roar its anger at the disturbance of this army's presence. Rain drizzles on us lazily.

Our side is just as quiet—though a quiet that has a feel of fear. It seems to affect even me as I bounce my leg and glance at Braun. He nods, agreeing that something must be done.

I adjust my stance and roll my shoulders; the armor we found for me is ill-fitting. I'll probably shed half of it within the first few minutes of battle when I need the freedom to move quickly and easily.

Braun, on the other hand, looks like the god of war in his armor. He wears plated metal with the Haratinian colors on it and a large broadsword strapped to his side I've never seen before.

I spot Marcus and some of the other royals farther down the wall. Next to us stands the Princess Kiera of Railen and her soldiers. Bedecked in bronze armor she is ready for battle.

Below us, a hundred thousand warriors are lined up in

perfect rows. Fifty thousand soldiers, both male and female, rest behind the retainer wall to refresh the troops on the battlefront. So many colors blur together in each section. I hope they are ready to fight together. Otherwise, we are going to have a big problem.

Thor hasn't shown, though he normally wouldn't show up until we desperately needed him. Classic Thor, but this time I fear he and Vali will be too late.

Braun bangs his sword against another elf's metal shield, startling me.

"Listen up!" he shouts, trying to extend his words farther.

"For all my life, I have fought for my kingdom against what I thought were injustices. But this—" He points to the massive army behind us. "This is the greatest injustice of all. One god, a lowly worthless god, does not think you should live. Does not think you are worth keeping around.

"Today we prove him wrong. We stand against Ragnarok, against the darkness that threatens to sweep over this land. Some of us will die, but we will not die in vain, knowing we did everything in our power to stop this..." Braun trails off, as if unsure how to continue. It's so quiet on the field you could hear a pin drop.

"Wonderful, really moving," Princess Kiera murmurs sarcastically. I pat Braun's shoulder in support.

Before Braun can scrape together this speech, Marcus picks it up, as if sensing Braun is just going to muddle it more. He clears his throat.

"This army we see is full of weak-hearted, arrogant creatures. Some who only lust for your blood and flesh." Marcus pauses and I immediately think of the harpies. They seem to watch us as though we are delicacies.

"You are strong, brave, and valiant elves. Let's show these pieces of shit how we greet unwelcome guests in Alfheim.

Fight with me. Fight with me!

"And we will water the sand with their blood. We will bring glory to all elves. Today is the day we show the gods—no the entirety of the Nine Realms—that we are not folly to their whims. We will not bow down to another race, to a god that is not our own."

Below us the warriors let out a deafening roar, so loud the retainer wall shakes beneath us. I am awed by his speech's impact on the elves below. Still, the dark army in front of us does nothing; doesn't even flinch at the show of force.

Light flashes at the back of the army, and I know *he* has arrived. I can feel it in my bones. Next to him is a dark wolf, as large as a horse. I huff a breath; shocked Loki got his son involved. Fenrir was always a grey area on where he stood with his father, but he was kind to me. Fenrir's betrayal to Asgard hurts more than Loki's.

I nudge Braun, but he's already seen it as well. The dark army parts as Loki walks through his ranks. The noise they make as he passes is thunderous. His jet-black armor matches his hair, allowing him to blend in with those around him.

Monstrous. He holds no weapon, but I know he rarely needs one to exact the punishment he finds most fitting for his victims.

"Well, well, I see someone warned you I was coming. I would say it's a pity, but I am excited to finally see some real action. Crushing Nidavellir and Asgard was almost too easy." His voice carries on the wind to us.

"Is that my dearest Vera I see?" I stiffen next to Braun as Loki squints his eyes and shields them, as if he's not quite sure it's me. "Eager to die?"

"Eager to finish what you've started." I murmur, knowing he can hear me perfectly. His eyes twinkle in delight.

He loves this part, the calm before the storm. I can see the terror on the soldiers' faces on the front lines, and I know he will mow them down in seconds. I glance at Braun who senses I'm about to do something reckless, but he's too slow as I jump over the side of the retainer wall, free-falling before I land amongst the soldiers below.

The impact jars my body, but only slightly, and I feel like I am floating as I walk through the soldiers towards Loki. Everything he has done to me flashes before me and rage bubbles just below the surface of my calm facade.

Braun curses as he starts to move along the retainer wall to the stairs. Harsh whispers reach my ears as Marcus stops him, just as I expected. *Good*, he doesn't need to be a part of this. I stop at the front lines, and the soldiers around me adjust to my presence.

"You don't have to do this Loki." I feel the madness roll off him in waves.

"Oh, but I do so enjoy it," he gives me a wicked grin. I take another step and another until we are practically nose to nose.

"Don't do this, Lo," I whisper. His smile falters, hearing my old nickname for him. Just as quickly his smile is gone, replaced by a sneer.

"It's time everyone knows my power and understands that it's my turn to rule. You will not stand in my way," he spits, stepping back.

He lifts his hand in the air and drops it. The army behind him lets out a roar of rage as its front lines sprint towards us, towards me. My sword shimmers into existence, but as I slash at Loki, he has already vanished. I grit my teeth as the massive wave of dark elves rolls towards me.

Blaster cannons from the retainer wall shoot out lasers and turn everything in their path to ash and dust. They are reliable, but they take ten minutes between each blast to reload with the energy needed.

Overhead, the roar of starships surges as the harpies take

to the sky, diving down to pick off our soldiers. The starship blasters are smaller and take less time to reload, but it doesn't take much for harpies to bring them down if they work together.

It has been so long since I've been on a battlefield, I've forgotten the chaos that ensues. I let out a cry and sprint towards the dark elves that charge us. The sands beneath us shake as feet pound towards each other.

The twang of loosed arrows fills my ears as they fall towards the dark elves, darkening the sky for quiet moments before they find their marks. And as the two armies collide, there is the sickening crunch of armor being smashed. Songs of metal hitting metal ring out. Swords and spears rip through flesh and armor all around me.

I block out the sound and focus only on killing as many as I can, as fast as I can.

I duck under the blade of one dark elf, slipping past him, and thrust my sword backward between his shoulder blades quickly, lethally. As I pull my weapon free, a spear comes at me from the side, and I step back, my sword snapping off the tip of the spear.

The dark elf doesn't seem bothered by this and he swings a dagger in his other hand. It catches my shoulder, but my armor deflects it. I twirl my blade and cut his head clean off. I don't wait for his body to fall to the ground before moving on.

I whip my head around to survey the area as a buzzing sound builds behind me. Our soldiers seem to hold the dark elves back better than I expected, but many of us are past the demarcation line and will surely be cremated to tiny bits of ash by the blaster cannons if we don't fall back. *Shit, shit, shit.*

My legs churn through the sand as I run away from the demarcation line. I continue to cut through dark elves that have slipped past our front lines as I go.

"Fall back! Fall back!" I call to the soldiers around me, pointing to the blaster cannons on the retainer. Some lookup and begin to run back as well, but not all. The buzzing grows louder, and I know the cannons are seconds away from going off.

The cherry-red laser light glows in the mouths of the cannons just before they shoot out another succession of blasts. I hit the ground and hope it passes above me. Heat singes the back of my armor, turning it molten hot, but the clothes underneath seem to keep my skin from melting off my body. I grunt in pain as the heated metal burns the back of my neck where it touches.

I lay there for a second longer until arms pull me up, and Braun's face comes into view. His eyes are full of white rage, probably pissed at me for starting the fight without him. Motion out of the corner of my eye catches my attention, and the view of more dark elves charging us turns my mood grim.

Fenrir gallops close behind them.

Braun pulls me behind him as if to protect me, but I push out of his grasp and move next to him. "Together, remember?" I say to him sternly.

"I've got the dog," he says, and I nod, thankful for Braun. While he doesn't know what Fenrir once was to me, I don't think I could take Fenrir's life.

We fight off the dark elves in our way, but we hold our position. We don't want to be in range of those blaster cannons again.

A yelp has me glancing to see Braun in a deadly dance with Fenrir. The large wolf lashes out then jumps away but doesn't make it out of range of Braun's sword that scores deep into his paw. I kick and punch whenever dark elves get too close to me before I slash through them and leave them in bloody heaps at my feet.

My armor is streaked with the blue blood of dark elves, and wherever I step my feet sink deep in the sand. It pulls on my boots, trying to suction them to the earth, and makes it harder and harder to maneuver. I push back against the dark elf in front of me, only to find myself being lifted off the ground.

Long claws dig into my armor on my shoulder, and the harpy laughs when I look up at it. I swing my sword and slice through its right leg with a wicked crunch. It screeches in pain as its black oily blood rains on me. It drops me moments later, and I tumble to the ground and land on top of two dark elves who fight against our soldiers.

Our soldiers help me up, and I am luckily unscathed other than bruised shoulder muscles. My chest plate is cracked, and the shoulder armor now pinches my skin. I pull off both.

Battle has an odd way of wearing on you. What feels like fifteen minutes is suddenly an hour; what feels like an hour is actually several. Time warps to condense yet slow down, each individual fight folding into the larger one. It has quieted on the battlefield as more and more of our soldiers fall right alongside the dark elves.

Daylight quickly fades, but the battle around us rages. The din of fighting has fallen into a steady rhythm: the rush of breath, the grunts of blows hitting their marks, and panting of soldiers slogging through wet sand. The sighs of last breaths taken, and the smell of refuse fills the air. The sand beneath us soaked in blood. The blue of the elves, both dark and light, turns the lavender sand a putrid brown.

I long for my wings as my arms and legs ache. To be able to soar above and ambush some of those damn harpies. My usual finesse is lost in the duration of the battle as I dodge blades lazily. Even with my enhanced strength that matches an elf, we are all weary.

It is unusual for battles to continue into the evening, but we all have night vision, outside of the harpies. There is no reason to stop, to not push the advance, if possible, though it feels like we've hit a stalemate hours ago.

More and more die around us, but for what? Loki's

fucking precious pride. Not that I care much for dark elves, but it blows my mind that they follow him so willingly. No fear. It may be the only feature of dark elves I'm jealous of.

I've long ago lost Braun, somewhere in the chaos of fighting. He could be ten feet from me or a mile behind, but I am constantly swarmed by the enemy. I cannot pause.

My breath becomes jagged, and my strength flags a bit more. I briefly consider just stopping, to sit down for a few minutes and hide among the dead that litters the ground around my feet.

Just then, a dark elf in front of me charges. I sigh accepting that the impact of this hit will be jarring. My eyes are heavy with the need for rest. As I ready myself to feint to the right, hopefully to avoid the worst of the hit, a arm wraps around my waist and hauls me to the left.

Even through the smell of refuse, of blood and death, familiar scents of cedar and sweat waft over me. I know it's Braun. He slaughters the dark elf while crushing my back to his chest. He lifts me enough that my feet dangle as he whirls us around heading back towards the retaining wall.

Soldiers take our places and hold back the dark elves. I almost push away from Braun, but he's managed to trap my sword against his arm. If I move too roughly, it will surely slice open his bicep.

Somehow, he manages to carry me in one arm, my feet dragging slightly over the dead bodies we climb past, while he mows down any that get in our path. His assurance that no one will attack from behind astounds me. He drops me once we are near the wall, where fresh troops start to march out.

"Rest," he grunts, taking my hand and dragging me behind him.

I'm too tired to protest, but I stop at the top of the retainer wall. The scene below is gruesome. Soldiers are dragged off the field by medics or other soldiers to be healed behind the walls if possible. Meanwhile the injured or dying dark elves are pushed away or stacked on top of each other in piles, regardless of if they are still breathing.

By their own kind. As if their inability to fight makes them worthless.

The screams coming from the piles of dark elves are almost unbearable. I briefly consider having the blaster cannons on the wall turned towards those piles and cremating them all to ash, just to put them out of their misery. It would be better than the slow death they receive currently. But then again, I'm not that decent.

I remind myself that they aid the god who has caused me such despair and heartache. I remind myself of the screams and death I saw on Asgard before it fell. They deserve this ending, and I will not feel guilty about it. I will not lose sleep over it.

Braun tugs my arm once, a silent plea to follow him. I turn away from the scene below and do not look back.

Chapter 29

I DON'T REMEMBER FALLING ASLEEP, but I do remember Braun yelling at a group of volunteers. "Find us a tent," he'd practically roared. They scattered like mice, and I leaned heavily into him as we stood there waiting.

He sheathed his sword and pocketed mine as the blade disappeared, before cradling me in his arms. I only meant to close my eyes for a moment, but I awoke to pre-dawn light filling a white canvas tent with shadows and Braun's heavy arm, roped with muscle, around my middle.

He must have been just as exhausted because both of us are still fully clothed and covered in the gore of yesterday. I shift out of Braun's embrace, needing to pee, and stifle a groan as I sit up. Every inch of my body hurts, as if I worked out all day yesterday.

Then I remember, that's basically what I did. I grab some clothes that have been left in the corner of the tent and locate bathing rooms set up a few tents away. While cleaning off the gore, I find sand in more places than I care to admit.

The clash of swords and the sound of laser blasters just beyond the wall echo through the bathing tent, setting my teeth on edge. Dread pours through me as I think about going out there only to sink into sand soaked with blood and entrails. I run my hands through my wet hair, braiding it efficiently.

As I walk back to the tent Braun and I shared, I find it

empty except for our armor, which is strewn about. I roll my eyes and pick up my sword hilt and pocket it. Next, I strap on the metal greaves across my shins and cinch the lower parts of the vambrace on my forearms over the light chainmail shirt. I lost the pauldrons and chest plate in battle yesterday, but I'm better off without them anyway.

I'm about to head out the flap of the tent when Braun comes striding in, nearly crashing into me. "Watch it," I huff as he grabs my waist and pulls me to him. He merely grunts, dipping his head to mine, and kisses me deeply.

His drenched hair splashes water on my cheek. My toes curl in my boots as warmth runs through me. Ideas flood my mind of what we could be doing in this tent instead of slaughtering dark elves. I frown when he pulls away and puts on his armor, but don't protest when he pulls me out of the tent moments later.

We walk to a mess hall, and I shove as much food down as I can manage, I'll need all the strength I can get. Today we will see the fire giants of Muspelheim and the ice giants from Jotunheim; I have no doubt of it as they were not present yesterday.

As I think to ask Braun about it, someone plops down on the bench next to me. I slowly turn to survey none other than the Princess of Railen. In full armor again today, Princess Kiera looks like a beacon of hope in a dark world. Her armor glints in non-existent sunlight.

She nods at me and Braun before digging into her plate that is piled high. Her soldiers sit down, acknowledging us as they do.

"We'll be using all sorts of magic today," the princess comments to Braun, her mouth so full of food as she talks it comes out garbled.

For a princess, she's incredibly unladylike and it makes me like her even more. She pushes some of her food off her plate and onto Braun's. I huff a laugh as I watch him decide whether to heed her advice or not.

When he starts eating, she adds, "Smart man."

I catch King Marcus and Princess Rowana staring at us from across the mess hall. Braun turns towards them when he notices my attention is elsewhere. He nods at them, and I frown as they nod back.

Rowana wears a cold smirk but harbors no ice in her lilac gaze. It would appear they had worked out their issues with Braun. Something I'll ask Braun about later. When they found the time to hash it out, I'm not sure. Maybe the silent conversations are a family trait.

We walk out together onto the retainer wall, and soldiers part around us as we survey the battle below. The dark elves have fallen back but dug deep into the sand, forming trenches. I immediately think of the Midgardian wars fought this way.

Our side continues to fire the blaster cannons from the wall, moving them slightly each time to evaporate more of the dark elves, but our forces remain behind the wall currently. The elves make almost no attempt to advance, so we don't either. I don't see Loki or the giants anywhere.

"They are waiting," I comment.

"For what?" Princess Kiera asks.

"Reinforcements," Braun adds. "Push the advance, get the starships in the sky and take out as many as we can."

He calls to the Montisan commander who stands close by along the wall. The commander gives a weary nod in agreement before motioning to runners behind the retainer wall to get the starships skyward.

"The minute those fire giants appear, we need to pull as much water as possible from the reserves." I think of the water we moved in massive vats to the sides of the retainer wall. "It's the only way to kill them. Loki will try to bring them in the middle of the battlefield and keep them away from the water's edge," I add.

The princess yells to the magic-wielding elves behind the retainer wall that have been reserving their energy for this. I feel their magic ripple through the tents on our side as the elves sit silently or even meditate, preparing to manipulate their element.

The flash of light behind the trenches alerts us. "They're here."

Braun's hand lands on my shoulder as the red-hot light of fire giants shoots up from the trenches. Even with how powerful Braun's magic is, it won't be much use today, it's too exhausted from the day before.

As the fire giants move out of the trenches, harpies shoot to the skies. More than double yesterday's numbers, but before they get too far, the low hum of engines cuts through the din of armies moving into formation. Starships circle around and fall into place next to each other from behind the dark army, the wings of each aircraft barely a few feet apart from each other.

One wrong move would mean death.

They thrust all forward engines towards the harpies, splattering many caught unaware from behind, while the guns on the ships rain hues of different molten hot laser light onto the dark elves below.

One starship dips too close to the ground and is immediately snatched up by a fire giant. Its flames melt the craft until the engine explodes.

"Now!" Braun commands. Laukaz elves rush to the retainer wall, their hands ready to manipulate the water we hid in reservoirs days ago. Water bursts into the sky from either side of the retainer wall. The elves work together with deadly accuracy. The clear liquid spirals and twists as it batters the first line of fire giants.

The fire giants crash down as their cores of flame are extinguished by the water, the lava morphing into hard rock. The

Laukaz elves step back with a cheer and leave room for the Veoor elves to take out the next row. They push wind through the giants' bodies, finding open pockets to shove air through to snuff out their flaming cores.

The earth trembles as the fire giants fall heavily to the ground. The elves continue to switch back and forth bringing down more and more fire giants. Harpies start to swarm above us, but archers are quick to pick them off.

Ignis elves move forward on the retainer wall when the frost giants of Jotunheim appear. The Ignis elves pull flames from the fire giants and punch them through the frost giants, using their elements against one another.

Finally, dark elves pour out of the trenches. For all we've killed there are somehow more than expected. Loki must have rallied more troops here. Just as I think of the god, he crests the lip of the trench and I flinch.

He wears the exact same armor he did when he tore down Asgard. His silver helm and armor are shot through with electric purple. Braun must have noticed the shift in my demeanor because he pulls me from view, behind the magic-wielding elves and the archers.

He runs his hand up my cheek and looks like he's about to say something heart wrenching. Something to distract me, but I know whatever he says will stay with me long after the moment ends. Something that will continue to distract me even in battle.

So, I don't let him.

Instead, I tug his mouth to mine and kiss him passionately before I take off along the retainer wall, down the stairs, and melt into the ranks of elves marching out of our side. I know he's next to me though he says nothing. I can feel his intense presence.

Princess Kiera and her soldiers aren't far behind us as we form lines in front of the retainer wall and avoid the harpies dropping from the sky to their death. Lava rock rubble and half melted frost giants lay in piles across the blood-soaked sand. The cloud cover breaks, drenching us the early light of morning.

I tilt my face to it for a moment, and when I look back, I see a limping Fenrir and Loki moving lithely between the remaining fire and frost giants. Loki didn't fight yesterday from what I can tell—just immediately disappeared after his arrival. The bastard.

A horn blasts across the field, our signal to start the ground assault. A growl bursts from Braun as we begin to sprint towards the front lines of the dark elves spearing forward. A glance at him tells me he isn't done fighting Fenrir. They must have gotten too tangled up in other battles yesterday to finish what was started.

Our front-line cuts through the first rows of dark elves' long spears, snapping them off at the tips, jumping over them completely, or hurtling through them. We are vicious in our attack today. So many of us are battered and bruised from yesterday, we want this done quickly. I am pushed to the ground by Braun as ice blasts towards us from a frost giant. It takes out just as many dark elves as our soldiers.

More than double the height of an average human, the frost giants' feet shake the sand beneath us with each step they take. Their mere presence chills the air here, so at odds with the fire giants. We maneuver around them as we stand to avoid their blasts and swipes of ice.

Fenrir engages Braun again and, to my dismay, Loki moves to the far right of the battlefield, far from me. The hum of a laser cannon charge makes me smile, and within seconds the two frost giants in front of us are no more than puddles of slushy water.

Dark elves rush forward to stand where the frost giants were moments earlier. I dodge a thrust of a dark elf, whipping my sword around so quickly its head rolls before I have time to process it. Another is upon me as I take a step forward. It wields a morning star, and the spikes on the ball at the end of the chain gleam wickedly.

The dark elf hefts it overhead, swinging it around, but it accidentally crunches a soldier next to us instead of me. As the dark elf moves to pull it from the body and swing again, I use the opening to my advantage. Flipping my grip on my sword, I angle it through the dark elf's shoulder, hitting the dark heart inside. I pull the sword free, and it staggers for a moment before dropping to the ground face-first.

I keep going and try to remain closer to Braun this time, though after what feels like moments, I find he is farther away. He skids under Fenrir's hulking form and pushes his broadsword deep into Fenrir's chest. Fenrir stumbles to the side, unable to get up, but I am engaged by more dark elves before I have time to see anything else.

Like the day before, time moves at an unknown pace, but I barely move from my spot. I don't want to be in the range of the laser cannons, so I let other soldiers rush past me to dark elves further behind the enemy's front lines. The elves scramble back each time they hear the charge of the cannon begin.

I am already hungry again, despite the large breakfast I had not a half-hour ago. Has it only been a half-hour? I look up to find the suns directly overhead and they beam down as if trying to lighten the grim mood I'm in. It has definitely been at least a few hours.

As I'm dragged back to the battle and scene in front of me, a grunt cuts clear through the mayhem of the battlefield, and I look over. Braun brings his sword down on Loki, still on the attack.

Fenrir lies close by on his side panting his last breaths. Braun must have finished him off this morning with renewed energy.

Loki toys with Braun. If he wanted Braun dead, it would

take only the swipe of his blade. Braun limps slightly and blue blood seeps through the armor along his thigh. Dread runs through me as I watch Loki's sword slip past Braun's guard.

I scream Braun's name as Loki's sword pierces his chest. The blade cuts through armor, flesh, and bone like butter. Loki laughs heartily as he pulls out his blade and Braun falls to his knees, but Loki's eyes are on me.

This is what he was waiting for.

I hurdle past dark elves and slash through whoever dares to stand in my way as I rush towards them. Just as Braun's about to fall forward, I slide on the sandy, muddy ground, pulling him into my lap. I apply pressure to Braun's chest, but warm blood continues to pour out of the wound.

I don't even care if Loki kills me now as my vision narrows the scope of battle to just this face. Braun's breath is shallow, and I know without a doubt that there is little I can do for him. Loki lets out a sigh and shakes his head as I glare up at him. Before I can scream at Loki, Braun tilts my face back to his.

"Vera," he whispers, "you have to know that I lo—"

I shush him as my blood-splattered hand cups his cheek.

He chuckles, but it's more of a cough as blue blood drips from the side of his mouth. His grey eyes are already dull.

"So stubborn. You can't save me this time, Vera, but all that I am, every piece of me is yours." His fingers squeeze mine. "Remember the promise you made Edda." He taps the tattoo hidden beneath my clothes on the inner part of my right arm. "Thank you for showing me true happiness."

I murmur words, pleading with him not to go. My forehead presses to his as he takes his last breaths and my heart crumbles as I watch the life drain from his face.

Loki laughs before mocking me. "Poor, poor Vera. Her mate is gone. What ever will she do now?" I stiffen at the word Loki uses.

Mate.

Valkyrie don't have mates, maybe partners, but the idea of an eternal bond of one's soul to another that is mating is not even in our vocabulary. Yet as I hear that word, I feel its truth. I kiss Braun's forehead and say the words in my mind that I can't say out loud.

I do not let my tears fall as I gently lay his body on the ground. I bottle them up as my rage consumes me. Loki has ruined everything for me again and again. Now he's mine to end.

"I will fucking kill you!" I holler.

My sword stabs air as he uses illusion to shift his position from my right to my left. He punches me in my side. I stumble but am not deterred. He could break every bone in my body and the pain would still be more manageable than the pain of losing all the people I love.

Our swords clash again and again, and he laughs as he relishes the game we play. It is not a game for me; it stopped being a game the moment I watched Loki push his blade through Odin's heart.

Around us dark elves stream forward towards Alfheimian soldiers, ignoring us. It's as if we are alone, though we have to avoid tripping over the fallen that litter the ground and the now black sand that tries to grab at our feet. I pull the small dagger from its sheath and will all my strength into it as I slip past Loki's guard and swipe across his arm.

I know I cannot kill him; I am not a god, but this blade, Baldr's blade, can at least do some serious damage. Loki howls in pain, and his arm is severed from the elbow down. The dagger hums with magic, and it begs me to seek the vengeance I crave.

Loki recovers enough to continually block my attacks. I pant and beads of sweat begin to fall into my eyes. I stumble in a hole in the sand and bark out in paid as I roll my ankle.

Loki doesn't wait and thrusts his blade into my ribs. I

hear the wicked sound of snapping as my ribs crack on impact and the wind is knocked out of me from the blow. I bellow in pain and anger as I swipe the dagger in a deadly blow that cuts Loki's chest from shoulder to hip. His blood splatters my face and neck, and Loki lets go of his sword as he falls backward in pain.

I try to pull his blade out of my ribs, but black spots dance in my vision and pain lances through my whole body. Blood pours out of the wound as the blade finally comes free. I grunt as I push my hand against the wound to stop the bleeding, but my energy fades, and my body becomes almost too heavy to carry.

I stumble forward and land on my knees as I watch Loki flail in front of me. Blood squirts from his missing arm and rolls down the gash in his chest plate. He curses at me and yells at his comrades for help, though none come. Even if I can't kill Loki, at least I did some irreparable damage.

Thank you, Baldr.

Thunder claps loudly as clouds gather overhead. I tilt my head to the sky when clouds collide together, and a new round of steady rain sets in. Water plops on my face in fat drops, washing away some of the blue blood splattered there.

My breath rattles in my chest and I am so tired, but I look back to Loki and pause as I see who stands in front of him.

Thor.

The bastard finally came through. Lightning wraps around him and he shines like a beacon on the battlefield. Thunder booms again as if to announce Thor's arrival. Around us, new gods and fresh troops from Vanaheim pop into existence.

Above Thor, harpies latch on to a starship blasting the dark elves below, but I spot white wings and a wicked blade slicing through the harpies and I smile.

Valkyrie.

I smile because I'm not the only one left. My sisters have come, and their vengeance will be a terrifying and magnificent thing to behold.

I smile because I watch as Thor's hammer crunches into the side of Loki's head so hard it rips it off his body and sends it flying through the air.

I smile as Thor doesn't even wait to see where it lands before turning to me. He murmurs something, but I can't understand him. Can't hear anything above the roaring in my ears, my vison cloudy and unfocused.

I smile knowing my tasks are complete and now, I can drift to Valhalla to be with my family and sisters again and maybe, just maybe I'll see Braun.

Chapter 30

WARM WHITE LIGHT IS THE first thing I register. I suppose this is what greets you in Valhalla. I slowly peel open my eyes only to quickly cover them with my arm and swear. Pain lances through my ribs at the movement. I frown, I thought I wouldn't feel pain here.

I blink my eyes quickly and find myself staring at the ceiling. A ceiling that looks far too familiar. Almost exactly like the room Braun and I shared in Merin on Alfheim. I pant when trying to sit up, pushing through the pain in my torso.

After a few minutes, I lean my head back against the headboard in victory. Footsteps sound and I look up to see a Valkyrie. Her wings and body are covered in blood of varying shades of black, blue, and red. Her red hair is pulled into tight braids, and her creamy skin is caked with sand.

"Axis?" I croak, surprised to see her.

She smirks at me before lightly sitting at the edge of the bed. She hands me a glass of water. I take a small sip and place it on the nightstand.

"I'm alive, aren't I?" I ask meekly. She nods solemnly. I sigh and run my hands through my hair to find it still coated with blood and dirt. "Care to explain?"

"Well, after you passed out, Thor brought you to medics behind the retainer wall." She smirks. "You were patched up by the medics there, plus your healing kicked in." Normally it would have taken longer to heal knowing a god blade pierced me.

"I figured you'd been injured, the martyr that you are." I pinch her for that, and she hisses. "Found you being shaken by some feeble female elf who kept trying to wake you and ask about someone named Braun." I snort realizing she's talking about Meli, who was unsurprisingly not concerned about my wellbeing. "So, I asked her nicely for directions."

"You yelled at her, didn't you?"

Axis merely shrugs. "You were injured, and you didn't need someone nagging you while you rested."

She watches me closely as my hands move across the sheets on the bed, the ones I've now ruined with blood and dirt, the ones I spent tangled with Braun in only the other day. Even hearing Axis mention Braun's name is like a punch to the gut. A shaky breath leaves my mouth.

"Someone you cared about?" she asks softly.

I nod, swallowing the lump in my throat. "What happened after Loki died?" I glance out the bedroom window to my right. There is smoke from the beach beyond, making it hard to see anything.

"We finished off most of the dark elves and harpies. The frost and fire giants somehow vanished." I nod knowing the goddess Hel, Loki's daughter, probably coordinated the retreat. "With Loki gone, it looks like our job here is done."

She smiles and I burst into tears, unable to reconcile the loss of another loved one with the fact that I'm still alive.

"I'm so sorry about your wings," she murmurs and awkwardly pats my hand.

"I lost them in Ragnarok," I explain when I realize she thinks I only just lost them, thus explaining my sadness. She brushes her own wings reassuringly as if unable to imagine being so nonchalant over the loss of them. "Where were you?"

"I got some Asgardians to Vanaheim, but Loki sent spies

everywhere to root us out. So, we hid high in the mountains there. We got your Valkyrien call, Vera. That's how we knew to find Vali and Thor. That's how we knew to come here." Even through my anguish, my heart soars knowing that some Asgardians did survive after all.

"We? Are there any oth—" I stop mid-sentence as two more Valkyrie walk in.

Kellin, whose dark skin and hair are also flecked in blood, comes into sight first, followed by Johanna. Johanna's platinum blonde hair and golden skin make her look like a poster child for the Valkyrie.

Once I would have hated for them to see me cry, the ultimate sign of weakness in Valkyrie, but I don't care anymore. I burst into tears for the second time and Johanna pulls me into a tight embrace. I feel another set of arms wrap around us, then another.

We hold each other as we mourn the loss of so many of our sisters, our families, friends, and lovers. We sit there for a long moment before they draw back, all of us still covered in the gore of battle.

They tell me of their time in Vanaheim and the loss of other transports that landed there, just like the one I found in Yulamic that held Rhodda. All in all, only one hundred and fifty Asgardians remain and three—now four Valkyrie.

I tell them about finding Rhodda and the graves on Midgard. I tell them about my new friends Mai and Braun and our adventures on Alfheim and Midgard. We all shift between crying and laughing through each story.

At some point, there is a knock at the door. A disheveled Meli appears, and Kellin has to hold back Axis from handing out another tongue lashing. Meli mumbles that they haven't found Braun's body. As much as I hate the female, I remind myself that I'm lucky I got those last few moments with him. I got to tell him how I feel. I gave him a Valkyrie's goodbye, a true warrior's burial.

I am lucky to get this confirmation, that he's somewhere in Valhalla finding eternal peace and someday I'll be with him again. I'm reminded of something Edda once said, 'In the end, we are all just stars crossing paths for a blazing second, but in that moment something magical happens...we are touched by someone else's light.'

Braun's light was all for me, even if it was only for a blip in time, I will cherish him forever. I nod to her and murmur my apologies as I see how distraught she is. She disappears down the hall, and Johanna is the first to use the shower to clean up.

I pull out all my spare clothes for them even though we aren't the same height or size. My fingers pause as I spot Braun's clothes sitting in the drawers beside mines. I glance at his pack shoved into the back of the closet and I want to go through it, but I'm so raw that I know better than to try.

Chapter 31

A FEW WEEKS LATER, I stare out a window of the Paris apartment overlooking the balcony and backyard. I'm glad I rented this place. It keeps my happy memories alive now that Braun is gone. Since my sisters-in-arms and I found each other, I convinced them to come to Paris with me at least for a little bit.

To my surprise, Mai was conveniently already here when we arrived, saying that she didn't want us to miss her too much. The Valkyrie stay in an apartment nearby with more beds and only go out in the evening because their wings are visible. I rub my chest at the sharp pain that hits me as my mind wanders to Braun and Edda.

"Seriously that outfit looks like trash." I roll my eyes, hearing Mai comment to Axis in the living room. Those two bicker constantly, like an old married couple, making the rest of us want to be somewhere, anywhere, else.

"Don't fuck with me today, Mai. I'm not in the mood," Axis' gravelly voice throws back.

"Pity," is all Mai says in return.

Someone pads into the bedroom. As an arm comes around my shoulders, Kellin tilts her head against mine, her floral scent encasing me. Her charcoal eyes take in the backyard below as well.

"Those two are minutes away from doing one of two things," she murmurs. I raise my eyebrows at her. "Fucking or fighting."

I snort. "I don't think I want to be here for either of those events."

"If it is the latter then Mai will be decimated," Kellin states.

"If it comes to that, Mai deserves it," I joke.

Just then Mai yells at me from the living room, and Kellin and I share a look before going into the other room. I wonder what topic Mai and Axis are arguing about now, though maybe Axis left to take a walk on the roof for the third time today.

We could hear her stomping on the roof at an ungodly hour this morning. As fiery as her hair, she's easy to push and Mai seems to enjoy it thoroughly. There is never a dull moment with Mai around.

I run my hands over my face. I am more tired than I should be, but sleep doesn't easily come these days.

Kellin and I walk towards the living room to find Mai nervously wringing her hands, and I see three men sitting on the couch. Axis and Johanna kneel before them. As I turn to face them, I gasp and drop to one knee, lowering my head.

Kellin follows suit. Thor chuckles, sitting casually, and picks off a piece of lint from his jacket. Next to him are two ancient men. Though 'men' is not the right word to describe them. *Gods*.

The left one smiles with kind emerald eyes. Vili, the god of creation and one of Odin's two brothers, sits there calmly. In robes of cream, he is resplendent even in his wrinkled age. Next to him sits Odin's second brother, Ve.

Together with Odin they were the gods of creation. I rack my brain to understand. They were supposedly killed over one hundred and fifty years ago. Odin even mourned for them for ten years after they were supposedly killed in the battle against the frost giants on Jotunheim.

"H-how?" I stammer after a long moment.

Ve gives me a terrifying smirk. "We knew Odin wanted the power for himself, so we hid off-world right when the fighting started on Jotunheim. Just before Ragnarok was brought to Alfheim, Thor found us." I shake my head, unable to think.

"You have fought for Asgard harder than any before. Come closer." Vili waves his gnarled hand towards me. He takes my hand and places his other on top, closing his eyes. "What sorrows plague you," he murmurs, and I swallow the lump in my throat.

I'll lose it if Vili mentions their names. He opens his eyes, and they are brilliant green. White power pushes through his hands into mine. I stiffen at first, but I relax when I realize it doesn't hurt. His magic flashes brightly and Mai gasps. Suddenly, I am exhausted, and my back aches as though it carries the weight of the world.

"For your efforts to find our people, to save our people and the elves. It is the least we can do."

I see white in the corner of my eye over my shoulder and tears prick the corners of my eyes. Not daring to believe it, I run to the hall mirror and practically trip over the added weight. As I stand in front of the mirror, my hands tremble when they reach behind me to brush the soft white feathers.

My wings. Tears stream down my face as I spread them wide. It takes more strength than before, and my back muscles already protest, but I don't care.

"I've made a small adjustment to them, something my selfish brother would have never thought of." Ve smirks as he hobbles over to me. "When you need to blend in, simply wish them away. We have given this to Johanna and Axis as well." He waves his hand as if clearing smoke.

I nod, unable to even vocalize my thanks. I look at my sisters who look at me in turn. Vili takes Kellin's hand, giving her the same power. I wish Braun could see this, and I am hit with a tidal wave of sadness as I think of that stupid elf.

"We have one more thing to discuss with you," Vili comments from the living room. I close my eyes and put on a brave face.

Epilogue

I AM MESMERIZED AS I walk through the streets. Unable to believe that this is real and here, I touch everything I pass. Only a few weeks have passed and now this entire planet exists again.

The city is quiet and waits to be occupied with more Asgardians returning home as well as new ones that have yet to be created or made immortal. Jane, Kellin, and Axis went back to Vanaheim to bring the Asgardians back. Mai made me promise she could join us here in Asgard soon, much to the annoyance of Axis.

This place is so different from the Asgard that existed before, but what Vili and Ve created is better. A fresh start, untainted by war, blood, and death. I fly towards the city center where a new palace now stands. It's made of stone, in varying shades of brown, orange, and white much like the rest of the city, and much more simplistic in its design, though it still feels just as important as the old one.

The Holy Mountains to the east and north have been resurrected, though the labyrinth of stone tunnels are long gone taking the old gods with them. Another piece we will need to rebuild.

The verdant fields to the south have yet to be tended to, and grasses and shrubs grow with wild abandon. So much like the Asgard from before and yet, now, it can be whatever we wish.

I can be whatever I wish. Whoever I wish. Still a Valkyrie, the call runs through me to protect, to ferry, to decide, but this time it will be different. We already decided. We would be different. We would be better.

As I soar past the towering palace entrance through the outer stone wall, there are no guards to monitor it. There is no one here to take up that job. I land and wander through the eerily quiet halls until I hear voices. I walk towards the sound, assuming I will find Vili and Ve.

"What do you mean she's not here yet?" a familiar voice demands just as I'm about to walk in.

I stop dead in my tracks. A muffled answer comes from another in the room. My heartbeat picks up speed. There is no way the person that voice belongs to is here.

"So, what am I to do, just wait?" the male asks. Someone stomps through the room loudly before flinging open the door. Thor looks surprised to see me but smiles.

"You're here, Thank Odi—" he winces, catching himself before finishing. Odin is long dead. We will not use his name anymore. "I thought I'd be doing you a favor having Vili and Ve fix him up, but now I'm not so sure. Really, I don't know how you put up with him. Just complains all the time." He jerks his head inside the room and winks.

My body trembles as I step into the room.

"You're welcome!" he calls from down the hall.

The male's back is to me, but his silver-white hair shines in light that floods the open room. I stop breathing altogether as he turns to me. He gives me a crooked smile, his grey eyes luminous, and he strides towards me. My feet move without thought as I run towards him.

I jump on him, knocking him backwards. His chuckle moves me to tears. Happy tears. He runs his hands through my hair and down my body, but I can only stare into those storm cloud eyes I love.

He traces his fingers across my cheeks and lips. "I-Is this real?" I stammer.

He chuckles and nods. His breath mingles with mine as he leans close. The kiss he gives me is full of passion, of love. A deep sigh of contentment slips out of Braun as I mumble his name in between kisses, over and over again.

Braun. Braun. Braun. I'm unable to fathom how he's here, how he's alive, but I realize in this moment, I don't care. My heart bursts with happiness. He sits up, pulling me onto his lap, and I rest my head against his chest.

"I missed you," I whisper on a shaky breath.

He kisses the top of my head. "I missed you more."

He runs a hand over my wings, causing a shudder to surge through me. "I love these," he murmurs in awe as he continues to lightly trace them with his fingertips, and I hum in pleasure at his touch. "And I love you," he whispers, and I shed more tears.

We stay like this for a long while before I take his hand and lead him out of the palace. Walking hand in hand down the cobblestone street, I am unable to keep a smile from my face. I want to scream and run through them, show him off to everyone. Yet no one is here.

As we walk, Braun explains, "The world was white and warm as I felt myself pulled to Valhalla. I stood on a grassy knoll; a crude stone archway just steps away." I nod, intimately knowing the gates of Valhalla. "I was..." He trails off as if not sure how to describe his emotions. "Excited and yet I was scared."

"You? Scared?" I smirk and he nudges me.

"I wasn't ready to leave you yet," he says, stopping to pull me close. "I took a breath and knew I would see you again someday. I could wait until you were ready."

I close my eyes and I focus on his heartbeat, rather than the emotions running through me. "Just as I took a step closer, placing my hand on the veil within the gate, the stone wards let off a blast and I..." Again, he is unable to find the words to describe the experience.

"Floated?" I provide, mumbling into his shirt, having heard similar stories from those on the brink of death and brought back.

He nods. "It took a long time to wake up, but when I did, Vili and Ve explained the extensive amount of creation magic used to heal me. To make not just my body but my mind whole again."

I stand there for a long while, wrapped in his warmth, the sun glinting off the stone buildings as it sets. We stay there as if there is no better way to say all the things we can't, all the emotions we have.

I know it all and I feel it all.

In the quiet moments, in the silence. Silence that halted me before, I now sink deep into, knowing it's a place where he and I are always together.

He laughs at something, and I pull back to glance up at him. He shakes his head before explaining, "Remember when we were in Yulamic and we found that book that explained Asgard would rise anew." He gives me a smirk and I roll my eyes at him.

"Don't you dare say it," I warn him playfully.

Our gazes lock, and he leans in as if to kiss me but pauses. "I told you so," he whispers, and before I can protest, he kisses me deeply.

In this moment, I am finally home.

Acknowledgements

First, to my readers, I cannot thank you enough for giving my book a chance!

Second to Katie Lea, one of the first readers/editors of my book, who saw the good, the bad, and the ugly. Who helped flush out my storyline and was just as excited to work on it as I was. Thank you for taking on the job of copy editing and pivoting to do all the developmental edits with me instead. Seriously, you motivated me to stay on top of it and keep moving forward.

A special thank you to Taylor Perkins, the first #1 fan of my book. Your excitement and love for this story was everything. You made me believe that someone might actually enjoy reading this just as much as I did. #teambraun

To all my beta readers: Heidi, Andy, Stefani, Enrica, Keita, Ashley, Taylor, Mira, Emily, Jessica, Lauren, Vanessa, and Dean. Thank you for your honest feedback, you are the reason a lot of changes happened to strengthen the story.

To my parents for their unending support and love. Thanks for reading the roughest draft version and telling me you were proud.

To Jaqueline, you brought my vision to life for the cover and galaxy map. I am in awe of your work and cannot thank you enough!

To Kelli at KDL editing, thank you for all the formatting, editing, and advice you gave!

To Amy at Imagine Ink Designs for making the formatting and layout absolutely perfect.

To the rest of my friends who had to listen to me talk about this for over two years. Thank you.

About the Author

Talia Clayton is a California native living in Portland, Oregon. When she isn't writing, reading, or working she spends time with friends and family and enjoys trying new restaurants, exploring coffee shops, and browsing bookstores.

www.taliaclayton.com
Instagram @author.tclayton & @taliaclayton
TikTok @taliacclayton

www.ingramcontent.com/pod-product-compliance
Lightning Source LLC
Chambersburg PA
CBHW021221310726
48971CB00006B/1643